BROCK

BRACKEN RIDGE REBELS M.C. SERIES BOOK 3

MACKENZY FOX

Copyright © 2021 Mackenzy Fox

All rights reserved. No part of this publication may be reproduced, distributed, or transmitted in any form or by any means, including photocopying, recording, or other electronic or mechanical methods, without the prior written permission of the publisher

Please purchase only authorized electronic editions and do not participate in, or encourage, the electronic piracy of copyrighted materials. Your support of the author's rights is appreciated.

This book is a work of fiction. Names, characters, places, brands, and incidents are the products of the author's imagination or used fictitiously. Any resemblance to actual events, locales, or persons, living or dead, is entirely coincidental.

Cover by: Mayhem Cover Creations
Formatting by: @peachykeenas (Savannah Richey)
Editing by: Mackenzie - nicegirlnaughtyedits.com

To all of my loyal readers out there, I'm so thankful every day that you are in my corner. I hope you enjoy Brock and the many more books I have yet to come, with love MF xx

AUTHOR'S NOTE

CONTENT WARNING: Brock is a steamy romance for readers 18+ it contains mature themes that may make some readers uncomfortable.

BRACKEN RIDGE REBELS M.C. – Enter at own risk…….

ABOUT BROCK – Bracken Ridge Rebels MC Book 3

Bracken Ridge Arizona, where the Rebels M.C. rule and the only thing they ride or die for more than their club is their women, this is Brock's story

Brock: For years I've let it slide. What she does to me, how she makes me feel. I've brushed it off like an annoying niggling habit that comes back every now and again to haunt me.

We came together once, then we drifted apart.

It's the story of my life.

We were best friends, but back then we were a lot of things. She was the fire in my blood, the elixir in my veins. My world fell at her feet, before it fell spectacularly apart.

She thinks she can run from the M.C. She thinks she can run from me. Little does she know that this old dog ain't learning any new tricks.

I've got my eyes on the prize. She will be my ol' lady.

I let her slip away once before, but I have no intension of doing that again.

Angel: I don't want to be someone's property. Nobody owns me. I belong to myself.

My life's been no fairy-tale, and I've had to grow up fast. I've worked hard to get here.

I can't fall for the V.P. of the Bracken Ridge Rebels.

What Brock and I had was a long time ago. What we had was young love, infatuation.

It wasn't real.

I wasn't going to be controlled then, and I won't be controlled now.

So he may as well stop. I'm not giving in. I'll never give in. He can't have what was never his to take.

1

BROCK

TWO MONTHS AGO...

The screech of tires outside my office alerts me to the fact that Angel's arrived.

I know the sound of her truck anywhere.

Of course, I also got the heads up from Gunner that she was hot on my tail after I threatened her date to fuck the hell off.

She's ungrateful. And I'm a jealous prick.

The two definitely don't mix.

Still, she's got a right to be pissed. I'm saving her heartache in the long run, though, she just doesn't know that yet. The guy isn't her type; he's your typical asshole who wears a suit and drives a fancy car he paid way too much for—an unworthy asshole at that. I get she doesn't wanna haul her cookies all the way over to church to find herself a man, but this is really scraping the barrel.

The guy had no balls.

"Brock!" I hear from the lot out front.

I sigh into my cold cup of coffee. Can't wait for the screaming match that's about to unfold. One thing about Angel; she can't be controlled. She'll speak her mind; she'll stand up for herself. I respect that, truly I do, but it doesn't mean I'm gonna be okay with some other guy fucking her. Nah, not this turn of the century.

She bursts through the door as I continue to stare at my computer screen, ignoring her.

"Brock!" she yells again, like I'm fuckin' hard of hearing.

I glance up. "I don't think they heard you over the other side of the Canyon, Ange."

I'm delighted to see she's furious.

Her long, pale blonde hair hangs behind her back like a cloak, her blunt fringe could literally cut glass. She's tall with glowing fair skin and has curves in all the right places. Her green eyes are unlike any that I've ever seen on another woman; not that I tend to look in their eyes when I'm doing what I need to do. I prefer them reverse cowgirl, truth be told.

But Angel… Yeah, I could stare into her eyes while I fuck her all night long. Trouble is, she won't let me.

I'm in the 'friends' zone and I've been tryin' for a mighty long time to get the hell out. A while back, we got close—not so close that I was able to score a home run, but we were flirting and touching and stuff—then she goes all cold turkey on me and says she doesn't want to 'ruin the friendship.' So, we stopped.

She's had me on a short leash ever since. One I definitely don't enjoy.

Fuckin' females.

Talk about flogging a dead man's horse.

"Don't play coy with me," she spits. "I've been running all over town looking for you!"

"Well," I sigh, like she's a nuisance. "You found me."

I don't need to glance up to know she's got steam coming out of her ears. She's so fuckin' cute when she's angry.

I try very hard not to burst out laughing at her annoyance. That won't help me here.

"I know what you did."

"Last summer?"

She comes closer as I start typing an email or pretend to.

She's wearing ripped jeans, a tight black tank and boots up to her knees. The woman's a fuckin' goddess.

My dick stirs at the thought of doing it with her in my office, over my desk.

I don't know why I torture myself. It's never gonna happen... then again, angry sex could be just what the doctor ordered.

"Don't be cute, Brock. In case you haven't noticed, I'm not in the mood."

I can't help my smirk. "That time of the month?" That should get her going.

"You really are a sexist, chauvinistic pig, aren't you?"

I glance up from my screen. "Jesus, Ange, the vein in your forehead looks like it's about to pop out of your brain any minute. Calm the fuck down."

"You have no right to interfere with my life! You drove my date away!" she yells. I can tell by the quick rise and fall of her chest—yeah, her beautiful tits do nothing to calm my raging hard on—that she's not kidding around. She's mad this time. She means business.

"Whatever you think I've done, I can assure you, I've only done to protect you."

She shakes her head. "Protection I didn't want, nor did I ask for!"

I shrug. I don't give a shit. The guy wasn't worthy of her, and I don't know what else to say.

"I don't know why you've got your panties in a twist; the guy was an asshole."

She may shoot lasers from her eyeballs in a minute; her glare is glacial. "That's not your call. Where do you honestly get off? If anything, it's *you* who's the asshole!"

I wouldn't normally let a broad come and yell at me like this, but Angel and I have a history.

This is what it's like with us.

We go way back.

We fight.

We used to kiss and make up.

We used to do a lot of wild shit.

Seeing her like this doesn't turn me off, far from it. I'm more turned on than ever.

I'm a sick fuck, what can I say.

"You know where and how I get off so that's a moot point. How is looking out for your best interests being an asshole?"

"You're sick, you know that? You've got a problem if you've got nothing better to do than spy on me and scare the men in my life."

"Men? So, there's more than one?"

"That's none of your fucking business!" she cries, poking me in the chest.

I look down at her finger that jabs me back and forth.

"Careful, babe, you know that counts as foreplay for me."

"You wish."

I've made no secret to her that I wanna give things another try, or at the very least, get to third base. But she just can't let the past go. I know she has feelings for me; it's why she keeps coming back, which is also why I can't let her ruin her life with some other schmuck.

Not happening. Not on my watch.

"In any case, do you really want a man who can't stand up for you?" I raise my eyebrows in question and begin to stand, and she immediately backs off. "Do you really want a grease monkey in a suit who runs at the first sign of trouble? A real man would fight me, tell me to fuck off, not run the other way and hide under his desk. You deserve better than that, a simple thank you would have been nice."

She shakes her head as she takes another step back. I lean back against the desk leisurely and cross my feet at the ankles.

"A simple thank you?" she spits. "I doubt any man on the planet is going to fight you, tell you to fuck off or *not* run the other way. You're intimidating and wearing an M.C. cut. Hell, you probably ran him off the road with your stupid motorcycle."

I wave a finger at her. "I'll have you know that's a Harley FXSTB soft tail night train you're dissing off. One of the most classy, luxurious, badass bikes around. I should wash your mouth out with soap or put you over my knee for that comment."

She does not look impressed.

"Oh, you'd like that, wouldn't you?"

I stare at her.

I know what I do to women when I look at them like this.

She can say what she wants, but she's affected by me. I know her too well.

"I can't imagine anything more disgusting!"

I snort. "Yeah, right. I bet you lay in bed every night thinking about what we used to get up to, don't you Angel?"

Her cheeks flush slightly but she stands firm. "I don't lay in bed thinking, I'm too busy getting busy to think about you or anything we used to get up to."

Another lie.

I don't stalk the woman, but I know she hasn't had *that* many dates. For one, she's a workaholic.

"You sure about that?"

She crosses her arms over her chest and stares back at me defiantly.

"Positive."

"Your panties wet?"

Her eyes go wide. "You'll never find out."

I smirk. "All you have to do is ask, babe. You know I'll give you what you want, how you want it, how I know you need it."

"You don't know anything about what I need."

"I know how you like to be touched," I remind her. "My memory's not that far gone."

She snorts. "Things have changed since high school, Brock. Women don't like to be thrown over a man's shoulder and dragged upstairs like some fucking sweet butt anymore. That's how it goes with you, isn't it? Caveman style?"

"Don't seem to remember you complaining or being *dragged* anywhere."

She tilts her head upwards, as if pretending none of it ever happened. "Maybe your memory is fading, or maybe I was just young and stupid back then. I didn't know any better."

I roll my eyes. "You keep tellin' yourself that." I snort "If you say it enough times, you might start to believe it."

"Leave me the hell alone, Brock. I mean it!"

I raise both my palms in surrender. "Fine."

She stands there as I take a long, hard look down her body. She's one fine specimen of a woman, especially in that tight tank top. I've never met a woman I'm attracted to quite like her.

I'd love nothing more than to touch her, feel her, make her come—right here, right now.

"Stop looking at me like that," she replies.

Mission accomplished.

I don't give her the satisfaction of a smile.

"Like what?"

"Like you want to fuck me."

"That wouldn't be a lie, babe. You know what you do to me."

She closes her eyes momentarily. "Brock," she whispers.

All her anger fizzles out.

It never lasts, she knows what we had, what we could have again, but she won't let it happen. She's Mrs. Mom now who only dates guys in suits that don't know how to treat her right, let alone fuck her right.

I push off the desk.

She glances up as I come toward her.

"Please..."

"Please what?" I stand toe to toe.

"Please don't."

I brush my fingers across her shoulder, her chest rising rapidly at my proximity.

My girl's no pushover, not by a long shot, but I know exactly how to push her buttons, more than she does mine.

I move my other hand to the back of her neck as I whisper in her ear. "You really mean that, Angel? Say the words, I'll fuck off, if that's what you really want, or…" I trail off.

She smells so sweet, like vanilla. The very scent of her makes my dick painfully hard. Imagining her on her knees before makes me want to implode.

But we have to do things her way. That's how this dance works, how it's always worked.

"Or what?" her voice sounds husky, raw. Just like mine.

"Or we could fuck."

I feel her chest beat against mine at my words.

"You know we can't."

I pull back so our foreheads press together. "You know we can."

I want to kiss her, devour her. It's been years since I felt her lips on mine. Since I sank my cock into her sweet pussy.

But I can't.

She's got to want this as much as I do.

"Brock, you know how this complicates things. I'm mad at you."

I hover my lips just above hers, so close that I can feel the heat of her breath on my tongue as I tell her, "Save that rage for sex. I can keep a secret, if that's what you want."

She shakes her head. "You know it'll change things, ruin things between us."

"We can keep it casual." I ignore the ruin part.

She laughs. "Yeah right, as soon as I meet another guy, you'll bury him."

Fuck, I want her. I'll say anything for her to give me a shot, to let me take what's rightfully mine anyway since I was her first.

"Only if he's not worthy."

"You think everyone's not worthy."

"There you go then."

She bites her lip. "I should go."

She turns to leave, and I grasp her wrist. She looks over her shoulder at me, in no hurry to leave it seems, all the fight in her gone, those green eyes killing me softly.

She's beautiful, so goddamn beautiful.

I move my head to her ear and whisper, "Wanna see if you're wet."

If she doesn't want it, she can stop me.

A guttural sound leaves her throat, and it really isn't fair. She of all people should know I remember everything.

She likes this; the dirty talk.

"You think your suit and tie asswipe knows how to give you what you want? What you need?"

"Brock, we can't…"

I move my mouth to her neck and bite gently on her pulse point, causing her to just about convulse in my arms.

"How long's it been since someone fucked you properly?" I ask into her skin.

Her hands grip my biceps, her touch sending heat through my body like an electric current.

"I… it's… been a while," she admits.

I kiss her where I bit her, and my hand comes up to grasp her breast. I've been wanting to play with her tits for quite some time; they've been the subject of many of my fantasies.

I continue to assault her senses, without kissing her on the mouth, as her grip on my arms tightens. I kiss all along her throat, nipping here and there, my other hand holding onto the back of her hair to keep her in place.

"You sure you want me to stop?"

"We can't fuck," she breathes.

I'm so hard.

I need her mouth on me.

I can't live without her fucking mouth on me.

"Let me make you come."

Her hands squeeze me again, tighter as I move my mouth down to the hard peak underneath my palm. I suck her nipple through the material of her tank top as one of her hands reaches into my hair and tugs. The motion goes straight to my dick. I push my hips into hers so she can feel the rock in my pants, and she gasps on contact.

I want in, I want in so bad.

"Lock the fucking door," she whispers.

I grin into her skin and hastily rush to the door, locking it quickly.

"Didn't take much convincing." I smirk, stalking back over to her.

"This means nothing," she tells me. "I just need to get off."

"Last of the romantics, we're cut from the same cloth."

I stand behind her and tug her hair back so her head's

resting on my shoulder, her ass grinds into my dick, just about sending me round the bend.

I reach around and grab both of her tits and rub my thumbs over her hard peaks.

"Fuck, Angel."

I quickly yank her top down and see that she's got a black, lacy bra on. I squeeze and pluck her nipples through the material as she moans.

"God, Brock."

"Yeah, babe, you're gonna be saying his name a lot for the next hour."

"Don't got an hour, Brock."

I nip her neck with my teeth as she pushes her ass further into me, grinding harder. I'm ashamed to admit I'm ready to take her hard and fast. I won't last long; she's my ultimate fantasy, and I can't fucking believe she's actually gonna let me.

I yank her bra down so I can see her tits, and they pop out; big, round, beautiful.

"Fuck," I hiss.

"Got them done after I had Rawlings."

Rawlings is her kid.

I don't fucking care, they're utter perfection and so much bigger than when I last saw them. All kinds of nasty thoughts run through my head of what I wanna do to make her come.

I spin her around and drop to my knees. I pull her to my mouth and suck one nipple between my lips, then the other, kneading and gently squeezing both at the same time.

I've dreamed for a long time about her tits in my face and now it's actually happening. I can hardly believe my luck.

She moans wildly while both her hands move into my hair, pulling at me, trying to get more of herself in my mouth. I reach down and begin to unbuckle her jeans.

"Pull them down," I say, in between sucks and licks.

"Jesus, Brock. Oh God," she whimpers as I gently bite her nipple and pull the other one with my thumb and forefinger.

She does as I say, pulling black panties down to her knees along with her jeans, and I glance down at her pussy.

Fucking perfection.

I continue to suck her tits while one hand moves to her wet center. I run two fingers down her crease, then back up, spreading her slickness around.

And don't I feel like a smug fucker.

My fingers find her clit and I circle it, biting down harder on her nipple as her breath hitches in her chest, her hands gripping my hair even harder. I rub, flick and lap at her clit until she's quivering against me. When she's almost there, I insert a finger, feeling her clench around me as I insert another, sliding them in and out. My thumb continues to rub her sweet spot until she comes long and hard around my fingers, and I ride out her orgasm, milking her for all she's worth.

She thinks she can fucking run and hide from me.

She's gonna learn.

She can't.

She's *mine.*

She's fucking mine.

2

ANGEL

I'd like to say I don't know why I'm here, but that would be a lie.

I know exactly why I'm here.

And he does too.

The bastard. He knows.

When the ripples of my orgasm begin to fade, I'm left a literal quivering mess, and I don't like it. Well, I like it, obviously. But I don't like him smirking up at me from his knees with his fingers still buried inside me and my tits out on display.

I like sex as much as the next person, but me and Brock?

We should not be doing this. We know better than this. But we're like magnets, magnets that cannot be separated.

I knew coming here would be a mistake, but I didn't know how much of a mistake until this very moment. Until I let him have his way with me.

I'm startled by the amount of feeling I have swirling around in my chest. I've always cared for him, but this feels different, like I could really fall, and that I can't do, not this time round.

He brings a wild side out in me like no other man can.

BROCK

Brock was my first.

We were friends all through junior high and then high school, fighting our chemistry and attraction until we couldn't anymore.

We were each other's firsts in a lot of ways.

"You say something, babe?" he smirks as I open my eyes and he goes to stand.

I glance down at his very hard bulge and my mouth waters. I haven't been intimate with him for over ten years.

"Shut up and finish the job."

He bites his bottom lip as he studies my state of undress, shaking his head. "She who couldn't be conquered."

"Anyone tell you you're a smug son of a bitch?"

"Yeah, but least I know how to make you scream."

He swiftly turns me around and walks me to his desk holding my shoulders.

"Plant your hands on the desk, spread your legs." He pulls my jeans down further and spanks my ass. By now he'll be seeing more of my ink. The vine of roses that runs along one side of my back, across my ass, and down to weave around the top of my thigh. Ink I got a few years ago as a present to myself.

He doesn't say anything but glides his fingers down the length of my ink slowly and gently causing a ripple on my flesh.

I hear him shuffle out of his jeans, then the unmistakable sound of a foil packet being ripped open. I don't even get time to see his cock as he moves a hand to my neck and holds it there firmly while his other hand directs his dick to my wet pussy and rubs it back and forth with the tip.

I'm so hot for him it's ridiculous.

I came here to tell him off and give him a piece of my mind, yet here I am naked in his office letting him fuck me against a pile of paperwork with the windows wide open.

Anyone could come right on past at any given moment. It's what makes it all the more thrilling, but being this cavalier is only gonna land me in more trouble.

"Not gonna last, Ange. Sorry in advance, but you're just too damn hot, and I can't fuckin' hold my load." He slaps my ass again. "So fuckin' hot."

I wiggle against him, trying to impale him because I need friction, but he holds my neck tighter, controlling the pace.

"Shut up and get in me," I order him.

I hear him snort as he lines me up and does just that. In one move, he's balls deep and thrusting in and out. He hisses obscenities as his other hand rests on my hip and he moves at a maddening pace.

It's hard. Harsh. It's so good I want to scream.

It's been a while for me, but he doesn't know that, and he doesn't care. He wants to get off just as much as I do.

He fills every inch of me and every nerve in my body is on fire as he hits me in all the right places.

He's right, nobody knows how to do me like he does. That's for sure. I'd just forgotten.

He moves in and out with fury as we fuck hard. I push my ass out further as his hand moves down from my head to cup my breast, then the other one follows. He fondles them while cursing and telling me how fucking beautiful I am, his dick plunging in and out as our skin slaps together. I feel the tension building again, this time to even more dizzying heights.

This time I know that I won't be able to hold in my scream.

"Come on, Angel. Tell me you don't like this, baby girl."

I pant, cursing him. "I hate you."

He laughs, then moves one hand down around the front and pinches my clit—hard.

I scream as I come with more force than a freight train as

he follows through, calling my name several times, emptying his load.

We stay connected for at least a minute as I struggle to get my breath back.

The one thing you instantly regret after mad, rampage sex is the reality of the situation.

We're not supposed to be doing this.

It's always hard to resist but even harder once I've let him see me unravel.

And I can't afford that.

I got screwed over once before and that was enough.

"Jesus, woman, you kill me."

I don't say anything for a few moments, then, "I have to go."

He pulls out abruptly as I immediately straighten and pull my jeans up. By the time I tuck my tits back into my bra and adjust them properly, he's cleaned himself up and has unlocked the door.

The reality hits me like a ton of bricks.

He comes back toward me and goes to cup my face. "What, no kiss goodbye?"

I realize then that we haven't even kissed.

I know he's mad at my rush to get out of here, but honestly, what does he expect?

"We didn't exactly have a kiss hello, remember."

"You always said kissing on the mouth is too personal."

He's right, I did say that. I still maintain it.

"It is."

He stares at me. "Want an encore tonight? I can come over after Rawlings has gone to bed."

I stare back wordlessly. "This was a mistake," I say clearly. There will be no round two.

"Didn't sound like it from where I was standing."

"You've just got me all figured out, don't you, Brock?"

His eyes harden. "I thought I did; seems I was mistaken. I got what I wanted, so did you. You can go now."

I try not to let his words sting but I know he's only reacting to my coldness, my unwillingness to go there with him. He knows deep down we won't work. We can't. We have too much history.

"Don't be shitty, Brock."

"I'm not. I wanted a quick, easy lay, and I got one."

I turn to him. "This is exactly why we won't work, why we never could."

He rolls his eyes. "Right. Keep tellin' yourself that, Angel. One day you might actually believe it."

I point at him. "Stay out of my love life."

His nostrils flare. I know better than to poke the bear, but he needs to be told.

I won't be owned by him. I won't be owned by anybody.

I belong to myself.

That's how it's going to stay.

"It'd take some long-suffering prick to put up with your array of shit," he tells me, his voice hard. "I won't be there the next time you almost make a mistake, though I bet secretly you're glad it was me and not him stickin' it to you."

"I didn't ask you to be there the first time."

I go around him, and he lets me pass without another word.

I didn't want this to end in a fight but how can it not.

He won't change.

He thinks he can claim me, then I'll be at his beck and call. He should know by now I don't roll like that.

Not anymore.

"Thanks for stopping by," he calls out as I get to the door. "You know where I am when your aching pussy needs me to release all that tension."

I slam the door, and while I'm tempted to sag against it in

sheer frustration, I don't. I march back to my vehicle, thoroughly annoyed and disgusted with myself.

So much for showing him who's boss.

I went right on in there and fell at his feet. Okay, so technically he fell at my feet, but I still gave it up on a whim, without any protest.

Goosebumps rise over my skin when I think about his dirty words and his throbbing cock inside me, pulsating as he called my name when he came.

Nothing could be hotter than that, nothing.

And it's why I have to run.

3

BROCK

PRESENT DAY

"All in favor of Colt officially setting up shop next to Rubble's joint."

Ayes ring around the table at church.

Hutch slams the gavel down. "More scratch stuffing the club coffers being the first matter at hand. There has been a big call in the community for security cameras in commercial businesses and buildings but also for residential homes. Pigs won't like it, especially if we have twenty-four hours on-call surveillance. Got the hotel and the Stone Crow, as you know, already lined up with the latest up to date cameras. Of course, we won't be allowed to wear colors on duty, but that comes at a small price."

"Sounds a bit too fuckin' reputable," Steel grumbles. "Colors are part of who we are. Should wear 'em, fuck the pigs."

"Yeah, but we want to be taken seriously," Gunner, of all people, pipes up. "Otherwise, it'll just look like we're outlaws and then the pigs will never leave us alone."

I turn to him. "You feelin' all right brother?"

Gunner pauses as he looks at me for the punchline. "Yeah, I'm doin' all right, thanks for askin'."

"It's just you never usually input anything useful into any of the meetings," I go on. "Just wondering what's changed."

"Got me a good night's sleep for once." He sighs, then adds with a wink, "Liliana keeps me awake most nights…"

I hold in my laugh, knowing that it'll only infuriate Steel, Lily's older brother. Last thing he wants to hear is all about his little sister and Gunner in the sack.

"Watch your mouth, Guns. I'll rearrange your face just like I did last time we talked about Lily," Steel grumbles.

And we're off.

"I've had harder slaps from my mother." Gunner rolls his eyes.

I don't know why he spouts such bullshit. He was hurting for days after that ass whooping when Steel found out they'd gone behind his back, and they brawled out in the parking lot.

"Well, I'm happy to have a rematch any fuckin' day of the week."

Nobody messes with Steel. He's the club's enforcer and he does his job well. When it comes to the women in his life, he's an overprotective son of a gun. I guess we all are, but Steel takes no prisoners. He doesn't give a shit who he pisses off or what he has to do to keep things smooth sailing.

Now that Lily and Gunner are officially together, things have been a little strained between the two of them, but I think Steel is slowly coming round. He just takes about ten years to warm up to the idea of anything new. He doesn't like change.

My mind wanders to Angel. She doesn't like change either.

I've barely even seen her since the day we fucked on my desk.

She's been out of town for a little bit; family problems, or so I heard. She doesn't tell me nothin' anymore. Ghosted.

I'm out of the loop, bam. Talk about flogging a dead horse.

This is what a quick, meaningless fuck can do to you. Great at the time, but now I'm payin' the price of her freezing me out.

I was afraid this would happen if we got together, and frankly, I am a little pissed she's gone AWOL on me, with not so much as a text message. She's practically glued to her phone, so there's no excuse.

We've always been able to tell each other anything, good, bad, or indifferent. Now I don't know what to think, but I definitely don't like being ghosted.

That crazy afternoon has been on my mind for the past two months.

How hot it was.

Unplanned and sexy as fuck.

She pushes all of my buttons, not all of them good, but that's how it's always been with us. We make each other crazy.

Maybe I have some kind of death wish because I know a woman like Angel can't be tamed. She can't be tied down, there's too much fire in her, too much rage. And she directs it all to the wrong people.

She thinks one really bad relationship defines her for the rest of her life, and even worse, it's ruined her for all others. Except me. I see past her bravado.

I knew the guy she married was a fucktard when I first laid eyes on him. He wasn't good.

But Angel wasn't in a great place back then and she'd moved away. When I found out she was pregnant with Rawlings, a surge of disappointment as well as rage flooded through me because I wished it were me. I wished I was the one she got to call dad.

Not that she would ever call the drug addicted sperm

donor that either. He did nothing for them, and when Angel wound up in hospital, the dude split. Just as well he did, and the pigs got to him first. Some said he OD'd in prison but that was just a rumor, unfortunately.

Fucking douchebag.

I've never touched the heavy hard stuff in my life, and I never will. I get my highs from booze, bikes, and pussy.

"You with us, Brock?" Gunner pokes me in the ribs with his elbow.

I run a hand over my face and snap out of my reverie. "Sorry, been a long week."

"You need a holiday," Gunner tells me. "You look a little pale."

"Yeah, and leave Bones in charge, I don't think so."

"Hey, what's that supposed to mean?" Bones, the road captain frowns at me from across the table. We run the scrap and junkyard together; the place is booming.

"Oh, nothin'. Be nice if you put in a days' work every now and again."

"Been operating the crane all week, asswipe, or did you forget that?"

"Lack of pussy," Gunner mutters, loud enough so I can hear him. "Clouding his brain."

"Least I'm not pussy-whipped," I throw back at him. I don't want to talk shit about Lily, period, and especially not in front of Steel. She's like my kid sister. Speaking of which, my little sister, Amelia, is talking about coming back to Bracken Ridge for a new job opportunity, if it works out.

We get along now but didn't for a long time. Having her back in town might pose as a problem if she's planning on being back for good. She and Deanna, Hutch's daughter, like to get a little crazy, not that I'm as over the top like Steel is. She lives her own life, but I wouldn't wanna see her hanging around the club or witness one of the brothers hittin' on her and shit.

I don't like to keep it in the family in that sense.

"Least I'm gettin' plenty," he fires back.

I shake my head and pinch the bridge of my nose.

"Gunner, shut the fuck up." Steel shakes his head in response, one frown away from punching somebody.

"Doc says I shouldn't be doin' anything strenuous until my back heals properly," Bones goes on. "Just following the good doctor's orders, while operating heavy machinery. I should be at home watchin' fuckin' TV with my feet up and a house mouse cleaning my place and cookin' my meals and shit."

"This is why you're single." Hutch shakes his head, looking over the desk at him.

"Best way to be, no strings attached, just how I like it."

Hutch rolls his eyes.

"How'd you put your back out, anyway?" Rubble chimes in. Rubble runs the Tow truck business next to Steel's garage with his wife Lucy.

"Yeah, you know the wild thing isn't meant for men your age." Gunner laughs.

"Very funny, asshole," Bones retorts. "It's all about stamina, Guns. Poor Lily only knows having five minutes till you blow your load. If you need any tips, brother, just hit me up, I got all the moves, wouldn't want you gettin' dumped for lack of performance."

That's a joke. Before Lily tamed the wild beast, Gunner was the biggest man-whore around. He outdid all of us when it came to chicks.

With his baby boy good looks, blonde hair, and what the chicks call *charisma*, he could sweet talk the panties off any girl. Now he's got Steel riding his ass making sure he doesn't fuck it up with Lily.

It's not gonna be good for him if he does but he's crazy about her, always has been.

Steel slams his fist on the table. "Will you shut the fuck up about my little sister before I break your face, for fuck's sake. I don't wanna think about it. Don't wanna see it. Don't wanna hear about it."

"So disrespectful," Gunner agrees, smirking. The little prick.

"Lily and Gunner's bedroom antics are not something I wanna hear about either," Hutch grunts, unimpressed. He points at Gunner. "You better be keeping your dick in your pants anywhere else," he warns. "I'll be sorely disappointed if Steel does get to bury you out in the desert. There's some fine-looking Cactus out west that could do with a hearty compost, I'd hate that to be you."

"Everyone's always threatening me with violence," Gunner complains. "There's no trust left anymore."

"Trust is earned," Steel grunts. "Not like you've proved yourself."

Here we go again.

Steel gripes a lot, but he looks after every one of us. He might moan about bitches nagging, but deep down, he means well, he just takes about ten years to get to know him.

"Told you I'll never hurt her," Gunner replies across the table. "Meant it."

Steel grunts again. "That remains to be seen."

Even though it's been a bit strained between them, I think Steel is slowly starting to get it because it seems Gunner and Lil aren't going away.

"If you bitches are all finished whining, I've got shit to do. Some of us actually work for a living," I say, looking pointedly at Bones.

"Like he'll ever quit bitching and whining." Rubble shakes his head. "Worse than any fuckin' female I've ever met."

"All of you make my fuckin' head hurt," Hutch grumbles. "Lucky the club coffers this month were outstanding. It's the only reason I put up with half your bullshit."

"That'd be thanks to me and Sizzle magazine," Gunner reminds us all.

Something I do not need stuck in my brain at any time of the day or night is Gunner in the nude posing for a women's magazine and them paying him for it. Pass me a bucket.

We've ribbed him endlessly of course, but the fucker doesn't give a shit.

Plus, he's got a down payment on a nice place in a new subdivision on the other side of town. He's doing okay for himself, the little shit.

"Oh please, don't remind us," Bones groans. "If I hear one more fuckin' thing about Sizzle magazine. I'm going to punch somebody. You'd think that chicks would have better taste than wantin' to look you with your tackle hangin' out, but clearly, they don't give a shit about girth anymore, it's all superficial pretty boy shit."

"Don't be jealous, my man, there's plenty of me to go round." He grabs his junk under the table and gives Bones a wink.

"Stupid fuck," Bones replies.

"Just wait for the calendar." Gunner turns to the head of the table. "Gonna bring in even more dough, Hutch. The profits are mine this time, I don't share a cut with the magazine, which means more money for all of us." He looks back at Bones. "So don't go spouting about tackle and girth while I pay for your upkeep. Not keeping tally, but I think I've earned my dues ten times over."

Bones just rolls his eyes, muttering under his breath.

"When you're bringing in a shit ton of money, son, I don't give a hoot what you're selling as long as it's legal. That reminds me, I've scored a meeting with Steph about the

Stone Crow, she may finally wanna sell her share after all these years."

"When's this happening?" Steel asks. "Thought she was set for life in that place."

Steph let us buy in when she was going to go under. She scratched our back when we had nowhere to drink, and then we scratched hers. She's good to the club.

"Her father's sick, so she may have to head back out west to take care of him. Will be sad to see her go, but it may be the opportunity we need to expand. Thinkin' of overhauling the place. With the new bar that's opened in town, the Crow could be more of a local's bar and grill than the decrepit ramshackle it is now. It won't attract some of the young ones, but we don't necessarily need that. We need locals back again, townsfolk. There should be one bar to drink in that everyone is welcome to with good, homemade food. One that don't serve fancy drinks and all this olives and tapas shit. Deanna could do the interior. Would be good practice for her."

Deanna's just started up her own interior design business. I must admit, the Stone Crow is long overdue for an overhaul. While it's never been an exclusive biker bar, we tend to drink back at church. The potential now that Bracken Ridge is expanding with new residential subdivisions means there will be more people moving to town.

It's a great opportunity.

"Sounds fuckin' fantastic," I say, knowing full well this could be a huge turn around for the club. To own the other half and the building outright, to expand and upgrade. The pub itself is historic and unique. People from out-of-town love that shit. "Happy to sit in if need be."

He flicks his eyes to me. "Will let you know when. Steph's been back and forth out of town, so we need to get onto this pretty quick."

I nod.

"Need to talk for a sec in private too," he mutters.

He bangs the gavel down and the meeting is adjourned.

The others leave and I stay seated.

When Gunner's finished shoving everyone around to try and get out the door first, Hutch turns to me.

"Got a call from Angel's folks."

My eyebrows lift instantly. "Oh?"

"You spoken to her recently?"

Not since we fucked two months ago, no.

"Nope, haven't seen her."

He frowns. "Some shit's going down, her father's worried about her, said she's got some trouble with the ex."

"What the fuck?"

He shrugs. "Just tellin' you what they told me; to keep an eye on her. It involves Rawlings, and the last thing I want is that motherfucker comin' to town. Ain't no way in hell the pigs gonna get to him before I do, if he knows what's good for him."

My heart hammers in my chest. "What the fuck? He's in jail, been there for a long time far as I'm aware."

"Yeah, well, it seems he may be gettin' out on parole or some shit. Talk to her. She might be keepin' things from her folks; you know how she is."

Parole? What the actual fuck? The prick almost killed her...

I rub a hand down my face and through my beard. "That's a little hard when she's ghosted me for the last few months. Been out of town for a bit, staff been runnin' the shop, keeping things afloat."

"She got money troubles?"

"I don't know, she doesn't tell me shit."

"Ron said she was back this weekend, go find out."

Great. Just what I want to be doing.

26

Getting a mouthful from Angel when I could be out on my property fixing it up.

I bought an old farmhouse six months ago with the intention of doing it up myself and living out there. Trouble is, the scrapyard's been so busy I've barely had time to take a piss, much less knock walls down and build shit.

"I'll stop by on the way home. You know what she's like, though. She probably won't tell me nothin'."

"Use your powers of persuasion." Hutch grins as I shake my head. "Need to know the angle. Could be nothin' or could be some shit goin' down we're not aware of. Find out if he's gettin' out on parole or not."

"Yeah, I think those powers I used to have are long gone, but I'll do what I can."

We fist pump and I get up to take a drive past Angel's Ink, her tattoo shop. If she's not there, I'll stop by her place. Not that she'll appreciate that after how we left things.

Truth be told, I'm annoyed.

We used to be so fuckin' close. She'd tell me everything.

Somewhere along the way, we just lost that friendship. She got busy with the business, I got busy with mine. We moved on.

I miss her.

She wasn't always the cold, hard bitch that she is now. She has a soft side; you just rarely ever see it.

I slide onto my custom Harley and fire her up. Angel's is less than a five-minute ride, and when I pull up outside the shop, I see her truck parked in the lot out back.

Bingo.

I take a few moments before I walk into the flames of hell.

Her shop is sensational from the front. The building is painted black with flames on either side of the brickwork.

She's a very sought-after tattoo artist and has built this place from the ground up. People come from far and wide for her to tattoo them, and she's even been featured in a couple of tattoo magazines as well this last year. She's done a lot of my work and most of Steel's.

It can't be money troubles; the place is always busy, and they charge a packet, quite rightly since you get what you pay for.

I push through the front door into the expansive, eclectic reception area. It features brick walls with black lounge chairs and a massive crystal chandelier in the foyer as you walk in.

Angel claims she was going for rock chick glam. Whatever that shit is. She and Deanna designed it together.

I have to say, Deanna might have a real talent for this decorating shit; I might have to get her to do my place once I get the walls up, doors on, and roof fixed.

Though, I obviously don't want rock chick glam. Something low key, beams and wood, concrete floors, manly shit.

A cute little blonde is at the counter. She's new.

"Hey!" she says with bright eyes, assessing me with interest from head to toe.

She's cute but a little young. And she's wearing a sparkly top that has sequins all over it.

"Hey," I reply flatly. "Angel in?"

For some reason I'm not in the mood for small talk.

Just being here, knowing she's back and hasn't even called me, ticks me off.

I'll usually flirt and mingle if the chick's cute and obviously into it, but I'm tired, not to mention, in need of some food and a decent night's sleep. I ain't really got time for this shit, but it's not like I can say no to Hutch. And I also wanna know what's going on for my own piece of mind.

She nods. "Out the back, who shall I tell her…"

I hold a hand up to stop her talking and proceed past her desk to the back storage area.

I hear the sound of Angel's voice. She's humming some tune as she puts shit away. I lean against the door jamb for a few extended moments watching her, clearly unaware of my presence as she lines up all the different inks and puts things into containers.

My eyes lock on her ass, not hard to miss since she's wearing skintight, leather-looking pants and a tank that's tied to one side.

She's got a fuckin' rocking body. She'd be even more perfect if she'd put a few pounds on. A man likes to have something to grab onto.

She turns to the door after a full minute of me staring at her from behind, and when she sees me, she literally gasps, jumps back and holds a hand to her heart, swearing loudly.

"Jesus, fuck, Brock! You scared the shit out of me!"

"You feelin' for your heart, sugar?" I reply, my eyes drop to her tits where one hand lays across her chest. "Cos I got a feelin' you ain't gonna find a beat in there."

She steps back, her eyes narrowing.

"Very funny. It's not nice to sneak up on people. You almost gave me a heart attack."

"Not sneaking." I defend. "Should be more aware of your surroundings, could have been a robber."

She puts her hands on her hips. I watch the annoyed movement, not that anything could really tear my eyes away from her chest.

Remembering sucking on her tits that day in my office has all the blood in my body rushing to my dick.

Fuck.

"What's up?"

"That's it? *What's up?*"

She stares at me. "I've been away for a bit."

"Figured that out."

"Dad hasn't been well; they're thinking of moving back so they can be closer to Rawlings."

I watch her carefully. She's never been a very good liar, and I don't doubt her dad's sick, but there's something more. I know it in my gut.

"That it?"

"Yeah, they want to come out this weekend and look at houses."

"Why'd you ghost me?"

Her brows furrow. "I didn't think I did."

It's my turn to look annoyed now. "After how we left things? You just up and fuck off out of town? I was worried about you, about Rawlings."

"You could have called."

She's right, I could have. But my pride wouldn't let me.

I have typical man syndrome and there ain't nothing I can take to cure it.

"*You* could have called."

She tuts at me, something I do not appreciate from anyone.

"Are we going to do this, tit for tat?"

"The only tit I got a barny with is yours. Last time I saw you, we fucked, you got mad at me, then you left. Now I hear some shit about your ex causing trouble. That true? What's going on, Ange? And why don't you tell me anythin' anymore?"

She glares at me. "I do tell you stuff, but we're not fifteen anymore Brock. I got my own shit to deal with. I'm a grown woman; I can handle it without running to you every minute with my problems."

"What problems you got?"

"Nothing I can't handle."

I sigh loudly. "This how it's gonna be?"

"You're not my old man, Brock. I can stand on my own two feet."

"Nobody's sayin' you can't, but you can ask for help if you need it, when you need it."

"I don't need it," she says firmly.

I move closer to her. "You're becoming a real fuckin' pain in my ass, you know that?"

She laughs without humor. "How? You've been here like all of three minutes."

"Three minutes too long."

"Very funny, there's the door." She wafts her hand toward me.

I shake my head. "We never used to be like this," I say quietly. I brush the hair back off her shoulder, and she trembles as my fingers brush her skin.

So, she does feel something?

It's so hard to say with her, she gives nothing away.

She's as stubborn as an ox.

This is why we butt heads. She will never submit, *never*.

"Yes, we did. We fought like cats and dogs and had great makeup sex if my memory serves me correctly."

That we did. Many, many times.

"So, what's wrong with that? The makeup sex makes it worthwhile. We could be that again if you weren't so pig-headed."

She shakes her head. "I told you, what we did was a mistake, Brock. I want to be friends with you again, but we can't be lovers. It's too messy, you know deep down that it is too."

I let out a deep breath. She won't fuckin' let me in.

"It didn't feel fuckin' messy when I was inside you, banging you against my desk." I move closer to her ear. "Felt fuckin' fantastic, baby girl. Haven't been able to stop thinking about it, bout your tits in my face, bout your sweet, wet pussy. Bet you been thinkin' about it too."

Her lip's part but no sound comes out.

I like that I affect her.

She can deny it, say whatever the fuck she wants, but she can't lie to me.

For some reason, she's keeping me at arm's length, I don't like it, but I can't exactly force her to want me.

"You have, haven't you?" I murmur when she doesn't respond.

"I'm sure you've been banging plenty of other girls in between."

That's a low blow. We're not exactly together. I've fucked a few girls these last few months, Tiffany mainly, and Chelsea on the rare occasion, but that's only because Angel's not been around.

The nerve of this woman astounds me.

"Let me get this straight, you ghost out of town without a word, and I haven't seen you in almost two months. You tell me how much you hate me, how much you don't want me and that we're never having sex ever again, and you expect me to be a fuckin' monk and pine for you in your absence and not have sex with anybody else?" I laugh in her face. "Yeah, you just want it all ways don't you, Angel? You're right, nothing's changed, it's just like the old days. You wanna control everything and shut me out, well it doesn't work like that anymore."

She looks momentarily wounded at my words but quickly recovers.

"Fuck whoever you want, I don't care. You're a free man, you never could be tamed, anyway. I learned that the hard way."

I bristle at her words. Another low blow.

"What the fuck is the matter with you?"

She steps back.

Tears form in her eyes, and I know something's wrong.

I don't know why she's keeping shit from me and bringing up the past. It's not like her.

"Look, we just bring out the worst in each other, that's obvious. I annoy you, you annoy me. Period."

"So, you're bringin' up the past again? We were different people then. I didn't know what I wanted after the military, it changed me. Neither did you. We dealt with it, we nutted it out and I thought we were good, and now you're throwin' it back in my face. Well, fuck you, Angel. I came to check on you, make sure you and Rawlings are okay, and you just fuckin' shit all over me. I thought we were family, but obviously, I was mistaken."

Her eyes go wide. "Brock, don't..."

I turn and stalk off out the door.

She calls after me. "I'm sorry, I'm just stressed, please, Brock..."

I've had enough of her shit, and I can't take any more.

If I stay any longer, I'll start saying stuff I don't mean, then we'll have a war on her hands.

She's so fuckin' stubborn, and it gets me beyond pissed. She gets me mad like no other woman can.

Like when she came shouting at me about ruining her date. Sure, it ended up in some pretty mind-blowing sex and some awesome flashbacks for my private spank bank when I'm alone, but this is different.

I care about her.

Or should I say, I *did* care about her. Now, I don't know what's going on with the ex, and I'll have to investigate without her help.

She can go and get fucked.

I'm the only goddamn stable thing in her life aside from Rawlings; her six-year-old kid.

Rawlings.

Pain hits my gut.

I need to see her. I miss that kid when I don't see her as much as I do.

I wish she were mine.

I wish her Momma was someone else. The person who used to care about me, who gave a shit.

She acts like what we did was wrong, but how could it be? It felt so fuckin' right.

And so what if we made a mistake, aren't we adults? I stupidly thought we could move on, I guess not.

She's got me so mad and worked up that I storm out of the office, completely ignoring the little blonde's well wishes. I hop on my bike and take off with a wild screech down the entire main street. I hope there's no pigs around because they'll handcuff me for this.

I curse her name as I ride too fast and head home.

Fuck me for caring.

I'm done.

She can go to hell.

What's worse; I'm rock hard and I'm done. I can't help my body's reaction to her, some things never change.

If she thinks she can walk all over me then she can think again.

This is the end of the line and I ain't biting.

4

ANGEL

I stare at my phone and go to hit dial, then decide not to, for about the five hundredth time. I feel shitty about how I left things with Brock.

I'm not just showing resting bitch face, she's in full force.

My anger is volcanic, and though I've directed it at him, it's not his fault. None of it is.

I just don't know how to cope with what I'm dealing with.

He was right about one thing: my ex. He's getting out on parole, and he wants to see Rawlings. I'm still in shock.

Since he's not allowed any contact or visitation, he's hired a lawyer. Clearly, he's out of his mind. I'm sure his drug money can afford a lawyer's fees, not that it'll do any good with an attempted murder charge and a restraining order, but I sure as shit can't.

When I get home, I sit at my kitchen table and stare at the lawyer's letter for the millionth time and can't believe this is even happening.

To make matters worse, his parents have seconded the appeal.

I never kept Rawlings away from them. Even if he was a

loser and a train wreck, I'd never keep her grandparents away from her. They've never taken an interest up until now.

He's acting like some born again Christian, back from the brinks.

I went to see a lawyer while I was out of town to get some advice, to see if any of what they're spouting has any merit. Now I'm gonna have to hire someone local.

I know this will probably blow over. They won't give him visitation or any kind of custody, the man almost killed me, he put me in hospital. The thought terrifies me, it's shaken me to my core, and any threat against my baby girl is the one fear that I can't control.

I'd run if anyone tried to take her from me. She's mine.

My heart beats in my chest so hard it may burst out at any moment.

Nobody is ever going to take my little girl away, that's a fact.

Added to that, I've sunk all my money into the business. I don't have money for lawyer's fees just rolling around at my disposal. I shouldn't have to.

I crumple the letter and toss it across the room.

I'm worrying for nothing.

I keep telling myself that. I know that there's nothing they can do, but it still has me rattled. That family is not right in the head.

My phone buzzes, making me jump. I glance down and see Deanna calling.

"What up, bitch?" she says when I answer.

"Hey, D, not much, what's going on?"

"Couple of us are going down to Zee bar for martinis, you wanna come?"

I'd love nothing more than to get smashed right at this very moment, but I can't.

"Can't, honey, I've got Rawlings and it's too late for a sitter. Give me more notice next time."

"You know mom and dad would be happy to baby sit, they love Rawlings."

I smile. Everybody loves Rawlings, she's the best thing that ever happened to me.

"Well, have an extra one for me."

"You know I will."

Deanna always knows how to have a good time.

"You okay? You sound weird."

I've been crying so I sound like I've got a cold, best to run with that.

"Not feeling too great, just got the sniffles, might be coming down with something."

"I'll come round during the week, we can get a coffee and catch up."

"Love to," I reply, wishing my life could be this normal and I didn't have all this stress.

I spend the rest of the evening ruminating about why I'm such a bitch to Brock.

I'm not as tough as I like to believe I am.

He's always seen straight through me, yet I know just how to piss him off.

And he's right. I have thought about what we did on his desk over and over in my mind.

He gave me what I needed, what I crave.

Yet, it's all I know. Men that are rough with me.

Brock never was. He liked control in the bedroom like any normal man does, but he was tender too. He was wonderful.

He's different now. Harder. I guess he's had to be with being in the military and now the club.

Life shits all over you and it makes you tough. That's just

how it is for most people. None of us grew up rich, we've all had to work damn hard for what we have.

There was nothing tender, though, about what we did in his office, and that wasn't all his fault. It's mine too for working him up and not walking away when I should have. We're both guilty.

I don't do the hearts and flowers shit, and I don't want a man to take care of me, but for once it would be nice to be made love to. To feel someone care about me.

I don't even know what that means anymore.

I've been through some real dipshits over the course of time, some worse than others.

I stare at the bottom of my red wine glass and call it a night. I'm not getting any answers from my bottle of Merlot any time soon.

By morning, I know I'm going to go and see him. It's eating away at me. I have to apologize.

I hate it when we're fighting. I hate that I'm the cause of it, that I'm so edgy and taking my anger out on the wrong people.

Brock's a good man.

I don't want to be on the outs with him.

He's done so much for me and for Rawlings over the years, and it would be so easy with him, so, why don't I let myself have what I want?

I guess old habits die hard and I'm the queen of self-sabotage.

I know what we're like together and we'd only end up completely messed up afterward. It's like we're damned if we do and damned if we don't.

I drop Rawlings off at school and take the turn out of town, toward Brock's place. I baked some banana bread last night when I couldn't sleep, his favorite. I've wrapped half of it up in silver foil. A peace offering.

He's renovating his big ol' farm and living in the upstairs loft while he gets his shit together.

As I hit the gravel and head down the dirt track, I can see not a lot has gotten done since I was here last. The guy's busy, and I really think if he wants to move in sometime this century then it might be an idea to hire some helping hands.

I park at the front; his Harley is nowhere in sight. He probably sleeps with it.

I snort at the very thought, and I bet I'm not far off.

All of the boys of the M.C. are not just obsessed with their motorcycles, but they completely try to outdo one another. They're like a bunch of teenage boys with something to prove.

I have to say, having been on the back of Brock's bike, I really do like it. There's nothing like a custom with roaring straight pipes rumbling beneath you to get the juices flowing.

There's something about the thrill of having the wind in your hair, being wrapped around a burly ass man, and a rumble of the engine, it's like nothing else.

Well, maybe one other thing.

My pussy clenches at the thought of me and Brock.

I've never done anything quite like that in the spur of the moment in a long time. It surprised me and scared me because I know I care about him, a lot.

That hasn't changed because we're fighting. But my need to protect my freedom and remain independent far outweighs any romantic notion of my happy ever after.

I'm my own crown of thorns, what can I say?

I don't know if I should try the front or go out the back; the whole place is like a construction zone.

I decide out the back is probably better since it doesn't look like the front door's been opened in a while.

I make my way around and hope to God he's not in bed still, or that he's got someone with him.

That would be super awkward.

My cheeks heat at the thought of seeing him naked. Even after all these years, he still does it for me.

I didn't so much as get a glimpse of anything when we were together last since he was quick to get the job over and done with.

I bite my lip at the thought of what his mouth did to me. Brock always was very good at pleasing me and knowing what I like. And having my titties played with is a massive turn on for me; I could let him do it all night long.

No! I need to pull myself together. *What the hell is the matter with me?*

I didn't come here to get laid; I came here to say freaking sorry, give him some banana bread, and hope we can be friends again.

It'll serve me right to not be such a pushover when it comes to him and sex.

I squash that thought as I hear grunting coming from the back porch and then I see a pair of legs sticking out from under the top part of the roof. Brock's up on a scaffold, shirtless and hammering away while the radio plays country and western in the background.

I stand and stare.

His body is a tribute to all that's sinful and seductive.

His chest muscles move as he hammers a nail into the wood, his thick arms clenching as beads of sweat run down his body.

His abs are rippled as my eyes wander lower to the V above his jeans and the smattering of hair that leads to something else I'd like to see.

My lips and throat feel dry as I indulge in the exquisite, fine male form in front of me and try not to imagine me riding him as he sucks on my... *No! Do not go there.*

"Hey," I call, hoping I don't startle him and give him a

heart attack. He doesn't hear me because the music's too loud. I can't reach the radio as it's too high up on the scaffold.

I have no choice; I grab his boot and give it a shake.

He immediately jolts, bangs his head on the roof, curses and scrambles up to potentially kill his would-be attacker... until he sees me.

With a frown, he reaches over and turns the music down.

"Jesus, Angel, you gave me a fuckin' heart attack."

I try not to give him a snappy come back.

Play nice, remember.

"Sorry, I tried calling out but your love songs for the single over 30's were just too darn loud."

He wipes his forehead with a bandana and sits up.

I try not to let my eyes drift down his sweaty body, but I fail miserably.

Neither of us say anything as my gaze lands on his again.

"I came to say sorry, about the other day." I hold out the silver package as his eyes dart to it.

"What's that?"

"Banana bread."

His eyes come back to me, his mouth purses. "You been bakin'?"

"It's a kind of peace offering."

He regards me coolly. "I'm listening."

I take a deep breath; apologizing isn't my strong suit. "I was a bitch, and I shouldn't have yelled at you."

"Been yellin' at me for the better part of twenty odd years, why stop now?"

I deserve that.

"We've all got shit going on, Brock, and I took it out on the wrong person. You were only trying to help." I suck down my pride because this is killing me. "My life's a bit messed up right now, that's all I can say."

"Wish you'd just have said that in the first place."

"I know. I bit your head off, that wasn't fair. That's why I came."

He runs a hand through his beard. "Anythin' I can help with?" His tone softens as he watches me.

I'm like an open book when it comes to him. I know he sees straight through me, but I shake it off. I'll tell him when I'm good and ready, and anyway, it's probably not something to worry about.

"If there is, you'll be the first to know."

He lets out a deep breath. "That wasn't so hard, was it?"

I shrug. "You know how I get. I don't mean to."

"How's your pop? They still comin' down here?"

"I hope so. Rawlings only sees them a couple of times a year. They're not getting any younger, none of us are." I look him directly in the eyes. "How are your folks?"

He shrugs. The unwelcome subject of his mom and dad is never a good topic of conversation but it seems rude not to ask.

They've had bad blood ever since Brock's younger brother, Axton, got locked up. His father blames Brock and the M.C. even though they had nothing to do with it. He and his dad have always had a strained relationship.

"Same."

"Have you seen them lately?"

He shakes his head and throws the bandana to the side. "Nah, mom calls every now and again. She wants to see me, but you know how dad is. Old fucker's too set in his ways. Amelia sees them so she keeps me up to date with what's goin' on. Like you said, nobody's gettin' any younger."

I shuffle on my feet as an awkward silence falls between us.

"You want me to make you a coffee? Before I get to work?" I offer.

The corner of his mouth turns up in a smirk. "Now you really must be groveling. You've
never made me coffee in your whole damn life."

"That's a lie, Brock Altman, and you know it."

He grins again and slides down off the scaffolding and lands on his feet. He's thirty-seven, almost a year older than me, and he's in excellent shape.

He towers over me as I try to keep my raging hormones in check.

I know he's been right under my nose this whole time, and it isn't like I haven't noticed, but I've steered clear. He's got his life to lead, and I've got mine.

Plus, he likes to go through a lot of women, like most of the boys in the club do. I've seen the hoes at the clubhouse, draped all over him. It doesn't bother me because he's not my old man, but a part of me does wonder what it would be like. If he were mine, if we were to make a go of it like we once promised one another.

But that is a dangerous thought. No good can come of it.

He goes for the back door, and I follow behind, marveling at some of his obvious new tats that I haven't seen before. To be honest, I'm a little miffed as I haven't tattooed him in over two years.

"You got some new ink."

"Yeah, brother down south owed me a favor. Does a good job."

I stay silent.

We walk through a rickety hallway to the makeshift kitchen. There's plastic sheeting hanging between the rooms.

"See you've been busy." I note, looking around the vast space. It's a shell, really. He's kept the old kitchen but the rest of what I can see is pretty much gutted.

"Too busy to work on it full-time, but I'll get there."

"Should get some prospects out here, get them doing shit for you. Make this place livable."

"I don't want my house fallin' down." He rolls his eyes and switches the kettle on. "I want it done properly, don't trust them to not fuck it up."

"Can't say I blame you. They aren't always the sharpest tools in shed." I glance around and through the kitchen window I see the vast, beautiful, sprawling landscape before me.

The porch wraps around all the way to the back so you can step out of the sliding doors and out onto the decking. It would be pretty to watch the sunset from here, surrounded by trees and nature. You don't get that a lot in Arizona.

He turns and rests his backside against the sink as I stand by the doorway. He makes no attempt to put a shirt on, not that I mind, but it's hard to keep my focus on his face.

I'm a woman, after all, and remembering what we did only fuels the fire inside my belly.

"Listen, I don't want us to be all weird around each other," I blurt out. His eyebrows raise in question. "After… what we did. Can we just move on from that?"

He crosses his arms over his chest.

"I take it that means you're not kidding; it really was a one-off."

"Brock, we can't continue it. We're not good for each other, not in that way."

"It felt pretty fuckin' good from where I was standing. Tellin' me otherwise?"

I shake my head. "It *was*, Brock, but that's just it, I'm not going to be your casual fuck buddy, you know that's never interested me."

He grunts. "I don't remember ever asking you to be that."

"You're not asking me to be your ol' lady, that's for damn sure."

BROCK

"Who says I'm not?" he challenges.

I swallow hard. "Brock, don't be stupid."

"You think I wanna be tied down to nag?" he says, and instantly I know he's lying.

"I know you don't."

"So, let's drop it. We can't be together, and you don't wanna fuck again, so I'll take my coffee two sugars and cream, extra strong."

His eyes are like fire as I struggle with him giving me orders.

Yes. I have control issues, and he knows it.

"Anything else, your royal highness?"

He waves his palms at me. "You're the one who offered. While you're at it, butter some of that damn banana bread. Don't just get me all the way in here and don't deliver."

"Didn't think you'd even be awake."

His eyes crease as he smiles. "So, you were planning on coming in to wake me up?"

I feel my nipples pebble at the thought of him naked in his big ass bed. It would be so easy to tug down his jeans and have my way with him in the kitchen. God knows I'm feeling all the feels where I shouldn't be.

"Very funny. I would have left a note."

"How touching."

Thankfully, the kettle boils and I have an excuse to stop staring at him. The sexual energy between us has skyrocketed to about a million.

This is what you get when you cross the line.

People who say you can be friends with benefits clearly don't know shit.

Now things are going to be really awkward between us every time we're together because for one, I can't stop thinking about him naked, and two, the way he's looking at me is like he's starving and I'm his next meal.

I have to stand my ground.

He doesn't really want me, not in that way. He wants what he can't have. And I can't let him have it because we will ruin each other. Just like the last time.

"Cups?" I reach for the milk, my back to him.

"Top cupboard, should be able to reach."

I'm not short, but the cupboards are high.

I stand on the tips of my toes and just get to the handle. I feel him behind me as his fingers touch mine. Safely grabbing one mug, then the other one, he places them in front of me on the bench. My whole body stiffens.

We're so close, I don't need him to press into me to know he's hard.

"There you go, sugar."

"Thanks," I breathe.

He goes to move back, but I reach out and hold his wrist.

"You know it's for the best, Brock, don't you?"

He moves back to face me, this time he steps closer so we're touching.

His hand brushes my hair to one side. "Nothing's as good as we feel together, Ange, but I respect your decision. I don't fuckin' understand it, but if it's what you want, then I can wait."

"Brock, that isn't what I meant."

"Man's allowed to wait it out, ain't he?"

I close my eyes. "I don't want to lead you on."

He grunts. "Little late for that, sweetheart."

"And I don't want to lose you again," I whisper.

His hands fall to my hips. "You'll never lose me. I'm a jealous fuckin' prick, and I can't say that'll change, but I'll try to keep out of your business, long as the guy's worthy."

I know that's not true either.

"I'm not trying to be a tease, Brock."

I feel his lips at my ear. "You come round here looking

like that and tell me you're no tease. C'mon, babe, we both know how hard you get me; you always have. Not that I should admit that, but I ain't afraid to admit the truth. You'll always get that from me, even when you don't wanna hear it."

He's breaking me.

He's been the one dependent thing in my life. I wish it could be different.

I can feel his hard on pushing against my butt, and I squeeze my thighs together.

I remind myself for what feels like the millionth time that I have to be strong. My walls are built high for a reason. Even for him.

The thought makes me sad, but I'd rather be safe than sorry.

Brock's always had the power to break me, and he wouldn't mean to do it, but he would, because I can't be who he wants me to be.

"It's just jeans and a tank. I didn't purposely dress provocatively."

I resist the urge to rub my ass back onto his hard on, though I want to. I want to go to heaven and back, lose myself in him for the rest of the morning. The urge to fuck him is so strong, I grip onto the counter for dear life.

"You'd be provocative in a paper bag," he says, then smacks my ass and moves away to a much safer distance. "Hurry up with my coffee."

I roll my eyes.

It's better this way.

When all's said and done, I have to believe that.

5

BROCK

I stand in the shower and let the water cascade over me. After Angel left, I did a little more work, then called it a day. I have to get to my real job mid-morning, and I needed those good few hours to get the nails in the roof.

Maybe Angel's right, I need to get some help. I really wanted to be in the house by Christmas, but that was six months ago. It's nowhere near being livable.

I wonder what Angel really thought when she traipsed through here.

It's all right for me, living amongst construction. I don't need anything fancy. But it doesn't feel like a home, and that's something I need to remedy.

I'm getting too old for this shit. I need my home to come back to where it's peaceful and quiet. The exact opposite to church.

I shudder at the thought of living in the room upstairs above the bar, it's too claustrophobic. Too loud.

I don't wanna hear the prospects fuckin' next door through the thin paper walls. Been there, done that, no thank you.

I've made a makeshift bedroom up in the loft, and it's fine

for now. The bathroom needs to be gutted, but at least it's got running water.

So many plans and so little time.

I was a fool to think I could do it all.

It's not like I don't have the cash, but I could save half by doing most of the hard stuff myself. Trouble is, I don't have the fuckin time.

I let the water run down my body as wash myself with soap.

Thinking of Angel in the shower is never a good idea.

My hand wanders to my dick, standing to attention.

I wasn't planning on whacking off this morning, but it's hardly my fault. She comes around in those skin-tight jeans with a tight tank, offering up her famous fuckin' banana bread, and I lose all control.

I close my eyes and remember the scent of her skin, the taste of her, how I wanted to do so much more with my mouth. How her not lettin' me only turns me on all the more.

What I wanted to do was devour her, all fuckin' night long. Then she'd keep her noisy trap shut for once because she'd be too exhausted to talk. I smile at the thought of gagging her while I fuck her.

Now I'm left like this, pleasing myself in the shower with a bar of soap, when it should be her in here with me.

I curse the day we took the plunge, because since that day when we were teenagers, there's been no goin' back. Not for me anyway.

I sheath my dick back and forth, gripping it tight, wishing it was her tight pussy milking me, taking me for all I'm worth while I pump furiously down her throat. That'd also shut her pie hole up for five minutes.

I don't see why we can't do the benefits part; she's making it way more complicated than it needs to be.

Shamefully, it doesn't take long to shoot my load all over the tiled wall. All I have to do is picture her perfect tits in my mouth and her hot, wet pussy and I'm a goner.

I call her name and close my eyes until I've drained every last drop. It's never as good as the real thing, but at least I won't be walking around with a big stiff one in my jeans all morning.

I quickly clean up, wash my hair and dry myself off.

I toss down another coffee and some toast and make my way to the yard.

Bones is fuckin' around on the computer when I get in.

"Yo," he says, without looking up. "How's it hanging?"

"Why you here? Thought you were bed-ridden."

He glances up at me then diverts back down to the screen.

"Better not be watchin' porn on there, asshole," I add. "Lucy's gonna be in today to do the books, better clear the browser history. She gets cranky if weird shit pops up."

Lucy, Rubble's ol' lady, does our book work once or twice a week in between the tow truck business.

"Fuckin' women, got our balls tied up nice and tight," he mutters. "Even the ones who don't belong to us."

"What are you complainin' about? Thought your balls were hanging free."

"If it's not Lucy, it's Deanna wanting shit done, if it's not Deanna, it's Fuckin' Lily, then there's your sister when she's in town, and don't get me started on Angel. Speaking of which, she back yet?"

"Saw her this morning."

His eyebrows pique. "Oh yeah?"

I roll my eyes. "Nothin' like that, she came over to make me coffee and suck up a little to get back in my good graces. We had a fight about her ghosting me, keepin' me outta shit I need to know about, it's gotta stop."

"She know that?"

"She's gonna."

He snorts. "You see what I mean, even when you don't have a ball n' chain, you got a ball n' chain, my friend."

"So fuckin' full of wisdom," I mutter. "Any other useful pieces of information I can swing my dick at?"

He pulls a disgusted face. "That's not an analogy I care to consider." He runs both hands over his freshly shaved mohawk, and I have to wonder what he's up to in here. Out of all the brothers, aside from Gunner, who hangs his ass out for a living so that doesn't count, he's the one who gets away with putzin' around the most.

If there was a gold medal in looking busy and doing nothing, then Bones would take the podium and win first prize, every time.

I glance at my desk and see the postmark on the letter and frown.

Stradbroke, Arizona.

My heart plunges into my stomach.

I take it with me to the lunchroom so I can read it in private and make a helluva strong coffee while I'm there.

I rip the envelope and begin to read.

Brother,

Well. It's been almost ten years since I wrote. Forgive me, things get a little rough in the joint.

Everything's done by email now, but you know me, I'm old school. Plus, they don't let us use computers and social media.

Shit's changed since I got locked up.

How're mom and dad?

I don't see them, obviously. Stradbroke isn't exactly the place for respectable folk, black sheep of the family and all that. At least they hate you less now that I'm gone, gotta be a flipside, right?

I'd like to say you're the favorite, but we both know Amelia is. She was eleven when I saw her last. She wouldn't know me now, hell, I barely recognize my own face. Some bastard stares back at me, wonderin' who I am, too.

I'm up for parole next month.

Fuck knows how that's gonna go, but I've been a boy scout this last year. Sometimes I don't know how ten years have passed.

I'm not that same seventeen-year-old kid anymore that made a mistake. A big one.

It cost me everything.

I regret it, brother. I want you to know that I'm not blaming anyone. I don't blame you; I made my own choices.

I've changed. I know people say that, brother, but I have.

I'm not the same kid I was when I went in, fuck knows I've paid my dues. I wish I could turn back the hands of time, but both of us know that isn't possible.

It gets me to thinking, and hear me out before you say no.

I got a lot of nerve, but I also got nothin' to lose.

I learned a trade in the joint, old school, they let me fix all the plumbing then I moved into electrics, got my ticket. I'm good at it too, earned some extra dough, though it's still not much. I got a certificate, can work for myself, damn proud of it.

I'm wondering if I get out, and that's a big "IF", that you'd maybe ask Hutch if I can prospect for the club.

Yeah, I know. A nearly thirty-year-old con that can plunge a toilet and fix leaky pipes, prospecting. But I'd work hard. I'd earn my keep. I'd make you proud of me like you once were.

I'm willing to shit kick. If I have to grovel, I will, but I can't go back there, Brock.

I won't go home.

Home is wherever you are, the only flesh and blood that's ever cared about me.

Always looked up to you, still do.

Nothing you did could have stopped me from making my choices. I was a stupid dick back then, I should've listened. But I didn't. I regret it, Brock. I regret it all.

I missed out on my teenage years. Missed out on seeing Amelia grow up. Didn't finish school. Disappointed mom and dad and lost our friendship. You're my best friend, always will be.

So.

Think about it, for me.

I get it if I'm too much of a liability, but I gotta ask the question.

Thanks for the cigarettes, they get me out of trouble. As for the rest, well, I've gotta have some stories to tell you when I get out of the joint.

That reminds me, if any sweet butts wanna pop by for a conjugal visit, just hit me up. Visitin' hours are the same. Be nice to see some pussy again. Fuck man, I barely remember what it's like, only in my dreams.

See you (I hope) on the other side.

Your kid brother,

Axton.

I stare at the words as they jump off the page at me.

Parole? He got fifteen years for armed robbery and aggravated assault. The thought he'd get out early never really crossed my mind, but if he's been on good behavior, like he says he has, who knows? Maybe this time they will.

I don't know whether to be elated or terrified; it's a little of both.

Axton and I were always close.

It killed me when he went inside. It broke me. He was just a kid. Yeah, he did wrong, but he's done his time. He was stupid.

I only see him a few times a year. Stradbroke is upstate, not that it's any excuse, but that place just gives me the creeps.

If anything screams at you more that you best walk the line, rather than do illegal shit, it's standing outside a prison waiting to go in.

When Hutch turned the club around when I was prospecting at eighteen, it was the best decision he made. In fact, he was one decision away from making the same mistake himself. When other members of rival clubs got caught with guns and drugs and other contraband, he was clean. He chose to walk away from that life, and the Rebel's ripped off the 1%er patch and hung it out to dry.

We're never going back there.

Hutch would no doubt still be locked up if he'd stayed, that or he'd be in a wooden box in the ground. Some heavy shit went down, members got shot in attacks of revenge, people disappeared, some never to be seen or heard from again.

The only reason the club still stands and stands strong, united with the brotherhood is because he walked away from all that shit. He gave it all up.

No amount of respect can be paid for what he did and continues to do.

He's like a father to all of us.

When I needed my own father in the past, Hutch was always there to fill that void.

When Axton got put behind bars, my father blamed me for leading him astray. Truth of it was, Axton did all of his stupid shit all by himself. Was nothin' to do with me or the club. But they didn't like me joining the M.C., so that was a good excuse to cut me out and cut me off for good.

Back then, he was hot headed, unruly, he got carried away quicker than you could blink, and his temper didn't help. He was just an angry teen, mixed up in drugs and people in all the wrong places. I did what I could, but I couldn't stop him in the end.

He was a good kid.

I run a hand down my face and wonder what Hutch will say. I mean, I don't think he'd say no.

Not if Axton really can prove himself. I'd be putting my name on the line, but that's a risk I'd be willing to take; he's my brother. There is also a very high chance he could just be using me to get a job, get settled and then high tail it, leaving me high and dry with a mess to clean up.

Plus, he's now an ex-con. Shit goes down in jail, it changes you.

I have to trust my instinct, and my gut says he deserves a second chance.

When I got out of the military, I never thought in a million years I'd be running a fuckin' scrapyard, but ten years later, here I am. Making good coin, making *very* good coin, even if dad thinks I'm just a no-good loser who should've taken the fall for Axton.

I should have protected him. But I had my own shit going on; it wasn't my job to babysit him, it was *his* job.

Maybe that's why dad hates me so much, because really, he hates himself.

I try to remember when the last time I saw them was. Two Christmases ago; that's the Christmas I put my foot down and said goodbye forever. Mom was devastated, bless her. She's the glue in our family.

I had the club, anyway. I didn't need his shit every time I turned the corner, standing there waiting for me to fuck up. To tell me he told me so. That I'd amount to nothing.

I don't know why he wants to live his life so bitterly, or why mom puts up with it. Surely, she must have had it by now.

Yet she's only seen me a handful of times in the last few years.

My parents are old school like most from that era. She let him disown his own children because he wants to save face at the country club.

We grew up fairly privileged yet here I am in Bracken

Ridge, the V.P. of a motorcycle club, or 'gang' as dad likes to call it, much to his disgust.

He can't grasp the concept of the club being legit or that we're as close as any family, more so than most, more so than my own. That's the sad part.

Maybe he'll never get it, and in the meantime our relationship is severed, and the one with my mom almost nonexistent. I know she only calls me when he's not around.

I always wondered what would happen if I ever did get an ol' lady and had a coupla kids. Would they still hold this grudge against me? Would *he?* Just because my little brother brought shame on the family name.

I cringe.

Axton was never a bad kid. Sure, he did some dumb shit. He fuckin' got busted for an armed robbery for fuck's sake, but he got caught up in the wrong crowd, got into drugs, lost his way. People fuck up, but to disown him? That ain't right. He never killed anybody. The gun wasn't even loaded.

I know him.

He wouldn't have done any of that shit if he wasn't high and trying to prove himself to the deadbeats he hung out with.

I think about his life and where he ended up and it could make a grown man cry. He had so much potential, he could've been somebody. He could have made a difference.

Axton had charisma. Charm. He was a lot softer than me growing up. He used to have a way with people that I just simply didn't—I still don't. That's why he was so easily led, he always wanted to please everybody, be everybody's friend.

I don't care to know anybody, except the people in my immediate circle. The rest I couldn't give a shit about.

I fold the letter up and put it in the inside of my cut pocket.

I'll talk to Hutch.

I know it would mean a lot to Axton to be prospecting for the club, but I don't know how Hutch would feel about it.

He's my brother, sure, but I barely know him anymore.

I know I'll have to sponsor him, which means he'll be on my watch. I'll have to kick his ass, and frequently. I can't go soft on him.

Deep down, I do lay some of the blame for not being there for him. For not being a better brother. I wish I could have just dragged him away from it.

He deserved better than that.

It's all up to Hutch. I respect his decision, even if it's no. Me sponsoring him will help, but him being an ex-con won't look good. Hutch doesn't want no trouble in the club.

It's risky, but it's a chance I'm willing to take.

I owe him that much.

6

ANGEL

I stare at the couple I'm about to tattoo and know it won't last.

I have a sixth sense for these things. It's like I just know.

Tattooing someone's name on your body, other than your kid or maybe your grandparents or mum and dad, is like the kiss of death.

"Tattooing each other's names is a big deal, guys. You break up, you got one big, fat, loud reminder of them right across your skin. Trust me, I do a lot of cover ups."

In actual fact, I'm known for my ability to do a very good coverup. I'm the best in the business, not that I want to brag.

The girl rolls her eyes.

Kids today. They got no idea.

"We're in love, and we're not gonna break up. Are we, babe?"

The dude's already been checking Jessie, my receptionist and ear piercer, out for most of the appointment. He's got a wandering eye. Why he'd want to do this is beyond me.

Chick must be good at something.

"It's only you, honey bun." He looks up at me. "Should get her name tattooed on my dick."

Firstly, I draw the line at private parts. And secondly, ew.

"Trust me, sunshine. You don't want me down there with a needle. Most men can't hack it on their biceps, much less the most sensitive part of their body. Would you stick a knife in your dick and slowly scrape it over and over until it's red, raw, and bleeding?"

His eyes go wide.

Didn't think so.

"That's what it'd be like, but by all means, go right ahead." I smile sweetly.

I sit and wait for the decision.

Stupid-scrawling-names-across-their-hearts or a dick tattoo. Choices, choices.

This is my life.

By the end of the day, I'm tired, not from working but from lack of sleep.

I know my ex hasn't got a leg to stand on but the thought of him being anywhere near Rawlings makes me want to commit blue murder. The fact he's getting out and will be around in society again, makes me more than nervous.

The last time he beat me, stabbed me... I ended up in hospital, I almost lost Rawlings.

Hurting me is one thing, almost killing my daughter is another.

It's unforgivable.

If he approaches me, I'll kill him.

There's no reasoning with crack heads.

It was a different time in my life back then, I was young and stupid.

And he'd never been like that when I first met him, he'd only dabbled with drugs, he was never hard-core, not in the beginning.

Aside from the fact he's a woman hater, he never wanted a kid to begin with. Rawlings was an accident.

It astounds me now that he's doing this. I don't know why, maybe to get back at me. It's the only reason, really.

He's never known her, and he never will. Over my dead body will he ever have anything to do with my sweet baby girl.

I've sheltered her from all of that shit. I'm the fucking poster child for turning your life around. I was almost going down that slippery slope myself, *almost*, but I got out. Luckily, with my life.

I get home after six and the baby-sitter, Kelsey, is playing video games with Rawlings. They're both screaming and carrying on like they're both six years old.

"Hey, guys, I picked up some Chinese on the way home."

Neither of them answers.

I walk into the den and both the girls still have their eyes glued to the screen, their fingers and thumbs madly working the controls.

"Is anybody here?" I say loudly.

"Hey, mama!" Rawlings says, her eyes not leaving the screen.

"Hi, Angel," Kelsey chimes.

"I've found a rich husband, and I'm running away to Paris. You'll have to fend for yourselves."

No response.

"Yeah, in fact, he's got his own private plane and his own private island."

"That's great, mom."

"So, I'll be leaving you to look after Rawlings, Kels. I'm sure you'll be fine. She rarely wets the bed."

Kelsey finally looks at me. "What the hell?"

I laugh.

Kelsey rolls her eyes. "Very funny, almost had me going."

"How about you pause the game and tell me how your day went, both of you."

BROCK

They groan and reluctantly pause the game until I get two minutes of garbled information, then Rawlings decides she's hungry, realizing I'm still holding the Chinese takeout. I go back into the kitchen.

"You want to stay for dinner, Kels?"

"That'd be great. Thanks, Angel, got nothing to eat at home except pop tarts."

Anyone would think I didn't pay her enough, which I do. I pay her well because she's reliable and Rawlings loves her.

Kelsey is seventeen and a really good kid. I've known her mom for years. She's helped me out a lot watching Rawlings after school two to three times a week. I'd be lost without her.

I'm just serving up dinner onto plates when I hear the sound of not one but two straight pipes getting closer and closer.

I don't know why I've got company but it's not unusual for Brock to stop by. That was before we did what we did, of course. But he still takes a lot of interest in Rawlings and making sure we're okay from time to time.

Sure enough, a few minutes later, there's a knock at the door.

When I go to open it, I see Brock and Bones through the peep hole.

I swing the door open.

"You guys smell the takeout?" I cross my arms over my chest, not letting them in.

"Hey, beautiful." Bones grins. "What takeout?"

I don't need to look at Brock to know he's staring right at me; I can feel it. He's tense, and I'm not sure why. We made up with the banana bread. We didn't make out or do anything. He seems to have accepted that we're friends again, and that's it.

He has to be okay with it.

His green eyes bore into me as I meet his gaze. "What's up, Brock?"

He thumbs to the porch. "Rawlings said she nearly fell through the deck."

I look to my right. I've patched the hole as much as I can, but I can't afford to get it fixed right now. All my cash is tied up, and while I make good money, I also have huge overhead and bills rolling in like there's no tomorrow.

"I'm waiting on someone to come do it." Well, I will be, when I get around to it.

Brock continues to regard me coolly. *What's up with him?*

"Who's that exactly?"

"I forget, but you know handy men. They aren't very handy, and they never show up when they're meant to."

"That's why we're here," Bones announces. "So, you don't have to worry your pretty little head over it. Now, what's this about takeout?"

I move aside and let him through the doorway. Rawlings is chattering away at the table, before I hear her jump up and Bones swings her around in the air and ruffles her hair with his hand. He's got enough knuckle duster rings to make Mr. T jealous, but he's harmless, and Rawlings loves him, like she loves all the guys from the club.

I turn back to Brock. "What's up your ass?"

His lips twitch. "You can ask if you need help, you know. Rawlings could've hurt herself. I'm pretty fuckin' good with my hands, or so I've been told."

I try not to let my cheeks heat with his innuendo. I know exactly how good his hands are, I've been on the receiving end.

"You don't have to come here and fix shit, I'm quite capable."

He frowns. "I know I don't *have* to. If we leave it up to you, it'll still be like that until Rawlings graduates."

I shake my head. "Very funny. I suppose I'll be feeding you, too."

He swallows hard, his eyes staying on my face but he's struggling with something; I don't dare to ask.

"You look pretty," he says quietly, then adds, "but tired."

I fold my arms back over my chest. "That was almost a compliment."

He grunts. "You gonna let me in, or do I need to have the secret password?"

I roll my eyes and let him in, except he waits for me to go first, shutting the door behind him, then, unnecessarily, he locks and bolts it.

Some things never change.

Bones is chowing down on fried rice and beef like his life depends on it. Luckily, I bought extra; these boys can put some food away.

Kelsey is giving him a look that I do a double take at. *No way in hell, girlfriend.*

I forgot how switched-on teenagers can be, and while Bones is pretty cute, he isn't into seventeen-year-old girls. He's also oblivious to her ogling.

When she meets my eye, I give her a pointed look. She blushes and digs into her chicken as I shake my head. God help me. I never want Rawlings to be a teenager. Nope, kill me first.

She's giving Bones the skinny on the video game she and Kelsey were playing.

I dish up Brock's plate as he takes a seat at my dining table.

It's been a long time since he's been around here, and I know he's just trying to help. I should feel grateful, but it kind of irks me too that he thinks I need him.

I can do shit for myself.

Okay, I can't fix decking, but he doesn't have to swoop in

here like some big hero on a white horse every time I have a problem.

He's always fixing shit. My broken fence. The outside porch lights. My lawn mower.

It's handy having him around, I concede, but I wish I could do these things for myself.

Relying on a man to do shit for me goes against everything I believe. I'm not a feminist, but I've been so let down by men in the past that I've learned to depend on nobody but myself.

I don't want to be ungrateful, though, and if I refuse Brock's help–I mean, why would I?–he'll just get mad and then we'll end up having a fight.

We've never fought like we have in recent years.

His eyes flick up to mine when I set his plate down as well as my own and sit next to him. He left the head of the table free for me to sit, rather gallant of him, must've killed him to do that. I know he likes to be in charge of things. *All* things.

I think about that day in the office, for like the hundredth time, and I suppress a groan.

So, he knows how to move.

Big deal.

He's not boyfriend material. And while I don't want a boyfriend or anything permanent right now, Brock would be all wrong.

We're too alike. We always have been.

Head strong. Tough. We both like control.

Even when we were kids, we were best friends forever, then we grew up and discovered sex and things changed between us, not in a bad way. But in a different way.

I admit, I don't enjoy seeing him with other women at the club, but I'm not going to lose sleep over it. Or, I wasn't, until we had sex in his office. Now I can't stop thinking about who he's been with since.

Now I want to fucking know. It's practically burning a hole in my brain just thinking about it. And it's stupid. Just because we fucked, doesn't mean that he's mine and I'm his and he can't fuck anyone else. Far from it. Brock will do what Brock wants to do and he always has. But a part of me can't help but wonder.

I know he favors the blondes, always has. With big tits and tattoos.

I shift in my seat and feel him glance at me.

"Everything all right?" he whispers as Kelsey, Bones, and Rawlings laugh over a joke Bones is telling. My mind is on other things, like usual, so I didn't hear any of it.

"Fine, how's your chow mein?"

"Bit rubbery, but better than eating cold pizza. That's all that's waiting for me when I get home."

I take a bite of my chicken; it seems nice enough.

"How are the renovations coming along?"

He frowns. "I'm getting a contractor team in; I need shit done quicker than I can get to it." He leans closer to me then whispers, "Axton may be gettin' parole."

My eyebrows shoot up. I glance at the others but they're not listening.

"When?"

He shrugs. "Next hearing is in three months. I think he's gonna get out, he's done his time. He's paid his dues, been on good behavior, got a trade now too."

I smile sagely.

Axton.

He was a good kid. He just got in with the wrong crowd, took too many drugs, got into trouble. Same old story you hear over and over, except Axton took a sawn-off shot gun and robbed a convenience store.

I wince at the memory. He was just a kid, and he paid the price.

"Is he planning on living with you?"

"Thinkin' about doin' up a room for him temporarily. Needs a place to land, maybe help out around here."

"Prospecting?"

"Club business, babe," he smirks.

Oh, right. I forgot.

Even though we've known each other since I was nine, *club business* supersedes everything with the M.C.

Women are just there to look pretty, put out and shut the fuck up.

"Right, the misogynistic boys club. Remind me again why women can't go into the meeting room?"

He grunts. "You get out of bed the wrong side?"

I roll my neck. "No. Just got a lot going on."

He watches me while he continues to eat, then nods at my food. "You on a diet?"

"No, just not hungry."

He grunts again. "Should put some meat on your bones, man likes a bit of flesh to hang onto when he's…"

"Anyone for seconds?" I ask quickly, kicking him under the table.

He rewards me with a devilish grin.

Rawlings raises her hand. "Me! Me!"

I get up and take her bowl.

"What's that on your face?" I hear Brock ask her, across the table.

She giggles. "Glitter, Kelsey put it on me."

He shoots me a look but doesn't say anything.

"Makes me pretty, Uncle Brock, but mommy won't let me wear makeup."

"That's because you don't need it, you're pretty enough

without all that sh… stuff on your face. How did swimming go, did you do what I told you?"

She nods enthusiastically. "Yep, and I held my breath for ten seconds. I'm going for a record." She beams at him, and he reciprocates.

He's always been good with her, taught her how to swim and hold her breath under water by holding her nose. He would have made a great father.

My stomach lurches at the thought.

I wonder why he never settled down and had kids of his own. While we were close once, we've never really had that discussion before. He was never ready to have a family. His home was here, and when I left town and got together with Marcus, we just kind of grew apart.

It was for the best. He was prospecting for the M.C., and I had shit of my own going on.

I do wonder though what would have become of us, but it didn't happen. No point dwelling on it.

I warm Rawling's food up in the microwave, then do the same for Bones who has another helping of noodles and fried rice.

After we're done eating, Kelsey takes off while I put Rawlings to bed. When I come back down from upstairs, Brock and Bones are outside working on the deck.

I clean up while they work and offer them beer in return.

"You know, you don't have to do it all in one night," I say, when an hour later, they're still hammering away.

"We aim to please," Bones replies, not looking up. "And Hutch would be on our case for not doing it sooner, especially if Rawlings fell through it."

Now I sound like a bad mom.

Brock ignores me.

I glance down and they're both on the ground,

hammering nails into the boards and Brock has a tool belt on that hangs so low on his hips it should be illegal.

I don't know why that does things to me.

I should be appalled.

It doesn't turn me on that he likes to fix things for me, I would have gotten around to it. But a fire lights in my belly seeing him with a tank top on, his muscles bulging as he whacks the poor, unsuspecting nail into the wood, while his mouth holds three other nails that hang out as he works.

Bones lines up the next board and they go full throttle as I sit down on the porch steps and look out onto the street.

It's quiet here. We live semi-rural. Neighbors are across the road but not right on top of us. It's how I like it. While the house may be old, it's got good bones. And I like it here.

It's cheap and Rawlings has plenty of yard to run around in. I want to get her a dog soon, but I worry I'm at work so much it would be home alone a lot, so it might not be the right time.

Another half hour goes by and then they're done.

I wrap my wool cardigan around my shoulders and stand.

The deck looks great. The big hole is now completely covered, while the wood doesn't match exactly, it's a damn sight better, and less dangerous.

"Thanks, guys, I really appreciate it," I say, as they dust themselves off and both stand.

It's not cold out, but I shiver slightly.

Brock tips his head. "Just need to wash up."

I nod as they go back inside and wash their hands. Bones makes a quick exit with his takeout container for lunch tomorrow and Brock stands at the door, shrugging his cut on.

"Next time, I wish you'd just let me know there's a big fuckin' hole in the deck."

I stare at him. What a jerk.

"I didn't realize I had to report to you about my repairs around the house, my bad," I shoot back sarcastically.

"Don't have to be a bitch about it."

I raise my hands to my hips. "Is this the part where I drop to my knees and kiss your feet?"

"Could kiss my dick, that'd make it worthwhile."

I shake my head. Not going to happen.

"We both know just a kiss wouldn't be enough, would it, Brock?"

He leans into my face, so close our lips almost touch. "It could never be enough with you, Angel, we both know that. Now quit bein' ungrateful and stop bein' a fuckin' tease. I'm on a short fuse as it is."

I lean back, best to not poke the bear. He's got that heat in his eyes, and that can only mean one thing, but he knows better. We had the talk. We're good now.

So, why's he looking at me like that?

"You were born on a short fuse, who's rocked your boat this week?"

He runs a hand through his hair. Come to think of it, he seems more tense than usual.

"Nobody. I just got shit goin' on."

"Club business," I drawl. "I got it. No place for a woman."

The corner of his lips turn up, but he halts his smile. "You always got a smart mouth, ever since you were fuckin' nine years old, nothin's changed."

"Yes, it has. I grew up, we all have to at some stage."

His eyes dance with mischief, and I know he wants me, but he won't touch me.

The thing is, we could do the sex thing. The friends with benefits. In a perfect world, it could work, but Brock's way too possessive and fiery for that kind of business. He can't even handle another man taking me out for dinner, much less any hanky panky.

He'd be able to keep fucking sweet butts and whoever else he wanted, and I'd be some piece of property at his beck and call.

Not happening.

I'm not going to be a club girl. I'm not going to allow him to claim me. Hell will freeze over.

"Goodnight, Angel," he whispers, too close to my ear. He sweeps past me, brushing my shoulder with his body as he squeezes by.

When his straight pipes flare up, I go back inside and lock the door behind me.

I'm doing the right thing.

There's only heartbreak where he's concerned.

It's for the best.

7

BROCK

AGED 10

I STARE AT THE TALL, BLONDE GIRL AT THE FRONT OF CLASS. Everyone laughs when she tells us her name's Angel.

I don't know why they laugh; she looks like one with her long, almost white hair that reaches her waist, and she's got pale skin and deep green eyes. They look a little startled, but this class will do that to you. She holds her head up high, but I can see her hands shaking.

I've never seen a girl so pretty before.

I kick Billy's chair, the idiot in front of me, and he shuts up without turning around. No-one needs a ringleader to act the fool.

I watch as she makes her way down the aisle, then takes her seat in the chair next to me and puts her small backpack underneath the desk. She pulls out a black pencil case with skulls all over it, and I arch an eyebrow as she takes her pens out, one by one.

She stills suddenly, glancing sideways and then flicks her large, green eyes up at me.

I don't know what she sees when she looks at me. Most kids are freaked out because I'm the biggest in the class, and, so I've been told, kinda mean looking. But she doesn't look at me like that. She looks... curious.

I'm also caught staring.

Instead of looking away like a fool, I do the unthinkable to make up for my mistake; I hand her one of my Twizzlers across the aisle. She stares at it like it's a foreign object, then, to my surprise, she takes it and offers me a small smile in return.

I shift my eyes back to the front and never say a word.

Angel.

Yeah, maybe math won't be so bad now that she's here. Not that I'll get any learning done.

∾

Some of the girls are mean to Angel.

She's pretty much a loner from what I've gathered from her first few days here. One of the girls, Miranda, sits with her at lunch but they don't seem to say much. Miranda is a bit of an outcast and is pretty new to Bracken Ridge herself. All the new kids get ousted by the local kids, like they own the place or something.

She stoops a lot, I think it's because she's tall, like she tries to blend in with the crowd and not stand out so much. She can't, though, she's not like anyone else.

I also find out she's good at games, not like the other girls who don't want to get their hands dirty. Angel is good at shooting hoops, playing all kinds of other sports, and prefers the outdoors to being inside the classroom. She helps the teachers, without being a total kiss ass, and doesn't talk back in class or cause trouble.

Maybe that'll change when she's been here long enough to suffer at the hands of some of the other kids.

BROCK

I find out all these things because we're in almost all the same classes, and ever since she moved to Bracken Ridge and started junior high, I've kind of befriended her. I guess I like the fact she's the underdog, unpopular because she's new and pretty, and she doesn't talk and gossip or snicker at other kids in class. She keeps to herself.

And I like the fact that she's not scared of me. She's not scared of anyone.

I take the usual way home, bouncing a ball along the sidewalk when I see a bunch of girls up ahead. When I look closer, I see they're behind Angel and one of the girls is shoving her in the back, calling her names. I begin to jog closer with the idea to intervene, to shut those girls up, turns out I don't have to.

I watch in sudden horror, just as she turns around to face her bully. The girl is taken by surprise, hardly expecting it, then Angel belts her in the face with her world atlas.

I stare in shock. All the girls behind her gasp in unison as Elise, as it turns out, holds her nose, blood squirting out of it all over her.

Holy shit balls, I think she broke it.

"I said, leave me alone!" she screams.

Everyone busies around the wounded girl on the floor as I approach and look down at Elise's crumpled form.

"Angel?" I call, rushing past the gaggle of girls without another glance.

She turns. "What do you want, Brock?"

She knows my name?

"Is that Elise?"

She looks over my shoulder. "I don't know, but she's been annoying me since I started school, Miranda too. She has to learn it's not okay."

I stare at her in wonder.

I bend and pick up the books that scattered out of her backpack as she rushed off, and I follow behind her.

"Here," I say, shoving her books into her open backpack. "You dropped these."

She looks over her should and gives me a small but wary smile. "Thanks."

"You need a bodyguard?" I laugh, shaking my head.

I've never seen anyone stand up to Elise Turner in my life. That has to be a first.

"Why would you do that?"

"My little brother got picked on. I don't like it. I don't like bullies. Elise had it coming, but I doubt she'll bother you ever again."

She smiles softly. It's hardly believable that the girl that just smacked Elise Turner in the face with her world atlas is not one bit upset about it. She actually looks quite pleased with herself.

"I don't like bullies either. My mom taught me to stand up for myself."

"She did right then. Can't let other kids push you around, if you show weakness then they'll use it against you."

She looks at me sharply.

I shrug. "My dad's military, sort of comes with the territory."

She keeps walking.

"Your mom sounds cool, if she's not gonna kick your ass for beating someone up."

She giggles. "She's a good mom."

I tag along next to her. "What about your dad?"

"He's good too, but he works away a lot, so it's me and my mom most of the time."

She sounds sad about that.

"Mine too, being in the military he's home a couple

months of the year. I'm gonna follow in his footsteps one day."

"Does that mean he goes to war and shoots guns?" She looks up at me, her eyes wide.

I look down at her as we walk. "It's all top secret, he doesn't talk about it much."

I know what my father does, but I don't want to scare her and think we're a family of thugs. My dad is a hard man, but he's not a totally horrible dad, not all the time. We barely see him. So, I'm the man of the house when he's away. My little brother Axton is five and is a real handful.

It's my job to look after mom and my brother.

I watch as she pulls out a cookie from the side pocket of her bag and unwraps it, breaks it in half and offers half to me. I take it gingerly.

"Thanks." I take a bite and realize I've no idea what to say. I've never really been friends with a girl before. They're all annoying and whiny. But not Angel, she's cool.

"What do you think about Mrs. Peterson's class?" I say to break the ice a bit.

Angel screws up her nose. "Pottery class?" She slaps her forehead. "I don't like that icky feeling on my fingers. It's gross."

"It's not like any of us are going to grow up and be sculptors," I agree. "I almost got kicked out for making an ashtray."

She giggles.

It's a nice sound. I like hearing her laugh, but I don't like seeing her frown or other kids picking on her.

"Do you smoke?" she asks me wide-eyed.

"Nah, I'm ten." I laugh. "Though, I had a puff once and it was pretty gross. I just did it so Mrs. Peterson would kick me out. All it got me was a can of whoop ass from my dad and detention for a week."

"Detention for making an ashtray?"

"Yeah, I engraved a bad word in the middle of it which she didn't appreciate."

She laughs again.

"What's the baddest thing you ever did?" I ask. She walks pretty fast, like she's got somewhere to be.

She thinks for a moment, then giggles again. "Hitting some girl in the face with my atlas."

I laugh with her.

"Don't worry, if you get into trouble, I'll tell them I saw it and it was self-defense."

She smiles again, crunching on her cookie. "Thanks, Brock. I'm Angel, by the way."

I smile back. "I know."

"You gave me a Twizzler on my first day."

Kill me now.

"There's nothing that can't be solved over a bag of Twizzlers."

We cross the street.

"You want me to walk you home? I'm only a few blocks away."

Good one, jerk face, now she'll know you know where she lives.

If she notices, she doesn't say anything. "I don't mind."

"Where'd you get these cookies?" I ask, shoving the last of it in my mouth. It's like the best thing I've ever eaten.

"Betty Crocker, dummy." She laughs, and I roll my eyes.

I've never let anyone call me a dummy before. Much less a girl.

"You're all right, Angel. If you need me to walk you to school, I'm right around the corner. Knowing Elise, she'll be plotting her revenge."

I don't like the idea of someone trying to hurt her.

"I usually get dropped off, but I walk home if my mom's working. I have a bike; I just need to pump the tires up."

"I have a bike too!" I say, feeling happy about that fact. "Maybe we could ride our bikes together?"

I haven't ridden a bike for a while, in fact, I'd probably have to pump the tires on mine too, but it'd be cool to hang out with her. For some reason, I like the idea, which is weird, I don't like many people.

"That would be cool, but won't your friends think you're a sissy hanging out with a girl?"

I give her a lopsided look. "None of them will think that, not if they want their front teeth for graduation."

She giggles again. "I'll ask my mom if it's okay."

"All right. Oh, and maybe bring more of those cookies," I say, hoping this walk never ends but knowing it has to.

She's cute and smart.

She shakes her head. "I'll see what I can do."

I smile.

Friends with a girl.

I can do that, yeah.

~

Needless to say, Elise doesn't bother Angel again. When her parents came to the school, I told the principal it was self-defense, and since Elise had been in trouble before for this kind of thing, she got suspended. It was all around the school faster than a firefly in a desert.

Angel was like the new messiah of our school.

She'd done the unthinkable.

Of course, I knew she was special the minute I saw her, it just takes some kids a little longer to catch on.

She sat at our table at lunch today. The other guys, Billy included, learned to mind their manners and as time went on Angel and I became inseparable. Best friends.

She helped me with the subjects I was struggling on, and I

taught her how to throw a punch and kick them where it hurts. We hung out at each other's places and even our moms became friends.

Things were awesome, the best years of my life. Until I hit puberty.

8

ANGEL

AGED 14

"I can't wear that!" I throw the dress on the floor, on top of the pile of other dresses that won't do.

"Why not? It's pretty," Miranda tells me, swinging her legs back and forth as she lies on my bed reading a magazine.

"He's going to hate it."

"Who?"

"Brock."

She begins to make kissy faces.

I roll my eyes. "I don't like him like that, but you know how he gets when other guys try to talk to me."

"I know. It's so weird."

"He says it's for my own good."

Miranda glances up at me. "I think he's right, you're not exactly dowdy, Angel. All the guys like you."

I frown, holding the next dress up to my neck in the mirror.

"That's only because I've grown boobs."

She giggles and shakes her head. "Yeah, they all trip over themselves watching you come down the hall."

I'm not interested in any of the guys. Well, maybe Chris

Marshall, but I'm not usually into the jock types. He is kind of cute, though.

"Nobody has even asked me to the dance."

"Brock did."

"Yeah, he's my best friend, which is kind of like your brother asking you out."

She looks up at me. "Brock is so cute, he's the cutest boy in school, Angel. And you get to spend all your time with him. It would be cool if you liked him like that; you've got a lot in common and you both like outdoorsy stuff."

The truth is, I *do* like Brock like that. I only said the brother thing to get her off the scent. But Brock doesn't think about me like that, he never has. He's treated me like a sister ever since we became best friends. There is no way I'm telling him I think he's cute and I want him to kiss me, though I have thought about it. Miranda and I practice on our hands.

"We shoot hoops, hang out at the arcade, and get yelled at when we come home covered in mud. Anyway, he doesn't like me in *that* way."

"Yeah? How come you're off limits then?"

I turn around sharply as she raises her eyes up to mine. "What do you mean?"

She snickers. "Come on, Ange, everyone knows that no kid within a hundred-mile radius is allowed near you. There's a reason for that."

I turn back to the mirror. "Yeah, he's just protective. He's like that with his little sister, too."

Amelia just turned four, though it's hardly the same comparison, it has gotten me to thinking.

"Uh huh. Well, he told Barry Matthews that if he even thought about asking you to the dance then he'd punch his face in."

"That's just Brock," I huff.

"Nuh uh, he told the whole class that you were his."

I look at her through the mirror as she watches me.

My head spins. "That I'm... *his?*"

She snickers again. "Yeah, that's what I heard. Just admit it, he's got it bad for you and you do for him, you should go together, like as a couple."

I tear my eyes back to the mirror and pretend to fiddle with the dress. It feels weird now.

I used to be able to wear anything I wanted, but lately, lately I've only worn things I know he likes.

"You're crazy." Is all I manage to say before she shakes her head and goes back to reading.

"Whatever."

My mind reels. He never acts like he likes me *like that*. It's usually the opposite.

I brush it off and decide on the black dress.

Mom will have a heart attack; dad isn't here to care.

Later, I walk Miranda home and decide to stop off and see Brock. I go around the back and that's when I hear loud voices.

I turn to leave, knowing it's his father, and though he's always nice to me, he isn't that nice to Brock. He's always yelling at him and that makes me angry.

"I didn't know he was going to follow me, the kid never leaves me alone," Brock pleads.

"That's no excuse, you know he follows every single thing you do. That's no defense and frankly I'm disappointed in you."

"That wouldn't be a first," I hear him mutter.

I can't see, but I can imagine his father getting up into his face.

"Don't take that tone of voice with me, son. Or I promise you it'll be the last time."

Poor Brock. He's a good kid. Axton is always following us

around, trying to get into all of our stuff and wanting to be part of our business. I don't mind him at all, but Brock finds him annoying.

He mutters something else, and I hear a clatter of a spanner or something crash to the ground.

"You want a poke at me, Brock?" his father sneers.

My eyes go round.

Did he just shove him?

"No, sir."

I cringe at his voice. He isn't afraid of him, not by a long shot, but he speaks like he hates him. Truly, truly hates him.

"You want to put up your fists like a man, like I taught you?"

"Why would I want to do that?" he fires back. "You won't let me hit you."

"You want to, don't you?" he prods. I can imagine him pointing his finger in his face.

"Sometimes, dad, yeah, sometimes I really do."

"You're not going to talk to me in that tone of voice, young man. You do, then you better be ready to back it up with a fist. Clearly, you're just a pussy. Maybe hanging around that little girl for so long has made you weak."

I literally push my back against the wall and bite my lip.

He's talking about me. Asswipe.

"Don't talk about Angel like that," he grits out. "Just don't."

Even I can tell that struck a nerve.

"What's wrong, son? Truth too close to home? What did I tell you about women?"

Brock doesn't answer so his father finishes for him; "That they weaken the knees. They make you soft. They belong in the home and nowhere else. Angel has too much mouth on her that one, uncontrollable, maybe that's why you like her, she's got a smart mouth, just like you."

"Shut up about Angel!" he roars. "She's nothing like that,

you don't like the fact that I can think for myself, that she doesn't make me weak, in fact, she makes me stronger!"

His dad guffaws with sarcastic laughter. I can imagine him, doubled over, taking it to the extreme. "Got you by the balls already, son, a fine first son you're turning out to be. Do you think that's a good example you're setting for your little brother? To show him that a little girl's got you right where it hurts and you're only fifteen?"

I can't take any more. I march around the corner and into the garage.

"Stop it! Just stop it right this minute!" I bellow at his father.

He and Brock's startled faces turn to me in unison.

His father's big, like him, and Brock is quickly catching up to his height. He's also been lifting weights so he's starting to get some muscles, too.

"Take those things back! And stop yelling at him!"

Brock stares at me with wide eyes and Jim, his dad, shakes his head and puts his hands on his hips. "Excuse me, young lady, it isn't appropriate for you to be yelling at me in my own house."

I see red. I could thump him one. "We're not technically *in* your house, we're in the garage, *sir*, and you've no right to yell at Brock. He's a good kid, he's always looking out for everyone else, putting everyone before himself, not that you would see that."

His dad narrows his eyes, clearly not impressed at my outburst, or me yelling at him.

"Always a little hot head, aren't you, Angel? Just like my strong-willed son, with a smart mouth to boot. Why don't you go along home now, before I have to call your parents and let them know how insolent you're being. The dance is coming up, I'm sure you don't want to be grounded, would be a shame to miss out on such an important night."

I stand my ground. "What about what you've said to me?" I challenge. "That women make men *weak*, that they make you *soft*, that I've got your son by the balls!"

His eyes brows raise at my tone. "That's enough, Angel, I mean it. I will march you home right now if I have to."

"You won't touch her," Brock snarls. "Over my dead body will you touch her."

I turn to look at him and I don't think I've ever seen him this mad. He's seething. I see his jaw clench, and I know he wants to hit his own father because his fists are balled up by his sides and his stance is rigid.

It strikes me how much I know about him. How I can tell his mood just by looking at him, and I can safely say I've never, ever seen him like this before.

His father rolls his eyes. "Very gallant of you, son. Can't put up a fight when it counts, though, can you? In front of her you're such a big, tough guy, but we both know you don't have the guts to follow through." He shakes his head, and it takes all of might not to leap over and punch him in the face.

He's such an asshole.

Brocks body stays rigid, but his eyes are fierce.

He hates him. I can tell in this moment that he's never hated him more.

Everything Brock does is wrong, and I don't know why his dad is like this. Brock is a good guy. He's a sweetheart. And he idolizes him, or did, up until last year.

His dad's changed a lot since coming back from the military. He's so angry all the time.

I realize this could get really ugly, and I'm suddenly glad I'm here because Brock won't fight in front of me. He knows I don't like it, yet something tells me he'd sock his father right in the mush right now if I weren't standing here.

I stare at his father, ready to pounce on him if he says one more word, but before I can blink, Brock has me by the wrist and is dragging me out of the garage.

His dad yells after us that we're suited for one another, or some shit, and I yank out of Brock's grip the minute we round the corner.

"What was that?" he demands, jogging to keep up with me.

"What was what?" I spit at him.

"You shouldn't have done that."

I feel tears sting my eyes. "He shouldn't speak that way about you."

His eyes soften. "It wasn't what he said about me that got me mad, Angel. It was about you. Son of a bitch had it coming. One day I'm gonna shut his mouth up."

I slow my pace and we fall into an easy silence.

"I'm sorry," I say after a while. "I just get so mad when he's like that to you."

"It's all right, I just wish he hadn't brought you into it. That's not cool."

Everyone knows about Brock's temper, and it seems his dad is the one who doesn't care about bringing it out in him. It's like the sick son of bitch enjoys it.

"Do you think something happened to him, when he was on his last tour of duty?"

He kicks the dirt as we walk. "Yeah. He changed a lot after his head injury. He's always been tough, but never mean. It's like he can't stand the sight of me."

My heart lurches for him. "It's not you, Brock, remember that. It's him. He doesn't hate you. He just doesn't know how to articulate his anger. And you're the easy target."

I feel him look at me. "When did you get so smart?"

I shoot him a glare. "Excuse me? I've always been smart. Remember how you passed Algebra; I'll forever hold that over you."

He snorts. "Yeah, like I'll ever need to use that out in the field."

I know he wants to join the military when he graduates, and I hate the thought of him going over to a war-torn country. I hope he changes his mind. Maybe seeing the changes in his dad will make him realize that it's not worth it. The idea that he could get hurt, that he… I don't even want to think it. I don't want to imagine a world where he's not in it.

We walk in silence.

"He didn't mean what he said," Brock says, after a while. "It's just how he is."

He can say what he wants, but Jim Altman has always been a sexist pig, and he always will be.

"I know," I reply. I don't want to make him feel any worse than he already does.

"What did you do today?" he asks as we round the corner to my street.

"I tried on dresses," I declare like it's nothing. "For the dance."

I feel his eyes on me again.

My mind floods back to what Miranda said, and I suddenly wonder if any of it's true. I decide to test the theory.

"Oh," he replies.

I keep my eyes straight ahead. "And I was thinking."

"Did it hurt?"

I shove him in the ribs. We always have this joke between us. Usually, I manage to get it in first.

I get to the big tree in my yard and sit in the swing. It's old and dilapidated now, but it still holds my weight.

Brock watches me carefully.

I can't believe I never really noticed how his muscles fill in the tank top he's wearing so well. And he's grown another half a foot.

Suddenly, butterflies rumble in my tummy. I don't know what that's all about.

I blame Miranda; she should keep her opinions to herself.

I suddenly don't feel as brave now that he's watching me.

"Very funny. I was thinking that maybe we should go together."

He narrows his eyes. "Eh, we *are* going together, Ange, unless you got a better offer?" He cocks a brow, challenging me.

"Billy…"

"Don't even say it, I'll kill him…"

I tip my head back and laugh. "Just kidding, you're so easy to wind up, Altman."

"Speak for yourself, you just yelled at my dad. Pretty sure that's your Christmas dinner invite gone out the window." He smirks and I smirk too.

"I really don't care. He can suck it. Pompous asshole."

He grins. "So? You were saying…"

I look down at the grass, and I can feel the heat burning in my cheeks. "I was thinking that maybe we could go… as like… a couple… if you want to…"

I don't know what the hell's gotten into me. It's like I've had too much Kool-Aid.

Maybe I just want to piss his dad off. Or maybe I liked what Miranda implied about us.

And for a second, it's bliss, until he folds his arms over his chest. Uh oh. Why is he frowning?

"Like, a *couple*, couple?"

I meet his eyes. "I mean, not really, just like pretend. Give them something to talk about, since we're apparently doing it anyway."

I mean, who has sex this young? The thought is repulsive. I've never even kissed a boy.

If it were to be with anyone, I'd definitely want it to be

with Brock. At least he'd be patient and wouldn't try to stick his tongue down my throat, I don't think.

"Who said we're doing it?"

I roll my eyes. "Everyone. Get with the times."

"Huh."

"Anyway, it's a dumb idea. Just trying to make the stupid dance interesting."

He doesn't like me like that. *Got it.*

His eyes flick to the ground for a moment like he's deliberating. "If I go as your date then does that mean I get to pick the dress?"

I roll my eyes. "No, Altman, it does not."

He grins. "Why? I'm much better at picking outfits than you are."

"That's only because I hate shopping."

"No, it's because you're a tomboy."

I glare at him. "Are you saying I couldn't pull off a dress?"

He unfolds his arms and runs his hands through his short hair, then rests them behind his head. His arm pits are hairy, and his pecs are just about bulging out of his tank top.

I can't tear my eyes away.

"I'm sure you could. But I'll bet fifty bucks that you wear pants."

"Ha!" I stick my hand out. "I'll take that bet, and I'll see you fifty, Altman." I laugh wickedly as he takes my hand and we shake, except when it comes time for him to let go, he doesn't.

My eyes flick to his again, and I almost wish they hadn't. His eyes burn with intensity. He's always had pretty eyes, for a boy, like smoky green sapphires.

My mouth goes dry.

He links our fingers together. His hand is warm in mine, and I feel that flutter again.

"I'll be your date," he says, softly. "I might even wear a suit."

I snort. "This I've got to see."

I part my lips but then close my mouth again. Unsure what to say.

"So, we're good?"

I squint at him. "With what?"

He squeezes my hand. "With this."

I swallow hard. "I thought we were pretending?"

His lips twitch. "What if I don't want to pretend?"

I feel my cheeks flush again. "You mean, you're actually serious?" Holy crap.

He shrugs. "If it keeps the likes of Billy off your case."

"Is that the only reason?"

He moves closer to me, and my heart literally jumps into my mouth.

"No." He raises my hand to his mouth and kisses my knuckles gently as I stare up at him.

"It's not the only reason."

I roll my lips inward, unable to think clearly.

So, he likes me?

"Then what is?" I press.

He smirks, letting my hand go. "You're the only girl I know who stands up to my father and doesn't bat an eyelid."

I shake my head as he backs away. "He doesn't scare me."

He nods. "I know. See you tomorrow. I'll wait out front. Gotta fix my brakes."

We still ride to school together.

"Tomorrow, then."

He smirks again, turning and jogs off down the drive and then disappears down the street.

I stare after him.

Does that mean he's my boyfriend now?

I've no idea, but I know that I'm not going to be able to act the same around him anymore. Things have changed.

Panic rises in me.

What if we have a fight? What if he doesn't want to be best friends anymore?

The rational part of my brain tells me that won't happen. It *can't* happen. But it still worries me. We've been through a lot, and Brock's always been my constant.

Maybe he feels sorry for me?

Poor Angel, she's got no one else to go to the dance with. Maybe he feels like his has to?

How mortifying.

"Angel?" mom calls as I twist and look behind me. "Are you out there? Come in now, it's getting dark."

"Coming, mom," I yell back.

I have a boyfriend. I think.

My heart leaps with joy as I skip to the front door.

Brock Altman is my boyfriend.

9

BROCK

PRESENT DAY

"What sort of mileage do Harleys have these days?" Melody's mom asks me as I lean against the school gate waiting for Rawlings.

If ever there was a pickup line, that's gotta be it.

She's a hot piece of ass, that's for sure. I never knew hanging around the school pick up que could be so good, should've volunteered my services years ago.

My sled isn't even here. Obviously, I'm not gonna put a six-year-old on the back of a Harley. So, I brought the truck. I didn't, however, omit my cut, and now all the moms are staring.

It seems Melody's mom, she never told me her name, is the only one brave enough to talk to me and is the only one with any sense of adventure. Gotta admire that in a woman.

I flick my eyes to hers as she quite openly flirts with me.

"About two hundred and forty miles to the gallon," I grunt.

She takes a long look down my body, sizing me up like I'm a lump of rump. "Never been on one before, they sure look exciting."

She's hot but not really my type if I'm being picky. She's

brunette for one, and I prefer blondes. Her tits aren't big, but they're decent enough. Yeah, under normal circumstances, I'd do her, but something has come over me since Angel and I can't seem to shake it.

It's like old times all over again on rinse and repeat.

Like senior prom when we both fumbled around, and I took her virginity.

Fuck, man.

Those were good times.

When Angel looked at me like I could save the world. I couldn't get enough of her. One taste could never be enough.

In all the years since, and it's been a long time now, she's only gotten hotter with age. She still has the ability to turn me on like no other woman ever has. It's our history, the fact that she's the first and only girl I really ever cared about, the only one I've loved. And all these years later, I can't seem to shake her.

She's stuck in my head like a damn broken record.

I stare at the woman eyeing me. "My straight pipes rumble so hard you'd come in seconds, one of the reasons I don't have chicks on the back of my sled, I prefer to be the one giving." I give her a wink.

Her eyes flare, I think she's unsure whether to be turned on or repulsed by me.

I wait for a reply, but I don't get one. The bell sounds suddenly, and kids start pouring out from everywhere.

It's not long before Rawlings sees me and comes running over.

I only know Melody because she's been over at Angel's place a few times. And her mom's been overly friendly every time I've run into her. This is the first time she's kind of hit on me.

Maybe I could fit in a little couch time after kid-sitting

duties are over. I wonder if she's got an old man at home and just wants a little action on the side. Shit like that never used to bother me, and I'd been happy to be the rebound guy. But lately, I've been questioning everything.

I glance down at her tits, and she squirms under my glare. Yeah, they're growing on me but I'm still limp.

If only I hadn't fucked Angel over my desk. Now there's every man's wet dream come true.

I'm cursed, I tell you, goddamn cursed.

There's no cure for what I've got. Well, there is, but Angel's not exactly serving her pussy up on a platter. So, that means I'm royally screwed. I had a taste of her and now she's got me all tangled up in a mess.

I need to get laid and clear my head of her.

She doesn't get time to answer because Rawlings runs up to me. Unlike most of the kids here, she isn't ever embarrassed by me showing up unannounced, instead, she runs into my arms. I pick her up and pretend she weighs a ton and set her down on her feet.

"Hey, Uncle Brock!"

"Hey, kiddo."

"Can Melody come over?"

I glance at Melody's mom, and she nods with wide eyes. Clearly, she's got orgasms on the brain.

Oh, brother.

Should've never taken the bait.

"Can't today, princess. Got stuff to do, maybe next time?"

Melody's mom pouts.

"Okay, but can we get ice cream?"

Kids are so fickle.

I take her by the hand. "There's always ice cream, baby girl." I nod to Melody and her mom as Rawlings says goodbye, then follow her around to the passenger side of my truck and strap her in.

I climb into my side and start the engine.

"How come you're picking me up?"

"Mom's gotta work late."

"Mom works a lot." She sighs.

"Yeah, she does, to give you all the things you have." She's a good kid. Angel's done a great job being a single mom, but it doesn't hurt to remind them. "And sometimes that means she gets stuck at work."

"I'm hungry," she whines.

I shake my head.

"Open the glove compartment, I got a stash in there."

She does so and pulls out a small bag of corn chips. "You always have the best snacks, uncle B. Mom never lets me eat this stuff."

"Yeah, well, let's just keep that between us, princess, yeah?"

"Are we going to my house?" She chomps on her chips and looks out the window.

I have to go meet with the contractors. Today wasn't a great day to collect her, but I didn't want to let Angel down. I'm trying to keep in her good graces, and collecting Rawlings is one sure fire way to do that. Not that I wouldn't do it anyway; Rawlings is no bother. She's practically an adult in a kid's body, and she's way smarter than me.

"No, sweetie, we're going to mine."

She jumps up and down in her seat. "I love going to the ranch!"

I laugh out loud. "It's hardly a ranch."

"It's out of town, isolated, and you've got wild animals, seems like a ranch to me."

I shake my head. *Six going on twenty-six.*

"You got homework to do?"

She shakes her head. "Nope. I did all my stuff in class."

Of course, she did. A chip off the old block.

Angel may have gone a bit wild in her youth, but that didn't happen until after high school.

She was a good kid, had even better grades, and like Rawlings, she liked school.

Rawlings, though, is a lot softer than Angel, delicate even.

"Where are we going? You missed the turn off," she wails.

I give her a sideways look. "Picking up something for dinner. Mom might stay and eat if we have something that smells delicious cooking."

She gives me a squinty look, just like her momma used to do. "Since when do you cook, Uncle B?"

"Hey, I've been cooking for myself since before you were born."

"Can't we just have burgers?"

Truth be told, a part of me wants to show Angel I am capable of more. I can cook, not saying it's anything decent, but it's kept me alive this long.

Since I live out of town, I don't have any sweet butts or club girls running around after me, much to my disappointment. I even do my own fuckin' laundry.

"How about your other favorite meal?"

Her eyes go wide. "Lasagna?"

"Yeah, and we'll make a salad, that way it'll seem sort of healthy."

She claps her hands together as we make our way to the store and get all the ingredients.

Once we're done there, I drive back to my place. Angel calls me on my cell just as Rawlings jumps out of the car and races to the door.

"Careful of the tools!" I yell after her, then to her mom, "Hey."

"Sounds like you've got your hands full."

"She takes after her momma, so that'd be a yes."

She laughs softly. It goes straight to my dick.

What the fuck is wrong with me?

"Very funny, what are y'all doing?"

I slam my door shut and haul the bag of groceries over my shoulder, along with Rawlings' school bag.

"Just got to my place, you checkin' up on me?"

"No, of course not, just making sure you got her okay."

"So, you're checkin' up on me," I grunt. "Kid's practically a saint, already done her homework, and she recited all the animals on the planet from A to Z. Should register her in one of those smartest kid in the world competitions, kids got smarts, and she can spell too."

"Must take after her momma then, right?" She snorts, throwing my words back at me.

"Did you call for something? We're busy."

"Busy doing what? You said you just got there."

I walk up the drive and to the back porch where Rawlings is chattering away to one of the contractors.

"We did. We got shit to do, you wanna speak to your momma?" I say to Rawlings.

"Hi, mom!" she bellows over her shoulder, making no attempt to come to the phone.

"Guess not." I laugh.

"Fine. I know when I'm not wanted," she huffs.

Oh, I almost forgot. "I've got something for dinner, so you don't have to worry about it."

"Brock, you don't have to do that."

"Kid's always hungry," I grunt. "Like you, she's got hollow legs, don't know where she puts it."

"Uncle B, we gotta go!"

One thing Rawlings loves doing is helping me in the kitchen. We've baked cookies before and banana bread, though it never quite tastes like Angel's.

"Yeah, sorry, Angel. We gotta go, we've got an afternoon here."

She laughs. "Sorry to be an inconvenience."

I wink at Rawlings. "That's okay, don't let it happen again. Bye, Angel."

"Bye, mom!" Rawlings yells.

I cut her off before she can answer.

"Can I grate the cheese?" Rawlings asks. I know full well that means she's going to eat most of it.

I frown. "Not sure if that's a little bit dangerous."

"It's not *that* dangerous," she scolds. "I'll be careful."

I bump her butt with her school bag. "You're just tryin' to eat the cheese before we get it on top of the lasagna."

"Someone's got to look out for quality control."

The contractor snorts, and I roll my eyes at him.

Yep, six going on twenty-six, just like her momma was.

~

It's almost nine o'clock when Angel gets finished and comes on over to collect Rawlings.

I kept her plate warm in the oven.

I forgot how much fun I have when Rawlings is around, she's a class act. Normally kids kind of annoy me. I've got no patience for their constant barrage of questions, but she isn't needy and as I say, is smarter than most adults I know.

Angel calls through the back fly screen door just as I crack a beer.

"Hey, Brock, sorry I'm late."

"You have a hot date?" I watch her as I drink from the bottle.

"I wish. Just locked up. Something smells nice."

I go to the oven and with the oven mitt, take out her plate and put it on the place mat on the table. Very fuckin' domestic. If the boys saw me now, they'd choke.

"This is all very fancy." She smirks, taking her jacket off. "Where's my child, by the way?"

I go to the fridge and take out the salad bowl and a soda and put that on the table for her as well.

"Rawls, momma's here."

"Hey, mom!" she calls from the makeshift den.

She rolls her eyes. "Netflix?"

I shrug. "We did shit first. And she ate all her dinner, kid needs to be rewarded."

She looks at me as I sit down opposite her.

"What?"

She smiles sagely. "You're a good man, Brock Altman, anyone ever tell you that?"

I scratch my beard and rest my elbows on the table. "Not as much as I like to hear it."

She tucks into the lasagna we made and makes appreciative noises as I watch her. "You guys made this?"

"I grated the cheese!" Rawlings yells.

"She grated the cheese," I mimic. "And I did all the heavy lifting. Mom's special sauce."

"You're a man after my own heart," she teases.

I try not to look at her like I want to fuck her across the table, but I've never been one to lie.

She pretends not to notice and opens her soda.

"You're making progress at least," she goes on, helping herself to the salad. "When do they expect to finish?"

I rest my head on my forearms, tiredness taking over me as I watch her. I'm glad she likes my food, or maybe she's just hungry.

"Eight to nine weeks, which is gonna be costly, but with Axton possibly gettin' out, it's made me want to get my shit together. And I want this dump to finally be a home."

She looks up from her plate. "It's not a dump, it just needs work."

"Yeah, a shit ton of work."

"You can get the prospects to come and do some manual labor, wouldn't hurt them."

"Already on it. Jax and Lee are gonna clean up all the yard, pour some concrete and make a pathway. Nothin' they can't handle." I wonder if I've given them too big of a job, but if they fuck it up, they can always shit kick for another year. That might be an incentive to do it properly the first time.

She still hasn't told me anything about the ex and it makes me wonder why she hasn't. I'm starting to get testy. I'm not a patient man. Time to broach the subject.

"So, I heard your ex may be up for parole already."

She looks at me sharply. I see the truth in her eyes.

"How did you hear that?"

"So, it's true."

"He's out, yes."

"He's out?"

She looks down at her plate and drops her voice. "Let's talk about this later," she whispers.

Anger boils within me.

"Let's talk about it now. Has he contacted you?"

I see the resolve in her eyes, and I know it's true.

"His lawyer did."

I bang my fists on the table and she jumps.

"His lawyer?" I lower my voice to a whisper. "What the fuck for?"

She sighs, and it's then I see the stress and worry she's been holding in unfold.

I'm pissed she's kept this from me, but if I know one thing about Angel, it's that if I back her into a corner and lose my shit, she'll run. She won't tell me shit. It's what she does.

Her hands tremble as she clears her throat. "He wants visitation, or some shit."

I stare at her dumbfounded. "Visitation?"

"You heard right."

"What the actual fuck? Does he not remember attempted murder charges and putting you in the hospital... you almost lost Rawls?" I shout whisper.

She winces at the memory.

"Yeah, I think I fucking remember, Brock. I was there, not like I could forget."

"So. Where is he? Sooner I know the sooner I can go end him."

She sighs again. "He's still in Minnesota, he can't leave the state. I've got no choice but to seek legal advice to clear it up. He says he's changed... I... I didn't think this was ever going to happen. I thought he'd be dead when he got out; he owed a lot of people money."

We don't talk a lot about that time of her life and how she got mixed up with him in the first place, I get too irate and want to smash something, namely his face.

I point at her. "If he sets foot in this town, he's a dead man. I'm gonna find out where he lives."

"No, I don't want you to do that. Promise me you won't do that; he won't even get into Arizona."

"Not promising shit."

She knows I'm not kidding. "He's just trying to rattle me, that's all this is."

"I'll fuckin' rattle him. I'm not kidding around here, Ange. I will fucking slit his throat and bury him out in the desert, let the coyotes finish him off." I want to add *for touching what's mine,* but I refrain.

"The lawyer is just a formality, if we cross the t's and dot the i's then it'll be fine."

"Then why didn't you tell me?"

She swallows hard. "I can't run to you every time I have a problem."

I baulk. "Every time? I think this qualifies for one of those times when there actually is a problem. The M.C. needs to know, then we can be prepared."

She fiddles with her knife and fork as I stare at her.

"You're scared of him," I state, knowing it's true.

Her bottom lip wobbles just slightly.

Only I get to see this side of her, how vulnerable she can be. To the outside world, she's a tough chick. She's got it all figured out and looks like fuckin' superwoman. But I know better.

"I don't trust him, he's slippery. Trying to mess with my head, and he's doing a good job of it. I never thought he'd get out..."

"Listen to me when I say, you don't have to worry about him. I'm here, I'm not gonna let shit go down, you have my word on that."

She smiles without humor. "You can't be around twenty-four-seven, Brock, and I don't expect you to be. I've got a restraining order against him, and he's on parole. He won't come here."

I hope.

"So then like I said, you've got nothing to worry about."

"I thought this was over," she whispers.

I reach over and place my hand over hers, giving it a squeeze. "I'll fuckin' defend you with my life, Ange. You have my word on that. I will do what needs to be done if he or his goddamn lawyer contacts you again. I don't fuckin' understand the justice system, what a fuckin' joke."

She looks slightly relieved at my admission, but her expression is still fearful. "I don't understand either, he maintains self-defense and that he was high, temporary insanity, I guess attempted murder doesn't get shit these days."

I lean toward her. "I don't like that you didn't tell me."

She shakes her head. "I didn't want you to go ape shit on me, that's why I didn't say anything."

Little does she know, I already knew from Hutch most of the details, I did not, however, realize he'd started legal proceedings and was already out. "This is kind of important. From now on I want to know everything when it comes to him and his sleazy lawyer."

"He can't take her away from me, Brock, she's all I have."

I pat her hand, feeling more protective than ever. "He can't do shit. You've not just got me, but the whole club too. We're your family, don't ever forget that. We won't let anything happen."

She smiles wistfully. "We should really get going, I've got a big day tomorrow."

I take my hand away and clear her plate.

"All right."

"Thanks for watching Rawlings." She stands and calls out to her daughter that it's time to go. Rawlings groans from the den, and I chuckle as I put the plate into the sink.

"Coming to church on the weekend?"

I know the answer already.

"I've got my parents coming out, so I said we'd house hunt on Sunday. Sooner the better, means they won't be staying with me when they move. I love them and all, but I don't want to live with them again."

Yeah, I know the feeling.

She goes in to fetch Rawlings and comes back out holding her backpack.

"What do you say to Brock for having you?"

"Thanks, Uncle B, I had fun."

I ruffle her hair and smile. "Next time I'll have some video games for you to play."

She jumps up and down and claps her hands. Angel rolls her eyes like that's the worst news in the world.

We make our way out to her truck and Rawlings climbs

up and buckles herself in while I hang around outside the driver's door.

"I really appreciate today," she says, looking down at the ground then back up at me.

I give her a chin lift. "That's okay."

Angel hesitates like she wants to say something but then refrains.

"Night, Brock."

"Night, Angel."

I watch her leave, the tires on her truck kicking up a steady stream of dust in her wake as she leaves.

I want her.

More now than ever before, but I have that sinking feeling that it's too late.

Years too late.

And I can't do a damn thing about it.

10

ANGEL

AGED 17

"What do you think of this one?" I say, spinning around in the short dress with a tulle skirt, knowing full well he'll hate it.

Brock sits outside the dressing room as I try and find something suitable for my cousin's wedding.

He cocks a brow, looking up from the magazine he's reading and when he sees my bare legs and the skirt barely covering my ass, he puts the magazine aside and stands.

My eyes go wide as I see the bulge in his pants. I squeal as he pounces and try to lock myself in the changing room, but he's too fast. His foot jambs in the door and he forces his way in and closes the door behind him.

"Now I've got you where I want you." He grins as I giggle and back up against the mirror.

"Shhh! They'll hear you!" I whisper as he cages me in, his mouth going straight to my neck where he bites it gently.

We've not gone all the way yet, but things have been getting pretty intense. He turns eighteen soon, a late bloomer, but we didn't want to rush into anything and though sex doesn't scare me, not with him, I want it to be special.

We have basically been to third base and when left alone, he can't keep his hands off me.

"You shouldn't wear skimpy little skirts, babe, it gets me all excited."

I giggle again, throwing my arms around his neck as he pins me against the mirror. I can feel his hard cock pressing into me.

"Jesus, Brock."

"He ain't listening, princess. I don't think he ever was."

He moves his mouth to mine and as soon as our lips meet, his tongue seeks entry. Him and his tongue are equally talented.

"We should stop," I pant as his head moves to my breasts, sucking through the fabric.

"No, we shouldn't."

I roll my lips. "They'll be wondering where we are."

"I don't care," he groans. "You should get this dress."

"Isn't it a bit short?"

He snorts. "Not to wear in public, to wear for me. When I finally get you on your back, you can be wearing it with heels and no panties."

Butterflies flutter in my stomach imagining it. "Sounds like you've been thinking about it."

He snorts again, bringing his face up to meet mine. I stare into his pretty eyes, and I can't help but grin back at him.

It'll always be us. Me and Brock.

I love him, though I've never outrightly told him that.

"Babe, it's all I think about. Not gonna lie, it consumes me day and night."

"Day and night, huh?" I laugh as he grabs me by the hips and lifts me, I swing my legs around his waist as he grinds his hips into mine.

"Yeah, you feel that? That's what you do to me, and I've

gotta take care of myself every time we part because I'm so fuckin' hard."

I gasp as his words just as there's a knock on the changing room door.

"Excuse me, you can't be in there!"

He turns his head to the door as I look over his shoulder.

"Shit!" I giggle.

"Now you've done it, Angel," he chuckles, turning back to me, then yells over his shoulder. "She just needed help with the zipper."

I slap him on the arm, and he kisses me chastely.

"Gonna get us kicked out."

He sets me down and points in my face. "I'm buying this fuckin' dress."

With that, he turns, unlocks the changing room door, and leaves. He doesn't apologize to the sales assistant, and instead, I hear him asking what heels they have in that same color.

I roll my eyes.

He's hurricane Brock. That's all I can say about him.

~

"I don't want you to go," I whine. "What am I going to do all weekend here by myself?"

We're at my place, lying on my bed, facing each other. Needless to say, my parents are out for the evening.

"It's one weekend, babe." He runs a finger down my cheek as I stare at him.

"Then you'll be gone for good."

"It won't be forever."

"What about the club?"

He's just started hanging out with the Rebels M.C., something I'm not entirely happy about, but he says they're good people. If his dad finds out, he's going to be toast.

"I can prospect after I get back. Hutch says there will be a spot for me after I enlist, so I can fall back on the club when duty is over."

I go to turn away from him, but he stops me, holding my chin with one hand.

"Why the cold shoulder?"

"You know why."

"Don't be like that, I've never kept it a secret I'm going to enlist. It'll be for a couple of years."

"And what am I to do?" I sulk.

He smiles, kissing my bottom lip gently. "Since when have you ever been the lonely-hearts type. You'll go to college and get your arts degree, then we'll move in together."

I stare at him. Something inside me screams that this is all wrong.

"What if we grow apart?"

He snickers. "You gonna wait for me?"

"You know I will."

He looks at me earnestly. "What about other guys? You sure you wanna commit to that?"

Why would he think I'd ever want anyone else?

"Do you want me to sleep around? Like some cheap slut?"

He nips my bottom lip with his teeth. "Of course not, you'd never be that."

"Then what? Do you want to be free and clear when you enlist? Is that it?"

He laughs, literally laughs in my face. "No, babe, that's not it."

God, he's so infuriating.

"Then what?"

He looks back at me. "I just don't want you to think you're missing out on the full college experience. I want you to have that, party and not hold back. I don't want another guy touching you, obviously, but I'm kidding myself if I think they're not gonna try."

"They won't get anywhere," I whisper. "I've known you half my life and we haven't done it yet."

"*Yet*, I like that word."

One thing about Brock, he's never pressured me. It's not that I don't want to, we almost have a couple of times, but I want it to be the right time, I want it to be special.

I know he wants me bad, and I want it to be the last thing I give him before he goes away.

"There's only ever going to be you," I tell him. He kisses me again, and I run my fingers through his hair.

"I love you, Angel, always have, since the day I first saw you."

I stare at him dumbfounded. It's the first time he's said that word.

I open, then close my mouth.

"Gonna leave me hanging, babe?"

I shake my head out of my reverie. "Brock… I… I love you too, that's why I don't want you to go, I'm afraid something will happen to you, and I'll never see you again."

I fold into his chest, and I can't stop the tears flowing.

He holds me close, soothing me and kissing my hair.

"Nothing's going to happen, princess, you'll see."

"You don't know that," I sob. "People die in foreign countries all the time, accidents can happen, you could be ambushed, shot, what about snipers?"

He holds me to him and moves his knee in between my legs then rolls me onto my back. He cages me in, hovering on his elbows as he kisses my tears away.

"Don't cry, babe. I'm a big boy, I'll be fine. I know how to look after myself, but I can't do the college thing, you know that was never in the cards."

I stare up at him. He's my world.

"I love you so damn much, Brock Altman."

He grins, pushing my hair back off my face. "That's the girl I know and love, my feisty little firecracker."

I roll my eyes. "Can you be serious for more than five seconds?"

"Depends."

"On what?"

He licks his lips. "You gonna give me a little sugar?"

I grind up into him and he groans. I can feel his hard on pressing into me. It'd be so easy to let go.

"Yes, but my parents will be home soon."

"I already got our textbooks open at the ready." He winks. "But do you really believe they'll think that's what we've been doing up here all this time?"

"I don't care what they think," I breathe, running my hands up his broad chest.

He kisses my nose. "Big words..." he stops as I stare at him.

"I'm ready, Brock. I want you; I want you in every way. I don't want to wait any more."

He swallows hard. "You just sayin' that because you think I'm going to die while serving?"

I screw my nose up. "That's a horrible thing to say."

He grunts a laugh. "I want you too, fuck knows I've never wanted anything more. But not here like this, I want it to be special, too."

"When then?" I moan, earning me a chuckle from him.

"Soon, babe," he tells me, bringing his lips down to crush mine. "Soon."

I had no idea then that in six months' time our lives would change forever.

The promises we made would be nothing but a distant memory.

Present day

I wake up with a start.

My heart's racing in my chest, and for a split second I don't know where I am.

I throw the covers off and moment by moment I gather myself and slow my breathing. I was dreaming. God knows what about.

I glance at the side table and press my phone to get the time. Two am.

I get up and pee and splash cold water on my face.

I can hear the wind howling outside, a storm's brewing.

I wander past Rawlings' room and peer in, her curtain is blowing so I let myself in and close it. As I glance outside, I see something by the tree. Someone. I can see the faint light of orange. The end of a cigarette butt?

My heart races in my chest as I rush from the room and back to mine, it has a better view from the large bay windows. When I get there, I look out and scan the yard, but I see nothing. Nobody standing there, no orange light.

Now I'm fucking seeing things.

A good few minutes later, I plop back down on my bed and sigh. Now that I'm awake, it's unlikely I'm going to get back to sleep.

Did I really see someone in the front yard?

Who would be freaking standing there watching the house?

I think the bad dream I had is making me paranoid.

I've always been tough. Ever since I had to grow up.

When I let Brock go, things changed.

I went to college, got my degree and worked in various graphic design places for a while. Brock came back once every six months, but each time he came back, he changed.

Then the last time, we ended things for good.

I shudder when I remember.

It wasn't like we had a huge fight, or we'd met anyone else, we'd just grown apart.

Being in the military had changed him, made him tougher, not that he needed to be any tougher than he already was. His dad saw to it that he was no *pussy boy*, as he like to put it.

I think back to that day in the garage when I yelled at him, and it still makes me smirk. His old man had it coming. Now he doesn't talk to Brock at all. All because he joined the M.C. and then when Axton got locked up, he got all the blame.

Stupid son of a bitch.

I haven't seen them in years, but I always liked his mom. It's because of her that he learned how to be a man, not because of his father. Sure, he knew how to throw a punch, defend himself, hell, even fire a gun, but his mom taught him respect, loyalty, and how to love. Some things his dad wasn't ever capable of.

I stare at the ceiling, unsure how I even got here.

It's probably not a great debate to have in my head at two am after waking up entangled in my sheets, but this is often where my mind goes.

To him.

To what we had.

Even if we were kids, it felt real.

Then I met Marcus, and everything changed.

Sure, I was old enough by then to know better, heck I was almost in my thirties for God's sake. But I'd never gotten over Brock, even after all that time apart. We just couldn't seem to get it together when he got back. the timing was never right.

Brock.

My God. We've been through some shit.

When Axton went inside, it really tore him up. He closed off a lot, he couldn't deal with it.

And it didn't help that his dad was constantly on his case. He felt guilty, for not being there for Axton. For not being a better brother.

But he's got it all wrong. It wasn't his job to take that on, and I know deep down Axton going to prison altered him, made him mad at the world, mad at himself.

He's proud. Too proud to admit it, but I know him. Sometimes I know him better than myself.

I grab my phone and go to my albums, looking for the photos I uploaded on here when we were seniors. We took some goofy pictures in the photo booth, ones I've always been meaning to get blown up because they make me laugh. I scroll through.

The last one is me looking at the camera, and he's looking at me. We look so happy.

So carefree.

Where did it all go so wrong?

But I know where.

The thing about being in love with your best friend is that when things end, you don't know what you are any more, or where you should be, and you wonder if you crossed a line that should have never been crossed because it very nearly could've ended our friendship. The loyalty and trust we have far outweigh everything else.

I've wished so much for Brock to be happy over the years. I really thought he'd find someone, settle down. He always said he wanted kids, so when I came back to Bracken Ridge when Rawlings was born, I was surprised that he wasn't there yet. Not even close.

Man-whore is probably how best to describe him, though he's tamed down a little bit now.

It makes me sad when I see the laughing, crazy, aloof seventeen-year-old in the photo. We had the world at our feet.

I regret a lot.

Meeting Marcus: I thought he was different, and at first, he was. I'd never been into heavy drugs, but I'd been drinking heavily and being with him only made me drink more and more. We got hitched on a whim, both drunk, and it was okay for a while. Then things turned ugly and violent, and I stayed. I stayed because I was too broke and felt ashamed and pathetic to go ask for help. Until that night when he beat me... when he cut me... and I ended up in hospital.

My biggest fear was losing my baby, getting pregnant was a complete mistake, and once I found out, it was more of a reason to stay. Until that night when he went on a bender, and everything changed forever.

He'd gotten a decent amount of time, not long enough considering what he did to me, but because I lived and so did Rawls, the sentence was lessened, then he made parole. It's so fucked up. I thought I was going to die, and I should have.

The other times he'd hit me, he was always sorry after, blaming being high and that he didn't know what he was doing, then things just escalated.

It's not like I thought I'd ever be one of *those* women, it just kind of sneaks up on you. The jives. The criticism. Then came the occasional slap.

I'd never been hit by a man, though Brock was twice his size, he's a teddy bear. He'd never hurt me, never. But Marcus was a junkie from way back, and the minute I knew that he was dealing again, I should have left, and I blame myself for not following through when I first had that thought.

I should have left him for good, it's not like he would have made a good father anyway.

I stare at Brock's photo, and I wonder what could have been.

I could have been a kept woman, and a part of me wants to be. But I fear being tied down.

I fear being an ol' lady because I know what it means.

I'm no one's property, and while I know it's just a formality, Brock takes control in all things. I'm not the same girl I was back then. I've changed.

And sometimes I just don't know how to get her back again.

11

BROCK

I stare at my mother as she looks around my office. She's never been here before and I've had this place almost seven years.

Her presence is obviously unexpected, so much so that I don't move from my seat.

I don't know what she's thinking, but when her eyes meet mine, there's a softness there. She's the polar opposite to my dad; she's nothing like him. Where she is kind, loving, and tolerant, he is mean, difficult, and impatient.

She looks good, it's been a while, but she still looks like half her age. Dad doesn't know how good he's got it.

My mom's like strawberries and cream. She was a full-time mom, preferring to raise us rather than work, not that dad would have allowed her to work, heaven forbid.

By the time Amelia came along, I was going into high school and dad was away more and more. Amelia is a lot like me, a little wild and a little bent out of shape, but she has a good heart. She looks like mom; sweet as pie, but she's got the devil inside her.

When she comes to town and gets on the cocktails with

Deanna, all hell breaks loose. I try not to take any notice, but it's a little hard when she comes to church and flaunts it.

I almost broke Lee's, one of the prospects, neck when he started hitting on her. Yeah, he learned the hard way, dumb fuck.

She might not be a little girl anymore, but I still ain't gonna stand for that shit.

"Mom," I say, purposely exaggerating the surprise in my tone. "What are you doin' here?"

Her lips turn up as she stands before me in her perfect wife outfit; a light pink pencil skirt suit and blouse with heels. Like she's going to the Kentucky Derby instead of through my wrecking yard.

If she made it from the car park to the office without falling into one of the potholes then she's made of tough stuff, but then again, she's married to my father.

"That's a fine way to greet your mother," she scolds. "Get up out of that chair and give me a hug this minute."

I want to tell her that hugs are earned, not just given, but I refrain. She may be small, but she'll still clip me around the head if I talk back.

I stand, towering over her, and come around the side of my desk. If I'd known she was coming, I'd have tidied up a little bit. Bones' desk next to me doesn't fare much better. At least I put my food wrappers in the bin. I dread to think what his place looks like at home. There could be something living in there and he'd never even know it.

I lean down and kiss her on the cheek as she puts her arms around me. "Hello, mother," I mutter. I'm just a little bit frosty; I don't know what she's doing here.

She holds me at arm's length and assesses me. "I probably deserve that." She clutches my cheeks and her eyes glaze over. "You look good, Brock Thomas Altman." She hesitates. "I know I've not been around much…"

"Much?" I snap. "You both cut me off at the knees when Axton went to prison."

"Brock, that isn't true."

"When's the last time I saw you? I'll save you the trouble; two Christmases ago when dad and I had that big fight and he told me to never set foot back in his house."

She lets go of my face and a light pink color, matching her suit, stains her cheeks.

"Can I at least sit so we can talk about it?" She sounds desperate and it makes me wonder what's going on. Why she's here.

I lean back on the desk. "What is there to say, mom?"

I mean, really, what the hell? She stood by him—so that says everything right there.

She sits anyway, crossing her leg over at the knee and placing her Chanel purse down on the mass of papers on my desk.

"A lot. And if you're going to stand there and fire spitballs at me then get it out of your system now, I've got all day, and I'm not going anywhere until we talk."

Spitfire. I used to think I got my temper from my dad, but no, I can see clearly how I resemble her in more ways than one.

I shake my head. "You think you can just waltz in here unannounced after two years of silence, talkin' your little talk, walkin' the walk, and then proceed to tell me off like I'm a child, like I'm the one who's done something wrong. I'm gonna tell you; there's nothing you can say that will make me change my mind."

"I've left your father," she announces, head held high.

Okay, except possibly that.

My eyes go wide. "What the fuck?"

"Manners, Brock," she chastises.

"You left dad?" I stammer, she may as well have just told me aliens just landed.

She nods, tears in her eyes.

I want to reach out to her, but I'm pissed, so I clutch the edge of the desk instead. Of all the things she could have said, I did not expect that.

She closes her eyes momentarily and then looks up at me. "We had a huge fight. I've been sitting on my hands for a long time, Brock, and it's all come to a head. I can't do this anymore. I'm sorry that I've been distant, you know what your father's like, he changed after Axton..." Her eyes well with tears again and a lump forms in my throat as I watch her. I never like seeing her upset. Even though Axton is the middle child, he really is like the baby of the family.

"He changed long before that," I mutter.

She nods, pulling a tissue from her sleeve as she dabs her eyes. "I miss my son," she whispers. "Both my sons."

I'm not sure I want to know but I still ask, "What was the fight about?"

She swallows hard. "You."

I let out a slow, silent breath. My heart races in my chest.

"I know it feels like I abandoned you..."

"Huh, you think?" I toss back, sarcastically. "Dad kicked me out of the house. He never could stand the sight of me; it was a relief truth be told to not have to sit there every Sunday and listen to him and pretend to care."

She dabs her eyes again. "You don't mean that."

I cross my arms over my chest. "I don't mean it to you, but I do mean it to him. I'm sure me not being around has been sweet relief for him, probably popped the champagne when I left."

"Brock, your father's a complex man, and I don't expect you to understand. I know I should have come sooner. I've done wrong, I've not been a good mother these past few years, I let him fill my head with rubbish about you and being in the M.C. and taking the fall for your brother. I'm not making excuses, but your father's a proud man, all he ever wanted…"

"Was for me to follow in his footsteps," I finish. "I know, and I did that, and it didn't get me anywhere, did it? I'm still a failure in his eyes."

"You're not a failure but joining the Rebels didn't help matters. A part of me used to think you did it on purpose just to spite him, to spite us. Then I met Hutch and I can see why you would warm to him, he's a good man, but so is your father, he just doesn't know how to show it."

"For someone who's just left her husband, you sure seem to be singing his praises an awful lot."

"I don't mean to, I know deep down he loves you, Brock. He loves all his children, but that's not what I came to talk about. I want to know…" she sniffles. "I want to know if you'll forgive me."

I know this is hard for her, she's a proud woman, not one to wear her heart on her sleeve so easily.

How the fuck her and dad got together, I'll never know, they're like chalk and cheese.

My eyes soften. "I don't blame you, but I'm your son too, and when dad made things really uncomfortable for me…" I trail off, gripping the desk with my fingers. "It was better to just stay way…" I finish. "For all of us."

"I know he's suffering, Brock. He doesn't know how to communicate without turning it into a fight, he can't be gentle, it isn't how he's made. I've tried over the years, but he's too set in his ways."

Ain't that the truth.

"Sounds like your making excuses for him," I chide. "Anyway, it's fine. My life is a lot more beneficial without him. I no longer get insults hurled at me, fists thrown at my face, cop the blame or am made to feel guilty for shit out of my control. I'm doing fine, in fact, I'm better than ever."

She nods her head. "I know it may take some time and I respect that, but I want to start again, if you'll let me."

"So, what now? You've left him and...?" I wait for the punch line.

"I don't know. But I won't be away from my children any longer. Now with Axton up for parole, I thought it may be a way to reunite the family, bring us back together. When your father baulked at the idea, I just snapped. I can't imagine a world where I don't get to see my kids, and I'm not having it. I want to be a part of your and Axton's lives again. I want to mend the bridges, Brock. I love you, you're my first child."

I stare at her wordlessly. Unsure of what to say. I'm not entirely comfortable, or used to, declarations like the one taking place, so I'm momentarily caught off guard. In order to change the subject, I switch to my little brother.

"Axton contacted you?"

"He wrote me. It made me realize how much power there is in forgiveness. He's done his time, he's not a bad boy. Well, he's a man now, and a part of me feels like your father and I failed him. None of that is on you, Brock, none of it. He was old enough to know right and wrong for himself, and I'm sorry your father shut you out. I can't say I'll ever forgive him for that, but I made the choice to not see you too, and that's on me."

I scratch my head and ask the unthinkable, "How's dad taking you leaving?"

She bites her lip. "He's not dealing with it very well."

"How long since you left?"

"I've been gone for two weeks."

My eyes go round.

"I've been with Amelia," she continues. "I've been trying to clear my head, and now that I've been away, it has made me realize a lot of things; one being that I won't miss out on being a part of my children's lives. If he wants to live by himself and stay in this toxic, self-absorbed bubble that he's created then he can do it alone."

Go mom. The old lady finally stood up to him.

I've waited so long to hear her say any of this, my head reels at the thought of that conversation going down.

I mean, he's never abused my mom, emotionally or physically, but he sure as heck wasn't easy to live with. Instead, he chose to toughen me up, taught me how to fight, how to stand up for myself, and for that I'm grateful. But not for all of it. Some of it was just downright harsh and uncalled for.

He wanted me to be his protégé. I only wish I'd not wanted to please him so much and had taken my own path in life, I'd do things differently if I had my time again.

It's water under the bridge now. I don't need his approval.

"Mom this is a lot to take in," I say after an awkward bout of silence. "But it was never you that I didn't want to see. Yeah, I'm mad as hell you didn't come around after he kicked me out, but I do forgive you, if that's what you want to hear."

She looks up at me with her big green eyes. "I only want to hear it if it's true."

I reach to her and take her hands in mine. "I missed you, mom."

She bursts into tears. "I'm sorry, son." She folds into my arms, and I encase her like she's the child and I'm the adult as she bawls, big, heart-wrenching sobs.

I still feel bitter, but I won't let her know that. I know what dads like to live with, and he'd make her life hell for even wanting to speak to me.

I get it, Axon disappointed him by holding up a store at gun point. That sucks. But it wasn't me. I thought I was doing everything he wanted, and even when I did, it wasn't enough.

The fact I'm a failure in his eyes does still sting. I've always wanted his approval, but once I turned into a man from a boy, I realized I didn't need it anymore.

"It's gonna be all right, mom," I say as she cries quietly. "I promise, we'll work it out."

I know she never got over her baby being locked up, what parent would? It was a shock to the system for all of us. I still can't get my head around it. But that's what happens when you get into drugs and get mixed up with the wrong crowd.

Dad always thought it was gonna be me that fucked up, I'm sure of it. As much as I assured him the club was legitimate and not 1%ers, he wouldn't hear about it. Joining the M.C. was the nail in the coffin, and Axton going away was the crematorium. I was dead to him in his eyes.

And really, it was fine with me. I was done with his shit, enough to last a lifetime.

I hold mom until she stops shaking.

"I'll make us some coffee," I say, holding her by the shoulders as she dabs her running mascara.

She cups my cheek. "Thank you, Brock. I mean it, I want to make this work. I really mean that, if you'll have me back."

"You know he'll come looking for you."

She shrugs. "He's been ringing me nonstop, but I told him I need time, that's as much as I can promise at the moment."

I'm shocked. I've never really seen my mom stick up to him, not like this, and it's definitely sending a message. Loud and clear.

"One thing's for sure," I say cocking my brow. "I know where I got my toughness from, and it wasn't from dad."

She smiles a watery smile. "You're a good boy, Brock. Always were."

I can't help noting the tinge of sadness in her tone, and I can't throw her out on her own. It took a lot to come and say those things, and fuck me, she left dad.

I make a mental note to call Amelia later and blast her ears off about why she didn't call me and tell me, the little sneak. I guess maybe mom thought dad would relent and she could go back, and we'd never know.

But dad will never relent, he'll never say sorry or admit to anything, it's just not his style.

And maybe it never will be.

~

Mom hasn't been out to my place before. She was booked in at the Lodge hotel tonight, but those plans are cancelled, now I'm slightly horrified that she's going to be staying with me.

I don't know how to tell her that's not a good idea, but she doesn't baulk at the house. She just steps over all the wood on the deck, the plastic sheets hanging up and even says hello to the prospects; Lee and Jax, who are busy cleaning up my yard.

"It's gonna be noisy here, mom, I've got contractors coming all week long," I say, as she flicks the kettle on, ready to make herself at home. "Might wanna extend your stay at the Lodge."

She swats me away. "Maybe I can help?" she glances around. "Do some cleaning, perhaps? I'll cook for you, too. You know how I like to make your favorite meals; it'll keep my mind off things."

I roll my eyes behind her back.

Shit.

It's like I'm ten years old again and she's promised me spaghetti and meatballs.

She stayed at Amelia's for two weeks, could that mean she's going to be here for the same amount of time? I love her and all, but I fucking hope not.

"You really don't have to do that, mom."

She frowns, running a finger over my bench top and eyeing the dishes from this morning in the sink. "You're never going to get a wife if you live like a pig, darling."

"Mom," I warn. "I don't want a wife, and I don't live like a pig. I just didn't tidy up this morning. Don't need you poking around my place criticizing."

"I'm not criticizing, I'm just trying to help."

I snort.

She turns to face me. "How's Angel doing?"

Here we go. That took her all of five seconds.

"She's doing just fine; you can ask her yourself if you pop on over to Angel's Ink."

"Such a clever girl," mom says, smiling. She and Angel always got along, but back then Angel was the apple of everyone's eye. "Never would have picked it that she'd own a tattoo shop, though."

"She's made a name for herself, she's worked hard," I grunt. I really don't want to talk about Angel, not to my mom, of all people.

"Anything still going on between you two?" There's hope in her voice.

"No, mom. If you just came down here to ask me five hundred fuckin' questions then don't bother. Angel and I are just friends these days, nothin's going on."

"Language, son, you know I don't like swearing."

I'm gonna have a lot of money in my swear jar if she plans on sticking around.

"Well, you don't have to hang around," she tells me. "I'll pop to the shops and get us some food for tonight. Would the boys outside like anything? I could make some sandwiches for lunch."

I put my hands on my hips. "No, mom. The boys outside would not like anything, and don't be talking to them, they've got work to do. You don't have to cook for me, I've kept myself alive for this long, pretty sure I can keep myself alive for a little bit longer without you fussin'."

It won't matter. She'll still cook. It's what she does; feeds everyone. And cleans. Then there's that gold medal in nagging.

Kill me now.

"All right, darling, if that's what you want. Don't worry about me. I'll be fine."

I don't know what she means by that, but by the looks of it, she's going to tidy up my kitchen and probably the rest of the house while she's at it. I'm not a total pig, like she claims, and once a month I get one of the sweet butts to come and properly clean the bathroom and vacuum the floors and shit, the rest of the time I do it myself.

I'm not totally useless.

"I'll be back after six."

She's not even listening; she's poked her head into my fridge and she's looking even more doubtful about its contents than she was about my dirty kitchen.

I wave a hand at her. "Hello, mom?"

"Fine, sweetie, I'll see you later." She gives me a kissing face as she concentrates on what she's doing, rather than at me.

I let out a low breath and stomp out of the kitchen.

As I pass by, Jax and Lee stop, and I point at them.

"Don't let her be feedin' you or chattin' like she's your fuckin' fairy godmother, got me?"

They nod, but Jaxon, always the smartass has to pipe up, "Your mom's pretty hot, Brock. She single?"

I turn and shove him in the chest, then point in his face. "Very funny, asshole. One more quip about my mom and you'll be eatin' your dinner out of a straw and shittin' into a bag for the rest of your life."

He grins but holds his hands in the air. "Sorry, man, just sayin'."

"Yeah, well, don't just fuckin' say, shut up and get back to work. This better be finished by the time I'm back, or I'll have an even better job for you lined up near the septic tank."

His eyes go wide. "Won't happen again, dude."

I shake my head, walking away.

Can't take the fuckin' woman anywhere, now I got my twenty-year-old prospect sniffing around like a dog on heat. Jesus Christ.

This is a bad idea. I can smell it in the air. Nothing good can come from my mom's meddling.

I want to make amends with her, but I don't want her fuckin' living with me.

My phone rings as I'm about to mount my sled.

"Steel," I say, running a hand through my hair.

"Hey, bro, got a sec?"

"Shoot."

"I got a big favor to ask."

I pinch the bridge of my nose. Why does everyone seem to want a piece of me today?

"Yeah, what?" I'm suddenly all out of patience.

"Faux Paws have a couple of horses they're desperate to rehome. I wouldn't normally ask but they're gonna be put to slaughter, and Sienna won't hear of it. Any chance I can bring them out to the ranch for a couple of weeks. We'll supply all the food, Sienna will come feed and exercise them, just till we get a new place."

I sigh feeling a migraine coming on.

Angel.

Mom.

Fuckin' horses.

Why not throw in a three-ring circus while we're at it.

"Sure, man. Whatever."

"Thank fuck, appreciate it," Steel says, sounding relieved.

"There's a gap in the fence, I can get the prospects on it tomorrow, that work for you?"

"Be a fuckin' life saver. If I don't come up with something, Sienna will move them into our place. Fuckin' women."

I snort a laugh. "She's got you where she wants you."

"Laugh all you want. I get food every night, my apartment cleaned, and sex on the regular. Plus, she wears my cut without any lip and is loyal as fuck, who's the fuckin' chump here?"

I think about my mom back in the house, cooking and cleaning, and a spark of jealousy that I didn't know I had lights in me fiercer than it ever has before.

He's right. I am the fuckin' chump.

"You got me there, bro," I mutter. "You got me there."

12

ANGEL

"I've filed a custody conjunction, there may be a hearing, but you'll likely won't need to attend," Kennedy, my new attorney, tells me, looking me in the eye. "The court will always rule in favor of what is best for the child, and in this case, she's been in your sole custody since she was born where she has a stable, loving, and secure home. Added to your ex-husband's current misdemeanors; attempted murder, the violence, past charges, and the restraining order against him, it's safe to say he's got a snowball in hell's chance at getting any kind of custody, he's living in some parallel universe we're not privy to. He's playing games, nothing more. The court will throw this out before the ink's even dried."

I sit back in my chair and relief runs through me.

I know it's true, I just needed to hear it.

"You don't know what he's like. He's a special kind of stupid, claims stabbing me was self-defense. He's a prick with no fucking conscience."

She stares at me. "It's just a tactic, meant to send a message. I don't like it, not one bit. There's no way he's getting anything, yet here he is filing court orders. I'd be inclined to question his mental state. With your permission, I'd like to contact the local P.D. to reinforce the terms of his release and the restraining order. He can't enter the state of Arizona as per terms of his release, but none of this can feel very good or comforting for you."

"He got seven years, he got out on a technicality, claimed temporary insanity and then the whole excuse that I was the aggressor. Apparently, he's been on good behavior, he's reformed."

She shakes her head, unimpressed. "I'm sorry, Angel. Sometimes the other side of the law sucks ass. In the meantime, I've advised his lawyer to not contact us again or we will file harassment and seek damages and compensation, you shouldn't have to deal with this, but two can play the game of cat and mouse."

"I'm not sure if it's a game I'm willing to play," I admit.

Kennedy's a strong woman, she's got to be to do this job and deal with some of the scumbags she has to. I take my hat off to her. "Then let me play it, that's what I'm here for."

I smile gratefully. "I appreciate it, Kennedy, more than you know."

She takes her glasses off and chews the end. "Seriously, Angel, I don't like the sound of this guy, but on the flip side, you don't need to worry yourself. He can't get out of Minnesota, so he's not coming anywhere near you. Plus, you have the M.C. behind you, that's gotta be a good scare tactic for anyone."

I nod. I know she's right.

I know that's true. One thing Marcus was always afraid of was my association with Brock and the M.C. It never sat well with him, and for good reason. I didn't realize it then, but the M.C. cared more about me than he ever did.

I don't know Kennedy well, but she knows the club by association. Her younger sister, Stevie, bartends at church, and Kennedy just moved back to Bracken Ridge and set up her own practice. She seems like the kind of ball-busting woman I need in my corner, since she doesn't know me well, she won't sugar coat anything, and that's what I need right now.

"I'll just be glad when this is filed, off my back, and he can leave me the hell alone."

She looks sympathetic; she's probably read my police report. I shudder at the thought. What he did to me can never be erased.

"It's going to be okay," she reassures me. "No court in the world will give him rights or access after what he did to you, he can sing like a canary from the rooftops, it won't make one iota of difference. If he does attempt to contact you in any way, shape, or form, you'll need to call the police immediately to lodge a complaint as he's in breach of his parole terms, then call me and I'll swoop down on him so fast his feet won't hit the ground."

I nod, feeling very out of my depth right now. "Thank you, Kennedy. You've been great with all of this, really."

She goes to stand. Her long, flaming red hair hangs almost to her waist. She's curvy and wears it well, her suit screams expensive, as does the luxurious office. She charges like a wounded bull too, but I need the best, and again, someone who will keep my business private from the prying eyes and ears of town. The last thing I need is my private life broadcast all over the place like its front-page news. It doesn't take much to get the folk around here excited.

"You're welcome, Angel. You have my card. I'll walk you out, I'm going to grab some lunch before my next appointment."

By the time I get to the front door I can hear the straight pipes.

I don't believe it.

Expecting to see Brock, I'm surprised when Bones appears in the parking lot. He revs his engine loud, so loud, some passersby look at him and shake their heads in dismay.

I roll my lips inward as I get closer to where he pulls up.

"Friend of yours?"

"Yes." I laugh. "Bones. He's harmless, honestly."

Kennedy smiles ruefully, then Bones pulls his brain bucket off and Kennedy's breath hitches slightly. I spare her a sideways glance. I guess he is kinda cute... in a rough and tumble, *I just rolled out of bed and didn't brush my mohawk*, kind of way.

"Ooh, they raise em' cute around here." She smirks. "Introduce me?"

I turn to look at her. "You sure you're ready for him? He's a bit of a wild card."

She doesn't get time to answer as Bones kills the engine and gives me a chin lift as we approach.

His eyes are all over my lawyer.

"Hey, Angel," he says, when his eyes finally meet mine.

"Hey, yourself, what are you doing here?"

He shrugs. "Brock asked me to swing by, make sure you're okay."

I roll my eyes. "I'm not a child, Bones. Of course, I'm okay."

Brock's overbearingness is going to earn him a slap upside the head. I know he means well, but I can handle this.

He raises both his palms. "Don't shoot the messenger, I was in the neighborhood."

I narrow my eyes, but before I get to say anything else, Kennedy clears her throat.

I glance at her. She's just a bit shorter than me and I'm five nine, she holds her head held high and eyes Bones like he's a piece of meat.

I mean, now that I'm up close, he's not an unattractive

guy. He's got nice, piercing hazel eyes and a very distinguished rugged look about him that the wrong sort of girls can't get enough of. Not girls like Kennedy Hart. She may be slightly taller than him which I find slightly amusing.

"Sorry, Kennedy, this is Bones. Bones, meet my lawyer, Kennedy Hart."

She thrusts a handout toward him, and he looks at it slightly taken aback. I try to hold in my smirk, but I just can't help it. She'll give good old Bones a run for his money.

When he's done recovering from the handshake thing, he grasps her hand and raises it to his lips. "The pleasure's all mine, sweetheart."

I roll my eyes at his gesture and his tone; both are equally repugnant.

He thinks he's smooth, then Kennedy says, "It's Ms. Hart, but I suppose you can call me Kennedy."

He smirks. "Ms. Hart." He gives her a very obvious once over, his gaze stilling at her ample bosom which, let's face it, are impressively huge. "Where've you been all my life?"

She frowns some more. "Do you greet all the girls you meet like that?" I sense a little bit of disapproval in her tone, but at least it's playful. That went south quickly, but really, what was she expecting?

He pretends to think. "No, actually. We usually get to third base." He gives her a wink, and I refrain from making puking noises.

Her eyes sparkle with wickedness.

"Well, this was... funny... but I've got to get going," I say, trying to make up for Bone's uncouthness, not that Kennedy really seems to mind.

"You comin' to church Saturday?" Bones asks, still looking at Kennedy slyly. Oh, I know what he's thinking, and I'm waving the white flag. I don't think getting it on with my lawyer is in any way a good idea.

"No, Bones, I have a child, remember."

He shrugs. "Pity. What about you, Ms. Hart? A beautiful woman like you is always welcome at the clubhouse. I can show you around, I have an amazing view from my room."

I almost choke. "Jesus, Bones, subtle much?"

"Wow," she mouths slowly. "Come on, I'm sure that's not your best pick up line, surely you can do better than that?"

He scratches the dark stubble on his chin. "I better do something bad this weekend so I can get arrested, if it means you get to come and bail me out."

She shakes her head. "Ahh, while bail bonds are my specialty, I doubt you could afford it."

"Try me."

"I think you'd better save all that sass for the arresting officer, you might need it."

He purses his lips and mouths an 'oooh' without any sound.

I chuckle. "Give it up, Bones, she's way smarter than you."

"Man's gotta try, ain't he?" he counters.

Even I can feel the buzz of electricity between them.

She narrows her eyes, and I can imagine her in court, cross examining the witness. Just that look alone would have them cowering into submission and spiling their guts. I don't think Bones quite knows what would hit him.

"It takes more than a cute smile, a loud, obnoxious bike, and a dubious looking mohawk to impress me, Mr. Bones. So, while I'm strangely flattered at your juvenile advances, I'll decline the enticing invitation of a view from your room and the tempting offer at avenging your no doubt impending arrest, and I'll bid you good day." Then she turns to me. "Angel, we'll talk during the week. Remember what I said, and call me if you have any questions, any time."

"Thank you, Kennedy," I reply, as she smiles at me warmly, she flashes Bones a scowl. And with that, she turns and stalks off in the other direction, her hips swaying as she makes her way across the lot to the café on the corner. She really does look hot in a skirt suit; flames practically follow in her wake.

I snicker as Bones watches her; his eyes glued to her ass. "You okay, lover boy?"

"I think I'm in love, Angel baby." He grins.

"Really?" I snark, hands on my hips. "You had to hit on my lawyer? I don't need you pissing her off. She's good and one of the few that let me pay off her fees in installments."

He turns back to me. "I wasn't hitting on her, I was merely being friendly, she's new in town, she might not know anybody. And she'd be even better sittin' on the end of my…"

"Eww, please no visuals."

He frowns. "You're right, though, she's way smarter than me."

"At last, we can agree on something."

"She really that good?" He nods back toward the café she's disappeared into.

"Very, she's a ball buster."

A huge grin spreads across his face. "I like ball busters."

"Don't even think about it."

"Why not? I may be batting way above my average, but I like a challenge."

I look down at him, assessing his attire with distaste. "It *is* a challenge, trust me. You're a good-looking guy, Bones, and a nice one most of the time when you're not being an ass, but I'll give it to you straight. You need to wash your jeans, put on a clean shirt, and don't ogle women's boobs just because they're big and in your face. If you do that, you might just get lucky with a broad like her, then again, you might get a punch in the face for your efforts, it could go either way."

He taps his chin. "Never had a classy broad," he admits.

"Might like to get me some of that. Tits are bigger than my head."

I facepalm myself. "Really, Bones?"

"What? Just stating the truth."

I don't know why I'm still standing here, seriously. "Bones, women like that like to be wooed. They like fancy dinners, to be wined and dined, chased for a little bit. They won't give it up on the first date, or the second, and they definitely won't be entertaining watching you hit on other women at church and boning them on the couch for all to see. May as well give it up now, you're fighting a losing battle, my friend."

He looks at me like I've grown two heads. "You think I stand a chance with her?" It's like he hasn't heard a word I've said.

I think about his disgusting room at church and how messy he is, never cleans up after himself, can't cook. I've heard he's hung like a horse and can move those swaggery hips, though, so there's that. And he's loyal too and not totally dumb all of the time, but snag a classy broad? Nah, not in this lifetime.

I pat him on the shoulder. "I think you'd have a better chance flying to the moon backwards, champ."

He pretends to look offended. "Should we take a bet on that? I think she checked me out at least once."

I put my hands on my hips. "Don't even think about it. I need her M.C. free, at least till my current mess is over with. Then do what you want. Listen, I gotta go. I don't know why Brock sent you. Remind him I'm a big girl, and I can look after myself. I don't need a freaking babysitter."

I flounce off toward my car.

"He cares about you," Bones hollers after me. "No need to act so ungrateful."

I flip him the bird. "When I want any of your help, I'll ask for it."

"No need to be a bitch!" he yells.

I walk away, laughing.

~

My parents come up for the weekend and tell me they're happy to babysit if I want to go out and catch up with my friends. They know I don't get out much these days; I'm either working or being a mom, or both.

I don't like being away from Rawlings for very long. She's not a needy kid, far from it, but my partying days have been numbered since I had her. And I don't regret it. Having her pretty much set me on the straight and narrow for good. But I always say no when Deanna asks me to come out and it might be nice to get out for a few hours, let my hair down. The only thing is, I don't want to go to church. Brock will be there and then I'll have to witness him around other chicks. Even I draw the line at witnessing that.

I call Deanna and she organizes drinks at the Zee bar with Summer, Sienna, and Lily.

It's been another long week at the shop. The business is doing well, aside from me I have two other senior tattoo artists, Gunner comes and does piercing a couple of times a week when he's not mooning over at Lily's salon, and I have Jessie on reception who's a machine at getting me organized.

It's been a long road, but the business is finally picking up. I've also done a few magazine features and that's helped things tenfold. We go to tattoo expos whenever we can, but those take me away from Rawlings, so I don't do that too much. When mom and dad move back to Bracken Ridge, I'll start going to more of them, anything that makes new connections and brings in new clients is a good thing. For the most part I'm doing all right.

When I arrive, the girls are already getting on it at the bar. I swear to God Deanna has a cast iron stomach. I squeal when I see Amelia has made the trip. We jump up and down like little kids as we hug each other.

"Hey, sister, I missed you." She kisses me on the cheek and hands me a shot of tequila.

"What the hell are you doing here?" I haven't seen her in over a year. Amelia and I always got along, she's like the little sister I never had.

"Long story. Mom's in town, though, so look out. She always liked you, and I know she'll be trying to meddle where you and Brock are concerned."

I gape at her. "Your mom's in town? Brock hasn't said anything." Typical male. Was he gonna wait till I run into her in the street or something? Asshat.

She picks up her shot and downs it. "Our parents split up, and I'm here to get shitfaced in the quickest time possible. Right, girls?"

Sienna, Deanna, Summer, and Lily all cheer and hold their shots up, downing them with various coughs and splutters.

"Lightweights," I mutter, then turn to Amelia. "What do you mean your parents split up? Are you shitting me right now?"

She shrugs. "Mom walked out on dad. She's had enough of all the fighting and dad cutting my brothers off. She gave him an ultimatum, and he wouldn't back down."

I gape at her. "But your mom's like so..." I'm lost for words. "*Normal.* I can't believe she left."

"Trust me, I know, Brock's just as shocked. Get this, she's moved into his place for a few weeks." She cackles with laugher and sobers, looking over my shoulder. "Deanna, Summer, hot dude alert, 9 o'clock."

I subtly look that way and see she's right. Couple of cute guys with buzz cuts that scream military walk up to the bar alongside us.

"Come on, Deanna, now's your big opportunity to prove to us you're not hung up on Cash." Sienna giggles, clearly, she's on her ear already.

"Woah, what's this? Cash as in...*Cash*, the Prez from New Orleans?" My eyes go wide.

Deanna rolls her eyes. "I'm not hung up on Cash. I find him interesting, funny, and he has an ass I could drink shots off, sure. And all right, I'm not saying he's not sexy, in a silver-fox- I've-got-a-huge-dick-and-a-swaggering-hip-roll-like-nobody's-business kinda-way, but my dad would kill him, and I don't wanna spill bad blood between the clubs just because I want to jump him."

"Ahh, so you do want to jump him!" Sienna declares triumphant. "See, I told you."

"I was there," Lily reiterates. "He had his eyes all over your ass."

Deanna turns to Lily. "What would you remember? You were too busy upstairs letting Gunner finally pop your cherry. A nuclear explosion could've taken place and you wouldn't have heard it."

Lily's eyes go wide as she slaps Deanna on the arm, and we all roar with laughter.

"I can't believe you just said that!" Lily cries, her hands over her eyes.

"Yeah, like puke." Summer winces, not thrilled hearing about her brother's sexcapades.

Deanna turns to her. "You can talk! What about you and Jett? He's hot for you, and I heard Tag saying if he hears your name come out of his mouth one more time, he'd ram his fist down his throat."

"Did he really say that?" Summer asks, sipping on her colorful drink.

"Maybe we should find some excuse to go down there, have a dirty weekend," I say, downing another shot. I forgot how good straight tequila tastes; it numbs everything. "Maybe you can hook me up?"

Amelia turns to face me. "Yeah, but then you'd have to deal with Brock when you got back."

I point at her. "Which is exactly why I'll never get involved with anyone at an M.C. because I don't belong to Brock, and once he gets it through his thick skull then we'll all be better off."

Sienna snorts. "You know that whole property thing isn't really a real thing, don't you?"

I turn to look at her. "Says she who wears her boyfriend's cut claiming you're *his* property, seems pretty real to me. You too, Lily," I say with an edge in my tone. "Property of Gunner, I mean, what is this nineteen fifty?"

Sienna shrugs. "Steel's a tough man, you all know what he's like, but he's really a big pussycat behind closed doors. If it makes him feel like he *owns* me when we're around church and that I belong to him and nobody else, then so be it. We both know I own him in the bedroom. I get what I want, so does he, we're both happy."

Lily wrinkles her nose.

I just about choke on my third shot and the girls all fall about laughing and clinking shot glasses.

"As for Gunner, he lets me be myself, he loves and supports me," Lily pipes up. "Why wouldn't I want the world to know he's mine and I'm his? I wear his cut with pride. I've always wanted it."

I smile at the way she says it. God, I remember being that

young and in love and look where it got me. "You two gonna get hitched?"

She bites her lip. "I'd like to, maybe one day. We're in no hurry."

"You're three days in," Deanna complains. "Sit his balls on ice for a while, girl."

"What about you and your old man?" Summer prods Sienna. "Sound of wedding bells any time soon? Or the pitter patter of tiny feet?"

Sienna looks slightly horrified. "Steel's been married before, so he doesn't care too much about that. I'd like to one day. Make it official. But kids, I don't think that's in the cards for us." She laughs. "We like our lifestyle too much, and we love our dogs, we want more fur babies, that's a definite."

"And horses," Deanna chimes, ordering more rounds from the cute bartender, then adds, "and whatever those two fine gentlemen are drinking." Nodding to the two hotties next to us who are checking us out.

"Oh boy," Sienna mutters.

"We're in for a long night," I agree.

Two hours later, we're half cut and heading to church. Okay, so I said I'd never go there but all my inhibitions are gone now that I've had shots and cocktails.

Deanna, Summer, and Amelia flirted with the two guys and invited them over here. I'm pretty sure Deanna wanted to drag one of them into the bathroom for a quickie, but the cab got here too soon. Wild, I tell ya. I smile at the way these girls party, knowing it used to be me and knowing even more that I suddenly feel old.

Well, I'm the oldest in the group, and the only one with a kid.

"You know, I always thought that you'd end up with Brock," Deanna slurs as she flings money at the cab driver, hooking an arm through Trent's- I think that's his name- bent elbow.

The other guy, Brandon, trots alongside Summer and Amelia, telling them some bullshit story about his submarine. I don't know if it's a metaphor for something, and I don't care because the minute I step into church, I hear the sounds of one of the singers from the Stone Crow Ally McCall crooning on the microphone.

Sometimes the clubhouse has a band and singers on a random Saturday night because they can.

The place is packed, and I see Stevie, Ginger, and one of the prospects Lee behind the bar.

I inadvertently look around for Brock, and when I don't see him, I feel a surge of disappointment flood through me. I don't know why. Maybe I've just had too much to drink, and I'm too nostalgic. I decide not to drink any more; I don't want to have my head stuck down the toilet for the rest of the night.

"Oooh, it's my favorite song!" Deanna cries, grabbing me by the arm, along with her boy-toy who she tugs with her other hand. She pulls us both to the dance floor, which usually holds the pool tables.

Deanna grinds against me, Trent settles in behind her as he grabs her ass, and I know for sure it'll be five seconds before someone comes over here and hauls his ass out.

Sure enough, I see a flash of tall, mean, and muscular as Steel approaches and shoves the dude in the chest. "Who the fuck are you?"

"Hey!" Deanna cries. "He's with me, I invited him."

Steel frowns. "She's the club president's daughter, if I were you, I'd take your fuckin' hands off her ass unless you'd like replacement front teeth."

Deanna's eyes go wide. "Dad's here?"

Steel looks down at her menacingly. "Yeah, your mom too."

She curses, pulling her skirt down just a little bit.

Steel shakes his head, then looks back at Trent. "I mean it, fucker, keep your hands to yourself. Everything in this building, except you and your friend over there, belongs to us, you got me?"

I roll my eyes behind his back, *here we go.*

"Yeah, man, sorry," Trent, very wisely, replies hesitantly. "I meant no harm."

Least he's not dumb enough to talk back.

Steel turns and looks me dead straight in the eye. "As for you, don't go fuckin' rollin' your eyes at me, woman, you know how it works here. I protect the people I care about, I protect this club, it's what I do. So, you don't like it, don't be here."

I stare at him blinking. "What did I do?"

He snorts. "Don't even get me started."

He stalks off, catching Sienna by the hand as he does and drags her toward the bar. When she looks up at him, his eyes soften. He reaches down and kisses her gently on the nose, then both her eyes, then her lips. Softly, though, not like a brute.

Huh.

Maybe she's right, he really is a pussycat when he thinks nobody is watching. It still doesn't take away the fact he's like all of the boys here; a neanderthal.

My gaze shifts, and I stare straight into the dark green, penetrating eyes that watch from the seat next to them.

Brock.

His eyes are all over me as he gives me a chin lift. I give him one back and I don't miss his casual assessment of my attire; my black, shimmery bodycon dress that fits snug and super tight. His eyes heat and all I can do is turn away.

It was a mistake coming here.

Like a magnet he draws me to him, and I need to get away before I do something stupid.

Like sleep with him again.

Clearly, I have no self-control where he's concerned, it's like my body has a mind of its own and takes over, rendering me powerless to do anything except become one with him.

And I hate myself for it. For wanting him. For needing him. For missing him.

I need to get out of here, fast.

13

BROCK

She stands in the middle of church looking like she just popped up from hell, not heaven. Oh no, heaven is where sweet, angelic things drop out of. In that dress and with her hair all teased and wild, she looks like she'd give the devil a run for his money.

Smokin' hot.

My eyes are all over her, and I can feel my dick harden at the very sight of her.

Her tits look fucking amazing in that dress, but it's plastered to her body and leaves little to the imagination.

"Yo, bro," Colt says, sitting to my right.

I give him a chin lift. "Hey, brother, when did you get back?"

Colt's been out of town getting some new equipment for the shop now that's he's finally about to open next to Rubble and Steel's joint. I'm happy for the guy, he's fit right into the club in a short amount of time. The girls like him too, out of all of us, he's the most respectful to the ladies and they seem to like that.

"Few hours ago." He looks tired.

"You get all you need?"

He looks at me wistfully. "Not all of it, no." Something in his tone tells me we're not talking about surveillance equipment anymore.

"What's her name?"

"Same one. Cassidy."

I snort into my drink. "She got beer flavored nipples or something?"

He smirks. "I wish."

"You never fucked her?"

He shakes his head. "Didn't say that."

I scratch my chin. "Shit, bro."

"Nah, man, wasn't like that. It's... fuck, this chicks got me all tied up in knots and my heads like ground hog day."

"That it? Sure as shit know that one of the sweet butts can help with that."

He shrugs. "We had a connection, dude. I know it sounds lame, but I can't stop thinkin' about her, night and fuckin' day, she's on my mind. It's driving me crazy."

"As I say. Plenty of available pussy here tonight," I reason. "The ladies seem to like your ugly mug, maybe you just need to forget about her."

He nods his head like he's considering the prospect.

I shake my head. "I used to be like that, there was only one girl for me, and when they get you, bro, you're fucked, let me tell you. You think you got your balls intact, hanging freely, you don't. My word of advice..." I bring the bottle up to my lips and take a swig, watching Angel shake her ass as Deanna slaps it repeatedly. "Get it out of your system before it poisons your blood, once they're under your skin, it's like an infection. You can't get rid of it, and there ain't no cure, ain't nothin' you can do except live with it."

"Fuck, bro." He laughs. "Think I need to order you a shot or two, along with my violin."

I grunt. "Mark my words, she'll come back to haunt you, they always do."

What I want to do is go haul Angel off the dance floor, take her down the back, bend her over the keg, and fuck her hard for dancing like that in front of everyone. Deanna slapping her ass and her laughing about it doesn't do my boner any good. Nah, it doesn't.

But I know her. I know she likes to think she doesn't want a badass biker hauling her anywhere, but deep down, deep down she's begging for the stability and the protection of a man like me, she just won't admit it. She's too fucked over in the head by what happened to her that she put me in the same category as her ex and all other men, and it pisses me off.

But I won't go to her, no I won't. I want it to be her decision. She knows how I feel, and I can't make it any clearer.

When the song finishes, they fall about laughing, and Summer skips up to them with a round of cocktails in her hands. Personally, I think they've had too much, but there ain't no tellin' these girls.

Steel's already had a go at the dude Deanna brought in, least he's keeping his mitts off her now. Haven't seen Hutch since he got here, suspect he's giving his ol' lady one in his office, Kirsty is still pretty hot and knows how to keep his attention, she's been doin' it for the last thirty years.

When my attention comes to, Angel is strutting toward me.

Brace for impact.

She sidles up to the bar, nudging in between me and Colt.

"Hello, Colt," she purrs.

"Hey, Angel."

She turns to me. "Hey, mister, you never called and told me your mom was in town."

I wasn't expecting that.

"Been busy," I grunt.

She narrows her eyes, taking a sip from her elaborate looking Stevie-made cocktail. I take a glance down at her and wish I hadn't.

That fuckin' dress.

There's a mesh panel that basically shows her tits on full display under the light and a tiny bit of fabric that keeps her nipples from being revealed. I feel my cock twitch as I think about fucking them.

I lean toward her. "That dress shouldn't be legal."

She looks up at me, a hand going to her chest as she heaves the fabric a little higher. It doesn't help, and now she's touching herself.

"Better?"

My eyes still on her tits, I shake my head. "Nah, babe, think you need to burn it when you get home."

"Can't go home," she says with an eye roll. "Mom and dad are babysitting."

"Didn't tell me they were in town," I toss back at her. Two can play at that game.

She throws me a glare, then drops her eyes down to my cut and lower. I'm not wearing anything special, same shit; a tight long-sleeved Henley, jeans, my cut, and my black boots. I'm a simple guy, after all.

"See something you like, darlin'?"

She licks her lips and when her eyes come back to me, I see heat there.

Interesting. The last time we were this close, she told me she hated me.

Of course, I know that's not true, she might wish she hated me, but she doesn't.

"Maybe I do," she counters.

My interest piques. What I'd give for another taste of her, for a whole night with her.

She moves her hand to my bicep, and I look down at it.

"Wrong muscle," I quip, she smirks as her eyes dart to my crotch.

"Jesus, Brock."

I turn to my side, resting one elbow on the bar as she keeps the hand on my bicep. I pull her closer by the hip, our eyes locked, and with my other hand, the one that's resting on the bar, I grip her breast and give it a squeeze. Nobody can see, her arm and my body blocking us from view and its dark in here.

Her eyes flame with desire.

I pinch her nipple and she bites her lip.

I'm so hard, imagining what I want to do with her, I know I'm not gonna make it out of here without a leak in my pants.

With no words, I silently pinch and caress her nipple subtly with my fingers, circling, flicking. Every single touch has her mewling, trying to fight the sensation as she grinds into my leg.

I lean into her ear. "You secretly missed me, didn't you, Ange?"

She doesn't answer, so I move my knee slightly to place it between her legs. She closes her eyes. In the darkness, we can be as bad as we want to be, and I want to get her off, right here, right now. I look around, nobody's watchin'. Colt's talkin' to a sweet butt next to him, and if people can see, so what.

I pull her further onto my knee, then slip my hand under her dress, she's soaked through the sheer fabric of her panties, and I curse a string of profanities. Silently, I slip my fingers under the fabric, pull her to me so her head's resting on my shoulder, and I flick her clit with my thumb, then insert two fingers and fuck her pussy, while holding her still with my other hand. To anyone else, it'd look like we're just hugging, enjoying a moment, and she will be enjoying it when she comes all over my fingers. It doesn't take long. She curses as she comes hard, whispering my name, shuddering under my touch as I ride her through it.

She rests on my shoulder when it's over, and I kiss the top of her head.

Though my dicks putting a hole in my jeans, I'm not gonna haul her ass upstairs. She's gonna have to beg me for it.

"Brock?" she whispers. I bring my head to her face and kiss her temple.

"Yes, Angel."

"I want you to fuck me," she says. "Like, now."

I tut. "Now, now, I thought we didn't do the friends with benefits thing, babe. Not sure we can keep crossing a line."

I feel her tense in my arms. "You just finger-fucked me in a room full of people, Brock. Now's not the time to play hard-to-get."

I grin. "Got five seconds to fix your dress before we get outta here."

She pulls her dress together, and I push off the bar. Joining our hands, I move toward the dorm rooms, and I'm up the stairs with her trailing behind me, five seconds later.

At my door, I pull her to me, then swirl her around so her back's against it.

"Doin' this my way, Ange, you got me?"

I don't let her answer, I move in and take her mouth. She gasps at my touch as I force my tongue between her lips into her mouth, kissing her for the first time in way too long. It feels so fucking good. Moaning, she grips my shoulders and I haul her by the ass against the door. My dick presses into her and she lets out another strained moan.

"Fuck, Brock. I'll wear this dress more often."

I smirk, pulling away from eating her face. "You'd look good in a paper bag, babe."

I move my head to her pulse point and bite. She whimpers as she wraps her legs around my waist, trying to gyrate against me, needing the friction.

"Greedy girl," I mutter against her skin. My mouth finds her tits, and I suck on her nipples through the material. She groans and grips my back, hard.

"Ahh, Brock."

I need to get her inside. I fumble with the door, and once we're in, I kick it closed behind me.

After that, we're like a couple of teenagers again. I lose my shirt, kick my boots off and pull my jeans and boxers off in one move. My dick's so hard, it's painful. I sheath myself a couple of times as she lies on the bed and watches me.

"This is what you do to me, babe, every single fucking time."

Her eyes are on my dick as I pleasure myself, fire in her gaze.

"Take your dress off," I order.

She complies, rolling it off her body, she flings it behind her in two seconds flat.

She's got no fuckin' bra on.

"Dirty girl," I mutter, my eyes on her pussy. She's got a thin scrap of material covering it, not doin' a damn thing. I drop to my knees, haul her to the edge of the bed and bark, "On your elbows, watch me, don't take your eyes off mine."

I rip the g-sting off and open her wide. Her pussy is so fuckin' beautiful, and she's dripping for me. I've waited a long time to do this, like a man starving. As I kneel, I push her knees out even wider. I blow onto her hot flesh, and she cries out, so sensitive from the orgasm I just gave her downstairs.

I lick her lightly, through her folds as she squirms. I keep her knees wide with my hands and I lick from the bottom to the top, sucking on her clit when I get there, then I do it again and again, nice and slow. I know playing with her gets her off so bad, so I'm gonna draw this out as long as I can.

"Brock!" she shakes.

I stare at her as she closes her eyes, then I stop. "Eyes on me," I bark.

Her eyes pop open as she tries to wriggle against me. I can't help but grin, and I start again, slowly as she protests, trying to speed it up. I plunge my tongue into her as she grips my hair with her fists and rides my face as I fuck her with my tongue. She doesn't last long, exploding like dynamite as I watch her unfold.

I give her two seconds reprieve. "Play with your tits," I tell her. I swipe my tongue over her clit, and she shudders.

"I'm so sensitive, Brock," she whines.

I ignore her, rubbing her wetness with my finger, slicking her all the way down to her asshole. Yeah, it's been a while since I've been there, too, and I will be again, but not tonight.

I latch onto her clit, sucking as I part her with my hand, watching her as she plucks her nipples and pushes them together. I'm so hard it's actually painful, and I'm leaking at the tip. I want her mouth on me so bad.

I pull her legs over my shoulders, and she tightens them around my head.

I quicken, sucking hard, then insert two fingers and fuck her with a vengeance, milking every drop of pleasure from her body as she screams, calling out, over and over.

When she's spent, she lets go of my hair and flops back down onto the bed. I remove her legs from my shoulders and crawl up the bed, over her body. I beeline straight to her tits, big, round and full. I suck on one nipple as she curses, scratching at my back. I toy with her as I straddle her body, and my dick nestles near her entrance, but I don't push in.

I want her to beg me to fuck her and beg me she will.

I move to the other one and punish it some more,

tweaking the wet nipple with my fingers, pinching and flicking as she bucks off the bed.

"Brock, oh God, Brock, I need you inside me."

I grin. "Need you to taste me first, babe."

She swallows hard, then I lift up to my knees while she moves down the bed and I hold my dick as she takes the tip into her mouth. She rests on her elbows and the sight of her doing that alone almost has me shooting my load down her throat, but I can't do that, not this time. This I want to drag it out for the rest of eternity. She grips my dick with one hand and jacks me off while her tongue lavishes my tip, then she takes me into her mouth, hollowing her cheeks, sucking me as I thrust a little, getting a little more into her perfect mouth when what I really want to do is shove it down her throat.

I move my hips as her tongue works me over while she sucks. I throw my head back and groan. It feels so good, how I've longed for this for so, so long. I can't last, though, I can't do any more. I pull out and grab her by the hips, yanking her out from under me. I flip her over, pulling her backwards so she's on her knees, her ass in the air.

"You like your ass bein' smacked?" I growl in her ear. "Turned me the fuck on watchin' you."

She spreads her legs wider and wiggles her ass.

I smack it hard.

She looks over her shoulder at me as I stare at her perfect body from behind.

I smack her other cheek; my fingers brush her pussy, and she yelps.

"I've been a bad girl, Brock," she cries. "Really, really bad."

Fuck.

Dirty talk with her is enough to make me come all over her back. The restraint I'm showing surprises me.

"Yeah, babe?" I rub my cock through her folds all the way from her ass to her clit. "What did you do?"

"I... I touched myself..."

I grin, dying to push into her, but I wait, driving her mad is something that I can't seem to get enough of.

"Did you think of me, baby?"

"Yes!" she yelps when I spank her right on the pussy. "Oh God, Brock, I need you, I need you now, stop fucking around!"

I lean over and bite her on the shoulder.

I laugh and move back to hold her hips, and I push into her with one move. She gasps and I don't even give her a second to get used to the intrusion. Fuck her, she can take it as good as she gives it.

"This is your punishment then, for turning me on. For letting me finger fuck you at the bar. For gettin' off without me watchin' you doing it."

"Oh God! Yes, yes, yes!" she screams while I drive it home.

I shift my hips and grind into her, her pussy gripping my dick like a vice. So tight, so perfect.

She grips the headboard as I pull her backwards, so we're both upright, and I grab her tits, squeezing them as my dick ploughs in and out of her at a maddening place. She screams, coming again, and I wish I could hold on and milk this pleasure for longer, but I can't. I come hard as I spurt inside her, hot and heavy, draining myself as I hiss and pull her ass to me and still, holding her against me.

Her heavy panting and mine mix together, and it's heady. Hot. Fucking divine.

"Jesus, Brock, we didn't even use protection," she breathes. I pull out and flop down on the bed. She immediately drops down onto the pillows next to me, and I kiss her shoulder.

"I'm clean, you're on the pill, yeah?"

She nods. "Still, we shouldn't take risks."

My heart pounds. Knocking her up wouldn't be the worst

fuckin' thing in the world. Having kids with her may be a long shot, but I live in hope.

"That's all you gotta say to me after that?"

She squirms and rolls around to face me. "That was hot, Brock, thank you."

I grin and kiss her. "Thank you? I think you knew when you put that dress on and dragged your sorry ass here things were gonna get heated between us, babe."

She watches me carefully. Her face is so beautiful. Her clear, pale skin like a vision. She's always been the most beautiful woman I've ever seen, even since she was girl. She captured my heart the day she walked into our classroom. I knew she was special.

"What am I going to do with you, Brock Altman?"

I give her a light slap on her delectable ass and get up, take a piss and come back to bed.

"You could use me for the rest of the night," I suggest.

She laughs, actually laughs, it's a nice sound. I haven't seen her this carefree in a long time. I know she's been drinking but she's not tanked.

"Yeah, big boy?"

I grin, circling my finger on her bare flesh on her shoulder. "You're not on a curfew?"

She screws her nose up. "No, but I'll need to text mom to let her know I won't be coming home."

Warmth floods me imagining her being in my arms for the night. We haven't been able to do this since we were kids. The thought excites me and makes me nervous at the same time.

I kiss her again. "I want you on top this time."

She smiles, and her whole face lights up. "I can't believe you spanked me."

I grunt a laugh as she straddles over me. "You liked it."

She doesn't disagree, and I watch as she pushes her tits

together and thumbs her nipples, watching me, biting her lip as she turns herself on.

"Love these," I say, reaching up as I suck on her nipple, teasing her lightly with my teeth, she throws her head back, grinding into me. "So fuckin' hot."

"I've missed this, Brock," she murmurs. "I've missed… us…"

It's like music to my ears. Okay, so we've both been drinking, and we're high on the euphoria we just gave each other, but fuck it, I'll take it.

"Ride me, Angel," I gruff, my eyes seeking hers. "Ride me like you hate me."

She grins as I grip her hips and lower her onto my hard dick as we go for round two.

"Your wish is my command," she breathes, and I give her full control. My body belongs to her when we're like this, and I'm at her mercy.

I always have been, and for tonight, that's all I need.

14

ANGEL

AGED 17

Brock stares at me, I wore the dress just for him, and when we're on the dance floor at prom, it's like nobody else exists but us. It's a strange feeling, I know after the next couple of weekends, this will be it. He's going to enlist, and that'll be that.

I still don't like the idea, but it's his dream, it always has been.

He had another fight with his dad about hanging around the motorcycle club.

I know Brock just does it to antagonize, but I don't want to be around when he tells his dad he's going to prospect. Maybe he'll be away too long to do his training and the club won't want him anymore. That'd solve one problem, the one it won't solve is that he won't be here, and I'll be going to Phoenix for college alone.

I've cried so many nights, but tonight I'm not going to cry. No, I'm not.

"What are you thinking?" he whispers in my ear.

I smile into his shoulder. "How cute you look in a suit," I whisper back.

I feel him kiss my temple. "I'm looking forward to you removing it later."

"Aren't you optimistic," I tease.

He grunts a laugh. "No, just hopeful."

He squeezes my hips, and I know he's the only man I'll ever love. He can say what he wants about me going to college and seeing other boys, but there will never be anyone like him.

I want to beg him to come to Phoenix with me. Maybe if I pleaded long and hard enough, he would, but I can't do that to him. He'd only resent me in the long run.

"You said forever, right, Brock? You and me, no matter what happens?"

His grip tightens. "What's wrong, Angel? What's going on in that pretty little head of yours?"

I swallow the lump in my throat.

"Nothing," I lie. "I just don't want tonight to end."

The last thing I want to do is make him feel bad, like he doesn't feel bad enough already.

He pulls back and pushes my chin up with his finger. "You want to get out of here?"

I nod.

He grins and we exit the gymnasium and run out to his truck.

"Where are we going?"

"I've got a surprise for us."

I laugh as he fondles my ass while helping me up into the cab, then he dashes around the front and hops in, guns the engine and we take off out of the carpark like a bat out of hell.

I snuggle close to his side, and he leans over and kisses me on the head. I half expect him to drive us to the nearest motel, but typical Brock, he does nothing of the sort. We drive north out of town and up to the Canyon. There's an awesome view of the town from up there, the lights twinkle below and it's like you're literally sitting on the horizon looking down on the world.

It takes about twenty minutes with the radio playing country songs lightly in the background, and I know I'll remember this night forever. Not because I'm choosing tonight to give myself to Brock fully, but because I know the friendship and love we have can withstand anything.

I love him.

When we pull up, he jumps out excitedly and then hauls me by the hands out of the passenger seat. He's reversed in so when he pops the back of the truck, I laugh out loud when I see the set up he's got in there so we can watch the lightshow.

Two pillows, a comfy looking duvet, and a bottle of cherry coke with two glasses.

I turn to look at him. "You got something planned, Brock Altman?"

He grins at me. "Thought we could come up here, look at the stars. I know you love it here."

I haul myself up and perch on the edge as he stares at me.

"What?" I breathe.

He closes his eyes momentarily. "Just want to remember this, tonight, how you look, how you feel."

I pull him by the tie, and he towers over me.

"I love you, Brock; I'll never forget anything where you're concerned."

Reaching down, he kisses me chastely before hopping up next to me. He pulls his tie off and loosens his top button, then pops the bottle and proceeds to pour us two glasses.

It's cold out, so I snuggle the duvet around me as he hands me my glass.

"Underage drinking at its finest." I laugh. "I haven't had this stuff in years." I wince, taking a sip; it's super sweet.

He shakes his head. "Been saving it for a special occasion."

I pat the space next to me. "Come sit closer."

He kicks his shoes off, moves behind me, and I lean back against his solid chest as his knees bend either side of hips. We stare out at the view.

"I do love it here," I whisper. "It's so quiet, away from everything."

"All that wasted toilet paper for one night," he muses, talking about the decorations.

I tut. "I'll have you know the cheerleading committee spent a lot of time putting all of those props together, if I never see papier Mache again in my life, it'll be too soon."

He rumbles behind me. "I think someone spiked the punch."

I laugh. "Yeah, I don't doubt that."

"Speaking of cheerleading outfits, gonna miss that."

I sigh and snuggle into him, taking a sip of my coke. "Don't remind me, but we said we wouldn't discuss anything tonight, right?"

He squeezes me, one hand coming around my waist. "Nothing's gonna change."

I squeeze my eyes shut and hope to God he means that.

We sit in silence for a while, watching the twinkling of the lights and the stars. The sky is always plump full of them on a night like this; it's like they all came out just for us.

"You're kind of romantic, you know," I say softly. "I think I like this side of you."

He kisses the back of my head. "Don't go yabbing about it, you'll ruin my reputation."

I giggle. "Yes, wouldn't want anyone thinking you were anything less than a brute."

"Best to keep up appearances."

I drain my glass and place it down next to me.

"Brock?"

He traces the top of my hand with his finger, tickling my skin. Every touch, every single one sends me into overdrive.

"Yeah, babe, you too cold?"

I shake my head. "No."

He kisses my shoulder. "What's up, baby girl?"

"I'm ready."

He keeps circling my skin and I close my eyes, pressing my thighs together. I'm starting to feel an ache between my legs, one only he can relieve.

"Ready for what?"

I rub my ass into his junk, and he chokes on his cherry coke.

"Holy shit, Angel." He coughs and splutters as I giggle uncontrollably.

"What did you think I meant?"

"I don't know," he says, when he's done choking. "That you're ready to go home."

I turn and reach up as he bends to meet me, and we kiss lightly. He tastes like cherry coke, and I smile despite myself.

"I don't want to go home, Brock; I want tonight to be special." I grasp his thigh with one hand and squeeze. "I want you, Brock Altman; I want it to be you."

He swallows hard. This is why I love him. He wasn't even expecting to have sex tonight, even though all the kids I know have been talking about who's going to do it with whom.

"You brought condoms, right?" I say, sudden panic surging through me.

His eyes go round. "Fuck, babe, I didn't."

"What!" I shriek.

It takes about five seconds before he breaks out into a shit-eating grin. I punch him on the shoulder.

"Very funny, asshole."

He leans down and kisses me, his body is rock hard behind me, his hands holding me tight. I feel the tip of his tongue and it sends a shiver through my body.

"Wanna be sure you're ready," he says, when we pull away breathless. I turn around and straddle over his lap, my skirt bunching up between us as he stares at me, his eyes heated.

"I never want you to do something you're not ready for, Angel, you hear me? Not ever. I can wait."

"I can't," I tell him honestly. "I don't want to."

"Angel..."

I place a finger over his lips. "Anyone ever tell you that you talk too much?"

He pretends to scowl and then bites the tip of my finger.

I move my hand down to the hem of his pants and pull his shirt out, I slowly begin to unbutton it as he watches me. When I get to the top, I spread it wide and take him in.

He's got a fine body, his muscles and six pack are hard and thick, and he has a small smattering of hair on his chest that's moving up and down rapidly.

I can't help my smile as I lean down to kiss his chest. "What's wrong, Brock? Seem to have lost your powers of speech."

He cups my ass with his hands. "Just enjoying the show," he replies, his voice low and husky.

I grind into his hard length, and he curses.

I lean down and kiss him gently. "I've waited so long for this moment," I whisper. "I love you, Brock, I'll always love you."

He kisses me back hard. "There's nobody but you." His grip tightens. "I love you, Angel, there's nothing I want more, but don't you want this to be in a hotel room somewhere... I don't know? Warm?"

"No, Brock, this is perfect, your truck has way more meaning than a hotel room."

He puts his hand on his heart. "I'm flattered." He chuckles.

I yelp as he all of sudden rolls me over, and I'm underneath him, his hand hitches up my skirt and rests on my thigh. His pretty eyes dance with delight and mischief.

"No way you're taking charge on our first time," he goes on. "Not happening, babe."

I look up at him, brushing the hair from his eyes. "So bossy."

He settles between my legs as I wrap mine around his waist. "You know what I love more than you in this dress?"

I shake my head, biting my bottom lip.

He grins. "You out of this dress."

I gasp as he growls into my neck and sucks hard on my pulse. I know he's going to leave a mark and I really don't care.

And it's there, in the back of his truck, that I give him the thing I know he wants the most. All of me.

I didn't know then that this was the beginning of the end, I didn't know that it would be years of waiting before I'd ever be with him again fully, and by that time, things had changed.

Everything we promised each other meant nothing, because the one thing about promises made when you're young and foolish is that they get broken, then put on a shelf and forgotten about.

But I never forgot Brock, never.

He was supposed to be my forever.

BROCK

PRESENT DAY

I wake with a start and all of a sudden, I'm suffocating with heat. I rub my eyes and it's then I realize why last night's tequila bout was probably not such a good idea.

Brock lies next to me, his arm, and a leg, swung over me as I try my hardest to roll him off. He's always been warm, even in those cold nights in the back of his truck, he was like a big teddy bear, my hot water bottle. Nothing's changed.

I slip out from underneath him and tiptoe across the room quietly.

Brock's old room has a small bathroom attached; it's tiny, barely big enough for one person, but I need to pee which I do super-fast and then creep back into the room.

I pick up my discarded dress, but I've no idea where my G-string ended up. Before I get my dress back on, Brock cracks one eye open.

"Not sneakin' out on me, are ya?"

I stop in my tracks like I've been caught doing something wrong.

I don't know why I try to cover my body up, he's seen it all, and then some, so I give up. Instead, I perch on the end of the bed and attempt to unroll my dress from its current state of disarray. Wearing last night's clothes is like the final humiliation in my walk of shame. I only hope nobody is downstairs to witness it.

"No, I'm just trying to reassemble last night's clothing, seen my G-string anywhere?"

He props himself up on one elbow. "That's my souvenir." He grins.

I cock an eyebrow. "Really?"

He beckons me to him with the crook of his finger. "C'mere, I got something for you."

"If it's your morning wood, I don't think so." I smirk back.

The sides of his mouth turn up. "You weren't sayin' no to my wood last night."

"I blame tequila."

Blaming something other than myself is lame, and we both know it, but I gotta try to dig my way out of it.

He grunts, flinging the duvet back and crosses the room to the bathroom buck naked. His cock hangs heavily between his legs at half-mast.

I momentarily close my eyes and remember all the fucking we did last night. In every position known to man. We were like rabbits, and I can feel where he's been and that's everywhere. He comes back a few moments later whistling a tune.

Fucking whistling!

I shoot him a glare. "You always so chipper in the morning?"

He grabs me by the arm pits and hauls me backwards as he climbs into bed, so my back is against his front. "After I just boned a beautiful woman all night, yeah. Just cos you're a grumpy ass bitch doesn't mean we all have to be."

He brings one hand around my body and rests it on my lower belly, the other one he places across my left breast.

"Still a charmer," I mutter.

"You know chivalry wasn't always my strong suit," he reminds me, settling back on the pillows. "Neither was being patient, yet here we are."

"When did you get so wise?" I quip.

He bumps me with his hips. "Less of the sarcasm."

"You used to love my sarcasm."

"Well, you said it differently then."

Something about the sentiment has me wakening from my hazy state of bliss.

"Shit, Brock."

He tightens his hold. "You're not runnin', I'll tell ya that for nothin'."

"You know this a bad idea just as much as I do."

He grunts. "No, *you* think that. You're pissed at me because I was away so long in the military, and when I came back, admittedly, I'd changed. But you're the one who ran off with that *asshole* and got knocked up."

I stiffen at his words. "That wasn't quite how it happened, Brock."

"Huh. Seems to me that you have a short memory cause that's how I remember it."

"No, I don't. At the time, he seemed like a nice guy, and I was lonely. I was wrong, okay. I made a mistake; I didn't know he was going to one day attempt to kill me..." I trail off, closing my eyes. I want to run, I want to bolt for it, but being in Brock's warm, calming presence has more of a hold on me than I could ever imagine.

"I didn't mean to... I'm sorry, I didn't mean to bring all that shit up. I'm pissed that he's even out, cocksucker's dead... I swear to God, Ange."

"Nothing's going to happen, he can't leave Minnesota."

"He better not."

"Let's just calm down and enjoy this." I reason.

He traces my stomach with his thumb, and I close my eyes, enjoying the sensation. "What are you sayin'?"

"I'm saying we're bad for each other, but I can't stay away from you, or maybe I just shouldn't drink tequila."

He grunts again. "We're not bad for each other, we've just changed. Tequila's got nothin' to do with it."

"We're not together, Brock."

"No?" He pinches my nipple, and I yelp. "Feels kinda like it."

"We had one night of passion, that doesn't qualify for a meaningful and lasting relationship."

"Doesn't it? So, any other guy you've been with that gave you that many orgasms before his dick even touches you?"

"You know my body, that's all there is to it."

He rumbles laughter beneath me, and I can't help but chuckle too. "Why do we fight it?" I wonder.

"I don't fuckin' know, but if you wanna take things slow, I can do that, we can reconnect. I know I haven't said much about it over the years. I've tried to stay away, but watchin' Rawlings grow up and get older, it's made me realize a lot of things."

"Such as?"

"Such as, you're the one that got away," he replies. "And I don't wanna make the same mistake twice. We're good together, Ange. You know that no matter what happens, we'll always come back to one another. We always do."

My eyes well with tears.

I can't be owned again.

"I'm not giving you an answer right now," I say. I need time to think this through when I'm not in a post-orgasm love haze. "I'm saying I'll consider it."

"That's big of you," he mutters. "What's a man gotta do? Tell me, and I'll do it."

"Fine. You asked. I don't want to be claimed at the table."

His hand stops tickling my skin. "You know that's not negotiable."

"See!" I cry triumphant. "We can't agree on that one little thing, so my theory is correct; we're a bad idea."

He reaches forward and kisses the back of my neck, sending shivers right through me.

"No, we're not. But claiming you at the table is a formality, you don't even have to wear the cut. Just knowing you're mine is enough."

I swallow hard. I guess… he may have a point.

"And it's no different to a marriage, a contract, you just

have it in your pretty little head that all women are property of the M.C., and there's no dissuading you otherwise."

"Aren't they property?" I challenge. "We both know they are, as much as Sienna and Lily like to think they're not, they are. If Hutch tells anyone in that club to jump, they all shout, *how high?* It's just how it is."

"So what? Hutch is a good man, he won't do anybody any wrong, you know him. You know what our club's about. Frankly, babe, if you don't wanna be part of the club then we may as well call it quits now. Hutch and Kirsty have been more a family to me than my own, especially those years after graduation when I came back each summer to prospect. My own father disowned me. Sure, we got our shit together for a while, then look what happened with Axton," he trails off.

I know Axton going away broke his heart. Hell, it broke all of us.

It hurts that he'd want to call it quits just like that. Choose the club over me, not that I'd ever want him to choose, yet I know that deep down, he thinks I chose Marcus over him. Even though he wasn't even around when we got together, and we'd broken up ages before.

You should have waited.

I try not to torture myself but waiting ten years is long enough.

"Fine, then we've got nothing more to say."

"Fine," he agrees. "But you can ride my dick before you stomp off all angry, take some of that energy out on me, babe. You know you want to."

"I do not, and that's disgusting," I retort, but before I can get up and do exactly that, he reaches down and feels between my legs.

"Feel pretty wet to me."

I can feel his boner in my back.

"Don't flatter yourself." I trail off as he begins to lightly rub my clit with his index finger, and I don't do a damn thing to stop him.

I should.

I should tell him to go shove his stupid club rules up his ass, but he's right about something; we have something. We have chemistry, it's undeniable.

And while I want to run and never look back, I'm afraid that if I do, it'll be the last time I do.

15

BROCK

10 YEARS AFTER GRADUATION

"V.P.?" I stare at the patch as Hutch holds it out to me.

"You've earned it."

A shit-eating grin spreads across my face. "Fuck. I don't know what to say."

"Say you want it, that'll make an old man happy."

I take it off him and hold it tentatively, like it's not real.

"Been voted in?"

"Obviously, with the spot open, it's time, Brock. You've earned your dues, and now you're back on a permanent basis. I want you by my side. The club needs you."

I look up from the dirty, worn patch and I've never been so proud. "I don't know what to say."

He grins. "Well, don't go gettin' all sentimental on me. The boys want to give you a goin' over before you get officially patched in, you know, one for the road and all of that."

"Better make myself scarce, then." I grin back at him.

"You're a good man, Brock. I'm one lucky son of a bitch to have you with me at the helm. You any further into talks with takin' over the junkyard?"

"Yeah, old man Marty is retiring, can get it real cheap

since he's run the place into the ground. I wanna make a go of it, can start off small, but there's nothing around for miles, no competition. It's a goldmine just waiting to happen."

"Well." He pats me on the back. "Make it happen. Proud of you, son. Be even prouder when your coffers double."

I nod, determined to make this work.

I leave the clubhouse and take off to Angel's place.

She's been distant since I got back. We've hooked up a few times since, but the last stint in the middle east left me away for over two years. It was hard on her.

Shit happens. Life goes on. The last conversation we had, I told her to make herself a life, find someone who could make her happy.

I didn't mean any of it, and she hated me for saying it, but we both knew it was true.

After I got shot and came home, everything was different. I knew what I wanted, I knew I'd missed out on a lot, but what I also didn't realize was that people move on too. They don't hang around forever, even when they say they will, and you shouldn't expect them to.

I text her and we meet at the diner.

She's cut her hair and I don't like it, but I don't say anything.

I've been back for almost a month, and I've seen her twice.

As soon as I see her, I know something's wrong.

"Spit it out, you look like the grasshopper who sang all summer."

She shakes her head and wrinkles her nose in that cute way she does.

"I met someone, Brock."

It hits me in the chest like a rocket blasting through orbit. Of all the things I'd imagine she'd say, I didn't expect *that*.

"When?"

"While you were away, we've been dating... you said..."

I know what I said, I didn't fucking mean it, not a word. But I'm selfish, always have been.

"Things move on, people change," I say, and I try not to make a fist under the table. "Is it what you want?"

She looks at me with tears in her eyes.

"I don't know, all I've ever really known is us."

I swallow hard. "I know I left a lot; I know I haven't been great, and we've gone our separate ways, but I'll always be here for you."

"That sounds like goodbye," she whispers.

I hold her hands across the table. "Never, babe. It'll never be goodbye, but if this is what you want, how can I stop you?"

"Maybe I want you to."

"Then don't go," I challenge. "Stay here, but you have to be sure it's what you want. If you're not sure then you'll always wonder if there could be someone else."

She knows it's true, so do I, even if it kills me inside to admit it.

A tear escapes her eye, and I watch it curiously. "I let you go once, and you never came back."

"I'm here, ain't I?"

"You know what I mean," she says, wiping the escaped tear away. "I want more than that, and I know how the M.C. treats women..."

"You don't know shit," I snark. "You only know what you've heard, and what you've heard is lies from small minded, red-necked idiots who like to gossip."

"So, they don't have women called *sweet butts* who hang around for sex?"

Okay, except possibly that.

"No different to anyone who hangs around any bar on a Saturday night looking to hook up, what's the harm?"

"Do you want other women?"

I take my hands away and glare at her. "What do you care? You met someone."

She tenses at my words, and we stare at one another.

This is what it's been like since I got back. We argue a lot.

We don't know each other anymore. Maybe she's right, maybe we did miss the boat. Maybe it is too late for us.

If that's true then why does my chest pound like I'm having a fuckin' heart attack?

"I'm moving," she whispers, looking down at her hands.

It's like I've been kicked in the guts.

"Where to?" I manage to grunt out between gritted teeth.

"Phoenix."

Not too far then, but not in reaching distance.

"I want to meet him."

"He's not here," she replies quickly.

"How convenient."

"What's that supposed to mean?"

I sigh noisily. "Well, I'm supposed to be your *best friend*, aren't I? Thought it might be important for your *best friend* to meet the man whose takin' you away from me, from your family, from what you know."

She points at me fiercely. "You of all people know there's a danger in what you know, Brock. And I'm over this town. Nobody does anything except gossip, put one another down, and judge you because you're different. I want to make something of myself. There are more opportunities for tattooing in the city."

If she'd have asked me to go, I might have considered it, but she's already gone, and I can't let her know she's hurt me. Hurt. Fuck. She's ripped my fucking heart out of my chest, and it lies bleeding on the table.

As my father would say, *time to be a man, Brock.*

Even his fist couldn't be any worse than this. This feels like fucking failure.

"Well, I can't promise I'll write you."

She stares at me, and I sit back and cross my arms over my chest.

"Is that all you've got to say?"

I roll my eyes dramatically. "What do you want me to say? Let's fuck for old time's sake?"

She shakes her head in disbelief. "I think I was wrong about you, Brock Thomas Altman. I thought you were a decent guy, but you've changed, and frankly, I don't like the asshole you've become."

I act like her words don't hurt me, like they're not silver bullets wounding me deep down to my core.

There will never be anybody but her, but if I ask her to stay, she will, and she'll never get out of this town. I want her to be something, I want her to experience life. Not with another guy, obviously, but I can't have it both ways.

She'd only resent me in the end. We both know it.

"Oh well, guess you won't be here to care about any of that, will you, Ange?"

I slide out of the booth and throw a twenty in the middle to pay for the coffees that never arrived.

"Brock... please."

I flick my eyes up to hers, they plead with me to do something, but I can't.

I'll forever miss her beautiful face, how she makes me feel and the way she bites her lip when she's nervous.

"You'll be fine, Angel. I nudge her chin with my knuckles. You always were the tough one out of the two of us. I'll always love you."

With that I leave her sitting there, staring after me as I walk away without realizing until much later that I've made the biggest mistake of my life.

Present day

"That should do it," Colt says, wiggling the camera that he's just installed at the yard, testing its flexibility. "All I gotta do is hook it up and we're good to go."

"Cheers, bud, this is something I've been meaning to do but upgrades cost a shitload."

"I doubt anyone could get over those gates," he replies, hopping down off the ladder. "But you never know, they'd need a serious pair of bolt cutters."

A few moments later, we both turn our heads to the door as Lucy strolls in. Her hair as high as Texas and her red lipstick is as bright as an Alabama sunset.

"Hey, beautiful, someone told me they knocked you up," I quip. "Don't look too fuckin' pregnant to me."

She swats her perfectly manicured fake nails in my direction. "You're a man after my own heart," she croons in her southern accent. "But I've put on ten pounds already, and if I blow up anymore, I'll be able to set sail. Hey, Colt, sweetie, how's it hanging?"

Colt smirks. "Hey, Lucy, hangin' just fine, thank you."

She turns to him, hands on hips. "Say, what ever happened to that little chicky related to Sienna, what was her name again?"

He looks mildly uncomfortable for a moment, but that won't stop her. "Umm, Cassidy."

"Ahh, that's it, Cassidy, why'd she leave town?"

He glances at me, and I just shrug. It ain't really club business, long as he doesn't mention the whole situation in the barn when Steel killed Sienna's ex-boyfriend, then we're good. Granted it was by default.

"Took off back home." He shrugs.

She narrows her eyes. "You end up tappin' her?"

He splutters out a mouthful of coffee he just took a sip of, and she rushes over to pat his back.

"I'm sorry, hon, I'm a real nosy little bitch, but really, I want to know. Did you?"

He looks uncomfortable. "Ah, nah, it really wasn't like that. She kind of formed an attachment to me while I took care of her after the abduction, but that was it…" He hesitates and I know then that something happened more than just sex. "She was pretty fucked up, anyone would be."

"Got a shitload of invoices for you," I interrupt, trying my best to get Colt off the hook.

Last thing he needs is fifty fuckin' questions from Lucy. She's wasting her time in book-keeping, she could have been an excellent interrogator. "Been fuckin' crazy around here as of late, everyone's renovating or looking for cheap shit. Got another haul next week, gotta go out of town."

She turns and marches over, then squints at me. "You getting enough sleep, sugar? Your eyes look really dark."

I look up at her. "Nice of you to notice. What's in the bag?"

She's easily distracted. "Ooh, I brought you boys some donuts from the diner. Thought you might be needing a little pick-me-up. Saw Angel this morning," she adds, tossing the bag on my desk as she goes over to Bones' side and stands there shaking her head. I watch as she sweeps the entire contents of one side into the trash can and then sets it on the ground. "She looked a little tired too."

Colt chuckles as I shoot him a glare.

"Is there anyone you're not going to interrogate today?" I ask, opening the bag. The donuts are fresh, and the paper is becoming transparent from the grease. I down one in two bites.

"Oh, hush, can't a girl have a little conversation around here? I have to listen to Rubble all day long, I need an outlet."

"Why not have an outlet down at Lily's or over at Angel's Ink?"

"Speaking of Angel's Ink," she drawls. Oh no. Should have kept off that subject. "Angel's a good woman, when you gonna sweep her off her feet, for real?"

So, I'm not off the hook.

I waggle the bag at Colt, and he strides across and takes a couple out. Damn, they smell good.

"Right, like Angel would ever want anyone to sweep her anywhere. She'd swing a machete at my head before that ever happened."

"You boys just don't get it, do you?" she sits down at Bones' desk while Colt works on the program on his laptop, licking his sugar-coated fingers. "Women want to be wooed, assholes."

I guffaw and shake my head, almost choking on my next donut. "You've been married way too long, buttercup. Clearly, you're a little jaded on what women want."

"Yeah," Colt pipes up. "They say they want one thing when they mean another, how's a man supposed to keep up?"

I point at him. "Well said. They get you spinning around in fuckin' circles and just when you think you're doin' somethin' right, bam, you're out on your ass, sleepin' in the doghouse."

Colt nods. I mean, I don't think he has any trouble with the ladies, but he's a damn sight more respectful than the rest of us.

"I'm gonna give you boys a little tip, on the house," she says, tapping on the keyboard. "Women are the same no matter where you go. They say they don't want this and that, but trust me when I say they do. They do want to be told they're pretty, they do want to be wooed and dined and chased, and they do want wild, crazy sex spontaneously and I don't know, maybe a bunch of flowers every now and again.

Not just a slap on the ass to say thanks for putting up with my shit day in and day out."

Colt looks like he might start taking notes. Fuckin' pussy boy.

"Should I give Rubble the heads up?" I mock as she looks up and gives me daggers.

"Fine, joke all you want. But don't say I didn't warn you. While we women enjoy a little somethin' somethin', it doesn't hurt to help out around the house. Nothing gets me more turned on than coming home to a house that's been vacuumed, and I wasn't the one doing it."

I laugh out loud. "I can just imagine Rubble in an apron, a feather duster in one hand, broom in the other."

She rolls her eyes, ignoring my joke.

Colt chuckles. "Not like either of us have an ol' lady, darlin'," he reminds her. "But if you know any that I can vacuum for in exchange for a little somethin' somethin' then send them my way."

I grin into my cold mug of coffee and my brain flicks to the flashbacks of me doin' Angel on Saturday night.

Her sweet, round ass cheeks as I spanked her. God, she was so hot for it. I fucked her so hard, she loves it too. Begging me for more as I tugged on her nipples. I can't decide which position I liked the most, though her on top is a sight for sore eyes because I love to watch her tits bounce up and down and her face contort as I make her scream.

I shift in my chair. I really don't need to be thinking about that, especially after she got a little chilly with me when I suggested we give things a go between us.

She rode me hard, mad at my suggestion though not mad enough to storm out. She loves angry makeup sex, and I want to be the one to give it to her permanently.

I don't know if it's nostalgia, being around Rawlings, seeing my mom, even Lucy being pregnant, but it makes me realize life doesn't go on for eternity. Things change. People change. We get older. We're not here forever.

And I want her.

I want her to be mine, and I want her belly to be round and swollen from carrying my kid. Yeah, she'll say she's too old, thirty-six, but lots of women are having babies later in life. She's still young enough, though I don't even know if she wants any more kids. She doesn't even want me to sleep over, much less impregnate her.

I chuckle at the thought as Lucy eyes me over the monitor. "Something funny?"

"Nope," I say, just as my phone rings. "Yeah, dude."

"Horses are being delivered this afternoon. Sienna will be there and Stevie's coming to help, she apparently rode horses as a kid," Steel says.

"Cool, I'll be there later, girls be all right for a few?"

"Yeah, I'll offload the feed in the barn and get all the troughs set up, you won't even know they're there."

I scoff. "Right, dude. I'll remember you said that."

"Owe you one."

I can't wait to tell Rawlings, she's always been a bit horse mad, though I know she'll want to ride one and that's not going to happen, not just yet.

Suddenly, a flash of little Rawlings on a pony trotting around the ranch invades my thoughts. Her mama walking along next to her, holding her hand as she waves to me while I watch them.

My heart longs for what it wants.

And I want them.

I know it's now or never. I have to do something.

I don't want to be forty years old and still on the wagon. Nah, that life doesn't interest me anymore.

Even if Angel is as stubborn as a mule, I could make it a

little harder for her to say no. I could kind of insert myself into her life a little more. A smile creeps upon my face.

"You don't even have to tell me why you got that big sloppy grin on your mush." Lucy sighs, not even looking at me. "But she sure as hell is one lucky girl."

I only wish Angel thought the same.

16

ANGEL

"What do you mean Brock has horses?"

Rawlings buckles her seatbelt and throws her backpack on the floor. "He didn't tell you?"

I dread the day my child is fully grown, seriously.

"I haven't seen him for a few days," I admit. Though, we did spend Saturday night together we were kind of busy. Horses never came up.

"Maybe I could take some lessons?"

"I don't know about that, horses are kind of scary,"

She laughs like I'm a fool. "Mom, they are not. They're cool. Lexie has a horse, and I've fed him carrots and hay and he nudged me with his nose, I think horses like me."

"Yes, but you've never climbed on one and ridden it around. They're high up and they sprint pretty fast, you could fall off."

She rolls her eyes at me.

"How did you know about the horses?" I wonder. She hasn't seen Brock since he picked her up from school last week.

"From Melody's mom."

Dread hits me in full force.

Melody's mom?

How the hell does *Melody's mom* know anything about Brock and his stupid horses?

Jealousy courses through me like a freight train. I'm not exactly known for my patience as it is, but imagining that he's been anywhere near her, or *any* woman, makes me want to break someone's face.

"Oh," I reply casually. "How does she know?"

She shrugs again. "I don't know, mom."

I don't know what annoys me more, imagining him flirting with Melody's mom or my impending rage of jealousy.

I'm annoyed with myself for letting him get under my skin, for drinking too much on Saturday, *and* falling into his bed like some cheap sweet butt. All it takes is one sexy little glance from those green eyes and I'm putty in his hands.

I've also considered his words about giving us a try, but coming back from that heartbreak, *again*, if things didn't work out this time… it would kill me.

Ever since the incident with my ex, I've distanced myself from anyone wanting more from me, even Brock, the one man I know would never hurt me physically, but he sure has the power to hurt me emotionally. He holds all the cards where my heart is concerned.

He says we're different people now, but are we really? I'm still me. I haven't changed that much. I just got a little tougher. A little disheartened. And maybe just a little jaded.

Having a near death experience from the hands of someone you thought loved you, the man who you thought would be the one protecting you, not the one trying to kill you, kind of alters you. I rub a hand over my stomach subconsciously.

Every time I look at my daughter, I'm reminded of what I

could have lost and that just makes me furious all over again. I have issues, big ones.

When I get home, I see a motorcycle parked in my driveway. Immediately, I assume it's Brock, but I'm surprised when I see Colt leaning against his seat.

"Hey, Colt," I say as I haul Rawlings' backpack from the floor of the truck. "Honey, you remember Colt, Uncle Brock's friend?" I guess it's the best way to describe anyone from the M.C.

"Hi," she says, waving her papier Mache sword at him.

"Hey, kiddo, what you got there?"

"A sword," she says proudly, swishing it through the air. "We made it in arts and crafts."

"This is my child." I smile as she goes running off toward the front door. "Could've made anything, she makes a sword."

"It's a special sword," she yells at us, disappearing inside.

"To what do I owe this pleasure?"

He smirks. "Hot date, don't you remember?"

I frown and he bursts out laughing. "Jesus, don't look so horrified, I'm just kidding. You wanted a quote for some security cameras on the porch."

"Oh." I realize, feeling like an idiot.

"Won't take too long. I can take a look, give you the best options, and I would suggest a sensor light, they work like a charm, long as you got no stray cats in the area."

I smile as I lead the way. I forgot I'd asked him to stop by after the night I thought I saw someone in the yard. It freaked me out, even if I was just seeing things.

He doesn't take too long, and when I get on inside my phone rings.

It's Brock.

"Hello," I say, still cranky about the Melody's mom thing.

"You sound like you had a rough day."

I roll my eyes. "No, just a busy one, what's up?"

"Mom wants to know if you'll come to dinner."

"I don't know, Brock, it's a school night for Rawlings…"

"It's at seven, not like I'm gonna keep you up all night."

My throat goes dry thinking about what he did to me Saturday, and most of Sunday morning, and while my body craves his touch, my mind is begging me to decline.

"How is your mom?"

"Ask her yourself, you know she won't take no for an answer."

I glance at my watch. I guess it would be rude not to go over there, and it would be nice catching up with her. It's been a long time and she's always been kind to me.

"I'll have a shower, see you over there later."

Silence.

"Are you there?" I say, pulling the phone from my ear to see if we're disconnected.

"Yeah, I'll see you then."

I shake my head, hanging up and call out to Rawlings. "Honey, you want to have dinner at Uncle Brock's tonight, his mom's in town."

She comes running in, and I have to laugh. She's pulled a tutu over her school uniform and is twirling the sword around like a ballet dancer with a vengeance. "What's he making for dinner?" she ponders, pirouetting around the kitchen.

"I don't know, honey, whatever we're grateful enough to receive."

"I hope it's lasagna again." She grins.

"Well, go wash up and if we have time, we can stop off and get a tub of rocky road to take with us."

"Yay!" she squeals. "Mom, you're the best!" She runs off toward the bathroom.

"I'll remember you said that when you're fifteen and hate me," I yell after her.

An hour later, I'm pulling up to Brock's place, and I see the front porch has all been cleared, a miracle in itself, and there's a new concrete path leading up to the front steps.

I'm actually pretty impressed, up until recently, you always had to go around the back to get inside. It seems like things are finally getting done around here.

"I want to carry the ice cream for Brock," Rawlings says, hopping out of the car.

"Uncle Brock," I correct. "And remember your manners at the table."

"I will, mom," she says, as I pass her the paper bag with the tub inside and we make our way across the front lawn.

We don't even make it to the steps when Sylvia Altman swings the porch door open and claps her hands together.

"Well, will you look at that." She smiles. "You're all grown up, little Rawlings. You probably don't remember me, but I'm Brock's mommy."

Rawlings looks up at her startled. "I brought ice cream." She shoves the bag out in her hands quite proudly.

Sylvia beams at me as she pulls me into her arms in a warm embrace. "Hello, my sweet, sweet Angel," she whispers, and tears form in my eyes.

"Hi, Sylvia, it's been a while."

"It has, and it's a pity I missed your parents this weekend, would have been nice catch up with them, how are they?" she pulls back and assesses me with sharp eyes.

"Good, they're good. Dad's had a couple of heart scares, so they want to move back here, retire and spend more time with me and Rawlings. They've put an offer in on a house, and they move permanently next month if all goes to plan."

She claps her hands together and crouches down to

Rawlings. "Isn't that wonderful? You're going to have your grandparents around all the time!"

Rawlings nods enthusiastically. "I really like Grandpa's car; we go play mini golf and then I have a kiddachinno."

I laugh and my eye catches movement at the doorway. Brock stands there, freshly showered, dressed simply in a black Henley and his usual ripped jeans with bare feet. His hair is loose and wet. He looks so damn sexy; I have to close my mouth from drooling.

No man ever makes me want to instantly jump their bones; not like he does.

"Hello, Angel."

"Hi, Brock," I reply.

Rawlings jumps up the steps and runs into his arms. Just as she does, he catches her and spins her in the air.

"How's my favorite girl?"

"Good, Uncle Brock, I brought you some ice cream." She squeals as he tickles her, then sets her down again.

"You did? Which flavor?"

"Rocky road!" she cries, both hands in the air as she waves the bag around excitedly.

It's so cute how she's taken to him, not intimidated by him or his size one bit. Then again, he's always had a way with kids, they just seem to swarm to him.

"My favorite," he says with a grin, holding the flyscreen door open for us. Sylvia goes in first, then Rawlings, then me.

He watches me carefully, he's even had a shave, and he smells like a fucking dream. I try not to notice, but it's a little hard not to.

"You lost your powers of speech?" he chortles as I close my mouth.

"Don't flatter yourself, bozo."

He laughs, then bends to my ear. "Wear that dress for me?"

"No," I fire back. "I just like teasing you."

He curses under his breath, and I don't need to turn around to know his eyes are on my ass. He's an insatiable son of a gun.

"Something smells good, Mama Altman," I say, knowing Brock couldn't have cooked anything this good. Even though, I admit, he isn't bad for a bachelor.

"My famous cottage-pie." Sylvia smiles. "Take a seat, I've set the table."

"I'll grab the plates." I hide my grin at her taking over Brock's house, and he shoots me a glare.

Brock takes the ice cream from Rawlings and walks behind me to the kitchen, placing it in the freezer.

"Mom says if I'm good you'll let me see the horses later," Rawlings calls, before we even get seated.

Brock looks at me and smirks. "We'll see, darlin'," he calls back.

"I said nothing of the sort," I tell him. *"Melody's mom* however sings a different tune."

He passes me the plates.

"What's the matter, jealous?"

"Ha! Hardly," I shout-whisper back. "But it's like Wednesday, Brock, couldn't keep it in your pants past hump day, could you?"

He waves a finger at me. "Someone sounds like they need another round of my whoop-ass."

I point a finger at him. "Don't even think about it and keep your voice down."

"It's my house," he argues.

"Yeah, and I don't need your mom listening to us fight."

He rolls his eyes. "Nothin' happened. She works at the stock feeders, and I was there today, but it's nice to know that you think so highly of me that I'll just bone anything that walks by at the drop of a hat. Real nice."

I shake my head. "Don't you? Saw Tiffany giving you cow eyes on Saturday night, bet it's been a hot minute since you tapped that."

I smile sweetly, and I can hear Rawlings babbling away in the next room to Sylvia.

"Could say the same about you in that dress. What did you do when you spray painted it on your body... think nobody's gonna notice how tight it was with your tits on full display through that sheer mesh? You wanted me to notice you, admit it, you liked it. Tits were beggin' for me."

"I like people looking," I snark. "Just not you."

He cocks an eyebrow. "You sure about that?"

I tap my chin and whisper, "Fine. You're still a good lay, Altman. I'll give you that. Plus, I had been drinking, you know how that hinders my judgement."

"That's because I know your body and how to fine tune it." He nips my ass as I squeal. "And you won't admit it, but you want me just as bad, you don't need alcohol."

"You okay, mom?" Rawlings calls from the dining room.

"Yes, sweetie, I'm fine," I call back, then turn to Brock. "Keep your damn hands to yourself!"

"Weren't sayin' that Saturday night when I had my hands all over you and my tongue was inside your pussy."

I bite my bottom lip. "That was a cheap shot, I was drunk, and lord knows the monumentally bad decisions I make when I'm drunk. Exhibit A." I waft my hand over his giant form.

It's all an act. His words and imagining where his tongue was only makes me hotter for him. Jesus, he's only gotten better with age, and in the sack, he's off the charts.

He comes toward me, his eyes ablaze with arousal. "Yeah? Well, you weren't drunk that day in my office, were you? A wild cat? Yes. Drunk? Nah, babe. We both know you can't get enough of me or my dick, and I know you want me to do it all again, and I will, soon. So, just shut your mouth, turn that finger around and get marching into the dining room, don't want to keep my mother waiting."

"You shut the hell up!"

I'm about five seconds away from throwing the plates at him and hitting him over the head with the frying pan for good measure when Sylvia pops her head around the corner.

"Will you two hurry up? Kid's hungry in here," she complains, giving Brock a pointed look.

"Sorry, Brock doesn't cook very often; it takes him a little bit to find the plates," I say sarcastically.

He hands them to his mother as she makes haste and disappears.

"I bet I cook more than you do. So quick to write me off, yet you couldn't get enough of my lasagna."

I try not to burst out laughing. His lips twitch, and I know he wants to laugh too.

"I admit, you do make a good lasagna."

He reaches for me, and I glance over my shoulder. "Brock, not when your mother's in the next room."

He nuzzles my neck with his nose. "Give me some sugar."

"Saturday night was a one-off, a hall pass."

He squeezes my breast through my dress, and I suppress a moan.

"A hall pass, huh? You think I can get another one?" he nips my pulse lightly with his teeth.

"You left a mark on the other side." I pull the collar of my jacket aside to show him. "I got a lot of shit for that at work, had to threaten everyone with their jobs just to get them to leave me alone."

He smirks. "I like marking you."

"Asshole."

"Dinners getting cold!" Sylvia calls out. Nothing like making it obvious that we're up to no good in here.

I march out, narrowly missing his palm as he tries to smack me.

My ass was sore for a few days after what he did with that palm on Saturday night, but I do like it a little rough. The thought of him doing it again makes me slick with want and I could curse myself for letting him affect me like this.

Dinner is really nice. Sylvia doesn't act like a woman who just left her husband. In fact, she's surprisingly upbeat. The subject of Brock's dad doesn't come up, thank God, but we talk about everything else, and she asks about Rawlings and school and how the tattoo parlor is going.

Every now and again Brock looks at me across the table and a couple of times he strokes my leg where no-one can see with his foot.

He's driving me wild, much to my disgust. If his mom weren't here tonight, I'd probably jump him once Rawlings went to sleep. Even I've got my limits, and he's definitely a hard one.

My daughter makes a big production about the ice cream, serving Brock the biggest bowl you've ever seen, and of course, he devours it and asks for seconds.

We wrap things up around nine. Rawlings is tired and it's past her bedtime.

I say goodnight to Sylvia, and Brock carries Rawlings to my truck, placing her comatose body in the passenger seat and hooking the seat belt around her little body.

When he's done there, he comes around to my side.

"Thanks for inviting me," I say, looking down at my feet. "It was nice catching up with your mom."

His lips turn up at the sides. "She misses you; you've always been her favorite."

I smile, meeting his gaze. "She seems to be doing well, considering."

"Yeah, well, my dad's a dick, what can I say."

"What's going to happen with them two? Has she said anything?"

He shrugs. "I don't know and thank God I'm not in the middle of things with them, that'd be so much worse. If he's any kind of man, he'll come down here and beg for fuckin' forgiveness and for her to take him back. She's a good woman, bout time he realized how good he's got it."

His words hit me in the chest at full force.

What have I been thinking?

Brock's a good man. A decent man.

And he loves me, and I'm pretty certain he loves my kid, too.

I can't look him in the eye, it's like a revelation.

Have I been a fool?

He tilts my chin up to make me look at him before I can turn around.

"What's goin' on in that pretty head of yours?"

I let out a slow breath. "So much, Brock. I don't even know where to begin."

He presses his forehead against mine. "Give me a chance," he murmurs. "That's all I'm askin'. You know we can be good together."

I close my eyes. "I'm scared. If things don't work with us, where does that leave us, where does it leave me?"

He holds my shoulders, caressing me lightly with his thumbs. "Angel, you know I'll never lie to you. You know me, the good, the bad, the downright ugly. I love you; I always have. I can't do this anymore. I want a fuckin' shot."

Old confessions come back from that night in the back of his truck. We promised each other so much and then it all fell apart.

I clutch him around his waist. "I love you too, but it doesn't make it any easier. You know how I am about your rules, about the M.C. I don't know if I can ever fully give myself to a man again. What he did…"

"I'm not him, get that through your head. You think I'd ever fuckin' lay a finger on you?"

"I didn't mean that." I start. "What I meant was, parts of me are broken, they don't work like they used to. I'm not the girl I was when I was seventeen."

He kisses my forehead. "And I'm not the same person I was either; we've both changed. We've done shit. I regret a lot of it, trust me, but I don't want to live my life alone, and I don't want to live it without you."

I let his words sink in.

"God, Brock, what if we fuck things up again?"

"Then we'll work it out, we always do."

I want to believe him. A big part of me wants to give my all to him.

"I'm installing a security camera at home," I whisper, out of nowhere.

He pulls back. "What for?"

"Security, dummy."

"I mean, why now?"

He's like a fucking sniffer dog, I swear to God.

"Don't get mad, all right?"

His nostrils flair.

"I just… I don't feel safe, knowing he's out there." I swallow my pride; it takes a lot to admit that out loud.

"He can't do anything; I won't let him. He won't get anywhere near you without me knowing about it. He can't set foot in Arizona, and if he ever does, I'll kill him."

I nod, knowing he means it. "I know that, but it bothers me he's out."

He brushes the hair off my face. "You can come stay here, if you want."

I smile as he looks at me quite seriously. "It'll be nice and cozy with your mom here too, one big happy family."

"Mom can go back to the Lodge; I can clear out one of the rooms for Rawlings."

"Brock, I'm not moving in with you."

"You are if you don't feel safe."

I want to throttle him as much as I want to fuck him. Seriously, the man is one hundred percent alpha, and I've got no business trying to pretend he's anything but.

"I'll be fine, I just wanted to be honest with you." I look up at him and he kisses me gently.

"I'm glad you're being honest with me. Could do with you bein' a little more transparent around here more often. You know I've only ever had your best interests at heart."

I scoff. "You say that to all the girls?"

He bumps me with his hips. "You always gotta ruin the moment, don't you?"

I laugh as he walks me back into the door and cages me in.

"Brock," I whisper.

"Yeah, baby?" He presses his erection into me. "I want you so bad."

He kisses me, sliding his tongue into my mouth as I surrender to him.

"I've got to go," I murmur, in between hot kisses.

He ignores me, sliding his hands around my waist. "Can't wait till the weekend. Come over tomorrow, after you drop Rawlings off."

"I can't," I pant, kissing him back hungrily. "I have a job, and you're not exactly a five second kinda guy."

He smirks against my lips. "You know me too well."

We kiss for a bit longer and my body wants more, so much more.

"I'll see you soon."

"When?"

"Soon." I press my hand against his chest, and he backs off. He's not happy about it, but there's not much we can do. We're not gonna go for it out here against the car door with my daughter inside and his mom looking through the kitchen window.

"Don't keep me waiting too long," he warns, smacking me on the ass as I open the driver's door. "And I mean it, about stayin' over, I don't like you feelin' afraid."

I start my truck and roll the window down. "I'll be fine."

"Call me, any time day or night, you got me?"

"I got you."

"Night, baby girl."

"Goodnight, Brock."

He taps the hood of my car as I pull out.

I feel happy. Happier than I have in a long time. And that's a first for me.

17

BROCK

STRADBROKE, ARIZONA STATE PRISON

I HATE THE SOUND THE DOORS MAKE WHEN THEY OPEN, I could never get used to it.

I hate everything about this place. It makes me glad I did nothing illegal growing up to land me in this fuckin' shit hole. A man like me wouldn't survive being a caged animal.

It's been a few months since I last saw Axton, and every time I come, this place just gives me the heebie jeebies. I'm like a cat on hot bricks, and I can't wait to get out of here.

I didn't tell mom I was coming; she'd only want to join me, and I didn't want to spring that on Axton.

I've still got to break the news to him about mom and dad, and I wonder if I should even say anything. They might get back together before Axton gets out, that's if dad ever comes to his senses. But I know how stubborn he is. He'll be waiting for mom to come running back, saying she's sorry, begging *him* for forgiveness. The funny thing is, I've never seen her like this. She actually seems happy. What does that tell you?

I sign in and wait in the visitor's area until I'm called through. Wishing I could be anywhere else, I glance around, my heart palpitating every extra second I'm in here as I try not to make eye contact with anyone. Fuck knows I don't want to get involved in chit-chat, nothing anybody has to say is going to make this feel any better, and lucky me, I get to leave.

They should seriously take teenagers into maximum security prisons to show them how much fun it wouldn't be if they get into trouble. This is enough to send my ass all the way back to boy scout camp without another word.

I try not to think about Axton and what he's been through. How hard it would be to call prison your home. Sure, he's learned how to be tough from bein' in the joint for so long. He sure as hell wasn't so tough when he first went in.

I shake off my anxiety, cracking my neck and refraining from getting up and legging it back out to my truck before my nerves take over.

Fifteen minutes go by before we're called through to the visitor's area.

Since Axton got moved to minimum security last year, we're allowed contact and we don't have to sit behind a glass window, talking through a phone. I get to spend some decent time with him, if you can call it that, but I'm thankful for small mercies.

I take a seat at the table the furthest away from the guards, not that they didn't just about give me a cavity search getting in here, but I don't wanna be on anyone's radar. I got nothin' to hide, but I'm sure they look at me like I'm about to do somethin' wrong. Maybe the cut's got somethin' to do with it.

I stare out the window, watching the people in the yard. There's a huge greenhouse, a large basketball court, and an outside gym. Looks more like a resort, I wonder where the fuckin' swimming pool is. A few moments later, Axton comes through the double doors and a guard stands to one side near the wall.

I stand and we clasp hands, then we one arm hug each other.

He's beefed up a lot since I saw him last.

"You been workin' out, bro?"

He grins as he sits, shoving me with one hand when I slap him upside the head.

"Not much else to do in here."

"You been keepin' your nose clean?"

He gives me a chin lift. "You know it. Fuckin' boy scout. I'm ready to get out, gotta be on my best behavior. I can't do any longer. I'll go fuckin' insane in here, and this ain't even maximum anymore. It's a walk in the park compared to that shit hole."

I glance around at the other visitors; one can't help but wonder what they're all in for. As for maximum security, I shudder at the thought. I've never asked him about it. Frankly, I'm not sure I wanna know.

"Talked to Prez."

His eyes light up. Me and Hutch had a conversation and he's agreed to Axton prospecting. But he's got to find reputable work and contribute to the club coffers, earn his dues.

"Yeah?"

He's already got the look of a puppy dog in his eyes.

"He's on board, but it comes with conditions."

Axton claps his hands together and woots at the top of his lungs, just like he used to do when he was sixteen and stupid. The guard frowns at him and motions for him to sit down.

He complies but not before fist pumping on the table.

"Calm down," I mutter. "I said it comes with conditions."

"Whatever you say, you name it, bro. I'm there. I'll do it."

I stare at him. "He's giving you this chance, which means that my reputation within the club is on the line. You fuck up that looks bad on me, and that can't happen. You get one shot, you hear me? *One.* Don't fuck this up." I point at him. "You may think you're all that 'cause you spent a shit ton of time in the hole and that makes you somethin' inside this joint, but I'm here to tell you that as a prospect, you start at the bottom. You're a thirty-something-year-old shit kicker, sure you're ready for that?"

He turns serious for a moment. "You think I ever wanna let you down?" He pats his heart with his fist; he's always been a dramatic little fucker. "You think I don't know what a big deal this is? That I'd rather die than fuck this up? I've let you down once before, and I regret it. I fuckin' regret it every day of my life."

"Okay, okay, calm down." I glance around before anyone can overhear us. "You've given me your word and that's enough. No fuck ups. and you'll need to prove yourself. It won't be easy, but you've got skills now, and if you play your cards right and work hard, there may be opportunities there for you, that's all I gotta say."

I'd like to say I know him as a man, but really, I don't. It's been a long time since we grew up, and it's been even longer since he was locked up.

Lucky for him, he has truly changed in prison, and I hope it's for the better. He's at least got a trade now and that could come in handy having an electrician in the club, and he can help with the plumbing. What's even better is that he can re enter society with at least some hope of a future.

"I want to grow some roots," he says, as if reading my mind. "So much shit has gone down, Brock. I wanna sink myself into something worthwhile, something you can be proud of me for."

"You mean you wanna sink yourself into some pussy." I laugh.

He smirks. "Yeah, that too, no conjugal visits for me over

the years. Been a long fuckin' time, bro. Itching to get laid, feel the touch of a woman again..."

I slap him on the back. "Don't worry, bro, plenty of chicks hang around club. Long as you stay away from the club sisters and ol' ladies, and no sweet butts unless Prez allows it, which he won't. There will be plenty to keep you occupied. We won't roll out the welcome mat, though, you gotta earn it. I should mention, Hutch won't stand for any ill treatment of the women. He's a tough fucker but this ain't a club of women beaters."

"Never touched a woman in vain in my life."

"Good, let's keep it that way."

He grins. "Can't fuckin' wait."

"You been okay, in the joint?" He knows what I'm hinting at, surely.

"Still a virgin in that department," he tells me. "Shit got real in maximum. Nearly didn't make it out alive. Some scary fuckin' shit goes down in there; you sleep with one eye open. Most don't last a few weeks without hanging themselves or getting into deadly brawls. Guess I just mixed in the right circles. For the most part, I kept on the downlow where I could and stayed in the good books with all the important people. Inmates that are feared the most are generally the ones to keep on side."

"Not like you're real pretty anyway," I smirk. He's in need of a good haircut and a shave. "Glad you had smarts, respect that."

"Thanks, fucker. So, what brings you all the way out here? It's not my birthday."

I contemplate whether I should tell him, it's not like he's close to either one of our parents.

"Mom and dad split up."

His eyes go round. "What the fuck?"

"Yeah," I sigh. "What's worse is she's stayin' with me,

rocked up at my place a coupla days ago, spent two weeks with Amelia."

"Holy shit."

"Yeah, she's doing well considering."

He looks off into the distance. "Why'd they split?"

I run a hand through my hair. "You and me."

"What's that supposed to mean?"

I give him a pointed look. "You're in the joint, and I supposedly put you here. You know dad hasn't spoken to me in years, blames me for not stopping you from goin' down the road you went down, he can't let it go. Moms had enough. She wants the family back together, and he said no, so she left."

He shakes his head, then links his fingers and rests his hands behind his head. "Holy shit. The old girl finally stood up to the old fucker?"

"You got that right."

"I wrote her, you know."

"She told me." I nod. "She never got over you goin' inside. She took it to heart, baby brother. There are bridges that need to be mended, so you should probably start with her. She didn't deserve it."

"What about dad? Has he not come looking for her?"

I shrug. "She says he calls all the time, but she needs space to think. She's one tough cookie, that woman, she really has had enough. I wonder how long it's gonna be before he comes crawling back into town with his tail between his legs."

"Probably never," Axton grunts. "You know what he's like."

"I do, and he's a damn fool. This thing he keeps inside, it's like poison. I of all people know what it's like to carry shit around with you for years. All it does is fester, makes you fuckin' miserable."

He nods, drumming his fingers on the table. "You think he's gonna change?"

"Hard to say, but he's got a hell of a lot to lose, stupid old bastard. I never honestly thought it'd ever come to this with them, but everyone has a breaking point. Even her. If you make parole, she wants to have a relationship with you, I thought you'd want to know."

His eyes light up.

Mom always wanted to come see him, but dad forbid it, which is why I couldn't bring her here today, she'd lose it. He's changed so much. No longer a wide-eyed, skinny boy with a chip on his shoulder. He's a man, a tough son of a bitch, and he's got a hundred and sixty pounds of muscle behind him.

"That makes gettin' out all that much sweeter. Can't blame her for any of it, as I say I regret a lot, I was a dumb fuck. But what about Amelia? How is she?"

"Same old, I see her a coupla times a year. She comes down to catch up with the girls more than she catches up with me, but she's good."

Amelia was only fourteen when Axton got locked up. She took it hard and copped a lot of shit for it at school. My parents moved away about six months later. Dad never said why, but I know it was because of the shame. Even though he didn't commit the crime in Bracken Ridge, that didn't matter. The news spread like wildfire like it does in all small towns—gossip runs wild.

"She wouldn't even know me now." He sounds sad, and I get a lump in my throat.

"You know this is no place for women," I say quietly. "Mom and Amelia…"

He holds up a hand to stop me. "I know, bro, I know. I wouldn't want them to see me like this. It'd kill me even more than it already does, I wouldn't want that."

"I know you wouldn't."

"What about dad? What do you think will happen with him?"

I shake my head. "Don't know, don't care. If mom wants to take him back, that's up to her, but her ultimatum didn't seem to do very much. Maybe he's ready for a whole new family, since we're all so easily replaced."

He frowns and I realize I should have kept my mouth shut. Last thing he needs is me shooting my angry mouth off, but one can hardly blame me. When it comes to our old man, it rolls right off the tongue so easily. Like second nature.

"You're right. Do you remember how dad used to be? Before he was on deployment the last time?"

I don't want to remember; he's not that man anymore.

I shrug. "What does it matter?"

"Makes you wonder what really happened over there. He never talks about it."

I stare at him. "Lots of people suffer trauma. Steel has PTSD, and he manages it. It's not a valid excuse for what he did to us, cuttin' you off, you're still his son, it isn't fair."

"So are you."

"I don't care about him, I don't expect him to support what you did, but to disown your own kid instead of tryin' to understand why he did it…"

"It's all right, Brock, I'm not angry anymore."

"No? Well, I am. Some things are unforgivable." He can go fuck himself for all I care. If mom never goes back, it'll be too soon, not that I want her living on my couch for the rest of time. But she has to stand her ground, stand up to him. I'm proud of her.

"You're right, it's his loss in the end."

Time's nearly up as I glance at the clock on the wall. "Keep your nose clean, kid, you hear me?"

He nods. For the first time in a long time of visiting, I see the resolve in his eyes. He wants to be better and that gives me hope. I just really hope and pray that he means it when it counts on the outside. It's all good now, the stars are all shiny in the sky, but that can just as quickly be taken away.

"Only a few more months, then I'll be your new shit kicker."

I grin. "Better be fuckin' certain of that. I'll be here, bro. I'll be waiting."

We clasp hands and go to stand.

"I'll see you on the other side."

I point as he walks away. "That you will, little brother, that you will."

As I'm leaving, my phone buzzes in my back pocket.

It's Steel.

"Hey, bro."

"Dude, Linc got a bead on Angel's ex."

I halt in my tracks.

"Where?"

"Still in Minnesota, hasn't left the state."

"Fuck face better stay there," I grunt, though I've got plans to pay him a visit in the very near future since he likes stabbing innocent women and their unborn children. I'll show him the meaning of fuckin' pain.

"If he knows what's good for him." He pauses. "Can make him disappear. Just say the word, it'd be an honor. In the meantime, I'll be in touch if anything changes."

"Thanks, bro. But if anyone's ending that fuckers life, it's gonna be me."

"Noted."

I hang up, and I can't help it when my mind wanders to that fateful night when Jenkins called me…

SEVEN YEARS AGO

"Brock?"

"Officer Jenkins, to what do I owe the pleasure?"

Jenkins is a good cop. By good, I mean he's not entirely in our pockets but he's half-way there.

"I got some bad news, unfortunately."

My mind races. *Angel. Mom. Dad. Amelia. Axton.*

I halt in my tracks, heart hammering in my chest.

"It's Angel."

The hammering turns to thumping, so loud, I hear the pounding in my ears and my head begins to spin.

"What about her?"

Please don't fuckin' say it.

"She's been hurt, Brock, she's been hurt bad."

"What? Where is she?" I stammer.

"Emergency... she's in emergency."

I halt. "She's here?"

"Was at her folks, she... she got stabbed, Brock."

I hang onto the desk like I may faint.

Bones looks up at me and then stands, asking if I'm okay.

"Who fuckin' stabbed her?" The words sound foreign to me, and of course I know who. That drug addict she ran off with and got hitched to just to spite me. He was never good enough for her, not in a million years.

"Ex-husband, she left him, he followed her back here. I shouldn't be sayin' anything but looks as if... shit, man... I fuckin' hate to be the one to say this..."

"Looks as if what?" My face pales. My life is in his hands with what he says next.

"It seems like she was carrying his child."

I pull the top of my hair in frustration and growl.

"*Was?* What do you mean *was?*"

"They're working on her now. You need to get over there, pronto. Just fuckin' go."

Time stands still.

"Brock?" he says after a few moments. "Did you hear me?"

"Appreciate the heads up, I owe you one."

I hang up and race out the door.

"What's goin' on?" Bones yells after me.

I turn but keep walking. "Angel's been stabbed, call Hutch and let him know. May need to round up the boys and take a road trip, I got a vendetta to settle."

"Holy fuck."

I don't remember how I get to the hospital; all I know is it involves speed and a lot of red lights.

When I get there, I see Angel's parents in the hallway of the waiting room, her mom's crying. When she sees me, she sags into my arms and sobs uncontrollably as I hold her up like a ragdoll. Angel's their life, their only child.

I look up at her father, his eyes are rimmed with red, glassy and haunted. Seeing another man like that is the worst kind of pain I could ever imagine; it says more than words ever could.

Deidre trembles in my arms, and I can't do anything else except hold her as her father holds his hand on my shoulder.

"What the hell happened?"

"She left Marcus," Ron says. "Came here to get away from him, and he turned up out of the blue, wanted to talk. We weren't home at the time. He forced his way in…"

"I didn't know she was home." She never fuckin' told me shit.

"She wanted to surprise you," he begins. "She… she just needed some time."

I nod like I understand, when really, I don't.

"And the baby?"

Deidre sobs even harder. As long as I live, I hope I never hear a sound like it again.

"We don't know, it's too soon to tell."

A flood of emotion sweeps through me.

I've always loved Angel, I always will, but hearing she's hurt and carrying a child, another man's child, tears me up inside. She's lying there dying and where is he? Wherever he is, he's just signed his death warrant.

"Where is he?"

Ron shakes his head. "Don't know, we came straight here as soon as we heard."

I hold Deidre by the shoulders and try to gently pull her away. "I need to go make some phone calls," I say quietly. "Find out where he is and get to the bottom of this. I'll be right outside."

"Son, don't do anything stupid," Ron warns, as if that could stop me. The guy's a dead man walking. I'm gonna fuckin' split him in half and laugh in his face while I do it. Nobody hurts my Angel, nobody.

I ignore him and stride outside. I take my phone out and dial Jenkins back.

"You get him?"

Please for fuck's sake say no. He's mine.

"Picked him up a few miles out of town. It's over, Brock."

"I just need a minute with him, that's all I'm askin'."

"Can't do it. You know how this works."

Is this fucker actually serious?

"Were you there? When she dialed 911?"

"Don't do this," he warns.

"Tell me, did you attend?"

He huffs. "I was first on the scene."

"Listen to me!" I bellow down the phone. "I just need a fuckin' minute with this piece of shit, you got me? Give this to me, I've never asked for anything before."

"It won't solve anything, and I'm not gonna do it," he says firmly. "You'll be locked up for life just for a few moments of satisfaction, that's not where you need to be. It's with Angel and her family. Don't make things harder for yourself. I know your angry, but this isn't the way."

"I'm comin' down there." I start toward my sled.

"No need," he tells me. "He's been transported to Minnesota as we speak under armed guard, he's long gone. Let it go."

Like it's that easy. I'll spend my life waiting to gut him.

I run a hand through my hair. "Don't do this to me, Jenk. Please, man, I'm fuckin' begging you."

"I'm sorry." He actually sounds like he holds a lot of regret in those few words. "But this is for your own good. He's goin' away for a long time, that's gotta be enough for now."

But it's not, it never will be.

I stare at the phone. Fucker hung up on me.

I feel a strange sense of foreboding. Anxiety sweeps into my chest and grabs hold of my heart, squeezing it like a vice. Maybe I'm having a heart attack?

Angel could die.

Her baby. She could lose it.

The reality hits me like a freight train.

I drop to my knees in the middle of the parking lot and howl like I've got the devil inside me.

18

ANGEL

PRESENT DAY

I stare at the roses in the vase on the counter. They came for me without a note.

A dozen red roses. Blood red.

Jessie said they got delivered but had no card. Must have been one of our happy customers, so she says.

Marcus used to buy me red roses, back when things were good. I feel my stomach churn, and I immediately take the flowers out to the trash bin and throw them in.

It's a little too close for comfort.

My phone makes me jump as I come back to the porch and let myself inside.

Kennedy's name flashes on the screen.

"Hello," I say, dropping my purse on the floor as I lock the door behind me.

"Hi, Angel. It's Kennedy Hart."

"Hey."

"I wanted to update you on the progress of the injunction. The family court ruled in your favor, no surprise there. And added to that, there will be no hearing and no contest. The guy's on drugs if you ask me, don't know what he's thinking aside from trying to spook you. I think that was his tactic all along, nothing more, it's a waste of everyone's time."

I sag into my office chair and let out a sigh of relief. Something about it being official that he can't have access to my child settles my nerves. I don't know why I needed it in writing.

"That's fantastic news."

"His lawyer has not come back with anything, so that's good news too. If he so much as pisses in the wind, he'll be wishing he didn't, trust me. I don't think I'll be hearing anything anytime soon. He just got out. It's obvious to me this is a powerplay, and all he means to do is rattle you."

"He's doing a good job of it," I sigh.

"I've reiterated the terms of the restraining order to his lawyer and sighted the original affidavit. I doubt he'll try to contact you directly, since that's the quickest way to get a one-way ticket back to the joint. Doubt he wants that."

I stare at the wall. "He tried to kill me, you know," I whisper. "He tried to kill me and my baby."

I know she knows this, but she hasn't heard it from my own mouth. Even saying it out loud doesn't even seem real.

"I know, and he's a full-blown asshole. He should rot in prison; I don't know how he only got seven years, it's still baffling."

"Would've gotten more if he succeeded," I go on. "And his sentence was originally ten years with parole. He only served seven because the charges were lessened to involuntary, being he was under the influence of drugs and alcohol. He's slippery, always was. Earned his way out on good behavior and no priors."

I don't know why I'm telling her this.

"Sometimes the loopholes of the job suck."

"You're not wrong there." I pinch the bridge of my nose.

"He's a piece of shit, Angel. I hope he meets his maker sooner rather than later."

I nod, even though she can't see me, and wonder if I should tell her about the flowers. What will she do anyway? I can't prove they're from him. Not like I'm hard to find in a small town.

My body goes cold, and I feel numb.

Brock was right. I am scared of him, or more like what he can take from me, the only thing I care about in this world —Rawlings.

He's never going to get anywhere near her again.

She should never have survived, she's my miracle baby. The only thing I regret is it's his blood running through her veins instead of… instead of the man's I truly love, and for that I have no penance for. I live with the fact that it should have been him. Every time I see them together, I'm reminded of it.

"Thank you, Kennedy," I say. "Appreciate the update."

"Talk to you soon."

We hang up and I toss my phone on the desk.

I don't know how I'm going to get through this. Him being in prison meant safety, it meant nothing could happen. Now he's out and free to roam. I feel powerless.

The fact the first thing he did was contact me about visitation rights just goes to show you how deluded he is. His request isn't worth the paper it's written on, and I don't know what kind of lawyer would even take a case like that. He was never going to succeed.

What a waste of money, and time. But he always did enjoy intimidating me, like Kennedy said, he's just trying to spook me, and if I'm honest, he's doing a damn good job of it.

I rub my stomach and don't dare to think about that night.

Jenkins.

He saved my life, without a doubt. He was first on the scene when I managed to dial 911.

I didn't know what real fear looked like until I saw it in somebody else's eyes. He kept me alive until the ambulance arrived.

I stare at the wall and wonder how I'm even here; it's not the first time I've thought it. I know how lucky I am. I knew from that point on that if I survived, everything would change.

I'd already left him, but I should have known he wouldn't let me leave him quietly. I'd put up with his excuses for his slowly increasing abuse for far too long. Without even realizing it, I'd become one of *those women*.

Of course, Brock didn't know the extent of what was going on, and Marcus had only ever slapped me around. I told myself it was only when he was drunk or high, like that was some excuse. Like that made it okay, not that it did, but I told myself he wouldn't have done that if he were sober. That's what I told myself for far too long.

The thing about domestic violence is it does creep up on you without you realizing it's even happening.

I've been to hell and back, with a lot of self-loathing in between, and a lot of guilt. I question my choices all the time.

Why didn't I leave? Why did stay so long? Why did I not see the signs?

But that's the great thing about hindsight; it's there to remind you of what you could have done better every waking moment, taking up space rent-free in my mind. It could drive me crazy if I let it.

I tell myself I survived, my daughter is happy, things are on track at work. I've got my own place. I'm doing okay.

I never want to be a victim, and I never want to rely on anyone else again.

When I eventually got out of hospital, I had nothing.

Nowhere to go except back with my parents. I was lucky in so many ways; I had them, and my friends, Brock, the club, and slowly, piece by piece, I picked myself up off the ground and made something of myself. And raised my daughter while doing it.

I've changed. I'm not that naive girl anymore.

Anyone comes near me, I'll shoot the motherfucker in the face if they try to take what I got, no questions asked.

Sometimes the demons inside me threaten to unleash. I have to keep them at bay because if I ever come face to face with him again, I know I will kill him.

And that's what scares me the most.

~

"I'm going to ask Brock if he'll do it." I hear Melody's mom, Trinity, say to the other moms at soccer practice. I'm not really close to her or anything, but hearing Brock's name has my ears perking up.

"He's not going to do it," says Kate, one of the kindergarten teachers.

"You don't know that."

She scoffs. "He's part of the motorcycle club, need I remind you. And I doubt the bachelor auction needs someone like him taking part. He would scare everyone away."

The way she says *someone like him* has me irked enough to go punch her square in the face.

They're talking about the charity fundraiser coming up.

Trinity glances at me a little worriedly at Kate's comment as I stare straight ahead, trying to keep my temper in check.

"I don't know, I think it's just what we need. I could ask him," she replies, all gung-ho for a bit of Brock. I almost want to laugh, and if I weren't so jealous thinking about her talking to him, I might actually do just that. "What do you think, Angel?"

I turn and look directly at Kate. "I think you need to shut your fuckin' mouth for starters," I warn.

Kate's eyes go round. "I'm sorry, Angel," she stammers, as if she didn't realize I was there. "I didn't... I didn't mean anything by it."

Trinity bites her lip and continues to pretend to watch the game. "So, is Brock like single?"

Now I want to smack Trinity in the face, too.

"How would I know that?" I reply with snark filling my tone. I don't know why she thinks we're friends, I never talk to her enough to give her that idea.

"Haven't you known him since like, seventh grade?"

"Yes," I reply. "We fuck occasionally too."

Several gasps happen at once and I feel Trinity's eyes on me, her eyes round in shock. What the fuck does she expect me to say? Stupid bitch.

"Holy shit," I hear someone whisper.

"Wow." From someone else.

Why not just shut them all the hell up?

"Hung like a horse, too," I go on. "Goes for hours. I guess you could put that on the flyer to attract a little more attention. Hell, you'd get a lot more money, but the committee might not approve, it's not exactly P.C."

Kate pulls a disgusted face.

Trinity keeps staring, probably imaging the size of his dick, and several muffled voices whisper behind me. The one thing I hate about this parenting shit is hanging around all the annoying moms.

I would literally die if Rawlings ever wanted to do the kiddie modeling or dancing lessons, she seems more like me as a child at the moment, a tomboy into the outdoors and basketball, rather than dolls and ballet.

A few moments later, I feel an arm come around my neck. I look sideways, and Deanna gives me a huge grin. "Hey, girlfriend."

"What are you doing here?" It's not like Deanna comes to Rawlings' games very often.

She shrugs. "In the neighborhood." She leans in close and whispers. "Why is everyone behind you shooting daggers at your back?"

I laugh and whisper back, "Just told them I fuck Brock and he's very well-endowed. They want him for the charity auction, so I was just giving them some pointers for their flyer."

She slaps her forehead. "You're worse than me."

"Hey, I'm just tellin' it like it is, babe."

She grins. "I think you've done enough damage, not that Brock would mind his reputation being catapulted into talk of the town. I notice he hasn't been spending any time with Tiffany lately." She gives me a pointed look.

"What?" I shrug.

She keeps her voice low. "You fuckin' him, for real?"

I look straight ahead and don't answer.

"Jesus, Angel. You haven't even said anything to me, thanks, friend."

"It just happened, nothing serious," I whisper back.

She gives me a lopsided look. "Does he know that?"

"What do you mean?"

She shakes her head. "He's been walking around church whistling, fricking whistling! Humming a tune as he swaggers around. Happy as a pig in shit and now I know why."

"Don't say anything, we're keeping it on the DL until I figure shit out."

"So, it might be a thing? Go you guys!"

"Shhh!" I clap as our team gets a goal. "I don't know how I feel about anything, D. I don't want to get in too deep. I mean, I know I've known him my whole life, but it's like we're just getting to know each other all over again."

She can't keep the grin off her face. "I always knew you'd be a thing."

"We're not a thing," I reply. "Trust me, I still don't know what we are, if anything."

"Well, all I can tell you is from what I've seen and heard, he seems pretty smitten to me." She squints at the field. "Shit, girl. Rawlings has a bit of sass about her on the field, just like her momma."

I smirk as I watch the tackle, and sure enough, the whistle blows. She's not a bully by any means, but being small, she doesn't like being pushed around and she'll fight back. Twice as hard.

"The apple doesn't fall far from the tree." I smirk.

We go back to church after the game because Deanna needs a ride. I drop her off and pull up as Colt passes us.

"Hey, Colt," Deanna calls. He seems in a hurry.

"Hi, D. Hey, Angel."

"You all right?" she quizzes.

He nods. "In a rush, see you later. Hutch is inside."

She narrows her eyes. "What's with everyone in this club secret squirrelling around? They think we don't know shit, but we know what's going on before they do. Men are such idiots, especially in this club."

I climb out of my truck. "What's going on this time?"

"Cassidy, Sienna's cousin. You comin' inside?"

I can see Brock's bike parked in the yard, and I don't think it's a good idea.

"I don't think so."

"Why not?"

"Yeah, mom, why?" Rawlings pipes up, popping her face up in between the seats as Deanna reaches in and plops her nose.

"Five minutes?" Deanna presses.

"I gotta get home, feed this kid," I protest.

I don't want to run into Brock, not until I work some shit out. Some stuff went down the other night out at my car that I haven't even begun to process.

All that talk about me moving in with him; the man is insane, as if it's that simple.

I don't think I'm quite at the point where I'm going to take him up on his offer. And I don't want to confuse Rawlings. It'll break her heart if I start something with Brock only to have it end and then leave her hurt and confused. I don't want any of my personal life interfering with her happy childhood. We're doing okay, why complicate things?

"Please, mom," Rawlings begs. "I want to ask Uncle Brock about his horses."

I want to slap my forehead. Ever since she heard about the horses, it's all she's been going on about. Since she fell asleep the other night at his place, we never got a chance to go see them.

"Fine." I relent as Deanna opens the back door and Rawlings happily hops out. She goes running up to the big wooden doors in her soccer gear and disappears inside.

We tag along behind.

"You're in so much trouble when she gets older." Deanna laughs.

"Tell me about it," I groan.

There's a couple of prospects inside playing pool. Stevie is behind the bar, cleaning the shelves, and Brock and Steel sit at the bar in deep conversation. They stop talking when we walk up.

Rawlings appears from behind the bar and runs up to Brock.

"Uncle Brock, can I see your horses?"

He looks down at her with a grin. "They're not mine, princess, they're Steel's. We could ask him."

She turns and looks up at Steel; he couldn't be more intimidating if he tried.

"Uncle Steel?"

His lips twitch. "Yeah, sweetheart?"

"Can I see the horses?"

His eyes shoot to me. "If your mom says it's okay."

I give him an eye roll just as Rawlings turns around, jumping up and down.

"Please, mom! Pleeeeaasse!"

"We'll see," I reply as she tugs on my jacket. "If you can behave for the rest of the day then maybe."

I can feel Brock's eyes on me, boring into my soul.

"Hi, boys," says Deanna. "Dad in his office?"

"Yeah," Brock grunts as he watches me intently.

Steel gives us a chin lift, his eyes on me too. It makes me think they've been talking about me before we approached, not that I'm paranoid or anything.

"Back in a sec," Deanna says, sashaying off through the clubhouse.

"What are the horses names?" Rawlings asks Steel, tugging on his cut.

He looks at Brock for help, but Brock just shakes his shoulders with laughter.

Steel looks back down at Rawlings, cute as a button in her soccer gear. "Doc, Sleepy, and Grumpy."

"Oh my gosh!" Rawlings squeals. "You have three horses?" She turns to me, beaming. "Did you hear that, mom? He has three horses!"

Even Steel can't keep the cranky look on his face for too long.

"Wow, babe, that's pretty cool."

"Can we go see them now?" she whines.

BROCK

I now want to smack Trinity for mentioning it in the first place. Not that I'll be invited to any P and C meetings from now on after my little stunt at the soccer game. Serves them right, they shouldn't be bitching about Brock, or in Trinity's case, be boning for him. It just looks desperate.

Before I can answer, Brock pipes up, "Of course, we can, but only if your mom says she'll come too."

I narrow my eyes, knowing what he's up to.

Rawlings then tugs on my jacket more urgently. I give her a look and she stops.

"Please, mom! I'll die if I can't go see them!"

I run a hand over her light-colored hair, I never stand a chance when she looks up at me like that.

"How much homework do you have?"

"A tiny amount," she declares. "I did most of it already."

"And you promise to do the rest when we get home, no arguments?"

"I won't argue, I won't!" she jumps up and down excitedly to prove her point.

"You're toast, Angel," Steel tells me, mischief dancing in his eyes.

"Tell me about it," I groan, then to my daughter; "Fine, fifteen minutes patting the horses, then we're going home to make dinner."

"Don't bother yourself with that," Brock says, pretending to take Rawlings' nose between his two fingers and thumb, making her laugh excitedly. "Mom's made a huge vat of pasta bake. It's like the woman thinks I don't know how to feed myself or eat anything that doesn't come out of a can."

"Need to get yourself an ol' lady." Steel smirks, his eyes in my direction. "Lots of fu... umm... *freaking* benefits, not just home cooked meals either. Cookie dough on the regular, extra topping. Sienna's not so great at housekeeping but makes up for it in the reverse cowgirl position..."

I roll my lips inward at his ability to not swear like a trooper in front of my daughter.

"Too bad I can't cook." I shrug.

"Can we go now?" Rawlings moans impatiently.

"Rawlings, don't be rude," I say, looking down at her. "Mom's talking."

"Kid's a lot like her mom," Steel grunts. "Got a bit of spitfire in her belly."

Rawlings looks up at him and laughs. "You're funny."

He makes a cross-eyed face at her, and she laughs some more.

"All right, time to go." Just as I say it Deanna comes back from her father's office.

Rawlings makes for the door, trotting like she's on a horse and I slap my forehead.

"Whose brilliant idea was it to get horses?" I mutter.

Steel glances at me. "They were meant for slaughter, if you must know."

Whoops.

"You rescued them?" I stammer.

"Ex-racehorses. Fuckin' tragedy. One of them, the big black surly one, won its owner six figures in its seven-year racing career. Fucker's left it lame and half-dead once they'd done exploiting it for money. Makes a man sick. Such a beauty too."

I forgot how passionate Steel is about animals for a second. I always knew he loved his dogs, hell, he shut the dog fighting ring down in one weekend with baseball bats and a sledgehammer. But I didn't know he had a soft spot for other animals too.

"That's awful, how do people live with themselves?"

"Quite easily," he grunts. "They don't give a shit, long as the coin's raking in. Beautiful animals too. Horses, like dogs, they've no reason to trust strangers, yet they do. They forgive, eventually, some take longer than others."

"Now Sienna's in on the act," Deanna pipes up. "It's a wonder she hasn't turned you vegetarian too."

He rolls his eyes. "She's workin' on it. Apparently, my blood sugar's through the roof. There's only so much salad a man can eat before he needs some pussy. I mean, meat."

Brock chuckles as Deanna and I groan in unison.

I shake my head. "On that note, I'm leaving."

"I'll follow you to my place," Brock says, standing.

"See ya later," Deanna calls. "Bye, Rawlings!"

She's by the door, impatiently waiting for us to leave.

"Bye, D! Bye, Uncle Steel! Come on, mom, hurry up!"

"You're welcome," Brock taunts, looking down at me with a grin.

I shove him in the side. "This better be good."

19

BROCK

I hold Rawlings up as she pats the smaller of the three horses. Its hot, heavy breath makes her giggle, and I laugh too.

"Uncle Brock, his nose is all wet," she says. "And he breathes funny."

I take her hand and place a piece of a carrot in her palm. "Hold your hand flat, don't curl your fingers, let him take it from you."

She does as she's told, holding her hand out tentatively, then she squeals when he uses his tongue to gobble the piece of carrot off her palm.

"See, he's really gentle."

Angel stands by watching us. I'd give a penny for her thoughts right now.

"When can we ride them?"

"Woah, slow down, princess." I smile. "First, we need to learn to look after them before we can go riding them, plus, they've been racing on tracks for a long time. Sometimes animals need to just be in the field, doing what they want for a while, learning all about their new home, you get me?"

She nods enthusiastically. "Gemma has a rabbit who gets

scared of the dark, they have to leave a light on for it or it won't go to sleep."

"Well, it's a lot like that," I say, patting the creature's large face. It sure is friendly.

This one's dark brown, there's a black one, the surly one Steel was talking about, and a white and brown flecked one. Both of those two are a lot shier than this one.

"Is his name really Grumpy?"

"No." I laugh. "You can name him if you like?"

"Did he not have a name before?"

Smart kid. "I don't know what it was, princess."

She stares at it and then turns to me. "I'd like to call him Harry."

"Harry?" I baulk. "Why Harry?"

She shrugs. "He looks like a Harry, and the spotty one looks like a Freckles."

She clings to the fence, still stroking Harry gently. I think he likes her.

"What about the big black one?" I thumb over my shoulder into the paddock where the big black horse grazes by himself.

She thinks for a moment. "What about Brutus?"

I snort and look at Angel. "Definitely your kid," I mutter.

She shakes her head.

"Brutus is a good name; he looks like you wouldn't mess with him."

"He's just shy," Rawlings tells me, suddenly the horse whisperer. "He'll come around."

My shoulders shake with laughter. Before Rawlings, I didn't really like kids at all. I didn't really get them. Then again, I'd never been around them for long periods of time, and the ones I saw in passing were annoying, whining brats. Thank god she's not like that.

A few moments later, mom wanders over from the house,

a shawl wrapped around her neck. It is getting a little cool out here.

"I was going to go into town and pick up a few things to go with the pasta bake, won't you stay, Angel?" she asks, a little too much hope in her eyes.

"We really shouldn't…" Angel begins, but Rawlings starts to protest.

"Well, whatever you think, dear."

"Mom, I can do the rest of my homework here," Rawlings says, tugging onto her shirt. "Please, can we stay?"

I stare at Angel, willing her to stay for dinner. Hopefully, if mom goes to bed and Rawlings passes out, we can have some free time together. Though sex is probably out of the question, and I'm not usually a man that likes to wait.

She looks at my mom and smiles. "That would be really nice, Sylvia, thank you."

As if solving all my problems at once, mom decides to save the day on top of all that. "Maybe Rawlings would like to come with me? If she's allowed?" Mom adores Rawlings like the rest of us, hard not to.

I hope to God she fancies a drive into town; I got some blue balls happening right now that I need to take care of.

"Yes, mom! Can I go, pleaaase?"

I swear all that kid has to do is turn on the charms and she gets whatever she wants.

"Fine, you can go. But no asking for things and no negotiating."

I stifle a chuckle.

Rawlings takes Sylvia's hand, and they head off back toward the house.

"Thanks, mom!" Rawlings yells like it's an afterthought.

I watch them go and turn to Angel. "You're in so much trouble when she gets to her teenage years."

"Tell me about it," she groans. "She's gonna give me hell."

She looks up at me with tentative eyes.

I give her a chin lift. "What?"

"You're so good with her, she loves coming out here."

I snort. "Of course, she does. She gets away with murder, gets fed whatever she wants, and renames horses instead of doing her homework. Kid's got it made."

"You'd have made a great father," she says.

The admission stuns me for a second.

I clear my throat. "There's still time."

She bites her bottom lip.

"You're killin' me with the silent treatment," I tell her. "Spit it out, for fuck's sake."

"You're a good man, Brock."

"Are you sure that's what you were thinkin'?" I frown in jest.

"There's so much I regret…"

I divert my gaze. I can't hear this.

"No regrets, babe. We're right where we need to be. Everything happens for a reason, can't change the past."

She smirks. "When did you get so philosophical?"

"It happens with old age." I shrug.

She grins, moving closer. "When's your mom leaving?"

My lips twitch. "Why's that?"

She runs a slender hand up my cut, fingering the dirty patch that bears my name and position. "Just asking."

"You wanna play?"

She laughs. "We've no time, they'll be back soon."

I reach down and cup her ass, bringing her body close to mine. "You have this wild notion that I can't be fast. I don't know why."

"You used to be fast in high school," she reminds me. "Remember our first time?"

I smirk, hovering my lips close to hers. "Remember? How could I forget. You jumped me."

"I did not jump you! If I recall, you packed that really sweet picnic and set the mood overlooking the canyon, when you used to be romantic."

I kiss her lightly. "*Used to be?* I can be romantic."

She swats me on the ass, hard. "Not in the last twenty years I've known you."

"Eating your pussy out isn't considered romance anymore?" I cock an eyebrow.

"See, ruined the moment right there."

I don't give her time to answer, I kiss her chastely and before she can protest, I throw her over my shoulder. She squeals and pounds on my back as I begin to walk.

"Brock Altman, put me down!"

"You're wasting time talkin', sugar, and I've apparently got to be romantic, eat you out and do you fast before we get sprung."

"We're not doing it in the barn!" she yells when she sees where I'm heading.

"Why not? The barns closer and I've always had this fantasy about taking you over a hay bale."

She pounds on my back again, but I don't care. I like her a little mad and wild, makes the sex all that much sweeter.

When we get in there, I set her down and she tries to back away, but I pull her by the hem of her jeans and kiss her hard. She moans into my mouth; I don't know why she fights it, we play this constant game of cat and mouse, but I know she's all over it.

I know she wants it.

She forcefully pushes my cut off, and I smirk at the fact I'm right. Before I can reach for her, she runs a hand over my dick, and I hiss at the contact.

"Hard for me already, big boy?" she teases, backing away as I follow her, led by my dick.

"I'm always hard for you," I grunt. Her legs hit the hay

bale and I waste no time in moving in and kissing her again, her tongue slips into my mouth and I just about lose my shit. Both my hands reach to her breasts as I knead them and squeeze hard. "Been dreamin' about these babies."

She gasps at my touch and reaches her hands up into my hair, pulling me closer. I roughly pull at her shirt, lifting it up, and pull her tits out of the bra that barely holds those things in there. I need just a little taste; I bend and suck one nipple into my mouth as she fists my hair, dry humping my knee as I push it between her legs. I tweak the other one, brutally teasing her as she groans at my touch, then move my mouth to suck it, rolling my tongue over and over on her hard peaks. Her tits are so big and fuckin' juicy, but I don't have time to stay here long. I wish I did.

"Need you hard and fast, baby."

She pulls my belt buckle, unfastens it, and unzips me in record time. Yanking my jeans down, she grips my hard dick and sheaths it with her hands. Dropping to her knees, she licks the tip and sucks me into her mouth, and I have to physically restrain myself from ramrodding down her throat and getting myself off in a shorter time than I planned.

"Fuck, that feels good." I push her hair back from her face so I can see her sweet lips taking me, and it's my undoing. I watch as she pumps me with her fist and I move my hips slightly, trying not to make her gag as she swallows my dick and works me over with her tongue.

I hold her hair and increase my pace, but I know I'm gonna lose it and the only place I wanna do that is deep inside her. I pull out of her mouth, and she gasps. I waste no time yanking her to her feet and undoing her jeans, then shoving them down. I spin her around and bend her over, perfectly disheveled over the stack of hay.

"Arms on the hay bale, stick your ass out."

"Hurry, Brock," she wails, wiggling her delectable ass at

me. I slap it hard, and she yelps. I run my hand through her slick heat, fingering her and rubbing her wetness all around. I rub her clit, circling it with my fingers and slap her other ass cheek with my hand.

"Gonna take your ass soon, babe."

She groans as I continue to pleasure her.

I replace my fingers with my dick, running it through her folds, rubbing her nub and squeezing her nipple with one hand while gripping her hip with the other.

"You want me bad, don't you, babe?"

"Fuck yes." She sticks her ass out even more as I move my mouth to her neck.

I'd be tempted to bite it but then mom will see and know what we've been up to. I kiss her pulse instead and move my dick to her entrance, entering her full tilt in one, swift motion. She gasps in surprise as I hold her by the base of the neck and clutch her hip tight, moving slowly at first, but I soon increase the tempo, fucking her over the hay bale as she sticks her ass out to meet my thrusts like the horny little bitch she is.

"Fuckin' like that, don't you my dirty girl?" I whisper in her hear.

"Oh God, Brock," she cries out. At this angle I'm goin' in deep, just how she likes it.

"You wanna give yourself to me now?" I demand. "Or you wanna keep fighting me?"

"Go to hell," she breathes.

I laugh and ram into her harder, faster. She gasps, and I reach around to rub her clit with my thumb until she squeezes me tight, then comes hard, gasping and calling out *fuck fuck fuck!*

I grunt and let go, coming violently, spurting inside her as I she milks my cock for all I'm worth.

When we're done, we're both left panting.

I'm pretty proud of my efforts. That was quick, but hell, I came like a freight train.

"That tight little pussy of yours can't get enough of me," I say, pulling out as she collapses on the hay bale. "As much as you try to deny it."

"Still waiting for the romance part to kick in," she pants as she turns and pulls her jeans up, buttons them, then tucks her beautiful tits back into the non-existent cups and puts them back in place.

"If my mom and your kid weren't comin' back from the shops, I'd drag you to my bed and suck those tits till you begged me to fuck you again," I breathe, moving closer to her.

"You have a one-track mind, Altman, but I suppose you are supplying me with dinner. I should be more grateful, right?"

I kiss her on the nose, just as I hear car tires on the gravel. Shit. They're back already.

"I'm just glad my mom fucked off for five minutes so I could have my way with you."

She tuts and then smooths her hair down. "Do I look liked I've just been bent over a hay bale?"

I pull some straw out of her hair and hold it up. "Nah, babe, not at all."

She whacks me again and sasses out of the barn, my eyes on her derriere as she retreats.

"Don't I even get a thank you for that orgasm?"

She turns around and shushes me, actually shushes me. I laugh out loud, and I try to catch up with her, but at the same time, Rawlings comes screaming around the corner with a bag of groceries in her arms.

The thing I love about kids is the sheer abandon they have. The few kids I have met have always flocked to me; I don't know why. I'm a mean son-of-a-bitch, but they seem to see something in me nobody else does.

I stare at the scene unfolding; Rawlings running to her momma and hugging her tight, like she's been gone for months instead of merely twenty minutes.

A pain surges in my chest and it isn't the first time.

When I look at them, I see my future, I see what I should've had. It hurts me that Angel won't see it, or she does, but she continues to hold me at arm's length. I don't like it.

I'll never quite understand it. I've always been open and honest with her, even when I let her go, it was for her, not for me.

When we're alone, she's putty in my hands, and I like that. I like that she lets me come in to bat, but I don't like how she won't commit to me, she won't let me claim her. It's like having my balls in a vice, and in the M.C., that is a problem. Women are supposed to know their place, not that Sienna or Lily, or heck, any of the women seem to. They seem to know more about club business sometimes than we do.

I can't help but feel like I know now what those other schmucks like Steel and Gunner crapped on about, when you find the one. Of course, I knew I'd found the one back when I first made love to her in the back of my truck, but that was a long time ago.

Like she keeps telling me; We changed. We grew up. We grew apart.

I don't know if things can ever get back to how they were. The passion we used to have, how Angel used to look at me. Sure, she looks at me with lust when we're alone. I know what she wants and how to give it to her, but back then, she looked at me like I'd hung the moon.

Imagining her innocent is hard to do, but I remember it. I remember when she was just a girl, inexperienced. Gangly and all legs. I chuckle at the thought. Those legs that go for miles.

I know I have to make things really fucking obvious. I mean, I thought I had. But with Angel, you have to tread carefully. If she feels pressured then she'll just run away, and I don't want her to do that. That's when we have real problems, and I just get mad.

I want her to feel safe with me, like she always used to.

She knows I can protect her, that isn't the issue. The issue is she wants to protect herself; I get it. After what happened to her, she wants to be in control at all times. But the real world doesn't work like that. Sometimes you can't do every fucking thing yourself.

What's more, is she pretends to be immune to me, to what we have and could have again, but I know the signs. I know how she works, and I know how I feel about her. No other woman has ever made me feel like this.

Mom comes around the corner, carrying another bag. What the hell did they buy?

When I get to her, I take the bag and peer inside.

"Feeding an army?"

She pats me on the arm. "You're a growing boy, and Rawlings couldn't decide what she wanted for dessert."

I roll my eyes. Seems she's got my mom under her spell as well as everyone else in this town.

"Good job, I'm hungry," I mutter.

I don't have the heart to ask mom how long she's planning on sticking around for. With Angel's parents in and out of town looking for a house, we can only steal sneaky fuck sessions in places like my barn. Not cool. I don't wanna smell like horse manure and fuckin' straw.

"When your brother gets home, we can have little soirees like this all the time," she muses.

I turn and look at her sharply, halting before we follow Rawlings and Angel in the back door.

"Mom, you know that may not actually happen, him gettin' out, don't you?"

She frowns ever so slightly. "But he will get out this time, won't he? He's been a good boy; he's done his time…"

Poor mom. She just doesn't live in the real world sometimes.

"It all depends on what happens at the hearing. You know how these things go; he's been up several times before."

"But he hadn't been on good behavior all those times," she argues. "He's really tried this time, and they moved him to minimum security. He's reformed."

I stare at her. "Mom. I think you need to understand the fact that it might not happen, you shouldn't set your hopes so high only to be shot down again if he doesn't get out."

She reaches up and pats me on the cheek. "I have faith, Brock, I always have."

I snort. "What about dad?"

Her smile drops.

"Have you heard from him?" I press.

She shrugs. "He's got nothing new to say."

Stubborn old bastard.

"Still happy pretending we don't exist?"

She gasps. "He'd never pretend that; he's just very set in his ways…"

I shake my head. "Mom, why do you defend him like that all the time? I get that he's disowned Axton, hell, what he did was a shock to all of us. But cutting us off like that."

"You mean you?" She smiles without humor. "Cutting *you* off like that."

Well, yeah, that's what the asshole did.

"Mom. I really hope dad comes to his senses, I do. But don't expect me to have anything to do with him when he makes this miraculous turnaround and expects me to just blow off what he did."

"There's no need to stoop as low as what he's done."

"Isn't there? Dad wrote the book on pigheadedness. Now you know where I got it from."

She nods like she understands, but really, she doesn't. She thinks dad will change his mind, get back in my good graces, and we can have some kind of relationship.

Not happening in this lifetime.

I've washed my hands of him; he's dead to me.

I tried my whole life to make him proud when really there was no way to make that possible. There will always be something wrong with me in his eyes, and I don't have to put up with that shit anymore.

"In time..." she begins, and for once, I'm thankful for my phone ringing so I can get out of this conversation without being rude. I don't want to fight with my mother, but I have no need to pacify her with convenient bullshit so she'll sleep at night.

I'm shocked my dad hasn't come crawling back, appalled even. Mom has and always will be the backbone of our family.

And that's what worries me.

She'll do anything to get this family back together, but what if we're just too broken to be fixed?

20

ANGEL

I stare at the girl sitting in Colt's office, and she stares back. I don't know who she is, but I think she might be Sienna's cousin, Cassidy. She looks like she needs a bath and a warm bowl of soup.

When Colt comes dashing in, he closes the door behind him, so she's out of view.

So, this is where he was fleeing off to the other day. Interesting.

"Hey, Angel, how can I help?" he asks in rushed tone.

"Who's that?" I whisper, just in case she might hear me.

He shrugs. "Cassidy."

"Is she all right?" I'm not usually a nosy person, but she looked like she'd been crying.

He looks uncomfortable. "She's a little... under the weather at the moment."

I wonder why he's dealing with her and not Sienna.

"You guys like..."

He shakes his head. "Nah, it's not like that." He leans closer and drops his voice. "I'm the only one she'll talk to. After the shit that went down a while back, she's been pretty fucked up."

"Maybe you should get her some help?" I suggest. "Talk to someone."

"Like a therapist?"

"Yeah, sometimes it helps if she's suffered from trauma." I don't add that I know all about that.

He taps his chin. "I'd have to run it by Prez."

I roll my eyes. "Of course, you do."

He narrows his eyes but smirks at me. "Brock told me you're a bit of a spitfire."

"Oh, he did, did he?"

"Yup."

"What else did he say? That I fire silver bullets too?"

He grins. "Actually, that's not far off."

I shake my head.

"So, what brings you over here?" he asks, finally.

"I can't seem to get any of the security cameras on my laptop. I downloaded the app like you said, and I just get blank screens."

"If you've got it with you, I can take a look," he says as I dig into my oversized purse and fish it out.

"I don't have time to wait, but I can come back later?"

"Sure." He nods, taking it from me. "I'll see what's goin' on. If I get it working, I can try and drop it over at the salon later."

"Thanks, Colt, I really appreciate it."

"No problem."

"And think about what I said," I add. "If she's really that fucked up, she should talk to someone. Whatever it is, it'll only get worse if it's left to fester. Trust me on that."

I like Colt. He seems like a good guy. Always respectful, doesn't sleep around like a pack whore like most of the guys do, and he treats the women well.

Something in my gut tells me that there's something more to him and Cassidy than he's letting on. I mean, it's plainly obvious that there is, but I don't think it's sexual. Then again, what the hell would I know. I can't even get my own shit together with a guy I've known for most of my life.

"Thanks, Angel, I'll suggest it to her."

His tone almost makes me feel sorry for him, kind of like he's lumbered with her. I wonder what's really going on there. Deanna mentioned she had some kind of attachment to him after all the shit that went down. I can kind of see why; he seems dependable, stable, and doesn't have any ulterior motives.

I'm making my way out when my phone rings.

It's Brock.

"Hey, Ange," he says, and I can tell he's just woken up.

"Bit early for you, isn't it?"

"I'm usually up hours before you are, sweet cheeks."

I roll my eyes because I know he only calls me those stupid names to annoy me.

"What's goin' on?"

"Got a mornin' wood, thought you may be able to help with that."

I splutter my coffee that I just took a big sip of and almost choke.

"Brock!" I chastise. Luckily, I'm wearing black and not white. "I'm on my way to work."

"Perfect, I don't need long with your sexy voice. Talk dirty to me."

"You're insane, and anyway, isn't your mom in the house?"

"Don't mention my mom while I'm touching myself, you'll make my hard on go away." He snorts. "Last thing I need, balls are still blue from last night. I needed about five more rounds with you to satisfy my appetite."

I feel his words go straight to my core and my pussy clenches. I'd love nothing more than to go over there right now and hop into bed with him instead of going to work, but for one, I'm not giving in to his demands, and secondly, his *mom's* in the next room. Not a good look.

I'd never be able to look her in eye again.

"Haven't you heard that abstaining is actually good for the libido."

He snorts again. "Where did you hear that? Some fucktard who doesn't know shit is my guess."

"Well, maybe if you tried a bit harder to get your parents back together then your mom would be out of the house."

He yawns. "Why would I want that? She should've left that fucker years ago."

Well, I can't argue there. The trouble is, Brock is a lot like his old man, stubborn as fuck.

"Brock, don't you think it's time to at least try and bury the hatchet? I know your dad's been a major douche, but sometimes you just have to let water roll under the bridge."

"Why should I? It's not like he's even sorry."

"He does love you, in his own way."

"I'll get out my violin, and by the way, I called to jack off to you tellin' me how much you wanna ride my cock, not listen to you preach to me about my fuckin' parents."

"Someone sounds like they need coffee."

"Well, go get some and come over here and ride me."

I roll my lips inward. "You know how well I do at taking orders," I remind him. "And some of us have to work today. I got bills to pay."

He grumbles something undecipherable as I get to my car.

"Is your mom calling you?" I laugh.

He comes back to the phone. "Yes, actually. And fuckin' Bones is here. Lucky for him, I lost my boner. You owe me, Ange. I'm comin' to collect later night."

"Will you sneak out after your mom's gone to bed?" I

giggle.

He does not sound impressed. "You think it's funny now, just wait till I tie you to your bed and spank that little ass red raw."

I bite my lip at the thought. He's definitely only gotten worse with age where the kink is concerned.

"To think I knew you when you were spotty faced and inexperienced, and I was your first kiss," I muse. "Those were the days." I can hardly even imagine it now. He's changed in so many ways.

He grunts. "First kiss? First everything. Can't get you out of my fuckin' head, woman."

"Miss me bad, huh?"

I hear Brock's mom holler in the background again as I climb into my car.

"Gotta go," he mutters. "Magic hour with me, my dick, and your sexy voice is all but a distant memory."

"Shoulda called me earlier. Bye, Romeo."

I don't wait for him to reply, I hang up with a smirk on my face as my phone alerts me to a new text message.

I read it and my heart plummets.

Kennedy tells me Marcus skipped his weekly parole meeting, and she needs me to call her immediately.

My hands begin to shake.

I just about drop my coffee trying to place it into the cup holder.

I should call Brock, but he'll only go apeshit.

I want to believe that it doesn't mean anything, that he won't come back here, but a part of being a victim of abuse means that you're never really free of your fears. They live with you.

The truth is, I wished he'd have died when he overdosed in prison that time.

I don't know how long I spend in the car, but when I

eventually pull it together, I drive to work without even knowing how I got there. I go straight into my office and close the door and begin to pace.

I need to call Kennedy first before I do anything else.

Without thinking, I pick up my cell and decide not to call Brock. He'll freak and find a way to track him down to kill him. Then I won't see him for thirty years. I know just the kind of man he is, and he's a dangerous one.

"Sit tight," she tells me. "They've put out a warrant for his arrest, and I don't think it will be long until they catch him. With these things, he likely has just forgotten about the appointment. He's only just got out, so I seriously doubt he's going to give all of that up so quickly."

If only I could really believe that.

"He's always had friends in low places, that much is certain. I'm trying not to freak out here."

"I don't think it's reason to cause alarm; he checked in last week without issues. I know that's easy for me to say, I'm not the one he tried to harm. I will update you the minute I hear anything more."

It makes me uneasy, that's for sure. At least he's out of state, that makes me feel a shit ton better.

"Let's hope that'll be soon."

"If you're worried, Angel, there is always witness protection. I know that sounds extreme and all, but it could be just until he's back behind bars."

Alarm bells go off. "I don't think that I need to do that."

"What about the M.C.?"

I swallow hard. "What about them?"

"I'm not stupid enough to believe that they won't intervene, if need be. It could be good to have their protection, just short term until he's arrested."

"Trust me when I say, Brock is an army of one, he's all over it."

"All right. Well, I'll be in touch soon. He can't cross any state lines, so please try not to worry too much. Ex-cons always try to dance around the law, it's not uncommon."

I know she means well, but she wasn't the one with a knife hanging out of her stomach while she almost bled to death on the kitchen floor.

Jessie calls over the intercom to tell me my next appointment is here, and I know I have to get my shit together.

It's all right.

Everything is going be all right.

I open the top drawer where I keep my gun and run my fingers over the cool gray metal. I've never actually shot a gun before, but I will if I have to. I fucking will. I'll do anything to protect myself and Rawlings. I hope he doesn't count on finding out just how much.

~

Brock texts me after work, and I tell him to come over. Rawlings is at a playdate, and I need to let out some pent-up frustration. The minute I hear the straight pipes, I get a thrill that runs through me, and I close my eyes, willing myself to keep all this shit to myself.

It'll not only ruin the mood, but Brock will make it his personal mission to go hunt Marcus down and hang him from the town square.

He knocks once and I fling the door open and pull him by the lapels of his cut into the house.

"Fuck, babe," he says as I press him up against the door as he shuts it with his boot.

Our tongues meet and we kiss like long lost lovers. I push my body into his, and I feel his hardening erection press into me. I moan into his mouth as my hand reaches his dick and I squeeze it through his jeans.

"Fuck me, Brock." I fumble with his belt buckle as he narrows his eyes.

"I take it you're kid-free?" he mutters, grasping my hair as I kiss and bite his neck.

"Yes, for an hour." I grasp his length and rub him hard with my palm.

"You rob a bank or something?"

"Touch me," I say, ignoring him. "Fuck me like you hate me, Brock."

He smirks, grasps me by hips, and lifts me, then turns and presses me into the door.

"You're a naughty girl, Ange. Bet you've been thinkin' about me all day doin' this to you, haven't you?"

I pull my shirt over my head and pull my tits out of my bra. His eyes dip low as he stares at them.

"You've no idea," I breathe, I just want his mouth on me. I want him to make me forget. I want him to take me to that place where everything is safe, and good, and warm.

He moves his head, sucking one hard nipple into his mouth, and I grasp his hair and pull him closer into me. He unzips his jeans, lets them fall and does the same to mine, then pulls my panties aside, brushing his fingers through my slick heat.

"So wet, I get you goin' just like that, Ange?"

"You know you do." I grind against him, and he hisses as he lines himself up and pushes into me. I let out a groan at how full he makes me feel.

"You been thinkin' about me fuckin' you like a barbarian, haven't you?"

I groan as he thrusts into me, rough and rugged, just how I like it.

"Jesus, Brock."

He smirks. "I keep tellin' you babe, he ain't gonna help you."

He grasps my breast hard and pulls on my nipple, his mouth going to my other hard peak as he sucks on me and pumps between my legs like a man possessed. His dark eyes bore into mine as he stares at me, never breaking contact.

I love you.

Jesus Christ, I always have. I always will. My beautiful, bad-ass biker who'll die trying to protect me. The fact is, I know he would. He'd die for my kid too.

Tears well in my eyes when I think about why I've kept him at arm's length, why I've pushed him away and been a downright bitch to him most of the time.

It kept him away.

Problem solved. But he was always in my heart, lurking, waiting. He's an itch I cannot scratch.

Sure, I had my reasons, but still. He didn't deserve it, and I drove him even further. I drove him into other women's arms.

But he's with me now.

He is, and that's all that matters.

I come hard in record time as he does not relent, he keeps pumping me hard, then moves his mouth to my other breast and sucks on that one just as hard as the first. I feel the tingle of his touch all the way through my body. There is no way I'll ever get sick of having him touch me. Never. He knows exactly what I like and exactly how to do it. He always has, and boy, can he move those hips.

I cling to him for dear life, like he holds all the answers, like this rough, hot sex isn't just an excuse to not think about my problems. I know they won't go away; I know they're all still there waiting, but Brock makes everything better.

He moves one hand down to my clit and circles it with his thumb, I explode again in seconds as he pumps hard, grunts his release, and slows to a stop as I feel him spurt inside me, hot and heavy.

He rests his head against my shoulder for a moment as we both struggle for breath.

"Did I hate you enough?" he mutters, close to my ear.

I nod.

"Come stay with me," he says, out of nowhere. "I'll kick mom out to the B and B, or she can come here, then you can be in my bed every night."

"Brock, we can't. What would I say to Rawlings?"

"That we're together. She's a big girl, she'll be cool with it. She loves me."

"She's six," I reply. "And it'll just confuse her if…"

"If what?"

"If things don't work out between us."

"Don't plan on that, Ange. Told you what I want, up to you if you want it too. I'm not playin' any games."

"So, that means you're done with other women? It'll be just me? Come on, Brock, you've been sampling the menu at church for a decade or more. Why would you give that up?"

He stares at me, and the look in his eyes is fierce. "Yeah, I'd give it up, hell, I *have* given it up. Haven't slept with another broad since we hooked up. I already told you all this. And none of those women are you. You're the one I want, the one I've always wanted. Let me prove it to you."

He pulls out and fixes himself as I slide down the door to my feet.

I stare at him and tears well in my eyes. When he glances back up, he frowns.

"Angel, what's wrong?"

I want to tell him about today. I want to tell him everything. But I can't. I know what he'll do, and I can't risk him getting hurt. This is our fresh start, and I don't want to mess it up by angering him into doing something he'll only regret.

"Nothing," I lie. "I just had a long day." *And I missed you.*

He brushes the hair back off my face. "Okay. You know

you can tell me stuff, right? If you need to vent or whatever."

I brush the nostalgia off and pull myself together. "That's what girlfriends are for," I remind him. "Isn't that all we supposedly do? Bitch and moan?"

"Long as you're moaning my name, I don't care what you do."

I shake my head and pull my clothing back into place. He stares at me while I do it. I also refrain from telling him that Colt needed more time with the app on my laptop. Seemed like something went wrong with the recording and he needs to figure out how to fix it. Brock won't be happy about that, either.

"Such a romantic," I tease.

He holds my chin with his thumb and forefinger. "Think about it, Ange. I want an answer and soon. And before you go spouting about that I can't tell you what to do, you're right, I can't. But I can give you the option of bein' with me. I won't wait forever, got me? It's already been too long."

For once in my life, I don't fire up and want to smack him. Mainly because I know he's right. He won't wait forever. This isn't some fairy tale, but it can be the best thing that ever happened to me if I look past my own nose.

I step toward him and wrap my arms around his neck. "I got you. But we've still got forty- five minutes, and I know just how I want to spend them."

He breaks out into a slow grin and walks me backwards toward the living room.

"Good, cos I plan on marking my territory all over this house, so you know where I've been and where I wanna be, all the fuckin' time."

I gulp as he bites his lip and looks up at me with those eyes that kill me.

"Fuck me like you love me," I whisper, and he does. For the next forty-five minutes.

21

BROCK

I STARE AT THE PHONE AND FOR THE FIRST TIME IN MY LIFE I don't know what to do.

My father's calling me.

I shouldn't answer, and I don't, but he calls back again fifteen minutes later.

"Yeah?" I grunt into the phone.

"It's your father," he says, like I don't know how caller I.D. works.

"Figured that when I saw your name on the screen. Why are you callin' me?"

"I'm worried about your mother," he tells me, and I almost smile at how much this must be killing him to admit. "I haven't heard from her in over a week, she won't return my calls."

"So, you thought you'd call me?"

"Amelia said she was staying with you. Seemed like the obvious choice."

I run a hand through my hair and take a deep breath.

"Well, you'll be happy to know she's just fine." *Enjoying life without you fuckface.*

He hesitates. "Well, tell her I called, won't you?"

Hey, dad, I'm fine, thanks for asking.

"Not your errand boy," I retort. "Tell her yourself. Maybe if you finally take your head out of your ass you might actually be able to see straight for once in your life. Mom's a good woman, you should never have let her walk away, but you're too pig headed to see that. Don't call me again, you got beef with mom then take it up with her."

I hang up.

I don't even know why I answered, but maybe I just enjoy the punishment.

He'll never change. He doesn't want to.

I text mom.

Brock: Call your husband, and don't have him call me again. Next time I won't be civil.

Mom: What!? Brock! What did he say?

Brock: Nothing newsworthy. He claims to be worried about you.

Mom: Did you speak to him?

Brock: Yeah. I told him to F off and not call me again. Should've blocked his number.

Mom: Brock! Please tell me you didn't.

Brock: Next you're going to say I'm acting like a child

Mom: Aren't you?

Brock: I like how this is sounding like it's all my fault.

Mom: That's not my intention, but two wrongs don't make a right. He's trying to reach out.

Brock: Didn't seem that way to me. There you are, still defending him.

Mom: I'm not. I just wish we could have some peace, that's all.

Brock: Well, call him. I'm busy. GTG.

Mom: All right, I will. Oh, and I'm making dumplings for dinner, sweetie. Love you x

I roll my eyes.

That's put me in a foul mood. Not even the idea of mom's famous dumpling stew can set me right again.

Why that asshat has to call me and ruin my day, I don't know. Maybe you should treat your wife better, *dad*, and she'd want to answer your calls.

When Colt rings me, my mood plummets even further.

"Someone's been fuckin' with the feed on Angel's security camera," he says when I bark a platitude down the phone.

I stop what I'm doing. "What do you mean?"

"She came in to see why the app wasn't feeding the footage to her laptop, and when I looked into it, I couldn't see a problem. So, I went to check out the installation, the wires have been cut."

A cold shiver runs through me.

"What the fuck?"

"Yeah, I know."

"Does she know?"

"I told her there's some technical problems I'm looking into, didn't want to freak her out."

I pace in the yard, feeling like I might kick the shit out of something any second. "So, if someone cut the wire, were they dumb enough to show their face?"

"Unfortunately, not," he replies. "I get a bad feelin' about this, bro. I mean, the wires were pulled out. It's a bit of a mess, but there's no attempted break in. I checked everything while I was there this morning, unless they got spooked. Isn't her crazy old man out of the joint or some shit?"

"Ex-old man," I correct. "Steels got Linc keepin' tabs. If he'd have set foot in Arizona any time soon, I'd know about it. It isn't him."

"Well, I'm just sayin', it's weird. Why cut the feed and then not attempt to break in? Like, thank fuck they didn't, but it doesn't make any sense. As I say, must've been spooked."

I have to agree with him, this all feels wrong.

"I'll take care of it," I grunt.

"She'll be pissed I told you first."

"I don't give a fuck. You goin' soft on me?"

"Just checked my dick, it's still attached, so I'd say I'm good."

I snort. "Speaking of women problems, you taking care of that wild one you got hangin' off your belt buckle? Heard she's back in town, *again*, time to tap in or tap out, bro, you know what I'm sayin'?"

"Good news travels fast," he mutters. "Tryin' to keep her safe. She's a danger to herself and she needs help. If she goes back home, she'll just get into more trouble."

"Why's that your problem?"

He hesitates, probably not used to my questioning. "I guess I feel a bit responsible for her. I feel bad for what she went through. She was banged up pretty bad, and it's keeping her busy helping me get the shop organized."

He's too nice, and now he's got a chick he can't get rid of, with problems to boot. Dumbass. Guess we all gotta learn the hard way sometimes.

"I just hope you know what you're doin', bro, chicks like that can be the death of you. This is just the start of it."

Don't I know it.

"I've got it under control," he assures me.

I snort again. "Now I know you're really in the shit."

"Later, dude. Gotta go."

We hang up, and I immediately call Steel and tell him what's going on.

"Need to put a prospect on Angel and the kid," he says, sounding as unimpressed as I am.

"I agree."

"Just to be sure, it's not worth takin' any chances. If the fucker's unstable and already sniffing around for visitin' rights—he's clearly off his rocker. The one thing about prison is it gives you a lot of time to let things fester."

"I'm not feelin' too thrilled myself. I don't fuckin' like any of it," I admit. "Angel's spooked out enough as it is. Long as he checks in with his parole officer, then we don't have reason to be alarmed, but I don't wanna take any risks."

"I'll send Lee to watch the school. Jax can watch Angel's Ink."

"Better make em' both incognito, dude. He gets sprung hangin' around the school, could pose a problem."

"He'll be discreet. You've got more to worry about with Angel if she finds out we're watchin' her."

"It's for her own fuckin' good, whether she knows it now or not." Tension floods right though me at not being in control of this situation, and I don't like it.

"Best you keep her bed warm until this blows over then," he says, making it sound so easy. "One less headache if you're with her at night."

He's right on one thing; I can't let her stay alone. The murky feeling keeps resurfacing, though I know she's not in harm's way directly, the fact she's worried has me worried, too.

"If she knows what's good for her, she'll come quietly and keep her smart mouth shut."

He laughs, something I'm not used to hearing very often. "You got a shit ton to learn about feisty women, bro, if you think that one will come quietly. I'll call you once I get an update from Linc."

"Later." I hang up and close my eyes. This isn't what I need.

There's no way I can convince Angel to come to my place. Plus, I'd have to kick mom out, which of course I would do if it meant keeping Ange and Rawlings safe, but then I'd have mom on my case about us getting back together. Last thing I need is my mom in my business.

I could stay at her place, that way if some little punks are sniffing around casing the joint, they'll get a nice surprise when I beat them to death.

I also don't wanna freak Angel out, so I can't tell her about the wires to the camera. I could say that mom is driving me nuts and I need some space. Yeah, she'd believe that. I really want to slap myself silly for even thinking about making an excuse just to please her, maybe I am pussy whipped after all.

Whatever I am, I'm not gonna let anything happen to them. The prospects better hope and pray they don't fuck this up because I really don't want to be the one in prison for killing them for negligence.

I decide to go home and clean up and then go see Angel at the salon, the sooner the better.

An hour later, I pull up outside and walk through the doors.

Angel's at her station tattooing some young chick; a blue butterfly spread across one shoulder. Angel's an amazing artist, she can draw anything. The lines and details are beautiful; it's a work of art, like everything she does.

I grunt at the receptionist as she asks me to take a seat. Angel glances up, and I give her a chin lift. She smiles as I watch her at work.

Seeing her tattooing someone turns me on big time. She's got a tank top on which shows off her own tatts up one side of her shoulder and down one arm, a long vine with roses that wraps around the whole side of her body.

Her ass looks great in the leather pants she's got on as she squats on a stool and continues her work. Thank God I'm at the tail end of the appointment. After she's finished, the chick cries and hugs her goodbye, then Angel waltzes over to me.

She gives me a look. "What are you doing here?"

"Hello to you too," I grunt. "Need to talk." I nod toward her office.

She looks at me quizzically, but without another word, I follow her to the small, cramped space. I try my hardest not to imagine doing her over the desk while she has a salon full of clients, so she has to be quiet.

I chagrin behind her back as I follow her inside.

"What's up? You look like you just got told there's no Santa Claus."

I shut the door behind me and move toward her, which makes her back up and I grin. I grip her chin and kiss her hard, not putting much weight behind it because I know she'll kick my ass if I try and fuck her here, even though I want to.

"Miss me bad?" I mutter, running my hands down her back as I grip her ass. "I like these pants."

"Brock," she chastises. "What do you want?"

I give her a lopsided look. "Is that a trick question?"

She rolls her eyes. "I'm busy."

"What and I'm not?"

She huffs. I love it when she gets impatient, makes me want to do very bad things. Lucky for her, I got shit to do too.

"Very funny, you look like you're up to no good, that's all."

"Got mom issues."

She frowns. "Seriously?"

"Seriously. She's all up in my business, and I need a break from her. Got enough shit goin' on of my own without listenin' to her talk about my dad nonstop. Get sick of hearing that shit all day long. She's now comin' to my workplace to 'tidy up' and be a general nuisance, I need a place to crash before I turf her out."

She baulks. "I know you didn't just ask me if you can sleep on my couch."

"You're right, I didn't, I want to sleep in your bed, with you wrapped around me. That's what I want."

She swallows hard. "Brock, doesn't this complicate things?"

"You said that to me when we kissed for the very first time. Life's full of complications, babe, we of all people know that." I'm an overbearing asshole, what can I say?

"I need to talk to Rawlings about us, explain stuff..." she begins, but it sounds like an excuse to me. I'm done waiting.

"I've been waiting my whole goddamn life, Ange. I want you; I want *us*. We can talk to her together if you want. She knows me, I'm not just some random guy who picked you up for the night and you'll never see again."

She looks indignant for a moment. "I've never picked up and taken a guy back to my place with my kid around. What kind of person do you think I am?"

I circle my arms around her shoulders and bump her with my hips. "Thrilled to hear it. You're a good mom, Ange. The best. And I'm not lyin' when I say I wanna be part of bein' with you and Rawls, a big part. I've always wanted that, a family, a family of my own."

It hits me deep, this longing I've had in the making for a long time. I don't want to grow old and be stuck doin' this shit for the rest of my life. Fuck that. Home is wherever they are.

She stares at me with those big, beautiful eyes. Eyes that have always been able to wrench at my heart and make it stop beating.

Why can't she just love me back? Like she used to.

She used to say it all the time. There was a time when she couldn't get enough of me.

She rests her head on my shoulder as I kiss the top of her head. "Why are you such an incredibly decent man?"

"You make it sound like a bad thing."

"It's not." She sighs, her voice muffled against my shirt. "But it's getting harder and harder to resist you."

I tilt her chin with my finger. "Then don't." I kiss her gently. "Stop fightin' me, we've wasted nearly twenty years over this shit. I don't wanna wait any more. If you don't want me or can't see a future with me then you have to tell me now before shit gets really real. I can't do this."

She bites her lip, resting her hands on my hips. "Brock, you know I love you, I always have, but if this goes south again, like it did last time, it'll break me for good."

"It was you who dumped me, remember?" I remind her, brushing her hair back off her shoulder. "I let you go because I thought it was what was best for you back then. I should've stepped up like a man and fought for you, for what we had. I didn't, and I regret that. I regret it every second of my life, every time I wake up alone in a house all by myself when I should have you by my side and a bunch of kids downstairs running around. I never wanted to be single and childless at this age. It's always been you, Ange, let's not kid ourselves."

"Wow," she exhales, pouting her lips into a slow smile. "That's quite an admission, never heard you say so much in one breath."

"Yeah? I remember when you were the one who did all the smooth talkin' in the back of my truck."

She smiles at the memory. "When you corrupted me?"

I laugh out loud. "You don't have a very good memory, babe. If I recall, it was you who jumped my bones and wouldn't take no for an answer. Dry humpin' me with that short dress on."

She knows it's true. She instigated our first time.

She brings her lips up to mine and kisses me gently. I keep mine still, letting her take the lead. "I worry we've waited too long," she whispers.

"You're overthinking it," I mutter. "Like always. You want me or you don't, it's pretty simple."

She tries to move in and deepen the kiss, trying to avoid talking to me. But I hold her back at the shoulders and stare at her. "What's it gonna be?"

The look in her eyes tells me all I need to know. "I want you, Brock Thomas Altman. I want you so damn much, I just don't know how to be what we were."

My heart soars by her admission as I nuzzle her nose. "We don't have to be what we were. We can be better than that. We can be so much more, but we have to be honest with each other. No more lies."

She stares at me, and I know something else is up.

"Spit it out," I say when she doesn't say anything.

She drops her head. "He didn't make his check-in with his parole officer this week."

My nostrils flair. Oh shit. "When did you find out?"

"Earlier."

"And you didn't call me?"

"Kennedy said not to worry, that this kind of thing happens..."

I feel the tension rising in my body. "Fuck Kennedy, easy for her to say sittin' in her cushy office without a mad man running around on the loose, a man who fuckin'..."

"He's not running around," she interrupts. "He can't leave the state, remember."

"Doesn't mean he won't."

She bites her lip and I smooth her shoulders, trying not to scare her, though I'm not doing a very good job of it.

"I need to sort my shit out, Brock."

I squeeze her gently. "Don't make excuses, I still want an answer."

"You know how I feel about you; doesn't that say enough?"

"Is that a backwards way of saying I can crash at your place, or you want me?"

"Both."

I nudge her with my hips. "Smartass."

She bites her lip again; it drives me crazy when she does that. "I really feel weird about freaking Rawlings out with you staying overnight. Kids are so impressionable at that age."

I frown. "I hear ya. If it makes you feel any better, I'll cover your screams with my hand while you ride me."

She slaps my butt and I grin. "Ha. Ha. That isn't helping."

"Fine. I'll sneak out before she wakes up if I have to. Don't know why you're so worried, kid loves me to bits."

"And your mom? She'll only ask questions and put more pressure on us."

"Let me handle her."

She groans. "God, it's like being in high school all over again."

"When are your parents back in town?"

"Probably next weekend. They've found a house and the offer got accepted."

I don't tell her that her father was the one who originally got in touch with Hutch. Last thing they need it Angel yelling at them too.

"One big, happy family," I muse.

She pushes me in the chest lightly. "I've got to get back to work."

"I thought we could celebrate?"

She shakes her head. "I'm at *work*, Brock."

I grin. "Scared they'll hear you?" I slowly drop to my

knees as I tug on the hem of her pants. "Promise I'll be quick."

She rests her hands back on the desk as I lower her zipper.

"Brock…" she groans as I nuzzle my face into her panties, and her hands reach into my hair as she pulls.

"We can practice you not makin' any noise," I whisper, looking up at her as I pull her panties aside and spread her legs wider.

"Jesus," she mutters.

"I keep tellin' ya, it's only my name I want to hear you callin' out, not his."

"Hurry, I haven't got all day!" she whisper-shouts, impatiently.

And there she is. The girl I fell in love with.

Oh, how I've missed her.

22

ANGEL

It's strange but comforting to have a man draped around you in bed. Especially when said man is Brock, and even more so now that I'm not used to having *any* man in my bed.

I've never been the type to be clingy, but I feel myself craving him more and more.

Brock can be very persuasive, and yes, he's brash, but I know he'd never do me wrong. He'd never treat me like anything except his queen. Maybe part of my healing from being assaulted and left for dead has finally made me confront my feelings and let go of the past.

Even with all the shit and turmoil going on at the moment, I feel so much stronger now than I ever was.

One of my favorite new things to do is stare at Brock while he sleeps.

He looks cuter than ever post all-night-sex with ruffled hair, naked in my bed, taking up most of the room.

"Anyone tell you it's rude to stare?" he mumbles into the pillow without opening his eyes.

Oops.

"Just enjoying the view," I say, sipping on my coffee.

"What time is it?"

"Just after six."

"Shit."

He groans, then rubbing his eyes with one hand, he rolls onto his side and cracks the other eye open, his eyes dancing over my body.

"Nice shirt," he says, his lips curling up at the corners.

"Thanks." I'm wearing his t-shirt, which on me it's more like a nightdress.

"I gotta get up."

"Why so early?"

"You not worn out from last night?"

Brock definitely made up for the lack of sex I've been having lately. Ten-fold.

"That's not what I meant. Where are you going at six am?"

"Already got me on a leash?" He gives me a salacious grin.

"Very funny."

"I gotta rig up the truck to get it ready for a pickup at noon at a deceased estate. Gotta get a head start."

"Sounds riveting."

He runs a hand up my thigh and reaches between my legs. "Like you in my shit. Like you even better without it."

"Don't start something you can't finish," I tease, setting my coffee down on the side table.

"I've got time."

Just as he says it, his phone goes off with a deafening ring.

"You sure about that?"

He cocks an eyebrow and barks down the phone as I tell him to shush. Rawlings isn't up yet.

"Said I'd be there at six thirty, now fuck off," he whisper-shouts, hanging up.

"Bones?"

"He hates bein' late."

He rolls on top of me, and I squeal in surprise.

"Brock, you're not a one-minute kind of man," I say in a hushed tone, trying not to giggle.

"More like you don't know how to be quiet, woman," he counters, nuzzling into my neck. "I can be fast."

He presses his hard on into me. "You better do your best then, clock's ticking." I pull his t-shirt off my body as his eyes drop to my tits.

"Fuckin' good morning to me," he muses as I close my eyes and wrap my legs around him once more as he takes me to heaven.

I think I could get used to waking up like this.

~

"Another hang up," Jessie says. "Keeps happening a lot this week, people love to pocket dial. Don't people know how to lock their phones?"

Every time something weird happens, I instantly get suspicious and on high alert.

I try not to let any of this affect me. I've got good people around me, and I'm in a good place. I can handle this; I can handle anything that gets thrown at me.

I know that the local P.D. know about Marcus. While I don't see Jenkins all that much, when I do, it always brings back the memories that I have fought so desperately to forget.

The fact this asshole is out after only seven short years just has my mind boggled at the justice system. If he'd have killed Rawlings, by me miscarrying, then he would have gotten longer because then it would have been murder. How fucked up is that?

No. Don't go there. Don't go there.

The last thing I need is that trip down memory lane. I've got the protection of the M.C.

If there was ever a time I'm glad I've been a part of the extended family at the club, then it's now. Maybe I haven't appreciated them as much as I should have. They've never done me wrong, not ever. Even if I don't agree with all of their archaic ways.

I have coffee with Lucy and Deanna the next day and we catch up on everything that's been going on these last few weeks, including Lucy's pregnancy, much to Deanna's disgust because she hates hearing about all that shit.

"You know you'll have all this to look forward to when you get knocked up," Lucy says, stirring her cappuccino.

"Eww, gross." Deanna shakes her head venomously. "I don't do baby poop or chunder, and anyway, I barely have enough time for me, let alone a kid. Also, finding a guy to procreate within a hundred-mile radius, let alone in this *town*, isn't going to happen anytime soon."

"You've got a point there," I agree. "Bachelors are few and far between."

"Ones I'd want to date anyway," she grumbles.

Lucy turns her eagle eyes to me and shakes her head. "You don't fool me, you know. I want to hear all about how long you've been bangin' Brock for," she says, pointing her finger at me.

I splutter my coffee.

"Don't play coy with us," she goes on, as I cough and grab some napkins. "Brock's been

whistling and singing and acting all kinda freakish these last few weeks. There's only one reason why a man comes to work dancing his own little tune with a smile plastered across his face, and that's because he's getting it on the regular with a woman he's crazy about."

"Why do you assume it's me?" I ask, feigning shock. "Brock's got a lot of women at his beck and call, not like he's short on admirers."

"Uh huh, and you're the only one capable of putting him in that kinda mood, honey. Fess up."

"This is a good thing; it means he's less grouchy than usual." Deanna agrees. "The sweet butts have been complaining they're hunting for scraps, the well's gone dry. Colt doesn't bone any of them these days either, did when he first got here, but seems he's gone soft too what with Sienna's cousin hanging around. Are those two a thing?"

"He says they're not," I reply. "But I don't believe him."

I really hope the conversation stays on Colt and doesn't get turned back onto me and Brock. I also know I can't lie, though Deanna kind of already knows.

Lucy shakes her head. "Men. Honestly. They think they can go stick it to whoever they want, then expect us to fall over with our legs in the air the minute they're ready to settle down." She turns back to me again. "Take some level-headed advice, Angel. Make him work for it, honey. Don't be lettin' him call all the shots behind closed doors. They may think they're big and tough at the club, but it's us that have to cook and clean and give them head. They should worship the ground we walk on for putting up with their array of shit. Accept nothing less."

"Wait, I thought Rubble does worship the ground you walk on?" I laugh.

She shrugs. "He does now. But trust me, honey, I had to train him to get that way, it wasn't all smooth sailing from the get-go. Men are work. You gotta set boundaries in the beginning, otherwise, they'll just think they own you and you'll do what they say."

"It's a little bit late for her," Deanna remarks, pointing her fork at me. "She's known Brock since they were little kids. I'd say if you don't have him where you want him now, you never will."

I roll my eyes. "Thanks for the advice, D. Since you're such an expert on men and all."

"Anytime." She shrugs. "I'm not totally useless, even if I do love em and leave em. I only use them for sex. Trick is to let them be the giver, not the receiver. Then as long as we both get what we want, that's all that matters. I'm sure if I ever meet Mr. Right, I'll come to Lucy for more words of wisdom."

"As opposed to Mr. Right Now?" Lucy laughs. "I can't wait for the day you fall hard. I'm going to waggle my finger in front of your face and say I told you so, too."

Deanna scoffs. "Since there are no available men in this town that I'd even consider sharing a zip code with, much less the rest of my life, I'm pretty sure I'm off the hook."

Lucy shakes her head, then glances at me. "Stop stallin', Angel. Tell us what we want to know."

"Are you going to keep nagging at me until I tell you?" I groan.

She nods enthusiastically. "I'm cranky and pregnant, this is the only out I get."

"She pretty much just confirmed it," Deanna points out. "She's doin' him, and we all know it."

"Fine. We've hooked back up, happy now?"

Lucy squeals excitedly while Deanna puts her fingers in her ears. Lucy leans over the table and squeezes my hand. "Good for you, sweetie, just remember what I said, though."

"We haven't made anything official just yet," I go on. "So just keep it on the down-low for the moment."

Deanna snorts. "Until the weekend when he makes it official at the table."

"He won't be doing that," I tell them. They look at each other with confusion.

"Of course, he'll do that," Lucy goes on. "Claiming you as his woman is part of the tradition of being an ol' lady and part of the club, ain't no way you'll get away with that, honeybun. You just need to learn to pick your battles, and this ain't one of them."

"Well, maybe I'm breaking tradition."

They both guffaw with laughter at the same time.

"OMG." Deanna chuckles, holding her sides. "You almost had me going there."

"Yeah, asking a man in the BRMC not to claim you is like asking him to hand over his balls."

I groan loudly. "Why does it have to be all or nothing? This is exactly why I stayed away from him for so long, because of the misogynistic, bear growling, chest thumping ways they expect us to adhere to while they sit around in their secret meeting room cooking up secret men's business, like we don't all know half the shit that goes on already anyways."

"Get used to it," Deanna singsongs. "They're all the same and none of them are changing anytime soon. They all beat the same drum."

Lucy wags her finger. "It's not all bad, girl. Just stand your ground, as much as they like to believe we're all nags, they'd be lost without us."

I can't say I disagree with her. Saying it out loud makes it seem real. Brock broke down my walls and reminded me of what we could have together. I know I need to communicate better with him, but that will take some time. I'm so used to living alone and relying on myself. And I definitely don't want him claiming me at no table.

At three o'clock while I'm at work, I get a phone call from the school saying there's been a fire and they've had to evacuate the classrooms.

I leave in a panic, dashing out the door. When I get there, the entire school is assembled on the front lawn while part of the boiler room goes up in smoke. Luckily, it's not near enough to do any real damage, though there are flammables in the neighboring cleaner's cupboard.

"Loose wiring." I hear one of the dads say as I rush to find Rawlings in her group with her teacher. "One of the dryers caught on fire."

She looks up at me as I take her in my arms and hug her tight.

"Hey, kiddo, are you okay?"

"Hi, mom, I'm fine. The storeroom caught fire," she tells me as I set her down.

I kiss her on the forehead. "It's okay, sweetie, everything's going to be okay. It was just an accident."

I look around at the other kids gathered, waiting for their parents and it's then that I notice Lee hovering around. I narrow my eyes as he makes eye contact.

"Wait here with Melody," I tell her as I head over to him. "Don't go anywhere."

"Okay," she replies.

I walk swiftly over toward the prospect. "Hey, Lee, right?" I don't know him very well, but I've seen him a few times at the clubhouse.

He looks just a little bit nervous. "Yeah."

"What are you doing here?"

"I was on my way to church," he says. "Saw the smoke, thought I could come help."

"Huh. Well, I guess that was lucky that you were in the neighborhood then."

"I guess it was."

He looks me right in the eye and he's either a really good liar or my instincts are getting a little rusty. This'll be Brock's doing, I'm sure of it.

"Did Brock…"

"Hey, I gotta go. Glad everything's okay." He takes off before I can say anything else.

I don't believe he was just in the neighborhood, not for a single second. I can smell bullshit about a mile away.

Brock calls me halfway home and of course he's heard about the fire already, bad news travels fast around here, especially with Lee hanging around.

"We're fine," I tell him. "Heading home now."

"I'll be there as soon as I can."

"Hi, Uncle Brock!" Rawlings yells through the speaker.

"Hey, kiddo. You want pizza for dinner?"

"Yes! I love pizza!" she calls back excitedly.

"Yes, please," I chastise as she rolls her eyes at me.

"Yes, *please*, Uncle B."

I want to facepalm myself but refrain. Brock's just weaving his way into her heart, as well as mine, and now he's bringing dinner home. For heaven's sake, it's not like I can say no now.

"Be there around seven, all right?"

"Fine, see you then."

"Bye, Uncle B!" Rawlings chimes, happily.

I hang up and she turns to me. "Uncle Brock is the best."

I can't help the smile on my face, now may be a good time to broach the subject of him being around a little more.

"Speaking of Uncle Brock," I begin. "How would you feel about him coming around a little more than he has been to spend time some with us?"

"That'd be cool."

Okay. That went well.

Then she turns and looks at me like my mother would. "Wait… you mean, like a boyfriend?" she says the words with her nose screwed up. Here we go.

I swallow the lump in my throat, I swear this kid is six going on sixteen. "Well, if he were, then how would you feel about that?"

She turns back to the front. "It's not that I don't like the idea, just don't do anything embarrassing like kiss in front of me."

My eyes go wide. "All right."

"Do I still have to call him Uncle Brock?"

"Yes," I muse.

She thinks for a moment. "But if you got married then you'd be my mom and he'd be my uncle?"

I count to five slowly in my head and try not to smack my head repeatedly on the steering wheel.

"I don't think we're quite at that point, honey."

"I mean, you can kiss him, just not in front of me." She pretends to gag. "Cos that would be really disgusting."

I turn to look at her. "Well, that makes sense, I promise not to embarrass you or kiss in front of you, deal?"

She nods. "Deal. But mom, boys are pretty gross."

I laugh. "You don't think Uncle Brock's gross."

"He's not six, mom. Boys my age are revolting."

I shake my head. "Best to stay away from them, then." For at least thirty years anyway, then I'll be too old to care.

"Aaaand Uncle B said I can ride the horses when I get older."

"Did he? I'm not sure the horses are staying long term, though."

"Well, he said he might keep them," she tells me. I swear this kid knows more about what's going on with Brock than I do.

"Well, we'll see about that. The horses he has are a little big for you to ride right now."

She sighs. "I hope I grow up to be tall like you, then it won't matter."

"It doesn't matter if you're tall or not, baby, I'll still love you."

She side-eyes me. "You're acting weird, mom."

"Why is saying I love you weird?"

"It's not... but I still want to be tall."

"I wasn't that tall when I was your age," I remind her. "I didn't shoot up until I was about nine or ten."

"When you met Uncle B for the first time?"

"Yes, how did you know that?"

"He told me."

"Oh yeah? What else did he say?"

She smiles. "That you were the prettiest girl in the whole school."

I roll my lips inward. "Did he?"

"Yes, and that you kicked the mean boys in the shins and broke a girls nose with your atlas."

My eyes go wide. "That wasn't quite how it happened," I say, remembering to clobber Brock later. "I stood up for myself, which you should always do... without violence."

"That is a pretty cool story, though," she giggles.

I try not to laugh too. "No matter what happens, you should only hang out with kids at school that make you feel good, kids that have your back."

"Like Uncle Brock did?"

I smile at the memory. "Yes, like Uncle Brock did. It is obviously a little... *different* having a boy as your best friend, but he was different from the other boys in school."

"Boys in my class are so dumb," she grumbles.

"Don't worry," I sigh. "They'll grow out of it."

I wish she'd stay six forever, but I know that's not going to happen.

"They're still gross," she says after a while.

"Can't argue with you there."

Glad we cleared that up.

I turn the radio up and we both sing to Miley Cyrus at the top of our lungs.

23

BROCK

We haul ass all morning. Colt came along for the ride since he's got weekends free, though I think he needed a break from that wayward broad that he's been housing. He should just bone her and get it out of his system.

Colt repaired the camera for Angel but installed a hidden one as well, that way if it gets tampered with again, we'll know about it.

I still don't like it, but Colt tells me that it isn't that unusual for kids to fool around with cameras and be little assholes, just because they can.

Steel hasn't had a bead on fuckface yet, but Linc is on alert and with the warrant out for his arrest, I'll feel a whole lot better for Angel's sake when he's back behind bars.

She won't admit it out loud, but I know this is a hard limit for her, and I can't blame her.

The only fear I have in the world is something happening to Angel or Rawlings. She thinks she can protect herself, but I know better.

I've got plans for us. When mom finally moves out and my place is finished, I want them to move in. It's bigger and has more space for all of us.

Plus, I'd love to teach Rawlings how to ride the horses. She's an adventurous little thing, just like her momma was at that age. Angel probably had a little more fire in her, truth be told, but I think Rawlings is going to be a chip off the old block.

Things shifted the other day when Angel pulled me into her house. We're on fire together, she can't deny it.

I know I'm an overbearing son of a bitch, but she knows this about me. She knows everything about me, not like I've got any secrets.

I can't turn back time, but I can make sure I do things right this time.

I came out here to look for stuff I can use on my house and since the club is buying out Stefanie's half of the Stone Crow, we might be able to pick up some materials for that too. This place has a lot of good junk. There's piles and piles of cherry oak flooring in one of the back sheds. The owner never got around to installing it, and it'd be perfect for the Stone Crow. That place needs an overhaul of epic proportions.

I send Hutch screenshots of the flooring and he texts me back almost immediately to pick it up and bring it with us.

Part owning the Stone Crow will mean I'll have a say in who gets hired, and I plan on putting Axton's name up for bartender when he gets out. Maybe he can do electrical on the side since I know there's a lot of rewiring to do there, too.

Sure, he's got to prove himself, but I know in my heart he can do it. I know he can make something of himself if he puts the past behind him and keeps his nose clean. I miss the little bastard.

"You thinkin' about pussy?" Bones asks, interrupting my thoughts.

I throw him a look. "Are you ever not thinkin' about it?"

He laughs. "Speakin' of which, Angel's lawyer, Kennedy what's-her-face, she can sit on my face any day of the week, she's smokin' hot." He makes thrusting motions with his hips, I wish he'd stop, he's giving me nausea.

"Stevie's sister?"

"Yeah, she's fuckin' hot dude. One of those stuck-up, snobby types with a high IQ and a rich boyfriend with a sports car. She probably takes tennis lessons and speaks several languages. Probably dying to be fucked sideways if the tension in her glare is anything to go by."

"Jesus fuckin' Christ," I mutter.

"No shit, her suit probably cost more than my first car."

"Heard she's been good to Angel."

"She's a ball buster. Don't take no shit. I like that in a woman."

"Should fit in well at church then," I snicker. Lord knows how the lot of us attract feisty and troublesome women.

"I should just ask her out," he goes on, like I care. "Or you know, fuck her stupid."

We continue hunting through the huge shed for anything else we may be able to use.

"Afraid she'll cut your balls off?" Like that would stop him.

"Didn't you hear what I just said? Her IQ is way higher than mine. She's a lawyer, wears sharp suits, probably carries a piece. She could cut glass with just her eyeballs. I'd have to ensure my ass before I got to first base."

"Oh, come on, every woman you've ever had has been smarter than you." I laugh. He punches me in the arm. "If you wanna catch this chick's attention, you gotta amp up your game a little bit. Chicks like to make you work for it."

He gives me a weird look. "Like what, what would I have to do?"

He really is fuckin' clueless.

"That shit Lucy's always harping on about. Women wanna be wooed, dazzled, and all that crap. Could be worth a bunch of flowers and some chocolates if she puts out and in turn puts me out of my misery cos I won't have to hear your whining all day long."

"You might be onto something there," he replies. "Yeah, I could do that shit. Chicks like candy and pretty shit. Maybe I could take her to dinner, the whole nine yards."

I point at him. "Now you're talkin', but it'd need to be somewhere flashy and expensive, not the burger joint."

I can't help my rumbling laughter imagining Bones in a fancy restaurant, he doesn't even own a nice pair of pants or dress shoes. A worried look forms on his face, and I realize he really does like this girl.

Colt comes out the back. "Shit, man, are these people hoarders or what?"

"Tell me about it," I reply. "Gonna be makin' a few trips, bro. If you can spare the time?"

"Yeah, of course."

"What about you?" Bones nods to him. "What do you think about women bein' wooed?"

Colt looks momentarily confused by the question and I laugh out loud.

"You mean like chocolates and dinner dates and shit?"

"Yeah."

"Could be worth it, if you really like her." He shrugs. "All chicks like that stuff, from what I've heard, though I'm not exactly Casanova."

"He doesn't like her," I interrupt. "He just wants to get into her pants, and he can't, so it's a challenge for him."

Bones flips me the bird.

Colt chuckles and shakes his head.

"Y'all can laugh now, but you'll see, I'll woo her any which way I can. I'll have her in my bed by the week's out."

"That's optimistic." I snort. "Better make sure you take a bulletproof vest, though, just to be on the safe side. She could be armed and dangerous."

"Who's the lucky girl?" Colt asks.

"Kennedy, the lawyer chick helpin' out Angel, she's Stevie's sister."

"Stevie's pretty cute, too," Colt confesses. "But she's got a boyfriend she seems pretty attached to, unfortunately, and I'm not gonna go near a club sister for obvious reasons. Don't need the black eyes or the headaches."

"Surprised Deanna hasn't tried to get into your pants," I smirk. "She's the wild child out of all the girls, the one you gotta watch out for."

Colt grunts. "She already did when I got patched in. Had to let her know I was her father's little bitch now, so it wasn't gonna work out between us. Plus, I don't wanna go on the run and live in Mexico for the rest of my life. The man's ruthless, especially when it comes to his daughter."

"I'd like to say Hutch is all bark and no bite." I laugh. "But that would be lying."

"That's something we can both agree on." Bones eyes go wide, as he scratches his beard. "The shit that went down before he turned the club around would make your toes curl. Was a shit storm. I wouldn't cross the man, unless I had a death wish."

Hutch has been more of a father to me than my own, he's stuck with me through thick and thin. That shit about blood bein' thicker than water is a load of shit.

My father will never know this, but I make six figures. More than I'd ever make in the military, and I didn't have to do anything questionable to get it. My record is clean, and I've worked hard to get this business off the ground. Seven long years working every single day of the week, but me and Bones made this a success, and I'm proud of that.

Sure, the dough might be better selling illegal shit, but I've never been one to be on the radar of the law or want to be lookin' over my shoulder forever, living like a ghost.

Selling drugs and guns and shit might be profitable, but it just ain't worth it. No way I wanna live like that, wondering when the next pay was goin' to come and at what price. Bones and I make a great living, it's how I was able to buy the farm. Well, it was the land I wanted, the house was always going to be a work in progress because of its run-down state.

"He's a good man," Colt agrees. "Gave me a chance when nobody else would. Look at me now, I'm running my own business and gonna be making good coin, got a family, chicks at the ready, a place to crash every night. I wouldn't have any of that without him. I'd still be bare knuckle fighting and doing whatever I could for scratch."

"He's like a father to all of us," I agree.

Lord knows me and Hutch go back a long way. He's seen me at my worst, when I got back from the military and things fell apart with my family. He's never ever questioned me, never judged me. I wish I could say the same for my own flesh and blood, but I'm not that lucky.

I think about my father, and I want to punch something. I'll never understand him.

When we get back to church, Hutch has a look in the truck and nods his approval, then pulls me aside and tells me about the settlement for the Stone Crow that's going through at the end of the month. It's sooner than we had planned but with Steph's ill father, she wants to get out of town as soon as she can.

"Gonna have to shut down for at least a month," he says, as I close the door behind me, and he stirs the ice around in his tumbler. "Gonna be a shit ton of work, place is a dingy cesspit. Not attracting the right sort of crowd. The restaurant is better, but the kitchen needs new fit out. I got a bead on some good secondhand kitchen equipment from a foreclosure, could be worth lookin' into at Stradbroke. Speakin' of which, how is your brother?"

"He's all right. Hearing's next month."

"He's gonna need a job ain't he?"

I glance at him; we've discussed this but not in any major detail. "He's got his electrician's license, fully qualified, could rewire the entire joint, save us a packet, and bartend on a night. Kid wants to work; he wants to prove himself."

"Gonna need a new bar manager. Leroy's out, he's goin' back to college to finish his degree, so that rules him out for the foreseeable future."

"How about offering it to Stevie? She's good at what she does, patrons seem to like her, and she's ballsy while still bein' sweet."

Hutch nods. "Not a bad idea."

"There's also two apartments upstairs, was gonna offer a bed at mine for Axton short-term, but he could move into Sienna's old place. Then he'd be onsite for security and could keep an eye on things after closing."

I know Hutch is hesitant with Axton. I don't blame him, he's an ex-con, and he's done hard time. Last thing we need are the pigs breathing down our necks, but this is Axton's one shot to get back on his feet, prove himself. If he makes an ass and a liar out of me then I'll bury him myself.

"Stevie and her boyfriend could move into Steph's place, nothing wrong with having a little bit of muscle around the joint. I'll bring it to the table, then you can talk to her, see what she thinks."

I nod.

He rubs his chin as he looks at me for a few moments. "I'm willing to give Axon a chance, it'll have to be voted in, but by a chance I mean *one*, Brock. You know me and how I feel about ex-cons. If this goes badly, it'll reflect on you. It's always harder to inflict punishment when the culprit is family."

"I wouldn't ask if I didn't think he was trustworthy. Puttin' my neck on the line isn't something I've taken on lightly."

He nods. "You want a drink? Look like you need one."

I run a hand through my hair. "Long day. Angel's ex didn't check in with his parole officer."

"Fuck."

"Yeah. Angel's freaked out. Got the prospects watchin' her and Rawls. Until he's caught again, it's best I stay with her, make sure she's safe."

He cocks a brow. "That the only reason?"

I look down at my boots. "We're gonna give things another try."

"About fuckin' time," he grunts.

I snort. "You gonna give me a lecture now about how to handle feisty women who can't be controlled?"

A slow smile spreads across his face. "Where would the fun in that be? Anyway, somethin' tells me you've already got a handle on your woman, otherwise she wouldn't be comin' back for more."

"You make that sound like I'm pussy-whipped," I mutter.

He chuckles. "Aren't you?"

"She knows who wears the pants; the same bastard who's been crazy about her since I was ten years old."

He shakes his head. "Gonna make me puke with that shit."

"How do you keep the magic alive?" I ask, getting up from the chair.

"You gotta let them play a couple rounds," he tells me, tapping a finger against his lips. "Way to a woman's heart is all the little shit. Be a man for her, that's your job, to protect her, but you gotta get to the nitty gritty, find out what makes her tick. You do that and she's loyal to you, then you're king. Relationships are work, my friend, *hard work*. Women will make you go gray fast, but if you get it right, you can have everything you want, get it wrong and you might just be payin' alimony for the rest of your miserable life."

"You ever thought about relationship counseling?"

He baulks. "Been with my ol' lady for thirty-two years, and we're still like teenagers."

The last thing I want is having visions about Hutch and Kirsty acting like teenagers.

"Please let that be the end of your speech."

He shakes his head. "Been meanin' to ask how things are with your old man. How's your mom doin'?"

I shrug. "I really don't know. She's not talkin' to him at the moment. Fucker called me the other day, tryin' to get me to tell her to come home."

"You're shittin' me?"

"Nah, seems like the old boy can't do his own bidding or act like a man. If he was, she wouldn't have run out in the first place. Shits me that he has to try and get around it through his children, should've tried Amelia, he woulda had better luck."

"Fuck me dead, prick should be down here on his knees beggin'."

I shake my head. "That won't happen. I told him to leave me the fuck alone. He's got somethin' to say, he should do it to my face."

"Coward's way out. I'm sorry son, for what it's worth."

I shrug it off. "Nothin' to be sorry for. Life's good right now, I got nothin' to complain about." *Except that fuckin' prick, Marcus, who I'm gonna gut if I ever run into him.*

"Send Colt in here before you go, I need to find out what's goin' on with this chick he's been housing, seems she's back in town and for good this time. You think she's gonna squeal?"

"I don't know," I reply honestly. "Need to ask Steel more about it, though, Sienna will know more, she's closest to her. Fuck knows why he's not cut her loose."

Last thing we need is some chick losing the plot and letting the authorities know that Sienna's ex's 'accident' wasn't exactly accurate.

"I can think of one reason why," Hutch adds gravely. "Softer than he looks, he's a good man, but seems to have a weak spot for the needy bitches. Not a trait I'm entirely comfortable with, but he seems to have a handle on it, for the moment."

"I don't think it's anything to worry about. He's got her workin' in the office, keepin' her nose clean and outta trouble from what I can gather."

He grunts but doesn't look too enthralled. He dismisses me with a wave of his hand. Before I close the door, he calls my name. I duck my head around the door as he raises his glass.

"Gonna need a date on you claimin' Angel at the table, didn't think I'd let that slide now, did you?"

I kind of hoped he would, but I keep my face stoic. "Get back to you on that," I reply, knowing how Angel feels about all of that makes me feel a little bit uneasy. "Just keepin' things on the quiet for a little bit until this shit with her ex blows over."

He nods, then gives me a grin. "Don't wait too long. Guys will think she really does have you pussy-whipped."

He laughs as I shut the door, shaking my head.

If only it were that simple.

24

ANGEL

I wake up in a ball of sweat, thrashing around as I feel hands come over me and clutch my shoulders. It takes a few moments to realize it's Brock, shaking me awake.

When I finally rouse and the fog clears in my head, I'm gasping for breath. Brock's wild eyes stare down at me as I try to collect myself.

"You all right, Ange?" he all but whispers.

I nod. "I'm fine. Just a bad dream."

He frowns. I don't want to worry him and let him know my worst fears have come true; that my attacker is free and now he's nowhere to be found. No matter what I tell myself, it doesn't take away from the fact that he's not under anybody's radar right now and he could be anywhere.

"Nothing and nobody is going to hurt you, you hear me?"

"I know that." I lie.

"I'm not leavin' you alone, that you can be sure of."

"You don't need to do that," I protest, but I know there's no point, he won't listen. "You've already got prospects watchin' me."

He doesn't even blink. "You figured it out."

"Yes, it's not like I'm stupid, might wanna let the boys know a disguise would be better."

He grunts and leans down, kissing me on the forehead. "Try and get some sleep, yeah?"

I nod but I know sleep won't come now.

I stare at the ceiling and the only thing that gives me any sort of comfort is the soft lull of Brock's breathing. I turn my head to look at him, side on, facing me, his hand stretched out across my body.

I'm lucky to have him, I know that. But it doesn't stop the unease inside of me, and the fact I carry that piece with me wherever I go. If it comes down to it, I will kill the son of a bitch and this time I will not hesitate.

∽

A few days pass and I drive out to the farm to help Sienna with the horses in the barn. I figure a couple of hours out in the country to clear my head might do me good. I haven't seen Sienna in ages.

"Hey," she says when I arrive, carrying a tray with two coffees.

"Hi, Sienna. I didn't know what you liked so I brought two cappuccinos."

"Thanks, that's exactly what I need." She smiles as I hand her a cup.

"How's it all going in here?"

I glance around and see the hay bales and a bunch of horse feed in large plastic bags.

"Good, I've kind of made a little area for them." She points to a corner of the barn away from the door where she's cleaned all the crap out and laid down some hay. "If they don't get rehomed soon then I might ask Brock if it's okay if Steel builds something a little more permanent like a pen. With winter setting in, they'll need some shelter. It will all be removable of course. We're just grateful they had somewhere to go, poor things. I can't imagine anyone wanting to kill them just because they got old and aren't useful anymore."

"That's so sad. They're beautiful," I reply. "Do you ride?"

She shakes her head. "Sadly, no, but I'd love to learn. What about you?"

"I used to, a long time ago, I'd probably fall off if I tried now." I laugh.

"We should look into horse riding lessons, could be fun. Keeps them stimulated and gives the horses some exercise as well. I think Stevie rides, we could ask her about lessons?"

"I'm keen if you are?" I say before I can even think about it. Well, it would be fun.

"Cool, I'll ask her, it'll get me out of the house. I seem to be tied to the place now that I'm there full time and live above the shop."

"Steel getting under your skin?" I snicker, taking a sip of my coffee.

She rolls her eyes. "I'm sure I don't need to tell you how overbearing he can be."

"Enough words spoken, I get it, any outlet to get away from them is a good one if you ask me. Least you don't have prospects following you around."

"Shit, are things all right?" she asks, setting her cup down and hauling another bag of feed over to the corner.

"Let me help you," I say, putting my cup down too. "And yeah, things are okay, just got some shit going down with my ex. He's not a good guy." I don't want to go into details, even if she may know some of it from Steel. Though the boys tend to keep their secret men's business to themselves for the most part.

"Urgh. Tell me about it, you pretty much know all the shit

that went down with me and my ex. He got what was coming to him in the end. This guy will too."

I don't know the facts, just that he stalked Sienna and kidnapped poor Cassidy. The boys intervened and he's not been heard of since. Nobody asks too many questions when there aren't any answers.

"Speaking of which, how is Cassidy going? I saw her at Colt's place."

Sienna frowns as we drag the bag into the corner and then go get another one.

"She's okay now. Colt's given her some office work to do, and I've been helping her where I can, she's going back to school. It's better when she keeps herself busy. She went home for a while but couldn't settle there, it was very hard for her after everything."

"Yeah, trauma can do that to a person, poor thing. Maybe we could take her out, have a girl's night, introduce her to everyone?"

Sienna brightens. "I've been suggesting that for a while, and I should really insist. She hasn't been up to it, but like I say, she's definitely getting better. I think she really likes Colt, though the pair of them are playing at keeping things on the downlow."

"You sure about that?" I say with a smile. "She seems to be around him an awful lot."

"Tell me about it. She's just got a lot of shit she needs to sort out in her head. Colt's been really good for her. I just hope she's not relying on him like her crutch, you know. He doesn't need that kind of responsibility, though he's already gone above and beyond what I'd consider normal, and he's not complaining. He really is just too nice."

"Not often you hear that," I agree. "But yeah, I'm up for girl's night if you can get her to come out. It would be fun."

"I'll suggest it again, thanks, Angel."

We continue to haul the feed and then top up the water troughs out in the field. I'm glad I came out here wearing old boots and jeans and not my good ones.

My phone rings just as we're coming back from the troughs.

"Hey," I say as Kennedy's name flashes across my screen.

"Hi, Angel. I've got some good news. Marcus was picked up about an hour ago trying to cross the state border, he's back in custody."

My heart soars and I almost drop the phone.

"Oh my God!" I just about squeal. "That's fantastic news!"

"I thought that would make your day. So, there is nothing to worry about, just like we said. He'll be going back to jail for relinquishing the terms of his release and also trying to leave the state. Violating his parole won't sit well. I'll update you once sentencing takes place, but that won't be for a while. He'll be held in custody."

My heart races and I feel so elated. "That's great, Kennedy, thank you so much for letting me know, best news I've heard today."

"I'll be in touch soon."

"Thank you."

I hang up and immediately call Brock as Sienna goes back into the barn.

"Hey, Ange."

"Hey, Brock, what's wrong?" I can tell by his tone that something's up.

"I was just about to call you."

"Me too, but you go first."

He pauses for a few seconds. "My dad's had a heart attack."

I stop dead in my tracks. "Brock, I'm so sorry, is he all right?"

"He's in the hospital, mom's got to get back there. She's a mess; she's with me right now."

"You should take her," I say, before he has the chance to make an excuse. "She needs you."

"I'm not leaving you, I told you that."

"You don't have to worry, Kennedy just called, she said Marcus has been picked up and he's in custody."

I hear him sigh with relief. "Thank fuck for that. Was almost about to set up a search party to go hunt him down myself, pigs did their job for once."

"So, I'm going to be fine, and you can drive your mom home. Did they say how he's doing?"

"I don't know much, but he's in intensive care. They had to restart his heart three times. It was a massive coronary."

"Oh God, I'm so sorry." I know I can't tell him what to do and he wouldn't listen anyway, but he needs to hear this. "I know this is hard for you, but if anything happens you will only wish you'd gone sooner, even if it's just to support your mom."

The line goes silent for a few moments.

"Brock?"

"Yeah, I'm still here."

"Just don't say anything you might regret, it's too late if the unthinkable happens."

"Maybe he should have thought about that," he grumbles.

"Sometimes you just have to be the bigger person, you know?"

I know this is hard for him, I get it. His dad has been such a bastard.

"I don't like leaving you with all this goin' on."

"I said I'm fine, he's not an issue anymore. So, there's no reason for you not to go, aside from your own pigheadedness."

"If I didn't know any better, I'd say that was an insult."

"It was a mere accurate observation."

"You and your fancy words," he mumbles. "You sure you'll be okay?"

I roll my eyes. "I'll be fine. I can take care of myself."

"That's my job now," he says matter-of-factly.

"It's not your job to follow me around like a puppy," I remind him. "We've never lived in each other's pockets, Brock, that's not who we are. Your family needs you, too."

He grumbles something else I can't decipher, and I know his decision is made.

"I'll call you tonight when I get there," he says eventually, as a smile creeps across my face.

"All right, if you need me then just call, okay?"

"I will."

"I hope he's going to be okay."

"He's more pigheaded than I am, so I doubt he'll fall off the perch without havin' the last word."

I shake my head. "Just try not to be your usual self. Your mom needs you right now, just think of the situation she's in. She'll be feeling a lot of guilt for leaving him and blaming herself, questioning if she did the right thing."

"He's brought everything that's happened on himself, mom shouldn't feel guilty for that. Even when he's not even conscious he has to have the last word."

"Relationships are complicated," I remind him. "Just be sensitive, for her."

"Any other wise words of wisdom obi wan?"

"That's it for now, but if I think of anything else, I'll let you know."

"How's the shit shoveling going?" he mocks.

"It's not so bad. Kind of therapeutic looking after the horses, they're pretty cool."

"Well, don't get too attached, they're gone the minute Steel gets somewhere else."

"Stop stalling, get gone. Call me when you get there."

He hesitates.

"I love you, Brock," I whisper so Sienna doesn't hear. "Drive safe."

"Right back at ya," he says and disconnects the call.

∽

I feel bad for Brock as I serve up Rawlings' dinner and help her with her homework. Poor Brock and Sylvia, I really hope that Jim is going to be all right. This may be just the kind of chance of reconciliation that the three of them need, if he survives. Lord knows this spat between Brock and his dad has been going on for far too long.

My mom calls later that night, and I fill her in on all the details as she tells me they've organized a moving van for two weeks from now. It's all happening so fast, but I'm so glad I'll have my parents around and they're more than happy to help out with Rawlings. She needs her grandparents around; it's good for her.

I don't tell her yet about me and Brock. I want to just test the waters first, make sure he's serious before we make anything official. Though he's only been gone for a few hours, I miss him already. I feel like a teenager all over again with butterflies in my stomach every time I think about him and what he likes to do to me. How he shocks me and pushes me to my limits.

He's always done that, he's always pushed me to be the best I can be, and I know that if his father passes away then I've got to be strong for him. No matter what he says, it'll be hard on him if this goes south.

He's always idolized his father, and I know that the last few years have been tough on him, even though he tries hard not to show it. His father's always been a big influence in his life; it hasn't always been like this, it's just worsened over the years. Jim can be a nasty bastard, don't get me wrong, but sometimes they are both as stubborn as each other and neither will back down.

I think about Axton and how much Brock needs him out of the joint. I've known him since he was five; I was shocked when he got put inside, it was so out of character for him to do what he did. I just hope that he's the man Brock thinks he is when he gets out because prison changes people. He's been in there a while. I dread to think about life inside a maximum-security prison and he's only just past thirty years old.

The Axton I knew was a good kid, a lot softer than Brock ever was, but he had a good head on his shoulders. It devastated the whole family when he got put away. Jim changed after that; he just couldn't get over it and subsequently Brock suffered with guilt and blame.

I really hate his father for that, for putting that on him when it wasn't his fight or his problem. He had enough to cope with knowing his baby brother was going away for a long time.

I try and shake myself out of my reverie and follow Sienna back inside.

Yeah, I could see myself here. I quite like stomping around on the farm. I've never minded getting dirty and I've always been a bit of tomboy. The more I look around, the more I can picture it, living with Brock out on the farm.

Maybe it's nostalgia and I'm just happy that Marcus has been locked up so now I can rest easy for a while, I don't know. But it makes me want all those things that I promised myself when I was seventeen, when I really didn't know what I wanted. Only Brock.

It's only ever been him.

BROCK

I wave goodbye to Sienna an hour later and pick up Rawlings, then head back to the salon. I've got a few things to do there before we head home. Jessie's locking the takings in the safe and tidying up before she leaves for the day. She really is a godsend around here; I'd never be organized or on time for anything without her.

"See you tomorrow," she calls as I set Rawlings up with her I-pad and give her a wave.

"Thanks, Jessie, see ya later."

After I get Rawlings video up and going, I settle in to do some work. I only have a few emails to send and a little bit of paperwork to finish, since I spent so long at Brock's place, I'm a little later than I intended and as always, behind on the boring stuff.

I make a coffee and when I come back out to the reception desk, I hear knocking at the door.

I roll my eyes as I set my coffee down.

Can't they read the opening hours sign?

I approach and open it, expecting to tell some kid to buzz off, tattooing's over today. When I open it, nobody's there, I glance down and see a single red rose has been placed on the door mat.

My blood runs cold.

Red roses.

Some asshole is obviously trying to spook me, for real this time. I swiftly shut the door but find myself being barreled backwards when a foot appears in the door jamb out of nowhere.

I look up into a pair of eyes that shouldn't be staring back at me.

I stop in my tracks completely caught off guard.

It can't be. It's impossible.

Shock hits my body like an old, unwanted friend. Now I know what they mean when they say your legs turn to jelly when confronted with something dangerous and you've nowhere to go, my feet literally feel glued to the floor beneath me.

"What's the matter, Angel, surprised to see me?" Marcus says as I open my mouth, then close it again.

"You... you can't..."

"Can't what? Be here? Seems I *can* and I *am*, it's nice to see you too, baby. I've missed you."

I stare at him. "How are you here?" I whisper, my vocal cords don't seem to want to work. "You got arrested..."

He smirks as we stare at each other. Maybe this is a nightmare, one I'm about to wake up from any minute...

"Mom?" Rawlings calls from behind me and his eyes shift to my daughter.

Fuck. My purse is in my car. I didn't bring it in with me. My gun's inside it.

So much for my big plans of shooting this cocksucker if I ever run into him again.

I thought we were safe.

I panic and try to shut the door on him but he's fast. He's inside in seconds and he pushes me back as I claw at him like a woman possessed.

"You just can't take a hint, can you, Angel? You know how much that infuriates me when you don't do what I want," he sneers, fending off my attacks. "Though you were never very good at taking orders."

"Mom!" Rawlings cries out.

"Rawlings," I screech, backing away from him. "Go into my office and lock the door, do it now! Go!" I yell. "Remember what I told you."

He tries to lunge past me to get to her, his eyes wild and crazy. I put all my weight into it and slam him in the chest with my shoulder, not knocking him over, but slowing him down and hurting myself in the process.

"Go!" I yell at her again as she runs down the hall, her I-pad dropping on the floor by the couch with a clatter.

All I want is her away from him, safe. Like I thought we were.

He comes toward me and swings, knocking me over as we both fall backwards. He's on top of me, and I knee him in the groin before he can get a good hold of me. He rolls off and clutches his balls as I try to scramble away, but he grabs onto my ankle and I turn and kick him, aiming for his face but missing and copping him in the shoulder. It's still not enough to stop him fully as I try again to get up and make it to the desk before he jumps on my back and pins me down.

"Gonna fuckin' kill you, bitch. I've been watching you, every fuckin' night for weeks. You and that biker you can't get enough of, yeah, I've been watchin'."

"No!" I cry out. "You're not going to do this to me…"

He laughs in my ear. "I gave you a chance, you stupid bitch, but you wouldn't take it. It was me that set fire to the school, by the way, pity I couldn't snatch her then cos you'd never find her. But here we are, Ange. You know, I should've gutted you better when I had the chance."

"I'll kill you," I groan out with the little air I have left. "I'll fucking kill you!"

He bends closer to me. "I'll slice her throat in front of you, that'll make you fuckin' shut your mouth real quick, always were the little hot head. That's what got you in this mess in the first place."

"You were arrested," I garble as I feel his hands around my throat. My vision becomes blurred as he applies pressure.

This is it. This is where he kills me.

"Paid some homeless guy to take my I.D. and try to get across the border. Pigs are so stupid. They'll realize eventually, of course, but it's bought me some time."

I feel his hands around my throat, and I struggle for breath, trying to bump him off me.

Rawlings.

Brock.

I try to reach out toward my office door, not that it'd do any good. I can't get to her, my baby.

I hear a commotion at the door, and a few moments later, a loud crack. Marcus falls off me and I cough and splutter as I try to get my breath back. I crawl away, holding my neck, only as I get to the wall do I turn around. It's Lee and Jax.

I've never been so happy to see low-life prospects in my life.

I pant, gasping, holding my throat, tears streaming down my face.

"What the fuck?" Lee yells, holding a crowbar that he's just socked Marcus with; he lies on the floor out cold as I stare at him wordlessly, still unable to comprehend what's happening.

I shake uncontrollably as Jax comes toward me. "Where's Rawlings?" he barks.

"In my office," I stutter.

He takes off to go find her as Lee crouches down in front of me.

"You all right?"

I sit there shaking. "How did you know?"

"We didn't." He shrugs. "Brock didn't get chance to tell us to stop following you when he left, we noticed a car tailing you from the school."

I stare at him wordlessly. They saved my life.

"She won't come out," Jax tells me, coming back from the corridor. I close my eyes as Lee takes his cut off and drapes it behind me and over my shoulders.

"I'll go get her; she won't come out until she hears my voice."

"You should really sit," Lee says, looking worried. "I think you need to just take a moment."

I shake my head. "I'm fine." I stop as I take a few deep breaths. "Thank you, guys, I don't know what to say. He's supposed to be in custody..." I trail off. My throat burns like a bitch, maybe he did some damage to my vocal cords.

"I know what Brock's gonna say," Lee mutters, shaking his head. "Gotta call Steel first, give him the heads up, no way he's gonna want the pigs involved in this."

I don't care if they string him up and bleed him out. I get up and walk toward Marcus without any thought and swiftly kick him in the balls, then the ribs, over and over until Jax holds my arms back and stops me.

"Go get your kid," he says softly. "We gotta get out of here."

I know he's right. I don't want to be around for whatever they have planned.

25

BROCK

I stare at my father's lifeless body and all the wires coming out of him as mom softly cries by his side. He's alive, that's one thing, but his heart's taken a beating.

He's lucky to be alive. I guess someone is on his side; he survived, and they got his heart started again. They've put him in an induced coma until his test results come back and they know more. Luckily, he was in a public place when he went down, otherwise, it could have been a different story.

He's a big man, like me, but he looks half his size lying there lifeless. I can't help but think mom leaving may have taken the final toll on him, not that any of this is her fault, bastard had it coming, but still, it's hard, seeing him like this.

I stand with a hand on her shoulder as she cries.

"Mom, it's not your fault, none of it is," I say, hoping that might ease her pain. "It's just one of those things, can happen to anyone."

She just shakes her head and keeps crying.

I wish I could say something to make it better for her, but I know I can't. No matter what I say, she won't hear it. She'll just maintain she should have talked things out with him, not left like she did. I know she did the right thing; it's just a pity dad had to go and have a fuckin' coronary.

"You're a good boy, Brock," she says, sometime later. "Thank you for bringing me back."

"Anything you want, mom. I'm right here."

"He wouldn't want you to see him like this," she whispers. "Despite his grievances, he's always loved you, Brock, always. I want you to know that."

I don't know why she always feels the need to sell him to me.

I know in his own twisted way he loves me, I'm his son, but he's got one hell of a way of showing it. I just don't know if I can get past him kicking me out and disowning me.

Even now, when I should feel all kinds of emotion and guilt, I just feel sorry for him. In the end, this is all we have; right now. And he's pissed so many chances away that I've lost count.

Maybe he'll never get to know me now, and he'll probably never get to know Angel or Rawlings. But that was his choice, and I can't make him change his mind, as much as I still want his approval. I've always wanted him to be proud of me.

Kicking me to the curb was the worst thing that could've happened to me back then, worse than getting shot in the Middle East. I could take that pain over this any day of the week.

"If he gets through this," I say, unsure if I really mean it. "I'll make an effort to try and mend things, mom. I'll give him a chance. For you. I will, if that's what you want."

Fuck. I know I shouldn't make promises I can't keep, but I'll say anything to stop her shoulders shaking like that. She sobs even harder, though, reaching over her shoulder to squeeze my hand.

It always takes some kind of shit tragedy like this to make

people come together, and I hate it. I hate that we couldn't just have a good relationship, that I wasn't good enough.

"You're a good son, Brock Thomas, such a good son."

I never wanted it to come to this.

My sister, Amelia, comes in with a tray of coffees in paper cups as I turn and give her a small smile. Her eyes are red and bloodshot from crying.

My phone rings, and I see its Steel. I let it ring out, but a few moments later it rings again.

"Gotta take this," I say, stepping outside. I give Amelia a touch on the shoulder on the way past. "Steel, what's up?" I run a hand over my face.

"I'm sorry man, but Marcus is here, he fuckin' attacked Angel," he says, his voice like shards of glass.

My blood runs cold, like ice in my veins as I try to take in what he just said. "What the fuck? That can't be possible, he's in custody," I bark.

"Wasn't him, he paid some guy to take his I.D. and purposely get caught, then he got across state lines in the back of a cargo truck."

I think my heart stops beating for a second when I ask, "Angel?"

"She's all right, the prospects were still tailing her."

I pinch the bridge of my nose and thank fuck that I forgot to call them earlier and relieve them of their tasks. My heart pounds in my chest.

"Fucking Christ. What the hell happened?" I pace the hall, ready to punch a hole in the wall.

"He got into the salon, the boys stormed in, got him off her."

"Off her, what the fuck was he doing?"

Steel clears his throat. "Strangling her."

I kick the plastic chairs in front of me.

"I'm sorry, bro," he goes on. "Couldn't have known."

My heart pounds in my chest as I ask, "What about Rawlings?"

My little girl.

I don't give a fuck that my blood isn't running through her veins. She's mine, too.

"She's okay, she locked herself in the office."

I pace the hall, trying to piece it together. "I left them alone."

"Wasn't your fault, bro, you know that."

"Where is he now?"

"Tied up in the salon, too risky to move him during the day."

"He's still there?" My mind whirls.

"Yeah, Lee knocked him out cold with a crowbar." He sounds pleased at that admission.

"Boys did good. I'm comin' back down. Now."

"I got this handled," he starts.

"He's mine. You keep him alive until I get there, you hear me? Won't be long before the pigs start sniffing around. I wanna be the first face he sees when he wakes up."

"All right. How's your pop?"

"He's gonna live; I'll be there in a few hours."

"Brock, you don't have to do this. You know what it means if you go too far."

Blood pounds in my ears as I think about what I'm going to do to this prick when I get there.

"Just keep him on ice, I'm leaving now."

I hang up and go tell mom and Amelia I got business to attend to and that I'll be back in the morning.

As I walk down the corridor, I try Angel's phone, but it goes straight to voicemail. I tell her to call me the second she gets the message. Fuck.

Nothing is gonna stop me from taking out my revenge on this prick.

I've waited a long time for this, and I'm gonna enjoy flogging his ass until his heart stops beating.

~

I drive like a madman back to Bracken Ridge. When I get to Angel's salon, I see Steel, Colt, and Rubble's sleds in the back lot away from the street.

I text Steel that I'm here so they can unlock the back door.

The fire raging in my bones feels like hot lava that may explode any second. This is the man who haunts my dreams, who took everything from me because I wasn't man enough to claim Angel when I should have. He didn't deserve her, what he deserves is to die. Painfully.

I try to calm myself as Rubble opens the back door.

"Where's he at?"

He nods to the front reception. "We got him tied up."

I step into the corridor and when he comes into view, he's gagged and bound to a chair. He's bleeding and unconscious, but alive. He's got blood oozing out of his nose, that's gotta hurt.

I slap Lee on the back. "You did good," I tell him. "You and Jax did me proud. Can't fuckin' thank you enough, you saved her life. My baby's too." My gut clenches at the thought of what they went through, at how scared she and Rawls would have been, it only fuels the fire.

He gives me a chin lift. "Fucker went down like a pussy boy. Angel fucked him up pretty good before we got her out of here."

"Where's Jax?"

"He took off, drove Angel and Rawlings to church."

Steel leans on the counter, and Colt sits backwards on

one of the stools on wheels while Rubble lurks in the hallway.

"How you wanna play this out?" Steel asks when our eyes meet.

"Don't wanna do this here," I say. "Gonna get blood everywhere."

"Well, there's always the junkyard. Could bury him in there and he'll never be found," Rubble offers.

"Pigs will be all over it if we don't fuckin' hurry," Colt pipes up. "Won't take long for them to realize they've got the wrong guy in custody."

"They don't know he's here. Angel didn't go to the hospital," says Steel. "We got some time."

I go over to him and yank him back by the hair as he groans. Great, he's waking up. I give him a couple of slaps around the face, and he begins to blink rapidly.

"He been out for long?" I bark over my shoulder.

"In and out," says Lee. "We've been fuckin' him over for a while."

They all snicker as I turn my attention back to him.

"Fucker had a burner phone," Steel grunts. "Slipped through the cracks. I'm sorry, dude. Fucker's as slippery as they come."

I crack my neck and roll my sleeves up, then slap him several times in the face to rouse him further. He grunts and groans a few times before opening his eyes fully.

When he does, his eyes go wide. Makes me think he'll beg like a little bitch. I'd be shittin' my pants too if I were him.

"Hey fuckface," I say, giving him a punch to the ribs, so hard I hear a crack. He cries out in pain. "Me and my buddies here are going to give you a little homecoming present, it's called; how slowly can we slice off your balls with as much pain as possible, and when I say slow, I mean slow. Steel here specialized in unthinkable torture; shit you can't even get your head around. You'll be begging us to kill you when we're finished, but don't worry, we won't oblige you, the harder you scream, the slower I'm gonna go."

His eyes go wide as he coughs and tries to get back his breath after the punch.

Steel gives him a menacing finger wave as I grunt a snort of laughter.

I stand and flex my knuckles.

"You think you can come into *my* town, hurt *my* girl, get *my* kid?" I shove him back in the chair as his terrified eyes dart around.

"Would've been safer in your cell," Rubble calls. "Pity you won't get the chance of ever going back there again."

I know I should go to Angel; I need to know how she is, but I can't step away from this. I want to fuck this man up. I've never hated someone so much in my life, and I'm glad the boys are here since I may not be able to stop once I start.

I turn and smack him in the face with my fist at full force; once, twice, three times until I hear the crack of his nose and he wails through the gag. Blood gushes everywhere.

Steel pats me on the shoulder. "Be better if we could get him over to the junkyard, more time to drag this out, nobody will come looking there, bro. But we need to move, it's gettin' dark."

I know he's right. I can't do all the things I plan on doing to him here.

"Be better if you didn't leave evidence in Angel's freshly painted salon," Rubble agrees, and I guess he does have a point.

I lean into Marcus's face. "What's the matter, tough guy? Not so fuckin' badass when you're tied to a chair, faced with someone your own size, are ya?"

He's a pussy, so fuckin' weak. He's barely conscious as his

head tips back and I grab him by the hair, about to belt him again when I hear an unthinkable sound... police sirens.

"Don't even fuckin' say it," I snarl, turning as Lee goes to the window and looks out.

"We don't got enough time, dude," Steel tells me, sounding as apologetic as I feel. "How the fuck they piece it together?"

"Fuckin' Jenkins," I mutter. Steam practically shoots out of my ears.

Everything runs through my head in two seconds flat and I don't like the feeling of being defeated. He's gonna get his own, I don't fuckin' care if they have to shoot the door down, he's not comin' out.

"Pigs are here," Lee confirms a few moments later.

"How many?"

"One patrol car at the moment."

"Fuck." I turn to Steel, hoping for a way out of this.

"I got nothin', bro. Game's over."

My phone rings.

Jenkins.

"Stay out of this," I bark as I hit the answer button. "Just walk away, brother. I got a score to settle, and you and me both know that I've waited a long time for this. Not you or anybody else is gonna ruin this for me."

"Not gonna do it, Brock. You can let me in, or I can break this door down. Think about what you're about to do, think about what you're losing in the process."

I begin to pace. This can't be happening.

Should've risked the boys moving him before I arrived. We'd be home free if he was at the junkyard, like Rubble said, plenty of places to hide a body there.

"Don't do this to me, man. You were there, you saw what he did to her, what he almost did to my kid, you fucking saw! Now he's tried to kill her, again, he tried to strangle her this time. You think I can let that slide? That he deserves to keep fuckin' breathing?"

A long silence ensues as I wait. "Yeah, I saw, and he's going right back to prison where he belongs. You don't need to be joining him, Brock. If you do this, you'll go down for murder in the first degree, you'll get life. It's not self-defense and the rest of the crew you've got in there will be accessories to murder. Just think about it."

"Just me here," I reply. "And I *am* thinkin' about it. I've had a long time to get revenge, Jenkins. You of all people know what went down. Shit like that haunts a man, imagine what it did to Angel."

"Well, just think about that, about Angel and Rawlings, how much this will affect them. You won't have the life with them that you want, it'll all be for nothing."

"Won't ever be for nothing!" I shout. "He deserves to suffer after what he did. I can't let that go unpunished; he deserves to die. And I'm gonna be the one to make sure he never hurts anyone else again."

"It isn't worth going to prison for the rest of your life. Your brother's gonna be getting out soon, think of that, you won't see him again until you're an old man. An old man whose dreams are long since dead and buried," he goes on. Typical pig trying to bribe me with all the things close to my heart. He's a good man, a fair cop, which is rare these days, but he can't take this from me. "There's no honor in that, none at all, it's a goddamn waste."

"Don't give me a pep talk I don't need." I run a hand through my hair as I look at Steel helplessly. "You don't know what he's put Angel through, you've no fuckin' clue."

He shrugs and mouths, "You gotta let it go, bro. Can't get locked up."

"You need to unlock that door, Brock, before I break it

down, I mean it. I'm not gonna let you kill him and go down for it. For Angel's sake, open the fucking door."

"Five minutes," I beg. "Give me five minutes, then you can have him."

A pause. "Will he be breathing?"

I turn to look at the man who's haunted my dreams and how much I want to take him to my yard and hang him upside down and torture him for days. Have him bleed out nice and slow. But the thought of going to prison and never seeing my girl and Rawlings again, leaving them unprotected, that digs at my heart.

I can't believe this is where the story ends.

Steel stands and comes toward me. "Bro. It's over."

I shake my head.

"Brock. I'll give you five minutes, broken bones and cuts I can explain, nothing else, got me. No deep wounds or bullets or missing limbs. I need him breathing, then I'm calling it in."

He owes me nothing, really. He could just break the door down and arrest us all.

"You're a good man, Jenkins," I tell him. "You'd be even better if you gave me more time."

"I can't," he says, and he does sound genuinely sorry. "Alert's gone out. Time's running out and you're wasting it talking to me. Five minutes, then open the door. Clock's ticking."

I hang up and close my eyes, breathing hard.

I hang up and turn back to the boys. "We get five minutes. Five goddamn minutes to fuck with him."

A slow smile spreads across Steel's face. Make no mistake, this man is dangerous. He killed Sienna's ex-boyfriend, after all, and I know he regrets not drawing it out. One punch and the guy fell backwards, hitting his head. Lucky for him, really considering the alternative.

I've never understood how a man would want to inflict

pain and misery on a woman, especially one he's supposed to protect.

The one good thing that my father taught me was that a real man protects his own.

Hutch infused it into my bones when I joined the club, too. You hurt women physically in our club, you get buried out in the desert and fed to the cactus. Ain't no place for women beaters at the BRMC, not if you wanna keep breathing.

"Best we get to it." Steel pulls out his knife from the inside of his jacket and kisses the flat blade. "This is my baby, slices through bones like butter."

Colt laughs. "Now we're talkin', this I gotta see."

"Didn't say anything about dismembering, did he?" Steel cocks an eyebrow, and I smile back at him.

"He said no missing limbs."

"Fingers and toes are technically digits." Rubble points out.

We both turn to Marcus as he literally shakes in his chair.

"How many fingers and toes does a man realistically need?" I wonder.

"I dunno, bro, but a man like this definitely doesn't need his balls, not where he's going," Steel replies coldly.

"You think you can choke my woman?" I bark as Steel flanks me. He's dying to get in on the act.

The heat in my veins begs me to take his life, and it takes all the restraint I have not to. Knowing that I won't ever get to see my girls again is the only thing that stops me.

They need me, but I need them more.

My life revolves around Angel and Rawlings and killing this little punk would only give me a life in a concrete cell. It would be worth it to rid him off the planet, but not at my life's expense. I'll find a way to get to him in prison, if he even makes it that far.

That will be my legacy, my wedding present to my wife, if she'll have me.

"Don't think he's got much to say," Steel chuckles, shaking his head.

"Time to find out…" I reply as Steel hands me the knife, Marcus tries to scream but Steel's hand is around his throat before he can blink.

26

ANGEL

I pace Hutch's office, unable to stay calm. He's instructed me to stay here and not leave. Under normal circumstances, I wouldn't undertake an order like that, but today I'm happy to.

Today, I'm happy to be anywhere where there are people in numbers, people on my side, and I can't thank the club enough for all they've done, even inadvertently, to keep me safe. All of it being Brock's doing of course, something I shouldn't have taken for granted and whined about at the time, even when I knew the club might be watching me.

I've never been so grateful for prospects. I'd be dead if they hadn't intervened when they did. I'll never look at them in the same light again. I could practically marry them both.

Imagining that prick's hands around my throat makes me want to shrivel up in the corner and never come out of this room, but if I do that, doesn't that mean he's won?

I can't stop my hands from shaking, even though Kirsty came over and gave me a glass of brandy and took Rawlings for a while to keep her busy. It didn't help nothing.

I can't seem to stop trembling.

I'm terrified of what Brock's doing right now, and

nobody at the club will let me leave and go over to the salon to find out. I'm not sure I want to find out, truth be told.

I heard the sirens over an hour ago. I know where they're headed.

I didn't want to go to the hospital, they'll only ask questions, and I'm never going to drop the club in it. So, I just have to wait.

I ball my hands into fists and try not to scream. I pull my phone out and try Brock's cell again. I know he tried to call me earlier, several times, but my phone lost charge. Now, I'll never get to tell him. Now, I'll never get to say that I don't want him to do it. I want him here with me, forever.

I know he'll kill Marcus; of that I have no doubt.

I need to do something.

I can't stay here; I feel like a caged lion. The only man I have ever belonged to is Brock; he's the only one I'll ever want. I know that now.

If he goes to jail, then my life is over. Everything I've ever wanted is over, and it's taken me until now to realize it. I'm such a fool.

Why did I wait so long? Why didn't I just tell him?

I bang my fist against my forehead several times, it's too late to knock some sense into my brain.

At least I told him I loved him, that was something, at least he'll know.

I drop to my knees and pray. I've never been religious, but tonight I might just see God. I pray that he won't kill Marcus, that he'll leave him breathing and come back to me.

I can just see him getting arrested, resisting of course, with Marcus' blood all over his hands. That's if he hasn't already buried him.

When I can't take it anymore, I sob on the floor, and I hate myself for it. For so long, I've been strong. I've had to be. My guard has been well and truly up, and I used to be proud of that fact, but now it just seems stupid. Now it seems as though I've let too much time pass me by being bitter and pushing Brock away.

It's not like I don't know who he is. I've always known.

I've had to be strong, for the sake of Rawls and try hard to get my life back on track. But now the floodgates open for what I had, and what I've lost, for all the bad shit that happened, and all the years I wasted with the wrong man. I weep like it's my last beating breath, and I don't even hear when the door pushes open.

"Angel?"

The second I hear his voice; I turn and look over my shoulder.

Brock stands in the doorway as I look up at him in disbelief, then he comes inside and closes the door behind him, leaning against the frosted glass.

His hands are bloody, and he looks like he's seen better days.

I wipe my face and scramble to my feet, and I'm in his arms before he can say another word, clutching to him like we have only seconds together, and maybe we do. Maybe they're coming to arrest him.

"Where have you been?" I sob into his cut.

"You know where."

I lean back. "What did you do?"

He frowns when his eyes drop to my neck. It's bruised and sore and my voice is hoarse.

"Not enough," he grunts. "Nowhere near enough."

My heart races in my chest. "Is he alive?"

Please God, say he is, and that Brock won't be going to jail.

While he deserves to die, I know that questions will be asked and there will be CCTV footage of him entering the salon. He won't get away with it.

"Just."

The air leaves my body, and I hug into his chest while his arms come around me. "Thank God," I breathe.

"Don't thank him, thank Jenkins. He got the tip-off, tried to talk me down. Reminded me of what I've got to lose. That's the only reason we stopped."

"We?" I mumble into his shirt.

He kisses my hair. "Less you know, the better. How are you? How's Rawlings?"

"I was so scared." I clutch onto his jacket, then I pull back, remembering the blood on his hands. "Rawlings is out there with Kirsty, I needed to pull myself together."

"There's shit to say." He doesn't sound happy.

"You're bleeding."

"Blood's not mine, well, most of it isn't." He runs his thumb over my neck and shakes his head. "If I'd seen this, I probably wouldn't have stopped."

"But you did stop, that's what matters."

"I'm sorry, I should have been here..." He trails off.

I shake my head. "Brock, your dad had a heart attack, and we thought Marcus was in custody. Don't start the blame game, please, just don't go down that road."

He leans down and kisses me softly. "I don't know what I would have done..."

I put a finger over his lips to quieten him. "It worked out. That's all that matters now."

He closes his eyes and breathes in deeply while he holds me.

"Take me home, Brock. I just want to go home," I whisper when he says nothing more.

He nods. "Sure, you don't need a doc?"

I shake my head. "I'm fine, really. I don't want to go there; they'll only ask questions."

He kisses me again, and I wrap my arms around him under his cut. "Scared me tonight."

I brighten, trying to not cry again. "The prospects, if it weren't for Lee and Jax, it'd be all over, they saved me Brock. I can't ever repay them."

"Think we're gonna have to find new ones," he says suddenly.

I pull back and look up at him. "Brock, you wouldn't?"

He chuckles. "They're probably gonna be patched in, well, Lee at least. He hit the winning blow. Can't get more loyal than that, babe. Loyalty in this club will get you everywhere, as will savin' my ol' lady."

I stare at him. "I want that, I do, Brock."

He grins. "Now you want it? Is that what it takes, a near death experience and me beating the shit outta that asshole?"

I shake my head. "Just glad they were there, when he went for Rawlings…"

He grasps my face gently with both his hands. "Don't, cos I'll go back down to county and drag his ass out and beat him to death for real this time."

I stare at him, my eyes glazing over. "I was so worried about you," I whisper. "I love you so much. I'm sorry it's taken me this long to admit it out loud, to tell you."

He bumps me with his hips. "I've always loved you, you know that, ever since that first time when you walked into class, when you agreed to be my best friend, when we danced at prom, when you grew a hot, sexy body and when I took your virginity."

"Oh, you remember that part," I muse. "Typical."

"I'll never forget it, best night of my life." He smiles down at me, his eyes full of warmth. Eyes I'll never get sick of looking at me like that. "I knew then we were meant to be."

"I knew long before that," I whisper. "I'm sorry, Brock, for everything…"

"Let's spend all night making it up to each other," he says, a smirk on his face. "I'm beat, I wanna go home."

"Shit, I'm sorry with all this commotion going on, how is your dad?"

He lets out a slow breath. "He's gonna be okay, long as he wakes from the coma which they say he will, I'll have to head back in the morning. They've got to do some scans and tests and shit, but he's gonna to have to make some major life changes if he wants to prevent another heart attack, they call it the widow-maker. If he doesn't; next time he won't be so lucky."

"Does this mean you might reconcile?" Hope blooms in my chest.

"Let's not get ahead of ourselves. He had a heart attack, doesn't mean that he's cured of hating my guts or me his."

I tsk. "He doesn't hate you, Brock. He never did. He just couldn't control you. I know how that feels."

He shakes his head. "You don't mind me controlling you when your bent over my bed with your ass in the air."

I sigh. "You always have to make it dirty, don't you?"

He grins. "You knew when you met me, I was pretty sick in the head. Nothing's changed, babe."

"Can't disagree there." He kisses me again chastely, urgently. I want him to be buried inside me. I want to wrap myself around him, hold him as close as possible.

"Let's go." He lets go of me and grabs my hand.

There isn't anywhere else I'd rather be than here, with him and my kid.

The past is in the past, and I'm so ready to let go.

～

I wake up the next morning, and my throat feels like I swallowed sandpaper. I roll over in bed and check my phone. It's past nine o'clock. I go to jump out of bed quickly, realizing

I've slept past my alarm and sit back just as fast as my head begins to spin.

A few minutes later, Brock appears in the doorway.

"Wakey, wakey, sleepy head," he chimes.

He comes toward me with a large mug of coffee in his hand as I sit up, propping the pillows behind me.

"I slept in... Rawlings..." I croak.

"Think the kid could do with a day off," he says, sitting down on the edge of the mattress. He hands me the cup. "Kinda been a rough coupla days for all of us."

I sip the hot liquid gratefully. "I need to talk to her, about yesterday. I didn't get to say much last night, everything happened so fast."

"She's doin' okay," he assures me. "She knows who he is, and that he can't hurt her, or you. Makin' pancakes if you'd like to join us."

He glances down at my neck and drops his eyes to the bed.

"Brock, it's all right."

"It's not all right, what he did to you..."

"I want us to move past this. What he did to me last time should have killed me, but it didn't. I've come so far since then, and I'll be damned if him resurfacing ricochets me back to where I was. I don't want that; I don't ever want to go back there. It wasn't a great place to be at the first time. I've spent too much time there already, and I refuse to go back."

He brushes the hair back off my face with one hand. "I hate that his hand marks are on you."

"It'll go away," I whisper. "I'll wear a turtleneck until it does so Rawlings doesn't see."

He looks back up at me, clearly something on his mind. "I've been thinkin'."

"Did it hurt?" I tease.

He rolls his eyes. "I want you and Rawlings to move in with me."

I stare at him as my heart pounds in my chest. "Brock…"

"Just hear me out," he says as I try not to smile at how endearing he's being. He's not a soft man, but I know he's trying. "Rawls loves it here, lots of room for her to play and do shit. You like the horses and bein' out here, we can keep 'em. It's quiet. The renovation will be finished in three or four weeks at a push, and my bed's a lot bigger than yours. I'd kinda like you in it. Permanently. Plus, did I mention that it's quiet here, no nosy neighbors and prying eyes."

"Are you done?"

"Depends, are you convinced yet?"

I purse my lips, but I can't hold back my smile. "You don't have to sell me on anything, I'd already made the decision that I want to be here. I want to be wherever you are. I don't want to wait anymore either. We've wasted enough time."

A slow smile creeps across his face. "Did I mention my big bed?"

"I'm lying in it," I remind him, as I see the hunger growing in his eyes. He reaches down from my face and grasps one of my breasts and squeezes it through my tank top.

"Fuck," he groans when I bite my lip. "Think I like havin' you at my beck and call."

"Ha!" I scoff. "Now when did I ever agree to that?"

He rubs his thumb over my nipple, and I feel my clit instantly come alive. He always does this to me with the lightest touch.

I make appreciative noises as he plays with me, his eyes never leaving mine, even when he yanks my top up and my boobs fall out.

"Love these things." He leans down and takes one nipple into his mouth as I set my coffee down on the side table and he moves closer. The throb between my legs aches as he tweaks my nipple while sucking on the other. He's right, he does love them, he gives them enough attention. "You make me so hard, babe."

"Brock..." I moan as he slips one hand into my pajama pants and rubs his fingers through my wet heat.

"So wet for me, Angel."

"When you do that, I am," I whisper, running my hands through his hair and down to his biceps. "God, I need you so bad."

He sucks on the other one, pulling, taunting, squeezing as he finger fucks me gently, so gently that it drives me mad.

"Fuck. Need my dick in you," he grunts, adjusting himself through his jeans.

A few moments later, we both freeze as we hear stomping footsteps coming up the stairs. There is no mistaking my child heading this way.

"Shit," I groan as Brock quickly slips his hand out of me and I pull my tank down.

She barges through the doorway two seconds later.

"What up guys? Pancakes are nearly ready." Her distain at having to come up here is apparent.

"All right, co-captain," Brock says with a grin. "You ready for me?"

She places one hand on her hip, just like me. "*Co-captain?* Uncle Brock, I've practically made them all myself." She rolls her eyes as we stare at her, trying not to laugh.

"We'll be down in a second, honey," I say. "You go set the table, okay?"

"Fine," she replies, drawing the word out indignantly as she turns on her heels and marches out, the door slamming behind her.

We both chuckle as she heads off and stomps back down the stairs.

"That's my child," I say, turning back to the beautiful man who loves me and my kid.

"Chip off the old block," he agrees with a sly grin.

"I hope you're not implying she's just like me."

"Well, she didn't get that scowl and stomp from anyone else."

"Come here," I breathe, grabbing a mittful of his shirt and pulling him closer.

"How long do you think we got?" he murmurs against my lips.

"About three minutes."

He moves fast and quickly drops his jeans, and it's then I realize he's camo under there. I stare at his thick cock, hard as steel as he grins at me, sheathing himself a couple of times as he looks at me like the big, bad wolf. I'll never grow tired of seeing *that* beautiful thing either.

"I'd better do my best then, huh?" he says. I squeal when he mounts me, pressing my hands against his chest.

"You don't know how to be quick." I laugh as he tries, and fails, to peel my shorts off.

"I'm gonna have to learn, if the wrath of Rawlings is anything to go by."

I roll my lips inward. "Learned that one from her mama, sorry to say." He looks up at me and I give him a shrug. "Least we'll hear her coming, that stomp is deafening."

He winces. "God help me, I'm really fucked."

"Changin' your mind already?" I tease.

He rolls his eyes as he shoves my tank top up again. "Kinda stuck with you now. Wouldn't want it any other way."

"Always the romantic."

He kisses me fast, his tongue in my mouth, leaving me breathless. "Babe, you didn't get with me because I'm a charmer, but I know how to drag out an orgasm, that's gotta count for somethin'."

I laugh as I help him by lifting my hips up so he can drag my shorts down, which he does, greedily.

"Wasting time talking." I laugh as he comes over me and we kiss like long lost lovers, which we are, in so many ways.

Lovers who found their way back to one another.

Or as they say, better late than never.

I'm right where I need to be and that's all I need to know.

EPILOGUE

2 MONTHS LATER

BROCK

I haven't ever been nervous like this in my entire life. But my mom and dad coming to my place for Sunday dinner, now that's enough to scare the pants off a man.

Dad has made a slow recovery and then my parents eventually got back together during that time; it was always going to happen.

I saw him a couple of times when he was in hospital, not that we said much to each other, but it was important to be there, for mom's sake if nothing else. So, him coming here, seeing my house for the first time right before Christmas, it is kind of freaky.

Things with Angel, Rawlings, and I have never been better. They officially moved in two weeks ago, which had me doing a rush job on the contracting, nothing my bank balance didn't take a hit for, but my priorities changed pretty swiftly after the whole Marcus incident. He's back in jail, and I'll see to it that he doesn't last there long. Turns out, he had a mental breakdown when he couldn't see the kid he tried to kill. Man like that doesn't deserve to ever get out, let alone breathe the same air as the rest of us.

Winter hit us hard, and I have the fire stoked, it's cozy and it'll be Christmas before we can blink. My first Christmas with Angel and Rawlings. I feel like the luckiest son of a bitch alive.

I've always loved Rawls like she's my own blood, and while Angel and I haven't discussed more kids yet, I definitely want to knock her up and give Rawlings a brother or sister. She'd love that. And I'd love to see Angel barefoot and pregnant with my kid, I can't imagine anything being better than that sight. If it doesn't happen, it's all right. I'm content with my girls. A man like me doesn't take much pleasin', but I'm happy as a pig in shit.

When there's a knock at the door, I can hardly believe the old bastard actually showed up. Rawlings runs to answer it; she loves my mom, they've grown quite close, but this'll be the first time she's met my father. I hope he reigns it in for her sake, she's just a kid.

"They're here!" she calls as I watch while my mom sweeps her up into her arms and she hugs her back and forth, kissing her face while Rawls tries to squirm away, wiping her cheeks, laughing all the while.

"Hi, my little princess, I missed you so much," she coos, even though we saw her two weeks ago.

Once she lets her go, she looks up at my dad and then just about bowls him over when she hugs onto his legs. Well, Rawlings has never been a shy kid.

Dad looks down at her, momentarily stunned. "Uh, hi, Rawlings," he says, a little stiffly. Nothing like the innocence of a child to break the ice. I don't think he quite knows what to do with her.

"Come and look at our tree!" she calls excitedly, grabbing my dad by the arm. He has no choice but to follow her into the den. The girls went to town decorating, it looks like Christmas threw up in there, talk about overload.

My mom hugs me and Angel, and I give my father a chin lift as he passes me by.

I've never bothered putting a Christmas tree up since I was a kid, but Angel and Rawlings make a big deal out of it, and I admit, I kinda like it. That too is weighed down with all the ornaments they could find. There isn't a spare branch that hasn't got something stuck on or hung around it.

We put presents all around under the tree for everyone in our family, even Axton. Yeah, he made parole. He'll be out next month. Nobody is happier than I am.

When Rawlings has finally finished making my dad guess all the presents wrapped up and what could be inside, it's time for dinner. We all sit around the table like civilized human beings, and if you'd told me last year that I'd be sitting here doing this, I'd tell you to go jump off a cliff.

I guess things change, you never know what's around the corner.

My dad asks me about the junkyard and the Stone Crow which has just reopened, ready for Christmas, and I fill them in on what's been going on around town. It's only small talk, but at least he can look at me, that's progress.

After dinner, I take them on a tour of the house and the stables. Yeah, the horses ended up stayin', big surprise. Angel and Sienna have been taking riding lessons in the field with Stevie. I have to say, they look hot as fuck all kitted out in their riding gear. Makes me wanna get a whip and spank Angel's cute little ass.

It's extravagant, but we got Rawlings a pony for her first Christmas. There's nothing I want more than to look out onto the pastures and see the two of them on horseback, happy and at peace.

Home.

It's all I've ever wanted.

We watch the girls pat the horses as I lean on the fence, and my father seems nervous, which isn't like him. He turns and leans his back against the fence while I face forward.

"Son," he begins as I stare straight ahead. "I have to thank you for being there for your mother, while I was in the hospital."

We've barely spoken about it.

"It's what any good son would do," I reply, rubbing salt in the wounds just a little bit.

"There's a lot that happens to a man when his whole life flashes before his eyes."

"You don't have to tell me that. It sucks it took you almost dying to realize it."

I'm not gonna go throw a pity party for him just because he's had a near death experience, but if all this has taught me anything, it's that holding grudges gets you nowhere.

"It makes a man think," he goes on. "About what's important to him, about what he leaves behind."

"Can't argue with you there."

He shuffles his feet as I wait. "I've done and said things I'm not proud of, Brock. I know that I blamed you for a lot of the shit that happened with Axton, when I should have blamed myself. It had nothing to do with you, for that I'm sorry."

I turn my head because I can't help it. I've never heard my father apologize for anything in his goddamn life. It shocks me to the core. He really must want mom to stay, big time.

"You cut me off." I can't help the bitterness in my voice. "You acted as if I were dead to you."

He looks at his feet, unable to face me because he knows it's true. "I was wrong."

I snort. "Did mom put you up to this? She make you do it?"

He kicks the dirt. "We both know that nobody can *make* me do anything. We're a lot like each other in that way."

"I'd never cut anyone off like that, never. So, we may look alike, but I think that's where the similarities end." Fuck you, *dad*.

He turns his gaze back to me. "We're more alike than you think, but you're right. You stuck by your brother when I couldn't. What he did… it was hard for us to accept. I wondered where I went wrong, we both did. For so many years, I blamed myself for not setting a good enough example. I was angry. He put shame on our family, shame we had to move away from, I couldn't deal with the fallout. And when you were discharged from the army and joined the M.C., it was the last straw."

Anger boils in my blood. More like he was ashamed of me too, even though I never held up a convenience store with a shotgun or got locked up. I'm not a fuckin' angel, but I like to think I'm not a bad person.

I realize I wasn't the easiest person to deal with after I got discharged. I know what anger feels like, and I got little to zero support from the government in the aftermath of being wounded, shot and then coming home. I had to rebuild my life again from the ground up, with no help from him, the man I idolized. Some wounds just never heal.

"All I ever wanted was to make you proud," I say, though the words feel lodged in my throat. "From as early as I can remember, I always wanted to be just like you."

We've never talked like this.

"You think you haven't made me proud?"

"I know it."

"That couldn't be further from the truth. You're my son, I've always been proud of you, even when I couldn't show it. I didn't know how; it wasn't how I was raised."

I think about Grandpa and know that part's true.

"You got a funny way of showin' it," I mutter.

We stand in silence for a long time. I stare at my girls from the open shed and dad follows my gaze.

"You were always meant for each other," he says eventually. "Couldn't keep you apart as kids."

"Next thing you're gonna say is you were wrong about what you said about Angel, too."

"Nope. I always liked her, even though she had a mouth on her."

"Still does," I mutter, if only to myself. "Only got worse with age."

"You gonna screw it up again this time?"

"Not a chance." Hell will freeze over before I let that happen.

He nods over to them. "Got a nice kid, she looks up to you."

I watch her babbling away to my mom and Angel and I smile. "She's six, she looks up to Hannah Montana and would gladly trade a kidney for her Nintendo switch, not sure I'm the best role model comparison."

Dad shakes his head. "A father knows these things."

I turn and face him. "This mean we gotta start bein' nice to each other?"

He half smiles. "Not if you don't want to."

"What about Axton? He's gettin' out. He's gonna be makin' a life for himself here, and I'm gonna sponsor him, get him back on his feet. A fresh start."

He pauses, like he's got a speech prepared, instead he says, "Despite what you think, I want what's best for him, I always did. He's done his time, it's something he has to live with."

"I don't know that he'll want much to do with anyone. You never visited him once," I remind him. "Shit like that sticks, and I get it, but he's paid his dues. He deserves a second chance."

"He said he didn't want us to visit. It would have killed your mother to see him like that, the trial was bad enough."

I shake my head. "Always so caught up on appearances."

He swallows hard. "I got a lot of makin' up to do. I know that. Rehashing all the mistakes I've made won't make up for lost time."

"No," I say. "It won't, only actions can rectify that."

"Isn't that why I'm here?"

"You tell me."

He nods slowly. "It's why I'm here. To at least try to make amends."

I lean my elbows on the fence. "So much shit's happened. So much shit I've buried because it was just too hard."

"I wish I could turn back time. I shouldn't have pushed you away when it was Axton I was angry with. You stuck by your own blood when I should have, too. For that, I'm proud of you, I've always been proud of you."

I turn my head to look at him. "If you burn me again, that's it. I don't give second chances, just because you're my dad and went and had a heart attack on us, doesn't mean shit."

He looks momentarily surprised. "Can tell you're my blood, you don't let up easily."

"I guess you taught me well then." I smirk, despite myself.

He chuckles. "Maybe a little too well."

"Nah." I lean toward him and slap him on the back. "You're still the meanest bastard I ever met."

"I guess I deserve that."

More silence ensues.

"Merry Christmas, dad," I say after a while, just as I hear Rawlings running up behind me.

"Merry Christmas, son," he replies as I catch Rawlings in my arms and hoist her over my shoulder.

Angel and mom approach and they smile at us simultaneously as they see the scene unfolding.

We can try, that's all we can do. I can't make any promises or see into the future, but what I have in front of me right now, it's all I ever wanted.

I'm the luckiest bastard on earth, and I'll spend the rest of my life making sure Angel and my kid know it.

ANGEL

6 months later

I stare at the plastic stick and gasp.

Two blue lines.

Holy shit.

I'm late but that isn't unusual, I didn't have any reason to panic because I've had no symptoms. Brock and I haven't been trying to get pregnant, but I have been off the pill for a while.

I sit on the edge of the bath and take deep breaths.

I mean, you hear about this kind of thing, but not *that* much. I'm almost thirty-seven, and I'm going to be a mom again. I honestly thought I was barren, definitely *not* fertile like I was in my twenties, obviously.

I feel a rise of excitement and terror simultaneously run through me as I think about what all of that means. Most of all, I think about Brock and how happy he'll be.

The ultimate gift. The thing he's always wanted, a child together. *Our* baby.

Though he dotes on Rawlings and spoils her rotten, he's

always wanted a brood of kids, a freakin' house full. I don't know about a brood, but this is a good start.

I shouldn't be surprised, the amount of sex we have is ridiculous. I guess we're like teenagers all over again and we're making up for lost time.

I wipe my tears as I hear the pair of them come through the door. I don't know how I can keep this a secret as I want to burst, but it's Brock's birthday in a couple of days, what an amazing birthday present this would be.

I need to think fast.

I quickly gather the pregnancy test, box, and instructions and shove them in the hamper, wiping my eyes quickly just as Rawlings comes barreling through the bathroom door. Privacy in our house is non-existent.

"Hey, kiddo," I say, washing my hands as she jumps up and down and shows me an invite to some kid's party in her class.

"Look, mom!" she squeals.

"Wow, baby-girl, that looks like fun. You get to dress up as your favorite book character?"

I can't tell you how much fun that's going to be.

"Dad's going to take me shopping for the best present ever," she tells me excitedly.

Yep. She's taken to calling Brock dad, totally her idea. Uncle Brock just wasn't gonna cut it.

The day she asked if it was okay, I swear I saw a tear in Brock's eye. I almost lose it myself at the memory. Maybe the pregnancy hormones are kicking in after all.

"Brock, in a kid's toy store?" I snort with laughter. "I'll believe that when I see it."

Though, Rawlings has roped him in for one of her pretend tea parties a few times, but he drew the line at wearing a tutu. I smile at the thought. He's so good with her,

I couldn't ask for a better father who loves us both unconditionally.

The man in question appears in the doorway and leans against it sexily as my eyes rake his body. He's so damn fine. I can see now how I got pregnant so fast; I'd get knocked up passing him in the hall.

"I've got ears, you know," he says, giving me a playful scowl.

"Yeah, mom, he is a pretty good present giver."

"You're just saying that because you got a pony for Christmas and a new bike for your birthday." I roll my eyes as Rawlings runs off, ducking under Brock's arm as he ruffles her hair on the way past.

I stare at him, and it kills me that I don't know if I should just tell him or not, the excitement inside me threatens to bubble up. I'm conflicted.

"You okay?"

"I'm fine." I lie.

"You look a little… flushed." Amusement dances in his eyes.

I try to give him my best frown, like I've no idea what he's talking about.

"Do I? Maybe I'm just hot from looking at you, all buff and brawny over there. You know what a man in ripped jeans and those boots does to me."

He comes over and gives my ass a squeeze and plants his lips on mine, pushing his tongue into my mouth.

"Better not get me too excited, kids had ice-cream. She's not gonna settle down for a while yet." He laughs when we break apart.

I roll my eyes. "Daddy of the year."

He shrugs. "King of the kids, what can I say."

We kiss again, and I run my hands over his shoulders and dig my nails in.

"Woah there, sunshine," he chastises. "Gettin' me all worked up when I can't do anything about it will only get you a spanking later."

I waggle my eyebrows. "Counting on it."

He narrows his eyes, smelling a rat. "You sure you're okay?"

Before I can answer, Rawlings yells out that the box isn't working on the TV.

He rolls his eyes. "Living with women is hard work."

"You love it," I say with a smile as I slap him on the butt before he stalks off, leaving me to calm my breathing and get a handle on myself before I blow it.

I don't know how, but two long, painfully slow days go by, and I've told nobody. I even made a doctor's appointment and had the pregnancy confirmed officially.

I'm six weeks along.

I hold my hands on my stomach as I sit at the traffic lights in my car, elated, scared, happy. All the emotions hit me, and I know it's the hormones because I'm not usually this sappy. I just want to tell him. I can't wait to see his face.

We eat dinner at the Grill, and Rawlings insisted we bake a cake, so I baked his favorite, banana bread. We decorate it with icing and serve it with massive dollops of ice cream when we get home, just how he likes it. And of course, we have to sing, because what's a birthday party with the three of us without an out of tune singalong.

Brock blows out his candles and Rawlings jumps for joy telling him to make a wish.

I wished for you, always.

Later when Rawlings has gone to bed, I go out to Brock, he's sitting on the back porch, looking out across the ranch. It's almost summer, the nights are longer and warmer.

I sit between his legs on the rocker as he sips on his bourbon.

"What are you thinking?" I say after a while as we sit in silence.

He kisses my hair. "How lucky I am."

I smile to myself. "Yeah? Are you just saying that because I baked for you?"

"You bakin' does a lot of things to me. Mainly, it gets my dick hard."

I roll my eyes. "Did you ever think this would be us?" I muse.

His hand comes down and squeezes my shoulder. "Always hoped it would. I got all I need right here."

Excitement builds in my stomach, and I think I might pass out.

"You sure about that?"

He bumps me with his hips. "What more could a man want? I got my girls, my house, things with mom and dad are good, Axton's doin' great. Shit's good, babe, shit's real good."

"What about another kid?"

"You wanna get some practice in, babe? Just say the word."

I close my eyes. "I'm pregnant, Brock," I blurt out.

He stills. "What?"

I let out the breath I've been holding in, so scared I'll ruin the surprise. "I'm six weeks, I was late, so I did a test." Even now, saying it out loud is still a shock.

"Are you shittin' me?" his voice is almost a whisper.

I turn in his arms and hold onto his biceps so I don't fall off, straddling across his lap.

"I'm not shittin' you, you're gonna be a daddy."

He stares at me dumbfounded. I've never seen this look on his face before. I'd say I got him good, finally.

I wave my hand in front of his face. "Hello in there?"

He grabs my hips and squeezes, his hands snaking up my body to cup my face.

"We're gonna have a baby?" he says. "For fuckin' real?"

I nod, tears forming in my eyes when I see his cloud over. "Yup. You knocked me up good and proper. Probably gonna have a ten-pound kid with huge feet, just like his or her daddy."

His lips twitch. "We haven't even been tryin'," he goes on, still staring at me in wonder.

I shrug. "Sometimes it just happens."

A slow grin spreads across his face as he pulls me into his chest, his hands wrapping in my hair as we kiss passionately. I feel his dick, hard and thick, pressing into me. I've never been kissed by anyone like him, it tells me everything I need to know about how he feels.

"That's what got us into this mess," I say breathlessly when we pull apart.

He hands skim back down to my belly, it's still flat, for the moment. He rubs his hands across it and stares down at me.

"You sure you got a baby in there?"

I laugh, running my hands up to hold his face. "Yes, and I'm gonna get fat, really, really fat. And whiny. Needy. Oh, and bonus, my boobs will get even bigger, and you'll have to massage my feet and get me shit when I demand it without question, and you're gonna love every second of it."

"This all sounded good until I became the cabana boy."

I laugh as his eyes shine with pride.

"It sounds better than slave-boy, doesn't it?"

He pulls me into a great big bear hug, almost knocking the wind out of me. "You don't know what this means to me, Angel. *Our* baby," he whispers. "I'm so happy, so fuckin' happy, babe. When did you find out?"

"Two days ago," I admit. "I wanted to tell you, but I thought it might be nice to surprise you on your birthday. Give you something special."

He kisses me again, then works his mouth down to my

throat and buries his head between my breasts. "Let's go to bed," he says, his voice hoarse. "I wanna show you just how happy you make me."

"I thought being the birthday boy, I was supposed to show you?" I tease.

He grins again and I yelp as he picks me up by the hips, and I swing my legs around his waist as he carries me into the house.

"I love you, woman." He grins as I wrinkle my nose.

"Guess I'm kinda stuck with you now, since you knocked me up and all."

He squeezes my waist as I begin to unbutton my dress with a free hand. His eyes drop to my breasts. "You're gonna pay for that comment."

"Hey, gotta go easy on the pregnant lady." I snicker as he begins to mount the stairs.

"You don't get no feet rubbin' and shit until you get fat," he tells me. "I know how it works. Heard all about it from Lucy non-stop."

I run my hands through his hair. "You know something, Brock Altman?"

We get to our room, and he doesn't let go. We slide on the bed together as he comes over the top of me. "What's that, beautiful?"

"That I love you more now than I ever could. It's always been you, even in your grumpiest days."

"You know how to get a man excited," he replies, unbuttoning the rest of my dress. "Hearing you say those words, minus the grumpy part, makes me the happiest man alive."

"Then fuck me like you mean it." I grin up at him. "Like I know you can."

"What about the baby? Can we still do shit?"

"Yes." I laugh. "Idiot."

He squeezes my hips gently. "Already demandin' shit and

back talkin', might have to get you a gag, then a man can worship your body in peace without all this lip."

"No arguments there." I grip his ass tight as his mouth covers mine once more. I'm lost in his touch, his every move.

We fit together, like missing pieces of a puzzle. Pieces that just needed to get their shit together. Finally.

And he does worship me, in every way, just like he promised.

ACKNOWLEDGMENTS

To my sister D – words can't describe how much I cherish your love and encouragement, especially when (at times) I felt like throwing in the towel and cried a lot, you're always there to spur me on and make sure I don't quit. Thanks for being my person.

Thank you, my lovely readers!! I have no words for your kindness, reviews and lovely messages and for giving this new indie author a chance. I'm so happy you are enjoying the Bracken Ridge M.C. series. They are all close to my heart and I have PLENTY more books to come so stay tuned!

Thank you to all the bloggers and my awesome ARC readers for your continued support. I'm so honored to be part of this author world and you make it so much fun! I'm really blessed to have you guys in my corner

Thank you to my P.A. Savannah Richey @Peachykeenas– you are amazing and I love ya guts sista

Special thanks to my awesome editor Mackenzie @nicegirlnaughtyedits (seriously she's great, check her out if you need editing services!) nicegirlnaughtyedits.com

Thank you to everyone who has supported me and helped me on this journey into authorhood. I feel so lucky to be in this amazing world of books and to be able to share it with you means the world to me.

Love MF xx

ABOUT THE AUTHOR

Mackenzy Fox is an author of contemporary and erotic themed romance novels. When she's not writing she loves vegan cooking, walking her beloved pooch's, reading books and is an expert on online shopping.

She's slightly obsessed with drinking tea, testing bubbly Moscato, watching home decorating shows and has a black belt in origami. She strives to live a quiet and introverted life in Western Australia's North-West with her hubby, twin sister and her dogs.

FIND ME HERE:

Tiktok: https://www.tiktok.com/@mackenzyfoxauthor
Face book: https://www.facebook.com/mackenzy.foxauthor.5
Instagram: https://www.instagram.com/mackenzyfoxbooks/
Goodreads: http://bit.ly/3ql07a7

Don't forget to join my private Facebook Group: The Den – A Mackenzy Fox Readers Group here

Find all my books, newsletter sign ups, book links here in one easy spot: https://linktr.ee/mackenzyfox

Checkout my website:
https://mackenzyfox.com

WANT MORE?
COLT– BRACKEN RIDGE REBELS M.C.
BOOK 4
EXCERPT (UNEDITED)

Bracken Ridge Arizona, where the Rebels M.C. rule and the only thing they ride or die for more than their club is their women, this is Colt's story…

Colt: She's the raven-haired beauty with bright blue eyes, eyes that could render any man to his knees with one glacial stare. The sight of her hurt, vulnerable, scared…it makes my heart thunder.

I want to avenge her, I want to keep her safe, I want to keep her for myself, even when I know the waters surrounding her are deep and perilous. It doesn't make me want to stop, it makes me want to kill every bastard whoever did her wrong, every single one of them, one by one.

And maybe I will.

That's if her dark soul doesn't torture me and put me out of my misery first.

Cassidy: I feel his presence before he speaks. His voice deep but soft, it washes right through me like a comfort blanket. It shouldn't be familiar. I shouldn't cling to him, it's wrong.

He may have rescued me from my dire situation, but that is no excuse to dig my heels in and cling to him.

My savior.

The trouble is, I can't help it. He's strong, masculine, sexy as sin, and I can't help the feelings awakening in me whenever he's around.

I wish I could, but I can't seem to stop, and it could be my final undoing.

27

COLT

FOUR MONTHS EARLIER

I STARE AT THE RAVEN-HAIRED BEAUTY BOUND AND GAGGED TO the chair and a ripple runs through my body of anger and pain.

She's bloodied up, terrified and shaking.

The fucker who did this is lying on the floor as Steel and Gunner stand over him, checking his pulse. Yep. Definitely dead.

I move closer to her. "Shit, is she gonna be okay?" I wave my hand in front of her face. No blinking, no movement, nothing. This isn't good.

Steel turns and unbinds her hands as she stares into space. The tears have stopped but her face is smeared with water, dirt and blood.

Fuck.

I want to kill this man all over again, with my bare hands this time, and I don't even know this girl. I don't have to; nobody innocent deserves this.

Brock sticks his head in the doorway after checking on the getaway vehicles. "Ready."

"She's not moving," Sienna cries, giving her cousin a solid shake. "Cassidy, are you okay? Shit! Speak to me!"

I move closer. "I've got this." Sienna moves out of the way as I bend and take her limp form in my arms, she hangs like a ragdoll as if she were dead too, if it weren't for her blinking and the occasional rise in her chest.

"It's all right, darlin', we're gonna to take good care of you," I whisper. "Nobody's gonna hurt you anymore, I promise."

"You go with Colt now to the car. Me, Brock, and Gunner won't be far behind," Steel tells Sienna. She tries to protest but he won't hear it.

Eventually she follows me and we leave the barn and get in Brock's truck, Bones is hot on our tail.

"Meetin' at the Lodgeway motel," he says as I give him a nod. "Bout four hundred miles. Better get goin'."

"All right, see you there."

Sienna climbs in the passenger seat.

"Buckle up," I tell her as I slide Cassidy into the middle of the seat and set her down carefully. I shrug my cut off and place it over her. Sienna cries silently and I pretend not to notice. Serious shit went down tonight when Sienna's ex held Cassidy capture and she's been held here for days. The shock of it all seems to be just setting in.

I climb in and start the truck. We need to get out of here sooner rather than later. Last thing we need is more trouble on our hands.

Sienna doesn't say anything and for a long time we just sit in silence.

"You warm enough?" I ask eventually, leaning over to adjust the fan.

She nods. "Thanks, Colt."

"You hungry? We can stop for food."

She shakes her head. "If I eat, I think I might throw up, I'm not sure Brock will appreciate that when he gets his truck back."

"Probably not," I snort. "But I can get coffee, if you'd like."

She turns to me. "You're a good man Colt."

"So they say." I give her a wink.

She gives me a small smile. "So, you ever going to tell anyone your story?"

I snicker. "What? Now why's there always gotta be a story?"

She shrugs. "Don't we all have skeletons in our closets?"

"You said a mouthful there, sister. Would you believe it if I told you, I was the son of a preacher?"

She smiles softly. "Like the song?"

I grin. "Kind of. My parents are very religious. Still live in the same small town in Ohio."

"What brought you all the way out here?"

"Passin' through, I got some work. Used to be a fighter, did alright, but got sick of having to patch myself up after every fight. Knocks to my head didn't help, though if you'd ask my parents, they'd probably pray it would knock some sense into me and go home. I stuck around, got in with the club prospecting. The rest is history."

"How did you get in with the Rebels?"

"Was drinkin' at the Stone Crow one night, got talkin' with Bones, he must've thought I was a semi-standup guy, while I didn't relish the thought of starting at the bottom, you gotta start somewhere. And I didn't want to go back to where I'd been. I wanted to plant some roots."

She nods slowly. "You're a real nice guy, Colt," she says after a while. "I mean it."

I give her a side-eye. "You're the only one who thinks so," I laugh.

She frowns. "What do you mean? The guys like you, the girls like you, too, but they said you won't go near any of them."

"I go near plenty." Not that I broadcast it.

"Not the club sisters, though."

There's a difference between sweet butts - the girls who hang around the club helping out in exchange for free booze, a free party and sex, and club sisters - women of the M.C. of higher rank by association, like Steel's sister Lily and Hutch the President's daughter Deanna. Ol' ladies, like Sienna, are property of their old man for want of a better term. They are completely off limits unless you want to end up at the bottom of a well.

"Yeah, I still wanna be able to breathe without apparatus," I chuckle. "No offense, ya'll seem great and all, but I don't need a nag and I definitely don't need any one of the brothers on my case because I've definitely got no follow through. I think the women of the M.C. will only get me in trouble and I like my balls where they are."

She smiles softly. "Follow through is a choice, you know."

"Yeah, and I'm technology challenged, that timed with remembering to call a woman is why I'm single."

She turns back to the front and after a long time in silence she asks; "What do you think is happening back there?"

I stare at the dark, desolate road. "Whatever it is, it's over now. Steel and the boys will sort it out, so no need to worry."

"I'm sorry for dragging the club into my mess," she confesses. "I never meant for any of this to happen."

"I don't know the details, but I don't see how that jerk stalking you and kidnapping your cousin and bribing you left you any choice, sweetheart. Plus you know the boys, they live for this kind of thing, payback's a bitch, haven't you heard?"

I hope she doesn't ask me anything else, we discussed taking him out before we drove down here. Brock is a very good shot being ex-army, luckily it didn't come to that; bullets are harder to cover up.

"Will they dump his body? I'm worried they'll get caught."

"You don't need to worry about anything," I say again. "It's all being taken care of, they know what they're doin', just trust that."

We stop for gas an hour later and I buy myself a burger and three coffees. Cassidy is still asleep and Sienna isn't hungry.

I stare at the girl slumped next to me, while her injuries don't look life threatening, it still bothers me that we can't take her to seek medical attention. She's barely moved from when I placed her on the seat, if not for the small lull of her breathing I wouldn't know if she were dead or alive.

Sienna helped her drink a little water when I pulled over to get gas, but she hasn't muttered one word or moved since.

Shock does weird shit to people, that's all I know.

Take my parents for example, they live in a very *different* community, the Amish community to be exact. Hence the reason they never come out here and likely never will, hence the reason I have to lie about where I am and what I do, not that I ever see them but sometimes I write home.

They'd never understand the M.C. lifestyle. They don't even understand why I left and it's not something I've discussed with anyone. I don't know how the M.C. would react if they knew about my childhood and teenage years. Only Hutch knows the truth.

I left when I was old enough to buy a bus fare. The only one I was close to, was my cousin Rebekah, but she ran away from home when she turned sixteen. It was after I had left.

I went back to look for her some years back, but knowing her, she wouldn't want to be found. She'd always talked about leaving to go to the big smoke, it had always fascinated her, much to her parents shame, she went through with it.

Rebekah was always the wild child of the community, she'd been punished severely on more than one occasion when she played up, namely sneaking out and meeting boys and smoking weed. That kind of shit is frowned upon in our community, as was the fist fight I got into, but that didn't stop me either.

I stare at the open road and I can't thank my lucky stars enough I got out of there. The Amish ain't for me, the only thing it taught me for real was how to work hard and how much I didn't want to be controlled by religion or by my parents.

I think about what Sienna said about the girls thinkin' I'm a nice guy, if only they knew.

I used to be good. Courting girls from the community, nothing ever happened because most of them were good girls, *most* of them, aside from one called Meri who I was steady with. She let me do stuff but we never went all the way.

Meri ended up married and she's got kids now. That's what you do in the Amish world; when you're a man you work till you die, find a virgin bride and have ten kids. When you're a woman you're a home maker, a baby breeding machine and you'll honor your husband.

I wasn't a bad kid, not until I got to about eighteen, the only way I could express myself was through fighting, because I liked the thrill of it. It filled a void, and it helped me release all of the pent-up anger I felt suffocating me. Meri wanted me to get serious, since I was the one she'd done the most with, and I thought I wanted that too, until everything changed.

At one point I'd wanted her to come with me, but that was a fools game. She'd never leave, it was all she knew.

The bright light of the Motel sign snaps me out of my reverie and I pull up and jump out to get us all checked in.

I got adjoining rooms so I can be close by if the girls both need me until the brothers arrive. Bones texted me an hour ago saying they were on their way.

I carry Cassidy into the room and lay her on the bed, I stand back and Sienna and I both stare down at her.

"I'm worried about her," she whispers. "She's usually a very verbose person."

"She was just kidnapped, likely tortured and traumatized," I remind her. "That shit's gotta take its toll."

Her hairs matted and wayward, the dirt and blood on her face tells me more than I would've liked to know. It makes my blood boil that someone could inflict this on another person.

I guess I have always had a protective urge. It's instilled into me from my upbringing that women are to be protected by the man of the house. Even within the Amish there are things that go on that shouldn't in any community, but in my household I was at least thankful my father was good to my mother. He never beat her or treated her with ill respect. I can't say the same for Rebekah's home.

"I need to wash her."

"I'll get the shower going."

Sienna gives me a look and I hold my palms up. "I wasn't insinuating that I'm going to stay, just tryin' to help." And I am. She needs to get the muck, sweat, blood and stench off her.

She nods and shrugs Cassidy out of her jacket and removes her shoes.

"You got any spare clothes?"

She nods. "I packed a change just in case, we're the same size."

"Okay. I'll be right next door, call if you need me, yeah?"

"I will." She smiles while helping her cousin stand. I turn to leave.

"Hey Colt?"

I turn as I open the connecting door.

"Thank you."

I nod once. "No problem."

I close the door and as soon as I get inside, I take my cut off and lay it over the end of the bed and turn the television on low. I need a shower myself but I'm so wired from tonight that it's unlikely I'll be able to relax.

I take a beer from the six pack I bought when I got gas and knock off the cap and take a long, well-needed swig.

Doing dangerous shit doesn't worry me, I live for it, but being alone with two women, one of who may flip out at any given moment, that freaks the hell out of me.

Least Sienna has a good head on her shoulders.

I sit on the end of the bed and flick through the channels. I settle on some late night horror movie, seems kind of fitting.

I'm just about to kick my boots off when I hear a loud thump and then Sienna screams my name.

I shoot off the bed as fast as my legs will carry me and charge through into the connecting room and into the bathroom. I see Sienna trying to pick her naked cousin up off the shower stall floor as she lies in a crumpled heap.

"Out," I say, as she lets me in. I switch the taps off as Sienna passes a towel to me. I step in and wrap it around her lifeless body and scoop her off the floor and into my arms.

"She just collapsed," Sienna cries, pacing as I carry her out to the bed. "I couldn't hold her up."

"Should've asked me for help, I'm not a total pervert."

"I'm sorry." She waves a shaky hand at me.

I hold her in my lap. "Get those clothes, need to get her dressed."

Sienna dives into the backpack and pulls out sweatpants and a hoodie. She swiftly pulls the clothes on her body awkwardly while I hold her. I try not to look but it's a little hard since I have to help pull the pants up. She's not as curvy as I usually like my women, in fact, she could do with putting some weight on. I try not to get a dry mouth seeing her bare tits. The thing that makes me see stars are the more apparent bruises on her body that we couldn't see before. The flesh around her wrists is red raw and bruised.

If that bastard wasn't dead already I'd turn around, drive back and put a bullet through his skull.

Though she's not cold she shakes uncontrollably.

"Shit Colt, I'm getting really worried, maybe she needs to go to emergency."

Cassidy flicks her eyes to her cousin and shakes her head. "No doctors."

I stare down at her, she speaks.

"Cass!" Sienna yelps, dropping to her knees in front of us. "Please talk to me."

She blinks rapidly. "Wh…where are we?"

Sienna rubs her hands up her thighs. "We're in a motel. You're safe Cass, everything's going to be okay."

"What happened?"

I exchange a glance with Sienna and shake my head once.

"You don't remember?"

She shudders. "I was locked in a trunk."

Sienna bites her lip. "It's all right, sweetie. You're safe now, nothing's going to hurt you, nobody will hurt you ever again." She brushes the hair out of her face as I still hold her in my arms. She sags back against me, seeming to not care who I am or what I'm doing holding her.

Maybe I should dislodge myself, let her rest, I go to move and prop her back on the pillows but she stiffens, tears well in her eyes as she looks directly at me for the first time.

"Wh…where are you going?" she stammers.

"I should probably let you get some rest."

Her shoulders begin to shake as tears well in her eyes. "Don't leave," she whispers as my eyes go round.

Me leaving seems to be setting her off again. "All right." I nod, quickly. "I'll stay for a bit."

Sienna stills, her eyes flicking to mine and back to Cassidy again. "Do you want anything to eat, or drink?" she asks, her brow furrowing.

Cassidy shakes her head and doesn't bother to wipe her tears.

I move and peel the covers back and pull her back onto the bed and cover her, she holds onto my arm, holding me in place.

"It's probably best if you stay with her," Sienna whispers. "Until she falls asleep maybe?"

"All right," I reply, I sit back on the pillows, I keep my body on top of the covers.

Sienna perches on the end of the bed and faces Cassidy.

"Do you want to talk about it?"

Cassidy huddles into the covers. She's stopped crying and she rests her head on my shoulder. At least I'm having a calming effect on her and not a hysterical one, it could be worse, I guess.

She closes her eyes and Sienna and I sit in complete and utter silence until the lull of her breathing tells me she's asleep.

"You should get some rest," I say. "Feel free to use my room if you want to lay down." There's no couch or even a chair in here, and it does kinda feel a bit awkward.

"I want to wait for Steel."

I glance at the alarm clock on the side table. "They're three or four hours behind us, might wanna get some shut eye till then. I'll wait up."

She rises from the bed. "Thanks Colt, I thought I could hold her up, but she just didn't have any will to stand."

I kinda know how she feels, while I haven't been kidnapped and beaten up, I know what it's like to give up and have little hope left.

"Leave the connecting door open, if she needs anything I can just wake you."

She nods. "Okay."

I give her a small smile and as she leaves, I turn the small lamp off and rest one arm behind my head. I glance down at the raven-haired woman lying in my arms, her hair splayed across my shoulder as she sleeps soundly.

I can't grasp what the heck just happened. She's definitely in shock, coming in and out of a state of consciousness that I don't understand. From zombie like to collapsing, vacant, then crying and holding onto me like I have all the answers; I don't.

I don't have one fuckin' clue what to do.

The brothers will be here soon, I just gotta stay awake and then they can take of this. Of her.

I sit back and rest my head against the wooden headboard and I don't fight it when sleep threatens to take me over.

Pre order Colt here (release 16th Nov 2021)

ALSO BY MACKENZY FOX

<u>Bracken Ridge Rebels MC:</u>

Steel

Gunner

Brock

Colt (preorder)

<u>Bad Boys of New York:</u>

Jaxon

<u>Standalone:</u>

Broken Wings

Printed in Great Britain
by Amazon